BLACKBURN

Also by Bradley Denton

Wrack and Roll
Buddy Holly Is Alive and Well on Ganymede

BLACKBURN

BRADLEY
DENTON

PICADOR USA
NEW YORK

Portions of this book have appeared previously, in slightly different forms, in *The Magazine of Fantasy & Science Fiction* and in *Pulphouse: The Hardback Magazine.*

Design by Dawn Niles

ISBN 0-312-13029-5

First published in the United States by St. Martin's Press

First Picador USA Edition: May 1995
10 9 8 7 6 5 4 3 2 1

For B.C.

CONTENTS

VICTIM NUMBER TWO

Blackburn was surprised that it was so easy. He hadn't thought he would be able to shoot another man. But here was Number Two trying to pull on his pants. The man was big, and his footfalls shook the telephone on the nightstand. A hole in his stomach pumped dark blood. The blood glistened on the man's skin, on the bedsheets, on the floor.

The woman on the bed was screaming. She scooted back against the headboard and stuffed part of the top sheet into her mouth. She screamed louder.

"Don't do that," Blackburn said. His ears were buzzing from the gunshot.

Number Two pulled his pants up as far as his knees, then fell. The telephone jumped. The man grunted. He lay on his side, and the blood ran down his belly to the floor. The woman continued to scream. Her screams were why Blackburn had come into the room. But there was no need for them now.

"It's all right," Blackburn said.

The woman screamed and screamed.

"What else could I do?" Blackburn asked.

Number Two began twitching. After a moment Blackburn realized the man was sobbing. He was in pain. Blackburn was sorry for that. He wasn't used to the pistol. Until today, he had never fired a real gun. He hadn't meant to hit Number Two in the stomach.

Blackburn stepped closer to the man. "Don't look," he said to the woman. The woman pulled the sheet over her head. Her screaming was becoming hoarse.

Blackburn pulled back the pistol's hammer to cock it. Then he pointed the muzzle at the side of Number Two's head.

The man was sweating. His twitching had become a steady tremble. His eyes rolled up to stare at Blackburn. He moaned.

Blackburn hesitated. It had been easy to shoot when he had seen the man beating the woman. It was not so easy now.

He turned to leave. This man wasn't Number Two after all. Wounding didn't count.

The woman's screams stopped as Blackburn started for the door. She was probably already reaching for the phone. He would have to get down the road in a hurry. He hoped that the junk Ford pickup he had stolen would start.

He heard the woman say, "Oh my God should I call an ambulance?"

He heard the man say, "Get you for this, bitch."

The pistol was still cocked. Gripping it with both hands, Blackburn went back to the man and fired into his head.

It was spectacular. Blackburn was shocked. He'd had no idea. The walls, the bed, the woman, his clothes. He'd had no idea at all.

The woman was screaming again. "I'm sorry," Blackburn said. He gestured at the walls with the gun. "About all this."

The woman's nightgown was hanging askew, making her body look twisted. Her hands covered her face. She was trying to say something through her own screams. Blackburn couldn't understand the words.

"Hey," Blackburn said. When she didn't respond, he yelled. "Hey!"

The woman stopped screaming. She uncovered her face and stared at him. Her hair was tangled, her face streaked. The flesh around her eyes was puffy and bruised. She was trembling just as Number Two had.

"He was hurting you," Blackburn said.

The woman rose to her knees. She clenched her fists beside her face and shrieked, "He was my husband!"

Blackburn was confused. "Did that make it okay?" he asked.

The woman crumpled into a ball and wouldn't say anything more.

Blackburn went out. Some people.

The lights were on in the motel office. The county sheriff's patrol must be on its way. Blackburn sprinted for the Ford and jumped in. It started on the first try, and he tore out of the gravel lot onto the blacktop. Six hours remained before sunrise. He would have plenty of time to lose himself in the Ozarks.

He had learned a lot since leaving Kansas that afternoon. He had learned that improving his aim was essential. He had learned that a .357 Colt Python packed a bigger punch

3

than he had realized. And he had learned that when a man deserved to die, killing him was not hard.

Only two cartridges remained in the Python. He would need more. His seventeenth birthday had been eventful, and he expected more of the same in the days ahead.

ONE

BLACKBURN AND THE BLIND MAN

The day before the blind man came to school, Jimmy Blackburn's father made his mother bleed. It wasn't much blood, but Jimmy's mother cried. His sister Jasmine screamed. Jimmy wanted to hit Jasmine in the mouth the way Dad had hit Mom. Jasmine's screaming was what had started the fight in the first place.

Dad went outside and drove off in his pickup truck. Jimmy would have gone outside too, but Mom said he couldn't leave the table until he had cleaned his plate. He didn't want to eat. His round steak and mashed potatoes were cold. But the longer he waited, the worse they would get. So he tried. Maybe if Mom saw that he was trying, she would excuse him anyway. Maybe she would even let him have some ice milk later on.

Mom dabbed at her mouth with a dishrag. She was still crying a little. Jimmy was afraid she was a sissy. He had been hit harder than that before and hadn't cried. Jasmine started pounding on her high chair tray, squashing her food, and Mom didn't seem to care.

"May I be excused yet?" Jimmy asked. Jasmine was making him sick.

"Five more bites," Mom said.

Jimmy forced down five bites of meat, then left the table. Jasmine threw a blob of potatoes at him as he went by. It stuck to his shirt. He threw it back, hitting her in the face. She screamed louder than ever, and Jimmy was sure that he would get in trouble. But Mom only reached over with the dishrag and wiped Jasmine's face. The blob of potatoes smeared and turned pink on the cloth.

He went outside and sat on one of the tires behind the garage. The sun was setting, turning the western sky gold, red, and purple. Mom said that Kansas had the most beautiful sunsets on earth. Jimmy wondered how she knew, since she had never been anywhere else.

The windbreak of evergreens murmured. Winter was coming. Jimmy couldn't wait for snow, because snow would mean canceled school days. He hated third grade. Mrs. Porter was fat, and her breath smelled like burnt newspaper.

A meteor streaked southward, its white trail pointing at the town of Wantoda. Jimmy hoped it would hit the grade school. He listened for an explosion, but didn't hear one.

After a while he got chilly and went back inside to watch TV. Mom gave him a bowl of ice milk, then made him go to bed at eight-thirty. She stood in his bedroom doorway and listened while he knelt and said his prayer: "Now I lay me down to sleep, I pray the Lord my soul to keep. If I should die before I wake, I pray the Lord my soul to take.

God bless Mom and Dad and Jasmine, in Jesus' name, Amen."

Jimmy got into bed and under the covers. Usually Mom said good night and closed the door as soon as he did that, but tonight she just stood there, centered in the rectangle of kitchen light. Jimmy's bedroom had once been a pantry, and it had no windows to let in light from outside. He couldn't see Mom's face. Only her shape against the yellow.

"Remember, Jimmy," she said. "A prayer isn't just something you say. It isn't like a poem you memorize for school. It's what you use to talk to Jesus."

"Yes, ma'am," Jimmy said. "I know."

"I'm sure you do. But sometimes we forget that we know something. So be certain to remember what Jesus said about praying: Anything you ask in His name will be granted."

"I know," Jimmy said again. "They told us that in church. On Easter." Easter was months in the past, but he still longed for the taste of malted-milk-ball Easter eggs.

"Yes," Jimmy's mother said. "Yes, they did." She started to close the door. "Sleep tight, honey."

" 'Night, Mom."

"Good night." The door closed. The room was black except for yellow lines marking the door.

As Jimmy lay waiting for sleep, he heard Dad come home and say he was sorry. Jimmy listened hard, holding his breath, but didn't hear Mom answer. That made him mad. She should say something. Dad didn't like it when she didn't say anything.

Jasmine started crying then, and Jimmy heard Mom hurry to Jasmine's bedroom. But Jasmine only screamed. She was probably seeing monsters again. Stupid three-year-old brat. She would make Mom and Dad start fighting again.

And she did. It was worse than before. There was yelling and crying. Then something made of glass broke.

Jimmy put his head under the covers and started praying.

He didn't pray in a poem this time. He prayed straight to Jesus and asked Him to make Mom and Dad stop fighting.

The yelling became louder. Mom was almost screaming like Jasmine. Jimmy realized that he wasn't praying properly. He got out of bed and knelt again, putting his hands together with the fingers pointing upward. That must turn them into an antenna, he thought. Beaming prayers to Heaven. He imagined his body as a radio transmitter. He squeezed his eyes shut and prayed the same prayer over again. Please make Mom and Dad stop fighting. Please make them be happy.

There was a smack, flesh on flesh, and a thump. Then the front door slammed and the pickup truck started. Its tires spun on the gravel, throwing some against the house. It sounded like BBs hitting a sidewalk. The pickup roared away, the sound fading fast, leaving Jasmine's screams. Then those faded too, leaving Mom's sobs. Bawling, Dad would call it.

Jimmy stopped praying without saying amen. Something had gone wrong with his transmission.

He got back into bed. He was mad, but he wasn't sure at whom. Everybody, he decided. Every stupid body.

The first, second, third, and fourth graders filed into the auditorium, their teachers leading them to their seats. There were rustling and squeaking sounds as they sat. The teachers took the aisle seats. Somebody laughed, and a teacher gave a warning. Then, except for coughs and sniffles, there was silence. The principal, Mr. Sturner, climbed the steps to the wooden stage and stood in front of the curtain. He announced that the school had a special guest who would present a special program. It was important, he said, that the children be quiet during the program, because the special guest relied upon his sense of hearing. Any chatter could result in serious consequences.

Mr. Sturner left the stage. The brown velvet curtain

opened, revealing the blind man standing at the rear of the stage. He was wearing a blue suit and black-framed sunglasses. Sunglasses indoors looked pretty strange, Jimmy thought. The blind man put down his long white cane, then walked toward the front of the stage. He raised a hand in greeting.

He walked steadily. His head was tilted upward. He didn't slow as he approached the edge. It was four or five feet to the concrete floor. He couldn't see that he would fall.

Jimmy wanted to yell "Stop!" The girl beside him gasped, and so did others. Then they held their breath. They were afraid for the blind man. But no one said anything, because no one wanted serious consequences.

Somebody had to tell him, Jimmy thought. Somebody had to warn him that in two more steps he would drop off the stage. Why didn't one of the teachers do it? Why were they sitting with their hands folded, waiting for him to fall?

The blind man stopped with his toes at the edge of the stage. He smiled. The children let out their breath and murmured to each other. The teachers glared at them, and there was silence again.

The blind man spoke. His voice was loud and rhythmic, like an auctioneer's.

"I just heard a voice," the blind man said. "A soft yet commanding whisper in my ear. Do you know who it was?"

The children, fearful of the teachers, said nothing.

"It was the Lord Jesus, children," the blind man said. "I cannot see with my own eyes, so I rely on Him to guide me. And He never fails me, so I never fear. Just now He warned me to stop lest I fall and do myself injury. So tell me, children: Where on the stage have I stopped?"

"Right at the edge!" Jimmy shouted. Mrs. Porter glanced at him, but her expression was only the usual frown.

The blind man turned toward Jimmy. "Thank you, young man. I didn't doubt it. Jesus let me get as close to you as I could without falling."

Jimmy was amazed. He'd had no idea that Jesus spoke to anyone who wasn't in the Bible. He had seen blind people on TV, so that was no big deal—but not even on TV had he ever seen anyone that Jesus had whispered to.

"And I'm glad to be as close to you as I can," the blind man continued, "because I'm here to show you that you can succeed in this world no matter what your human limitations may be. I, for example, cannot see; and yet I live a full and productive life. Some of you may have your own handicaps as well. Some of you boys may not be as strong or as smart as others, and some of you girls may not be as pretty as your friends. But with hard work and faith, those limitations don't matter.

"I lost my sight when I was in the second grade, and the years that followed were difficult. I remember one time that some boys spun me until I was dizzy, and I walked into the girls' rest room by mistake . . ."

Some of the children gasped, and others laughed. Some of the teachers laughed too. No one got in trouble. The blind man went on with his story.

Jimmy was impressed. Here was a man who was brave and funny, who made teachers forget that they were supposed to make kids shut up, and to whom Jesus talked directly. Here was a man who knew some things, a man to be listened to. When the girl next to Jimmy started whispering to the girl next to her, Jimmy punched her arm to make her shut up. Mrs. Porter didn't see him do it.

The girl rubbed her arm and glared at him. "I'm telling," she whispered.

Jimmy knew she was lying. If she told, she would have to admit that she had been talking. He punched her again. She yelped.

Mrs. Porter glared down the row of seats. "Cynthia," she said, "hush."

The girl's eyes welled up. Jimmy was disgusted. What a sissy.

The blind man retrieved his cane and demonstrated how he used it to avoid running into streetlights and mailboxes. Its metal tip scratched back and forth across the stage. "And if I become bored," the blind man said, "I can always pretend I'm Zorro." He raised the cane and slashed an invisible Z in the air. Everyone laughed.

When the blind man finished his talk, he asked if the children had any questions. After some hesitation, quite a few raised their hands. Principal Sturner called on the ones he wanted to, since the blind man couldn't call on them himself. Jimmy noticed that Mr. Sturner only called on the teachers' pets.

The first question was "How do you eat without missing your mouth?" and the second was "How do you drive a car?" Jimmy was peeved. It was obvious that the teachers' pets were all going to ask really stupid questions.

He had a question of his own, and it wasn't stupid. It was, he thought, the only important question anyone could ask the blind man. But he didn't raise his hand. He was afraid to ask the question in front of everyone else. Mr. Sturner wouldn't call on him anyway.

The last question asked was "Do you have a job?"

The blind man smiled. "Yes. I am an evangelist. That means that I spread the good news of Jesus and His love to everyone I meet. You see, despite all that I've had to learn in order to live without eyes, the fact is that none of it is worth a plugged nickel without the help of Jesus. His voice guides my life, and I assure you that I listen."

He pointed his cane at the children. "As should you all. Thank you for your kind attention."

The curtain closed as the lunch bell rang. The children and teachers applauded. Jimmy watched the curtain sway as he waited for Mrs. Porter to herd them out of the auditorium. His question would have to remain unasked.

* * *

It was a miracle. It was as if Jesus had known what Jimmy wanted, and had given it to him. But Jimmy hadn't prayed for this. So how had Jesus known?

The blind man had come to eat lunch with the children, and he was sitting right next to Jimmy. His white cane was propped against the bench between them. Its handle was wrapped in red tape, darkened where the blind man's hand had gripped it.

Everyone watched the blind man eat. He opened his mouth wide and brought a spoonful of macaroni to it as if his arm were a machine. He chewed with his mouth closed.

Jimmy could see behind the left lens of the sunglasses. The blind man's eyelids were closed, the skin around them dark and puckered. Jimmy wondered if there was any eye in there at all, or just an empty hole. And if it was a hole, would the brain be exposed if the eyelids opened?

Mrs. Porter sat at the end of the table. She was watching the blind man too. She was also watching Jimmy, and scowling. She didn't want him to say anything to the blind man.

He would do it anyway, but he was scared. It would have been easier in the auditorium after all. Up close, the blind man was big, bigger even than Jimmy's father. And he had an odd smell. Jimmy thought it might be soap, but he wasn't sure.

The blind man swallowed and turned toward Jimmy. Jimmy saw his own face in each lens of the sunglasses. "And what's your name, youngster?" the blind man asked.

Jimmy was surprised. He had to think for a minute. "Jimmy Blackburn, sir," he said at last.

"That's a nice name," the blind man said. "Have you been saved?" He asked this question in the same tone as Mr. Sturner asking who had flushed the wad of paper towels in the boys' rest room.

"Yes, sir," Jimmy said. "Last Easter." Every child in the Fairview Baptist Church had been saved that day. The pastor had made them come up to the altar and accept Jesus Christ as their personal Savior in unison. Jimmy hadn't felt any different afterward, but now he was glad it had happened. He would have hated to tell the blind man that he was one of the unsaved.

The blind man smiled. "That's wonderful. What better time to be saved than on the day the Lord arose. You'll remember it for the rest of your life."

"Yes, sir," Jimmy said.

"And He'll never leave you now, Jimmy. He'll live in your heart forever, and if you need help, he'll tell you what to do. He's the one friend you can always count on."

Jimmy glanced at Mrs. Porter. She seemed to be concentrating on her food now. He leaned closer to the blind man and spoke in a quiet voice.

"Did Jesus really talk to you?" he asked.

The blind man's smile faded a little. "He talks to me all the time, Jimmy." His voice boomed.

Mrs. Porter looked up from her food and gave Jimmy a warning look. He pretended not to see her.

"I mean when you were on the stage," he said, still keeping his voice quiet. Maybe Mrs. Porter wouldn't hear him over the lunchroom babble. She wouldn't like what he was saying. It was almost as if he were calling the blind man a liar. "Did Jesus really whisper in your ear to warn you? So you wouldn't walk off the edge?"

The blind man's smile came back full and strong. "Oh, that." He picked up his napkin and rubbed it around his mouth. "Yes, He did, Jimmy. He saw that I was about to do myself harm, and He stopped me. He'll do that for you too, if you keep Him in your heart and study His Word."

Mrs. Porter's look had become fiercer. It was telling Jimmy to shut up and behave himself. But he couldn't stop now. This was too important.

"You mean Jesus was right there on the stage with you?" he asked. "Invisible?"

The blind man chuckled. He tapped a finger against his sunglasses. "Everything is invisible to me, so I must rely on what I can hear and feel. And I tell you truly, I heard the Lord's voice, and I felt His presence, just as I hear your voice and feel your presence right now. So don't be fooled by what your eyes tell you, Jimmy. The Lord may be invisible to your eyes, but not to your heart."

Jimmy was excited. "Is it true that anything you ask in His name, He'll give to you?"

"Why, of course," the blind man said. He seemed surprised that Jimmy would ask such a question. "That's promised in the Bible, in the Lord's own words. If you open your heart to Him, there's nothing He won't do for you."

Mrs. Porter cleared her throat. "Jimmy, you had better finish your meal now. Lunch period is almost over, and I'm sure you've pestered our guest quite enough."

The blind man chuckled again. "Ma'am, I only wish more youngsters would pester me as this boy has." He smiled down at Jimmy. "I'm going to be talking to the fifth, sixth, seventh, and eighth graders this afternoon, Jimmy. I hope that they can still believe in the invisible too. Sometimes older children can't, you know. The world has poisoned them. That's why it's good that you're already saved. For some people, it's too late. They've become too scarred to feel, too deafened to hear."

"Yes, sir," Jimmy said. He wasn't listening hard now. His question had been answered. He took a few more bites of macaroni, then drank some milk. The blind man was still talking, but not to Jimmy. He was addressing the children across the table, repeating some of what he'd already said.

Mrs. Porter's lips were twitching. She kept looking up at the clock on the lunchroom wall. "Finish your meals, people. Lunch is over in six minutes."

Jimmy raised his hand. Mrs. Porter stared at him as if he had just pulled a booger from his nose. He kept his hand up until she asked what he wanted.

"May I go to the rest room, please?" he asked.

Mrs. Porter pressed her lips into a line and looked up at the clock again. "Have you finished your meal?"

"Yes, ma'am."

"Very well, then. You may throw away your trash and go to the rest room. You have five minutes."

"Yes, ma'am." Jimmy stood.

The blind man touched his shoulder. "It was a pleasure to meet you, Jimmy," he said. He held out his hand.

Jimmy put his right hand into the blind man's grip. The blind man's hand was big and soft. It was as if Jimmy's own hand had been swallowed.

"Remember to listen and feel, Jimmy," the blind man said. "With your heart."

"Yes, sir," Jimmy said. He was anxious to leave. He didn't have much time. The blind man seemed to want to hang on to his hand forever. Jimmy pulled free, picked up his tray, and hurried to the garbage can. He dumped his trash and leftovers, put the dirty tray on the counter, and walked out of the lunchroom as fast as he could.

He would have started running as soon as he was in the hall, but Mr. Sturner was standing beside the lunchroom's double doorway. Jimmy could feel the principal's eyes on his back. The blind man was right. You didn't always have to be looking at people to know they were there.

He turned the corner and stopped at the door to the boys' rest room, his fingertips touching the wood. He looked behind him. Mr. Sturner had not followed. The glass wall of the school office was right across the hall, but the secretary had her back to him. She was eating a sandwich. There was no one else in sight. The only sound was the murmur from the lunchroom.

Jimmy took his hand away from the rest room door and ran down the hall to talk to Jesus.

* * *

The auditorium seemed deserted. Only the stage lights were on. The door swung shut behind Jimmy with a reverberating *kachunk*. He waited a few seconds for the voice of a teacher to ask him what he was doing there.

"Hello?" he called. His voice was too loud in the big, empty space.

He walked down the sloping center aisle past the curved rows of metal-and-wood chairs. His shoes squeaked. The wooden seats were all standing up against the metal backs. They had made a lot of noise when everyone had stood to go to lunch. Jimmy had enjoyed it. He wished that he could hold down twenty or thirty at once so that he could listen to the clatter when he released them.

When he reached the gray-enameled cement apron between the front row and the stage, he paused to gaze at the spot where the blind man would have landed. It would have hurt a lot. He might have broken his arms or legs. He might even have been killed. Jimmy was amazed all over again at the blind man's bravery and faith. So what if his hands were like dough? Jesus didn't care.

Jimmy crossed the apron to the right side of the stage and climbed the steps that Mr. Sturner had climbed. His shoes were as loud as hammers. He stopped halfway up and looked out across the rows of seats. No one was there. The doors remained closed. He continued upward.

His footsteps were loud on the stage too. He started walking in a shuffle, and the noise was like the sand blocks in music class. He headed for the split in the middle of the brown velvet. When he reached it, he stuck his head through. Behind the curtain, the light was orange.

"Jesus?" he whispered.

His whisper didn't echo. It was if he had said the name to himself, under the covers in bed. No one but him could hear it. He would have to speak up.

He stepped through the split. "Jesus?" he said again, louder. He pressed his hands together and swiveled as if he

16

were a radar antenna. He pointed his fingertips first at one part of the stage and then another. "Jesus?" he called. "Are You here, Jesus? Come in, Jesus. My heart is open to You, Jesus. Come in, please. Over."

There was no answer, no whisper in his ear. He went to the center of the stage, held his arms out straight before him, and turned around and around so that the prayer beam from his fingertips swept the entire stage. "Jesus, this is Jimmy Blackburn," he said. "I accepted You as my Savior last Easter. I have to talk to You. Over."

Still nothing. Jimmy became dizzy, so he began turning the other way. "Jesus, I have a prayer," he said. "I have something to ask You for, in Your name. And anything asked in Your name You promised to do. I know You're here. You whispered to the blind man. Come in, Jesus."

Jesus didn't answer.

Jimmy stopped turning. He pointed his fingers skyward, then closed his eyes tight. "Jesus, please make Mom and Dad happy. I pray this in Your name, Amen."

He listened for the Lord's voice, but all he could hear was the swoosh of blood in his head. All he could feel was the stage rocking under him, trying to make him fall.

He opened his eyes. He was alone on the stage. He had been too late.

Jesus was gone.

Jimmy knew that he had to get back to the lunchroom. He called "Jesus?" once more to make sure, then parted his hands and let his arms drop. Maybe Jesus had gone to the lunchroom with the blind man. Maybe, Jimmy thought, he should have spoken his prayer there instead. But then everyone would have heard.

His dizziness subsided. He walked back through the split in the curtain, into whiter light. The empty seats were spread out before him. He raised his right hand and stepped forward, toward the edge of the stage. His footsteps were as loud as a giant's. He imagined the gasps and the fear.

Would he know when to stop? Would he fall? Would Jesus save him?

Something crackled under his foot. He both felt and heard it. He stopped and looked down.

His toes were four inches from the edge. He was standing on a long strip of brown paper tape that was stuck to the stage. It was almost invisible against the wood. It lay parallel to the edge of the stage.

Jimmy put his other foot on it too. It crackled again. The tape had ridges and air bubbles.

He stepped off the tape and squatted at one end of it. The end had curled a little. He grasped the curl and stood, pulling. The tape came up with a sucking sound. Jimmy wadded it into a ball and then compressed it in his hands as hard as he could. Sharp corners of tape jabbed him. After he stuffed the ball into a pants pocket, his palms were red and sticky.

He hurried down the stage steps and out of the auditorium. The doors banged shut behind him. As he passed the office, he saw Mr. Sturner and the blind man talking inside.

Jimmy made it back to the lunchroom before the bell rang. He'd had more time than Mrs. Porter had said. He sat in his place at the table and stared down at a spot of ketchup so he wouldn't have to look at anyone else. All he could hear was his own breath. All he could feel was the ball of tape in his pocket, biting into his leg.

When the bell rang, Mrs. Porter marched the class back to her room single file. As the children settled into their desks, the bell rang again. That meant that the fifth through eighth graders were going to lunch. They would have twenty minutes to eat. Then, Jimmy knew, they would have an assembly to hear the blind man speak.

He sneaked glances at the clock all through the reading lesson. The twenty minutes lasted what seemed like hours. When the bell finally rang to signal the end of the older children's lunch period, Jimmy forced himself to wait five more minutes before raising his hand.

"What is it, Jimmy?" Mrs. Porter asked. Her voice was angry.

Jimmy didn't let it stop him. He couldn't. "I'm sorry, ma'am," he said. "I have to go to the rest room again."

Several of his classmates giggled. Jimmy ignored them.

Mrs. Porter's face reddened. "Jimmy, you just went to the rest room not half an hour ago."

"I know, ma'am, I'm sorry, but—" Jimmy weighed humiliation against success, and chose success. "—but this time it's Number Two."

The class erupted in laughter. Mrs. Porter slammed her hand on her desk and glared at the entire class. "That will be enough!" she said, almost shouting. "There's nothing funny going on in this classroom." Her eyes shifted to Jimmy. She looked disgusted. "You may go, Jimmy. If you aren't back in ten minutes, I'll call Mr. Sturner on the intercom and have him check on you."

Jimmy hurried out of the room, walking in a half waddle for authenticity. His classmates snickered, and Mrs. Porter yelled at them again. Jimmy was glad. If she was mad at them, maybe she would forget that she was mad at him.

He strode alone down the cool, empty hall. The ball of tape pressed into his thigh. He passed the rest room and went straight to the auditorium.

One half of the center double door was propped open with its metal foot. Jimmy slipped inside and stood against a concrete pillar embedded in the wall. If he remained still and quiet, he wouldn't be noticed. Everyone was looking the other way.

Principal Sturner came down from the stage. The curtains parted. The older kids murmured.

The blind man stood alone at the back of the stage. As before, he put down his cane before stepping forward. As

19

before, he strode without hesitation, without fear. He was courageous in his faith.

Jimmy didn't watch the blind man's feet. He concentrated on the face. The smile. The ears. The sunglasses, shining with twin spots of light.

The older children and their teachers gasped as the blind man came close to the edge of the stage. The blind man raised a hand in greeting, and his smile broadened, revealing his teeth. Then he stepped off, and fell, and landed on his face on the cement.

Girls screamed. Boys yelped. Teachers rose from their seats.

The blind man twitched. He raised his head. His sunglasses hung from one ear. Jimmy saw his milky, blank eyes.

Mr. Sturner rushed to the blind man and tried to help him up. But the blind man was big, and Mr. Sturner couldn't do it. His feet slipped, and he fell too, landing on his bottom beside the blind man. Somebody laughed. Everyone else screamed or yelped again.

The upper-grade boys' P.E. teacher ran down a side aisle. By the time he reached the apron, Mr. Sturner had picked himself up. Together, they pulled up the blind man. The blind man stood, but swayed as if he would fall if the other men let go. His mouth was open. He was making sounds that were almost words. Jimmy could see blood under his nose and inside his mouth. Spit gleamed on his chin.

Mr. Sturner adjusted the blind man's sunglasses so that they covered his eyes again. Then Mr. Sturner and the P.E. teacher helped the blind man up the center aisle. The blind man moved his feet, but they weren't helping. The other men were dragging him.

"Let's get him to the nurse's office," Mr. Sturner said. Then he looked around at the staring, murmuring children and their teachers. "Everybody back to class! There's been an accident!"

When the three men reached the center doors beside Jimmy, the principal and the P.E. teacher jostled to get through the one open door. While they jostled, the blind man pulled a hand free and reached out, grasping air.

"My cane," he said. His voice was slurred. Jimmy could see his tongue. It looked chewed. "I need my cane."

Mr. Sturner ran to get the cane. The blind man and the P.E. teacher waited. The murmur in the auditorium began to subside as teachers told their classes to be quiet or else.

Jimmy stepped away from the pillar and went to the blind man. He could feel the P.E. teacher staring at him, but he didn't care. He was looking through the blind man's sunglasses. Now that they had fallen once, he knew what was behind them.

He touched the blind man's clenched hand, and it opened. Jimmy reached into his pocket and pulled out the ball of brown tape. It was covered with pocket lint. But its points were still sharp.

"Jesus says hi," Jimmy said, and pressed the ball into the blind man's soft palm.

He returned to the pillar. The P.E. teacher was still staring at him.

The blind man trembled. His hand closed over the ball of tape and formed a fist. His mouth opened wide, as if he were about to yell, or scream. Then it closed without making a sound. The blind man opened his fist, but the ball of tape didn't fall. It was stuck.

Mr. Sturner returned with the cane then, and he and the P.E. teacher took the blind man away. The teachers began telling their classes to stand up. Jimmy slipped out before they started up the aisles.

The hall was empty. The blind man was gone. Jimmy pushed his inside-out pocket back inside and headed for Mrs. Porter's classroom. He stopped at the boys' rest room on the way. This time, he really had to go.

VICTIM NUMBER FOUR

The amps thundered, and a white strobe froze the jumping bodies with each flash. The club was a roofed-over alley with walls of spray-painted brick. It was like dancing in a pizza oven. Blackburn liked the place. His ears throbbed. The girl he was dancing with kept bumping into him. He liked that too. She laughed every time she did it. He couldn't hear her over the roar of the band, but he could see her teeth and eyes flash with the strobe. She was happy. He would have to find out her name.

The band played on a plywood stage at the back of the alley. They weren't good, but they were loud. Two electric guitars, bass, and a mismatched drum kit. The beat was fast, the feedback painful. Disco, Blackburn had discovered, was anathema in Austin. That was fine with him. He had tried on one of those white suits with the black polyester shirts a few months ago, and his chest and back had broken out in boils. Tonight he was wearing jeans and a LET'S GET SMALL T-shirt. The girl he was dancing with was dressed as he was, except that her T-shirt depicted a Harley-Davidson eagle. He didn't think she was wearing a bra. He couldn't tell for sure, because her long hair kept flying around and hiding her chest.

The band called itself the Dead Gilmores. Their leader, a short-haired guitar player in black jeans and a tuxedo jacket, had introduced them. Every word after that had been unintelligible, dissolved in amplification. Blackburn rather enjoyed that. He thought that any band that believed its lyrics were crucial was kidding itself. Kids out on Saturday night wanted to drink, dance, yell "Wooooooo!" and have sex with somebody. They didn't want to hear a bad poet bare the angst in his tortured and immature soul. They could go to college for that shit.

The Dead Gilmores ended whatever song they were playing—all of their songs sounded alike—with an apocalyptic crash, and then their leader announced that they were taking a ten-minute break. The house lights, six yellow bulbs suspended from the corrugated-tin ceiling, came on. The crowd applauded and yelled "Wooooooo!" Blackburn's ears ached. The crowd was almost as loud as the band. The girl he had been dancing with bumped against him and laughed.

He leaned down and yelled into her hair. Did she want a beer? She raised her eyebrows and nodded. In the improved light, he saw that she had a lot of pimples. Her face gleamed with oil and sweat. She was gorgeous.

The bar was being mobbed, so Blackburn told the girl that she should wait while he plunged into the maelstrom. He used those words. The girl laughed. Blackburn was pretty sure that he had it made.

He struggled through the crowd, turning one way and then another to slip past the clumping bodies. It took awhile. When he came up against the particle-board bar, he found himself standing next to the Dead Gilmores' leader. The musician gave him a sidelong look and nodded. Blackburn nodded back. The musician wasn't wearing a shirt under his tuxedo jacket, and his pale stomach moved in and out as he breathed. His skin was streaked with sweat tracks. The hollows under his eyes were blackened with what looked like charcoal. It was running down his cheeks.

"How's it goin'?" the musician shouted.

"Okay," Blackburn shouted back. "You in line?"

The musician nodded. "Bartender's slow."

Blackburn nodded back again, then glanced around at the crowd. He could feel that the musician was watching him. He tried to ignore it. But the bartender was taking a long time, and the musician kept on looking at Blackburn. Blackburn gave up and returned the stare.

"That chick you were dancing with," the musician said. His eyes didn't blink.

"What about her?" Blackburn asked.

"I fucked her."

Blackburn said nothing.

"I fucked her yesterday," the musician said. "You can have her tonight, though. Got my eye on the one in the pink." He jerked his head to the left.

Blackburn looked. Several people away, a blond girl in a pink halter top was listening to a scrawny boy in denim. She looked bored.

"Looks like she's with someone," Blackburn said.

The musician glanced at the boy in denim. "No contest." He looked back at Blackburn. "No matter who. You. My drummer. The best-looking guy in here. Wouldn't matter. She'd leave with me."

Blackburn wished that the bartender would hurry the hell up. He liked the Dead Gilmores just fine, but their leader was going to sour him on the whole band in about two seconds.

"Know why?" the musician asked.

Blackburn said nothing.

"It's because of my eyes," the musician said. "The music gets them interested, but then it's my eyes. I'm not bragging. This is just what they tell me, man. There's something about my eyes. Something about the way I look at them. Some kind of hypnotic light in there, you know? That's what they say."

Blackburn looked hard at the musician's eyes. The irises were pale blue, and wet. The pupils were like small black olives. The whites were oiled plastic. The capillaries were so red that they stood out in relief.

"They just look stoned to me," Blackburn said.

The musician sneered. "See your chick? She's looking over here right now. She's looking at me. She's trying to see my eyes."

Blackburn didn't turn to look for the girl. He stayed focused on the musician's eyes. They weren't anything special. Fiber and jelly.

"Yeah, you're afraid to look," the musician said. "You don't want to see. Better learn to play guitar, man. Your eyes ain't got it. Most don't. That's why guys are always ripping me off for shit. My last bass player stole my amp. Same old story. I was cool, he was a dork, and his girlfriend wanted me. So he stole my shit and took off. But I fucked his chick before they left."

Blackburn laughed. The musician had started out as irritating, but he had become funny. Blackburn turned away and gestured to the bartender, who finally took notice and came over. Blackburn ordered two Shiners.

"Hey, man!" the musician yelled. "I was here first! My

break's almost over!" The bartender had already turned away to get the beers.

"He'll be back in a second," Blackburn said.

The musician glared. "Same old shit," he said. "You feel threatened, so you rip me off. Just like the guy who wouldn't let me back in his cheap-ass nightclub because he said I bothered the women. Hey, man, I *fucked* the women. That's what pissed him off. He felt threatened. And he didn't pay me for my last gig. Fuckin' ripoff. All because the girls like my eyes."

"They just look stoned to me," Blackburn said again.

The musician jabbed a finger into Blackburn's chest. "All right, man. You watch." He turned and shoved people out of his way until he reached the blond girl in the pink top. He gazed at her and said something that Blackburn couldn't hear. The girl frowned.

The bartender put two bottles of beer on the bar, and Blackburn looked away from the musician while he paid for them. When he looked back, he saw that the girl in the pink top was heading for the door. The musician was following her. She said something over her shoulder to him. She didn't look happy.

The musician caught up with her, grabbed her arm, and pulled her through the crowd toward the stage. "Time to party!" he cried. "Time to dance!"

Blackburn took a sip from one of the beer bottles and watched. The blond girl was trying to pull free of the musician's grip. The crowd parted for them as they neared the stage. Some of the males cheered and hooted. Some of the females did too. Blackburn started squeezing his way through the packed bodies.

The blond girl was furious. Her face was red. She was screaming at the musician. He pulled her up onto the stage with him.

"Let's hear it for this sweet little rock-and-roll mama!"

the musician shouted into his microphone. The crowd bellowed.

The musician pulled the blond girl to him and stuck his tongue in her mouth. Then he shoved her away and picked up his guitar. He and the drummer kicked off the next song while the blond girl struggled toward the door. She passed right by Blackburn, who was heading the other way. He saw that she was crying.

The yellow light bulbs went off, and the strobe started again. Blackburn found the girl he had been dancing with and handed her one of the bottles.

She pointed toward the door. "Sorry, but I'm gonna take off," she yelled. "I'm too pissed to stay. That guy's a good player, but he's a shit."

Blackburn nodded. The girl started through the jumping bodies toward the door. Blackburn started toward the stage.

When he got there, the Dead Gilmores were cranking fast and loud in a final frenzied bridge. The noise from the amplifiers was like an extended bomb blast. Blackburn's skull rattled. He jumped onto the stage at the crash of the final chord and headed for the drum kit. As the sound decayed, Blackburn grabbed the sticks from the drummer's sweat-slick hands. The drummer yelled.

The band leader's right arm was still raised from striking the chord. Blackburn came up behind him and crouched. The musician stepped back from his microphone and toppled. The amplifiers squealed.

Blackburn climbed onto the musician and knelt on his belly, just below the guitar. The guitar was glitter-specked lavender. In the light of the strobe, each speck was a different color. The musician stared up at Blackburn.

The strobe flashed, and the drumsticks were poised above the musician's face. The strobe flashed again, and they were sticking up from his eye sockets. The crowd squealed with the amplifiers.

Blackburn leaped from the stage, and the people began

clapping and cheering. "All right!" someone yelled. "Alice fucking Cooper!"

Blackburn glanced back at the Dead Gilmores. The bass player, rhythm guitarist, and drummer approached their leader in stop-motion animation. One of them squatted beside him and touched his face. The strobe gleamed from it. It was like oiled plastic. The drumsticks pointed toward the corrugated roof, toward heaven.

The strobe stopped as Blackburn reached the door, and the yellow lights came on. The voice of the crowd started to change. Blackburn went out and ran for his car.

As he unlocked the car door, a voice behind him called "Hey!" He looked back and saw the long-haired girl he had been dancing with. She came up beside him.

"You got tired of the Gilmores too, huh?" she asked.

Blackburn nodded.

"Yeah," the girl said. "They kind of suck."

Blackburn smiled. "Yeah. They did."

The girl seemed to be studying his face. "You have a nice smile," she said.

"How about my eyes?" Blackburn asked.

The girl laughed. "Well, they aren't hypnotic."

He opened the car door, and she got inside. They drove out of town and spent the rest of the night in the country, where it was quiet.

TWO

BLACKBURN FLIES A KITE

The south wind sang through the catwalk. Jimmy lay on his belly with his head hanging over the edge, listening. He worked up a gob of spit and let it ooze from his lips like syrup. When it fell, he closed one eye and watched. It curved away from the tower's east leg and stayed airborne almost ten seconds. Then it burst on the Potwin road, just missing a motorcyclist coming into town from the north. Better luck next time, Jimmy thought.

He stood and walked around to the north side of the water tank, sliding his hand along the rail. In the field below, Jasmine sat apart from the others, playing a five-year-old's game in the dirt with her Doll-Baby. She showed no interest in the brown paper kite he had made. It was lying in the weeds beside her, its shop-rag tail coiled. That was fine with him. As long as Jasmine was all right, he could stay up here awhile longer. Mom had told him to watch her, but she hadn't said to stay close.

The other three kids were flying their own kites, or trying to. Chrissie Boyle and Kyle Thornton were struggling with a green batwing, but it never rose higher than eight feet before diving. Jimmy wasn't surprised. Chrissie and Kyle were only seven, and they didn't understand what was necessary for a kite to fly. Kyle kept trying to throw it, and Chrissie kept running with the wind.

Chrissie's brother Todd had his kite soaring high. With nothing to do now but hold the string, he was spending his time laughing at Chrissie and Kyle. Todd was almost twelve. He was more than a year older than Jimmy, and liked to think of himself as Boss Stud of any group. Being Boss Stud meant having the right to ridicule everyone else.

Jimmy didn't mind. Compared to Dad, Todd was an amateur. Besides, Jimmy preferred solitude over groups. It was only when Mom made him look after Jasmine that he had any use for other kids.

He looked up, squinting at the July sun, and watched Todd's kite for a minute. It was a shield-shaped piece of plastic decorated with the face of a roaring tiger. Below it, a knotted black tail lashed. The tail looked as if it were brushing the top of Clay Hill a half mile away.

Jimmy headed west around the tank, reading for new graffiti beneath the letters that spelled WANTODA. Ever since he had realized that there was no useful truth in either religion or textbooks, he had relied on the water tower and other popular media to teach him what people really thought was important. DRINK MORE WHISKEY, the tank said. '68 RULES. WORLD'S BIGGEST SPITTOON. A-BOMB THE GOOKS. CHERYL SUCKS TO THE HILT. FORD = FOUND ON ROADWAYS DEAD. JOEY + HOLLY. SKOOL DONT TEECH DIK. '70 IS BEST YEA! LARRY + JU-

LIE. KING GOT WHAT HE DESERVED. TOMMY + SUSIE OOOH! SALLY WARDERS IS A CARPENTER'S DREAM (FLAT AS A BOARD). EAT SHIT. DAVID P. + SAM O. = QUEER BAIT. DORIS IS A PIRATE TREASURE (SUNKEN CHEST). KILROY WAS HERE & CHERYL SUCKED HIM. SO LONG BOBBY K. DOPE IS GOOD. KILL ALL COMMIES NOW! GARY + MELANIE. FUCK NIXON. '69 FOREVER! Last weekend, Jimmy had put a sandwich and some notebook paper into his army surplus backpack, and he had come up here and copied everything down. He was sure that if he took it all to heart, he would know how to live in the world.

But he wouldn't add anything to the jumble. Placing his own words among these would be like placing himself among their authors. He had to live in the world, but he was also separate from it, as if he were a starship crewman beamed down and left behind. Or, as Mom had told Mrs. Boyle last week at Nimper's IGA, as if he were a devil child swapped at the hospital for the real thing. Jimmy guessed that meant there was a kid his age stuck with a bunch of demons in hell. Trade you, he thought.

He had almost decided there was no new graffiti when, on the south side of the tank, he found something written along a seam. This was in magic marker instead of spray paint, and it was too small to be seen from below. It said:

JIMMY BLACKBURN IS A PUSSY.

He rubbed the words with his thumb, and they smeared. A thunderstorm had come through yesterday evening, so the insult had been written since then. He began to have suspicions. Chrissie, Kyle, and Todd had all been goofing around beside the tower fence when he and Jasmine had come to the field. But neither Chrissie nor Kyle had the guts to climb the ladder.

Jasmine's voice rose to Jimmy in a shriek. He returned to the north side of the tank and looked down.

Todd had pulled in his kite, and now he was standing

over Jasmine and thrusting the tiger face at her. He roared as the plastic touched her skin, and then he yelled, "I'm gonna eat your baby! I'm gonna eat your baby!" Jasmine held Doll-Baby close to her chest and bawled.

"Hey!" Jimmy yelled. "Big man!" The metal wall behind him rang. His words echoed from Clay Hill, and it was toward Clay Hill that Jasmine looked.

Todd held his kite in one hand and snatched Doll-Baby from Jasmine with the other. He rubbed Doll-Baby's head against the tiger's mouth. "It's eating your baby!" he cried. "It's eating your baaaabeeee!"

Jasmine, screaming, lurched to her feet and reached for Doll-Baby. Todd danced away, mimicking her cries. Chrissie and Kyle continued to try to launch their batwing.

Jimmy walked to the hole in the catwalk over the south leg. He wouldn't hurry. If he hurried, he might make a mistake going down the ladder. Besides, no matter how quickly he got to the field, Todd would be sure to stop torturing Jasmine before he arrived. Then, if Jimmy tried anything, Todd could claim self-defense.

Todd thought he was smart.

But if Todd were smart, he wouldn't be messing with Jimmy Blackburn.

When Jimmy walked into the field, Todd was back to flying his tiger. Jimmy only glanced at him on the way to Jasmine, who was sitting beside the paper kite again. She was kissing Doll-Baby.

"You okay?" Jimmy asked.

Jasmine looked up. Her face was wet. "He tried to eat Doll-Baby."

"No, he tried to bug you. You need to act like you don't care."

Jasmine glared. "He took *Doll-Baby*."

"You're getting too old for Doll-Baby anyway."

Jasmine stood and kicked Jimmy in the leg.

"Want to go home?" he asked.

"And never come back. I hate Todd Boyle."

"Waste of time." Jimmy looked down at the kite he had made. There was a hole where he had drawn the eagle, and the support sticks were broken.

"Todd Boyle stomped it," Jasmine said. "And he threw the string." She pointed at a white line that zigzagged off among the weeds.

"I can make another kite," Jimmy said. "I can make a hundred." He looked across at Todd, who was ignoring them. "Did he do anything else?"

"He said you wouldn't fight and he called you a pissy."

" 'Pussy.' Say it right or you'll get made fun of."

"Are you?" Jasmine asked.

Jimmy picked up his broken kite. "Am I what?"

"Are you going to fight Todd Boyle!"

"No." He started walking.

Jasmine toddled beside him, dragging Doll-Baby by one arm. "But he was mean to me."

"Lots of people are mean."

As they passed Chrissie and Kyle, Kyle said, "Jimmy, our kite won't go up." He sounded as if he were about to cry.

Jimmy stopped to help. As the batwing ascended, Chrissie said, "We have a new baby at our house." She spoke with defiant pride, as if the baby made up for not being able to fly a kite. "Her name is Tina, and she's only four weeks old."

"So?" Jasmine said.

"Be nice," Jimmy said, helping Kyle pay out the string.

"So my mom says Tina is the prettiest baby in the state," Chrissie said.

"Me and Jimmy saw her at the store," Jasmine said. "She looks like a mashed turtle."

Chrissie shoved Jasmine. "You take that back!"

Jasmine swung Doll-Baby at Chrissie's head.

"Chrissie, look!" Kyle shouted. The batwing was almost as high as Todd's tiger.

Jimmy pulled Jasmine away from Chrissie, and Chrissie begged Kyle to let her hold the string. Things blew over fast when you were little. When you got older, they didn't. Jimmy guessed that someday, they wouldn't blow over at all.

After Jimmy and Jasmine crossed the Potwin road, Chrissie and Kyle cried out behind them. Jimmy looked back and saw that the tail of Todd's kite was smacking the batwing. Kyle was trying to pull the batwing away, but it only bobbled in place. Todd was going "Moo-hoo-HA-HA-HAAAA!" Chrissie and Kyle began yanking on their string together.

Jimmy knew what would happen. The batwing's string snapped, and the kite tumbled backward until it crashed on the road. A farm truck ran over it. Kyle began to cry, and Chrissie screamed at her brother.

"That's what happens," Todd shouted. "That's what happens when you get help from a pussy."

For the first time since Jimmy had come down from the tower, Todd looked at him. And grinned.

Jimmy turned to resume the two-mile walk home. Jasmine went into the ditch, her shoes squishing on the wet ground at the bottom, and ran ahead. She thunked Doll-Baby's head on fence posts as she went.

"Won't that hurt her?" Jimmy asked.

"She likes it," Jasmine said.

As they passed the shattered batwing, Jimmy threw his own kite into the road with it. He kept the tail.

When Dad got home that evening, he came into the kitchen and said "Supper fixed?" to Mom. This was a sign of trouble. Jimmy tried to get out the back door.

"Where you think you're going?"

Too late. "Nowhere."

"Nowhere what?"

"Nowhere, sir."

"You get your chores done? You smash those cans like I told you?"

"Yes, sir. I put them in grocery sacks."

Dad looked as if he were trying to think of something wrong with that.

"He was good today," Mom said. "He took care of Jasmine this afternoon so I could get some things done."

Jasmine popped into the kitchen. "He was too pussy to fight Todd Boyle."

Jimmy heard his heartbeat in his head. He tried to open the door, but Dad gripped his arm before he could turn the knob.

"You say that word to your sister?" Dad shook Jimmy so hard that his shoulder popped.

Jimmy was mad. "I didn't do nothing."

Dad opened the door and dragged Jimmy across the yard into the garage. He propelled Jimmy facefirst against the pickup fender and told him to drop his pants.

Jimmy let his jeans and briefs fall around his ankles. Then he gripped the rim of the wheel well, palms up. He would not cry.

He heard Dad take the piece of fiberglass fishing rod from its nails. It *whish*ed through the air twice. Jimmy shut his eyes and clamped his teeth. He would not cry.

The rod hissed a third time and bit into his buttocks. He sucked air through his teeth.

"You gonna teach your sister nasty words?" Dad asked.

"No," Jimmy said. *Eat shit.*

The rod hit the backs of his thighs. Jimmy yelped before he could stop himself. Dried mud inside the wheel well crumbled between his fingers.

"No what?" Dad asked.

"No sir," Jimmy answered. He heard his saliva drip onto the fender. *Queer bait.*

The rod hit his thighs again, with an even hotter sting. His nose began to run. Tears squeezed past his eyelids.

"You gonna backtalk me any more?" Dad asked.

"No sir." *Fuck Nixon.*

"Carl." It was Mom. Jimmy knew better than to look around. "Jasmine says that James didn't say that word to her. She says it was another boy, being mean."

"I ain't whipping him for talking dirty," Dad said. "I'm whipping him for talking back."

Mom's shoes crunched on the concrete as she left.

The rod *whish*ed through the air twice.

Jimmy cried.

When Dad was through, he put the rod back on its nails and said, "Turn around."

Jimmy did as he was told. His legs and bottom burned as if matches touched them in a hundred places.

Dad put his thumbs in his pockets. "Was some punk bothering your sister?"

"Yes, sir."

"Did you whip his ass?"

"No, sir."

Dad looked at him for a long time. "Guess I raised a sissy," he said then. "Didn't I?"

Jimmy had to answer. "Yes, sir."

Dad went to the door. "Pull up your pants," he said, and went out.

Jimmy lay in bed reading a *Green Lantern* comic book. He had already read it ten or fifteen times, but he wanted to keep its events sharp. The new issue was on the rack at the IGA, and he would buy it on Saturday after Mom gave him his allowance.

He was sweating in his windowless room, and the sweat made his welts sting. In a few weeks, when it was hot enough, Mom would let him sleep on the couch in the living room.

After he finished the comic, the welts hurt worse. He wondered how Dad would like it if *he* were the one who was whipped every time he said something wrong. Jimmy looked at his own fishing rod in the corner. Maybe in a few years, he would see if he could give as good as he got.

He sat up and pulled the rod onto the bed. It was a six-foot length of thick black fiberglass. Its Zebco 404 reel was loaded with a hundred yards of twenty-pound test monofilament. At Christmas, Dad had said he'd chosen the sturdy pole and strong line so that Jimmy could catch some really big ones. So far, though, they had only gone fishing once. Dad had gotten disgusted with Jimmy for having trouble threading a worm onto a hook. "If you ain't going to fish right," Dad had said, "you might as well not fish at all." Then he had thrown their stuff into the pickup and driven them home. Several times over the next week, Jimmy had dug up worms near the septic tank and practiced. But it had been for nothing.

The door opened. "That's it, James," Mom said. She pulled the string to turn off the light. "Time to go to sleep."

Jimmy put his fishing rod back in the corner. " 'Night, Mom."

She stood framed in the doorway. "You aren't bleeding, are you, honey?"

"No." The cut on his thigh was small. His jeans had been stuck to it, but it had only bled a little when he'd pulled them down.

"All right," Mom said. "Just be sure to be respectful from now on, and you won't be spanked any more."

"Yes, ma'am."

"That's a boy. Good night, dear."

" 'Night."

She closed the door, and Jimmy lay still, listening. As usual, Jasmine threw a fit at having to go to bed. Also as usual, Mom soothed her until she settled down. Then Mom and Dad had a fight. Jimmy scrambled the words in his head.

When the fight was over, Dad watched the end of the *Thursday Night Movie* and Mom took a bath. Jimmy tried to hear the movie through the noise of running water. There were sirens and gunfire. Usually these sounds put him right to sleep, but tonight his welts kept him awake.

He was still awake after Mom and Dad had gone to bed and Dad was snoring. Jimmy waited until he was sure that Mom must be asleep too, and then he got up. He dressed without turning on the light. When his shoes were tied, he opened his door just enough and slipped into the kitchen. He closed it so that there was no click.

At the back door, he paused. Dad was still snoring, so Jimmy took the key from the nail over Mom's wringer washer. He couldn't unlock the deadbolt without making noise, but he didn't think Mom and Dad would hear. If Jasmine did, she might wake up crying for fear of monsters. But that wasn't unusual. If she kept it up long enough, Mom might come to tell her it was only a bad dream. Jasmine had lots of bad dreams, and Mom no longer looked in on Jimmy just because his sister was bawling.

Jimmy unlocked the bolt, opened the door, and stepped outside. He closed the door and relocked the bolt, then crept around the house into the front yard. When he reached the road, he jumped into the ditch and ran toward town.

He could see the water tower ahead. It was like a silhouette of the Tin Woodman, black against the purple sky.

Dogs in town barked at Jimmy, and a few lights came on. The dogs didn't scare him. He and dogs got along. Some of their owners, though, might call Officer Johnston, the Wantoda cop. Johnston loved grabbing kids out after curfew. But only one car passed Jimmy before he reached the Boyles', and he was able to hide behind a parked van. The car wasn't Johnston.

The Boyles didn't have a dog. A white cat ran from Jimmy as he came up the driveway, but he wasn't startled. The house was dark, as were all the houses on this street. He went to the backyard gate, stopped to listen, and climbed over. The chain-link rattled as if in a breeze.

Jimmy crawled through the grass like a lizard. He kept close to the flower bed that Mrs. Boyle had lined with chunks of granite. He would be chigger-bit, but that was better than being seen. Some of the windows above him were open, so he was careful to be quiet. He slithered behind the house, hoping Todd's window wasn't open too. He wanted to break glass. He had been invited over here once, before Todd had turned into Boss Stud, and he remembered that Todd's room had blue carpeting on the floor and a portable TV on the dresser. If the TV was still there, maybe he could hit it with the granite boulder he would heave inside.

A wail made him freeze. It came from the window directly above. Jimmy remained still until he heard voices from deeper within the house, and then he crawled over the rocks into the flower bed. He pressed against the house's foundation. A yellow rectangle shone onto the grass where he had been.

"Are you dirty, sweetheart?" Mrs. Boyle's groggy voice asked. The wail continued. "No? Hungry?" A moment later the wail stopped.

The foundation was cool and gritty against Jimmy's cheek. Petals tickled his nose.

Mrs. Boyle began singing. "Hush, little baby, don't you cry. Mama's gonna sing you a lullaby . . ." She was accompanied by creaking wood.

Jimmy got to his knees. Then he stood. He could just see over the windowsill. Flower-print curtains hung on the other side of the screen. There was a gap between the curtains, and he could see Mrs. Boyle in a rocking chair beside a white bassinet. The top of her robe was open and pulled to one side. Baby Tina Boyle was sucking on the exposed breast. When Baby Tina stopped for a second, the nipple stood out bright red.

Jimmy was fascinated. When Jasmine had been a baby, he had never seen Mom feed her with anything but a bottle. And he had never seen a lady's breast, although he had seen pictures. The real thing was more amazing.

The door behind Mrs. Boyle opened. Jimmy almost ducked and ran, but then he saw Mr. Boyle's sleep-puffed face. He hadn't been spotted.

"She okay?" Mr. Boyle asked.

"She's fine," Mrs. Boyle said. "Go back to bed."

"Seems like she wants to eat twice as often as Todd and Chrissie did."

"About the same. You're just waking up more."

Mr. Boyle grunted. "Is she gonna starve while we're at Chrissie's whatchacallit on Saturday?"

"It's a tonette concert. That plastic instrument is a tonette, and don't you let Chrissie hear you refer to it as a whatchacallit. I want to buy her a flute when school starts." Mrs. Boyle shifted Baby Tina in her arms. "I'll get a sitter for Saturday."

"Why? We'll be gone, what, from one to two-thirty? Todd can handle it."

"She's a month old, and he's just a little boy. Besides, he'd rather be out playing with his friends."

"He's gonna be twelve in September. He can watch a baby sleep for an hour and a half, or I'll know the reason why." Mr. Boyle yawned. "Well, have fun." He closed the door.

Baby Tina squeaked, and Mrs. Boyle began singing again.

Jimmy sank to the flower bed. He waited until the singing stopped and the yellow rectangle disappeared, and then he returned to the grass. He crawled back to the gate.

He didn't want to break Todd's window. That would only make Boss Stud mad.

What Jimmy wanted was to make Boss Stud dead.

Before going home, he went to the water tower. He squirmed through the hole in the fence, went to the south leg, and began climbing. He had never done this in the dark. The rungs were wet, and one of his feet slipped when he was halfway up. The sensation of almost falling was wonderful. He tried to re-create it after a few more rungs, but it didn't work. The slip had to be unexpected.

On the catwalk, he leaned against the rail and gazed over the town. He hadn't realized that a tiny burg like Wantoda had so many lights. They were spread out below him like a field of stars. It was as if he were an astronaut a billion miles from home, and the water tank were his spaceship. Down on the Potwin road, Officer Johnston's patrol car cruised past without slowing. It was a sign to Jimmy that he could do anything.

He made it back home and into bed without being caught.

Jimmy left his room as soon as Dad drove away. The garage would be his until six o'clock. He took his fishing rod and pocketknife with him when he left the house. He came back for crayons, Scotch tape, and Mom's stapler.

In the garage, he tore a huge sheet from Dad's four-foot roll of brown paper. He was measuring it on the floor when Mom came looking for him.

"What are you doing, James?"

He looked up. "Making a kite. The other one got busted."

"Don't you want breakfast first? We have Wheaties."

"Could I wait and come in at lunch?" He resumed his measurements.

"I suppose so. Does your father know you're using that paper?"

"Yes, ma'am." Dad had granted permission for him to use it for the first kite, and he had no reason to think he couldn't use it for a second.

"Well, don't use too much. We don't know what he wants it for."

Jimmy doubted that Dad wanted it for anything. He had probably found it at work and taken it for no reason, as he had done with other stuff. But Jimmy knew better than to say so.

"And be sure to put that tape measure back where you found it. You know how your father is about his tools."

"Yes, ma'am."

Mom went away. A while later Jasmine came in carrying Doll-Baby. "Whatcha doing?" she asked.

"What's it look like?"

Jasmine cocked her head. "Why's it so big?"

"To make up for the busted one."

Jasmine lost interest. "I wish I had a bicycle," she said.

"You're too little."

"If I had a bicycle, I could give Doll-Baby a ride."

"If you'll go away," Jimmy said, "I'll give Doll-Baby a ride for you."

"You don't have a bicycle either," Jasmine said, and left. She took Doll-Baby with her.

At lunchtime, Jimmy went into the house and ate macaroni. He watched Jasmine try to feed Doll-Baby, and he helped Mom with the dishes. Then he took one of Dad's saws and set off for Stranger Creek.

After returning to the garage, he measured and whittled two of the willow saplings he had cut. When they were finished, he put the kite together. He attached the tail from the first kite, but added ten more shop rags from Dad's barrel. Then he used a length of monofilament to bend the crosspiece into a bow. Finally he tied the kite to his rod and reel line and took it outside.

It worked. It worked so well that it almost dragged him across the pasture. He let it fly at low altitude for a few minutes to be sure the paper wouldn't tear, and then he reeled it in and took it apart. He had the pieces stashed under his bed, and the garage cleaned up, fifteen minutes before Dad came home.

He made a special effort to be polite that evening. He didn't want to be more sore tomorrow than he already was.

Jimmy didn't care that it was daytime. If he was caught, Dad would whip him. Or maybe he would be sent to reform school. He could live with either one.

He sat on the curb down the block from the Boyles' and read the new *Green Lantern*. After a while Mr. and Mrs. Boyle and Chrissie came outside and drove away. Some older kids were riding their bikes toward Jimmy, so he stayed put until they were gone. Then, except for a man mowing his lawn two blocks away, the street was quiet. On a nice Saturday, the people of Wantoda liked to get out of town.

Jimmy stood, folded his comic lengthwise, and put it in a back pocket. Then he picked up his backpack and crossed the street. At the Boyles' front door, he reached into the backpack and took out the sack of cow chips he had collected that morning. He placed it on the stoop and lit it with a match. He donned his backpack. When the bag was burning well, he rang the doorbell and sprinted to vault over the gate into the back yard.

He was under Baby Tina's window with a piece of granite in his hands when he heard Todd open the front door. As Todd yelled, Jimmy heaved the rock through the window screen, tearing it partway from its frame. The rock hit the carpeted floor with a thunk, but Todd was still shouting.

Jimmy grabbed the sill and hauled himself inside. The door to the hallway was open, but he wouldn't stay long enough for that to matter. He threw the rock outside and went to the bassinet. Baby Tina's face was squinched up. She was wearing only a diaper, and Jimmy worried that the tough canvas of the backpack might chafe her skin. But speed was essential. He shrugged off the pack, placed its open mouth beside Baby Tina, and rolled her inside. He buckled the flap.

Todd's shouts stopped. Jimmy grabbed the backpack's shoulder straps, went to the window, and leaned out to lower the pack as far as he could. When he let go, Baby Tina only had to fall a few inches. She began to wail anyway. Jimmy heard the front door close.

"If you think I'm gonna come in there and change your pants, you're crazy!" Todd yelled.

Jimmy clambered through the window and dropped to the flower bed. He reached up and pulled the torn screen more or less back into place. Then he picked up the pack and ran to the gate.

Seconds later he was walking down the street, whistling as loud as he could. But that wasn't loud enough to drown out Baby Tina, so he shifted his weight from side to side to make the pack sway on his back. Baby Tina's cries subsided.

No one was on the street, and Jimmy saw no one watching from windows or doorways. Even the lawnmower man had gone inside. Jimmy turned a corner and headed for the kite-flying field.

He found Jasmine where he had left her. She was sitting on a bare patch of ground beside the water-tower fence, spitting into the dirt and using her finger to draw muddy squiggles.

Jimmy glanced at the wrapped bundle beside her. "Did you do a good job guarding my stuff?"

"Uh-huh." She looked up at him. "You help me find Doll-Baby now?"

Jimmy shook his head. "You have to do one more thing first." Baby Tina squirmed and began to cry again.

Jasmine tried to peer around Jimmy at his backpack. "Whatcha got?"

"A bloodhound puppy," Jimmy said. "It's howling because it wants to track Doll-Baby, but I won't let it out until you do what I say."

Jasmine scowled. "No fair."

44

Jimmy looked at the sky. "I guess you're too little anyway."

"Am not!"

Jimmy shifted his weight to quiet Baby Tina. It didn't work this time. "Okay," he said to Jasmine. "I'll let you try. You know how to get to Chrissie's house?"

"I went there for birthday cake."

"Then you can go there again. But you have to promise to be careful crossing the streets." He paused. "Mom might not want you to go by yourself."

"Would too!"

"All right. Go to Chrissie's house and put this on the doorstep." He took a folded piece of paper from a pocket and handed it to her. He knew its words by heart:

Todd Boyle look in Baby Tina's room and be at field south of Clay Hill by Potwin Road at 1:45 P.M. to take her home or else we will kill her and your dad will kill you. Bring this to prove identity, signed, Some Friends. P.S. We are from Emporia so if you don't show up or if you call fuzz we will take her to beef plant. Wantoda fuzz Johnston is drunk on Saturdays and won't answer anyway and if you call sheriff they will take three hours and she will be hamburger.

Jasmine unfolded the paper and stared at it. Jimmy had written the note in cursive, and Jasmine couldn't read cursive yet.

"After you put it on the step," Jimmy said, "ring the doorbell and run away. This is a secret message, so you have to run before anyone sees you. If anyone does, say that you saw some men drop the paper. Can you do all that?"

"Uh-huh."

"Tell me what you're going to do."

"Go to Chrissie's. Put the paper on the porch and push the doorbell. Then run back here and you help me find Doll-Baby with the puppy."

45

"Right. Get going, Agent X-9."

Jasmine refolded the paper and left. Jimmy didn't like sending her off alone, but it was the only way.

When Jasmine was out of sight, Jimmy took off his backpack and brought Baby Tina out for some fresh air. She squalled worse than ever. She was moist and red.

"It's okay," Jimmy said, jiggling her. "Hush, little baby, don't you cry. James is gonna sing you a lullaby. . . ."

After a few minutes Baby Tina calmed down. Jimmy replaced her in the pack.

The kite was flying at the full length of its line when Jasmine returned. Kyle Thornton was with her, and he was immediately interested in the rod and reel. Jimmy had stuck the handle into the ground and braced it with clods. The shaft was propped on a forked stick, and it quivered with the wind. The monofilament, barely visible, curved upward in a blue arc. It was as tight as a banjo string.

"Neat!" Kyle exclaimed, reaching for the reel.

Jimmy pushed Kyle away, knocking him down. Kyle blinked, about to cry. Jimmy had never been mean to him before.

"Sorry," Jimmy said. He held out his hand. "You can't touch anything."

"I won't," Kyle said, pouting as Jimmy helped him up.

Jasmine shielded her eyes with her hands and gazed up at the kite. "Hey, what's that?" she asked. Her mouth opened wide.

A hoarse cry came from the road. Jimmy turned and saw Todd Boyle charge into the field. Todd's face was flushed, and his eyes were wild.

"You kids stand back a ways," Jimmy said. Staring at Todd, Jasmine and Kyle did as they were told.

Jimmy stood still until Todd was almost on him. Then he dropped and rolled forward. Todd fell over him, just missing the rod and reel. The rod shimmied, and the kite dipped. Its tail swung heavily.

"I'd be more careful," Jimmy said, standing. "You might make it crash."

Todd leaped up. "What did you do to her?"

"I didn't do nothing."

Todd held out the note. "Then what's this, you fucker?"

Jimmy snatched it away and tore it up. He let the wind take the pieces. "Nothing," he said.

Todd grabbed Jimmy's shirt. "Where's my baby sister?"

Jimmy pointed at the giant kite.

A pink form was suspended from it. The kite was so high, and the day so bright, that no features could be seen. But the drawing on the kite was clear. The baby was in the grip of an eagle.

Todd gaped.

"There were two men," Jimmy said. "I was across the road, and I saw them. I didn't know it was a baby they had until it was in the air, and it wiggled and bawled. When they got it up where it is now, they left. I came over, but I've been scared to do anything."

Todd turned back to Jimmy and let go of his shirt. Then he punched him in the face.

Jimmy didn't flinch. The sudden pain in his nose shot into his eyes, but he forced them not to cry. He was used to sudden pain. He was getting better at not crying.

He pointed again. "Is that your baby sister?"

"I'm not stupid! A kite can't hold a baby!"

Jimmy looked up at the kite. "I dunno. It's awful big." He made his eyes widen. "Jeez, look! She just squirmed!"

Kyle began crying. "She did! I saw her!"

Jasmine stared up with an expression of horror.

Todd looked at Kyle and Jasmine, then at the kite. The change in his face made Jimmy want to yell like Tarzan.

"That ain't my sister!" Todd said. His voice trembled. "She weighs too much! She weighs eight pounds!"

"But, God, it's a big kite," Jimmy said.

Jasmine began to cry with Kyle.

"A baby weighs too much!" Todd said.

The wail of an infant came down from the sky.

Todd bumped against the rod and reel, and the baby flailed in the eagle's claws.

"She's still squirming!" Kyle cried.

The wail came again.

Todd yanked the rod and reel from the ground. As the kite started to pull him forward, he cranked the reel frantically.

Far up, the line snapped and floated toward earth in a squiggle. Kyle and Jasmine screamed. The kite shot northward, and the baby jerked.

Todd made a noise that was part moan, part whimper. He dropped the rod and ran across the field.

The wailing from above continued.

Kyle and Jasmine started to run too, but Jimmy caught them each by an arm. "There's nothing you can do," he said.

Todd reached the Potwin road and ran north down the middle of the pavement. Jimmy watched him shrink.

The wailing became weaker, and weaker, and stopped.

The kite vanished behind Clay Hill.

Jasmine kicked Jimmy in the leg. "I hate you," she said. "You put Doll-Baby on your stupid kite."

"That was a *real* baby," Kyle said, sobbing.

"Doll-Baby's a real baby," Jasmine said indignantly.

Jimmy released their arms and picked up his fishing rod. He brushed dirt from the reel. "I'll find Doll-Baby for you now," he said.

"Liar."

He began to reel in the line. "I said I'll find her. You don't even have to help." He looked at Kyle. "And you don't have to feel bad. I'm sure that baby wasn't real."

"It was crying."

"It was fake. I saw the men put a tape recorder in its stomach."

"Oh," Kyle said.

The broken end of the line reached the tip of the rod, and Jimmy stopped cranking. "Mom was going to make oatmeal cookies," he said. "I bet if you guys went to our house, you could get some. I'll stay here to look for Doll-Baby."

"I'm not supposed to go home by myself," Jasmine said. "Kyle'll go too."

Kyle tugged Jasmine's arm. "Come on," he said. "Cookies."

Jasmine allowed herself to be dragged along, but she glared back at Jimmy. "I still hate you."

"Big deal," Jimmy said.

He watched to make sure they crossed the Potwin road safely, and then he looked north. Todd was climbing Clay Hill. As Jimmy watched, Todd fell twice.

Jimmy let the pain of his hurt nose get through and make him cry.

"Serves you right," he said.

The south wind sang through the catwalk. The whole tower was vibrating with an intensity that Jimmy had never felt before. As he cut the fishing line that held the backpack against the boards, he said, "Worth the climb, wasn't it?"

He opened the flap. As the sun lit Baby Tina's face, she opened her toothless mouth wide. Her eyes shone. She liked this vibration, this brilliance. She was smiling, maybe for the first time ever. And because no one was watching, and no one would know, Jimmy lifted her from the pack and hugged her. There was mealy yellow stuff on her legs.

Jimmy looked north and saw that Todd had vanished over the crest of Clay Hill. When Todd found the kite, he would be in a big hurry to get home, so he would probably leave the wreck where it was. Jimmy could retrieve Doll-Baby later.

The kite had crashed well beyond the hill, which meant there was no way that Todd could return home in less than thirty minutes. But Jimmy could be there in ten. If Mr. and Mrs. Boyle were back early, he would say that he'd found the baby in the field. And oh, by the way, he had seen Todd climbing Clay Hill.

If the Boyles were on schedule, all the better. Long before Todd showed up, his parents would have found their soiled infant alone in the house. Todd's troubles were just beginning. Jimmy took Baby Tina to the south side of the tank and showed her the place where the words JIMMY BLACKBURN IS A PUSSY had been written. There wasn't even a smudge now.

Baby Tina gurgled, and he decided to do one more thing.

He put her into the backpack so that her head stuck out. He molded the canvas around her body and snugged it with the piece of monofilament that had held it to the catwalk. Then he took his rod and reel line, looped it through the shoulder straps, and tied it.

He released the brake on the Zebco's reverse. A firm grip on the crank would be important.

He kissed Baby Tina's ear and whispered, "You're an eagle."

Then he stood and swung her into the sky. He braced the rod on the rail and let Baby Tina fly toward earth as fast as he dared. For this one moment of her life, she would know how it felt to be free.

VICTIM NUMBER FIVE

Blackburn walked into the U.S. Army recruiting office at the strip mall on East Kellogg and brought a blast of cold air with him. Papers on the Recruiter's desk went flying. The Recruiter, a burr-headed man in an olive uniform, left his chair and started picking them up.

"Sorry," Blackburn said.

The Recruiter grinned. "That's okay, son. Have a seat and I'll be right with you."

Blackburn sat in one of the two plastic chairs in front of the desk. His coat billowed and settled like a parachute. He picked up a model cannon from a stack of brochures and pointed it at the Recruiter.

"Boom," Blackburn said.

The Recruiter settled into the swivel chair on the other side of the desk. He stacked the papers on the desktop and placed a model of a Sherman tank on top of them. He nodded at the cannon in Blackburn's hand. "That's an authentic reproduction of a Civil War field piece."

"Union or Rebel?" Blackburn asked.

The Recruiter looked puzzled. "Either, I reckon."

Blackburn pointed it at him again. "Boom."

The Recruiter chuckled. "Are you interested in an Army career, son?"

Blackburn replaced the cannon on the brochures. "A friend of mine joined."

"I see. And that's inspired you, right?"

"Yes," Blackburn said. "That's a good way to put it. I'm feeling inspired."

The Recruiter frowned for an instant, and then his expression was all grin again. He held out his big, red right hand. "Master Sergeant Don Riggle here, son."

Blackburn stared at the Recruiter's hand. "You're the one," he said. He reached out and placed his hand in the Recruiter's. The sergeant's grip was like granite. Blackburn winced, and then was angry with himself. He pulled his hand back.

"And what's your name, son?" the Recruiter asked. His grin was still there, but suspicion crinkled the corners of his eyes. His eyes matched his uniform.

"Ernest Tompkins," Blackburn said.

The Recruiter pulled a piece of paper from under the tank and began writing on it with a steel pen. "And how old are you, Ernest?"

"I'm nineteen."

"High school graduate?"

"Yes." It was only a partial lie. Blackburn hadn't even had a senior year, but Ernie had.

"Which high school, son?"

52

"Wantoda Unified. East of here, in Tuttle County."

The Recruiter wrote it down. Then he looked up at Blackburn, his whole face smiling. The suspicion lines were gone. "And what sort of career training do you think you'd be interested in, Ernest?"

Blackburn considered. What would Ernie have said?

"I'm not sure," Blackburn said. "What have you got?"

The Recruiter's body made a gaseous noise. "You name it, son, and today's Army has it." His right forefinger, the size of a carrot, tapped the brochures under the cannon. "Communications technician. Air traffic controller. Smoke operations specialist. Automotive mechanic. Helicopter pilot. Chaplain's assistant. Sanitation specialist. Electrician. There's no end to the possibilities." He spread out the brochures. One of them was entitled *Field Artillery: The Career with a Future.*

"Lasers too?" Blackburn asked. Ernie had expressed an interest in lasers.

"Absolutely," the Recruiter said. "Laser technology out the wazoo." He laughed. His body made another gaseous noise.

Blackburn stared at the Recruiter. "Do you like the way I have my hair cut short, Sergeant?" he asked. His sandy hair was trimmed above his ears and collar. Ernie's hair had always been trimmed like that. Blackburn had never seen Ernie look shaggy.

The Recruiter frowned, then gave a chuckle. "Well, it's better than most young men these days, Ernest. Of course, it'll be cut shorter than that when you get to boot camp. More like mine." He ran a hand over his stubble.

Blackburn reached up and grasped the strands of hair hanging down on his forehead. He twisted them and looked past his hand at the Recruiter. "When I was thirteen I tried to grow it down to my waist," he said. "That was 1971. The sixties had just come to Kansas. That was the year the Student Union up in Lawrence burned."

The Recruiter's face turned stony. "I remember. I was at Fort Riley. Sure wanted to go over there and straighten things out. Looked for a while like we might get to."

Blackburn kept twisting his hair. "That was also the year Lieutenant Calley went to prison."

The Recruiter's eyes narrowed. "Are you here to sign up, son?"

Blackburn nodded. "Sure. Don't you remember?"

"Excuse me?"

Blackburn yanked out the twisted hairs and began to braid them. "This is what I wanted to do that year," he said. "I wanted to braid my hair and hide the braids in my coat. A long coat, like this one. This is Army surplus." He looked up from his braid. "The Army makes good coats."

The Recruiter scratched his jaw. "Thanks," he said.

"You're welcome." Blackburn looked back at his braid. "See, I figured that if anybody gave me any shit, I'd whip out those braids and snap the son of a bitch in the face. Pop his eyes out."

The Recruiter opened a desk drawer and pulled out more brochures. "Now, just take a look at these opportunities," he said.

"Infantry," Blackburn said.

"Excuse me?"

"I want to be in the infantry," Blackburn said. "That's where the shooting is, right? I know how to shoot."

"Well, now, son," the Recruiter said, spreading the new brochures on the desk as if they were a deck of cards, "there isn't much shooting these days. We're at peace."

"I know. We lost the war two years ago."

The Recruiter's nostrils flared. "We didn't lose anything," he said. His voice was low and hard.

"The communists took over South Vietnam," Blackburn said.

"The United States Army has never lost a war," the Recruiter said.

Blackburn considered. "I can respect that," he said. "If it's true, I can respect that a lot."

The Recruiter's eyes were steady. "It's true. No matter what you read in the papers or see on TV, you remember that. The U.S. Army doesn't lose. Ever."

"Would you stake your life on that?" Blackburn asked.

The Recruiter nodded. "I already have, son."

"Then sign me up."

The Recruiter and Blackburn filled out the rest of the form. Blackburn lied where necessary. Then he signed at the bottom of the page. The name he signed was "Ernest T. Tompkins III."

The Recruiter looked at the signature. "Carrying on the family name, I see."

"You don't remember?"

The Recruiter raised an eyebrow. "Excuse me?"

"My name. 'Ernest T. Tompkins III.' You don't remember it?"

The Recruiter's stomach made a grinding noise. "No, son, I'm afraid I don't."

Blackburn reached into his coat, into the pocket he had cut into the lining. "Then you lied. The Army has lost."

"I'm not following you, Ernest."

"The Army has lost its memory. It doesn't remember Ernest T. Tompkins III."

The Recruiter pointed at Blackburn. "But you're right here."

Blackburn shook his head. "You shouldn't have forgotten that name. Not after what happened. He sent my mother a letter a year and a half ago after you went to Wantoda Unified and signed him up. He hoped I would call her sometime, and last month I finally did. She told me he'd joined the Army."

"Who?"

"Ernest T. Tompkins III. Who wanted to serve his country after its ignominious defeat. Who was interested in lasers. Who had asthma, and told you so. And you said come on ahead.''

The Recruiter stood. ''Now look here, son—''

Blackburn pulled the Colt Python from his coat. ''So you sent him to boot camp last year, in the summer. In Texas. He died. He died running. He couldn't breathe.''

The Recruiter backed away from the desk. He held up his granite hands. ''Now look, son,'' he said, his voice soothing. ''Every recruit is given a physical. If that had shown anything serious, he wouldn't have been let in.''

''The physical must have missed it,'' Blackburn said. ''But you didn't. Ernie told you. His letter said so. And you don't remember.''

The Recruiter licked his lips. His stomach rumbled. ''Sure I do, son. I told him that the doctors would check it out and make the decision. It wasn't mine to make. You can't kill me for that.''

''What color was his hair?'' Blackburn asked.

''Excuse me?''

Blackburn stood and pointed the pistol at the Recruiter's abdomen. ''You say I can't kill you for not keeping him out of the Army because of his asthma. So I won't. I'll kill you for lying. You say the Army never loses anything. That must include memory. So what color was his hair? It was wavy on top. Very distinctive. What color was it?''

The Recruiter was sweating. He farted. ''Look, son, I talk to hundreds of young men a year. I can't possibly remember everything about every one of them.''

Blackburn cocked the pistol. ''But this wasn't just anyone, Sergeant,'' he said. ''You signed him eighteen months ago. His name was Ernest T. Tompkins the Third. He told you that he had asthma. He died at boot camp. It was reported on all three TV stations and in the Wichita *Eagle*. When I called my mother, she told me that she has the clipping, and that it includes a quote from you. 'It is always a tragedy when a young man dies,' you said.''

"Oh," the Recruiter said. His gut moaned.

"What color was his hair?"

"Dark brown. Almost black."

Blackburn lowered the pistol. He looked at the floor. He wished he still knew how to cry. "Ernie had asthma. He died at boot camp."

The Recruiter stepped forward. "I'm sorry, son," he said. "These things happen. All we can do is grieve, and go on." He held out a hand. "Give me the gun."

Blackburn looked up. "Red," he said.

"Excuse me?"

"His hair was red." Blackburn raised the Python and shot the Recruiter in the belly. The Recruiter stumbled backward, then lurched forward, yelling. Red ooze bubbled from the olive cloth. Blackburn shot him again. There was a hissing noise and a smell of shit. The Recruiter dropped to his knees and rested his cheek on the desktop. His fist smashed the tank. His eyes glared at Blackburn. They didn't blink.

Blackburn put the gun away. "Ernie had asthma," he said. "Ernie died at boot camp. Ernie's hair was bright red." He reached down and pushed the model cannon across the desk. "Ernie was my friend."

He stopped the cannon a quarter of an inch from the Recruiter's nose.

"Boom," he said. Then he turned and went out to the sharp wind of the Kansas autumn.

THREE

BLACKBURN AND THE CHICKEN-KILLER

Jimmy had been in town to see Ernie that Wednesday, so he didn't know that his mother and Jasmine had left until he got home. He figured out that he had been reading comic books in Ernie's room when Dad had smacked Mom for the fifth time that week. Mom had taken the old Chrysler station wagon, leaving the GMC pickup. Jimmy was sure that she would have taken him along too, if he had been home. She would at least have given him a choice.

Summer vacation didn't end for three more weeks, and Dad would be home a lot since he had been laid off. Jimmy didn't like the prospect. Not that he liked the prospect of school either. He had been dreading eighth grade. At the end of seventh grade, he had noticed that some of the girls were growing breasts, and some of the boys were getting hair on their faces. These were not good omens. Still, he would have preferred school over staying home alone with Dad. It wasn't even that Dad was a bad guy. It was just that he didn't know what else to do with his tough breaks but pass them along. With Mom and Jasmine gone, Jimmy would be in for more than his share.

He was sure of that right after Mom left. Dad tried to cook hamburgers for supper, and started a grease fire. He picked up the skillet and ran outside, burning his hands. When he came back in, he cussed Jimmy for not helping. Jimmy said that he hadn't known what to do, and Dad smacked him and told him to get to his room. Jimmy went into the hot little room and shut the door. He read the Spider-Man comic book that Ernie had given him. After a while he had to pee, but Dad hadn't said he could come out. He waited until he heard Dad's snore, then crept out through the kitchen and down the hall to the bathroom. He peed sitting down so he wouldn't have to turn on the light, and aimed so that the stream hit under the rim instead of in the water. He didn't flush.

In the morning he stayed in bed until Dad yelled for him to get up and do his chores. He got up and put on a T-shirt, cutoffs, and sneakers, then went out to feed the chickens.

The chickens mobbed him. Jimmy hated them. They were loud, smelled bad, and crapped all over the place. Dad had brought them home as chicks in March. There had been fifty of them. They had been cute, fuzzy little things. Some of them had even seemed smart and had taken to following Jimmy or Jasmine around. Then half of them had died, and the rest had grown up fast and gotten stupider. By the time they'd reached their growth, they had become brainless. Now they were eating and shitting machines. They laid eggs too, but broke a lot of them and covered the rest with chickenshit. Jimmy dumped a pile of feed on the ground for them to swarm over, then stepped away to drop a handful for the rooster.

All of the chicks had grown up into hens, so Dad had brought home a rooster in June. It was hideous. None of the pictures Jimmy had ever seen of roosters had looked anything like it. The pictures were of strutting, broad-chested birds with bright red combs and gold and green feathers. But this rooster waddled like a duck, had a dull pink comb that was torn, and feathers the color of old cornbread. It dragged its tail in the dirt. The hens often ganged up and pecked the hell out of it. It had lost a lot of feathers in the past two months, and the bare patches were scabby. It waddled over and gobbled a few mouthfuls of the feed Jimmy dropped for it, and then three of the hens ran it off.

Jimmy went into the plywood coop and gathered the eggs. There were ten that weren't broken. That was better than usual. He cleaned up the rest as best he could and took the ten to the well pump to wash them.

Ten. Farm eggs sold for thirty cents a dozen in Tuttle County, when people bothered to stop and buy them. Most folks just spent the extra dime to get them at the store with the rest of their groceries. Where Dad had gotten the idea that chickens would make money, Jimmy didn't know. Someone had lied to him. Or maybe things had been different when Dad was a kid, and he hadn't been able to figure out that the world had changed. The chicken feed alone cost more than the eggs brought in, never mind the trouble of dealing with the chickens themselves. Jimmy wondered what was wrong with Dad's brain.

He took the eggs into the house. Dad was eating toast in the kitchen.

"How many?" Dad asked.

"Ten."

Dad shook his head. "Don't know what's the matter with them." He eyed Jimmy. "You been chasing them?"

"No, sir," Jimmy said. He put the eggs into the bowl in the refrigerator.

"You been breaking any?"

"No, sir."

Dad put more bread into the toaster. "Want breakfast?"

"Sure." Dad gave him a look. "I mean, yes, sir."

The toast popped up. Dad rubbed each slice with a stick of oleo and handed one to Jimmy. Jimmy said thank you and sat at the table to eat.

"I'm going into Wichita," Dad said.

"Can I come?" Jimmy asked. Once in a while Dad would take him along to the hardware or auto parts stores. Jimmy liked the men who worked there. They were the kind of men who would say hi to a guy even if he couldn't drive yet.

"No," Dad said. "And don't go into Wantoda either. I want you here when your mother gets home. You tell her I'm checking on a machine shop job. I'll be home for supper."

"Yes, sir," Jimmy said. "Would it be okay if Ernie came out?"

"Long as he doesn't eat anything," Dad said. "I work hard enough to feed my own kids." He left the kitchen. The front screen door opened and banged shut. The pickup started and drove off.

Jimmy finished his toast, then put a pan of water on the stove. When it was boiling, he took an egg from the refrigerator and dropped it in. It hit the bottom of the pan and cracked, sending white streamers through the bubbling water. Jimmy let it boil until the water was almost gone. Then he shut off the stove and took the pan to the sink. He ran water over the egg and tried to peel it. It was still hot, and it stung his fingers. A lot of the white came off with the shell. He ate what was left. The yolk crumbled hot and dry in his mouth. The August day was heating up outside.

*   *   *

61

He phoned Ernie, and Ernie asked his mother for permission to ride his bike out. Jimmy heard Ernie's mom say that she guessed it was all right. Ernie's mom had a quavering voice and always sounded as if she were about to cry, so Jimmy could never tell how she felt about what she said. His own mother's feelings were always clear. She laughed when things were good, and she bawled when things were bad. She bawled too much.

Jimmy took his BB gun outside and shot at sparrows to kill time until Ernie showed up. There was a hot wind, and his shots curved wide. Sometimes he could see the BBs swerving as they flew, going into orbit like tiny golden satellites. Some of the chickens came running, expecting more feed, and he shot one of them in the rump. They took off squawking. Dad would switch him to within an inch of his life for an offense like that, but Jimmy sure as hell wasn't going to tell him about it. The stupid chicken wasn't hurt, anyway. Jimmy would have liked to put one through its head, in one eye and out the other.

Between shots, he looked down the Potwin road toward Wantoda. Finally he saw Ernie. Ernie was coming slow despite having the wind at his back. Jimmy took his BB gun to the porch and rode his bike out to meet his friend. He put his head down and stood to pump against the wind. The pavement was oily, cooking in the sun. His bike rattled.

When he came within fifty yards of Ernie, he charged him as if to collide head-on. Ernie yelled and stopped where he was. Jimmy whizzed past, then turned and coasted back, letting the wind push him.

"Hey, pussy," he said, coming alongside.

Ernie's wavy red hair was damp, and his face was flushed. He was wearing a blue nylon backpack that made his narrow shoulders look even narrower. He was wheezing. "Pussy yourself," he said. He was hoarse.

"What's the matter?"

"Dust or something. Can't hardly breathe."

"Come on and get a drink." Jimmy pumped ahead and waited in the driveway until Ernie arrived. They went into the house together and made Kool-Aid lemonade, then drank it with ice and ate the bologna sandwiches and Cheez Curls that Ernie had brought. They discussed the Spider-Man comic book that Ernie had given Jimmy and agreed that the Green Goblin was not a worthy adversary. He acted like a queer.

When the food was gone, they went outside and took turns shooting at the sparrows. They had trouble hitting within a foot of their targets.

"Too much wind," Jimmy said.

"You should do it at night, anyway," Ernie said. "You put a flashlight on them. They get hypnotized and can't move. We can try it tonight, if you want."

"Maybe. My Dad'll be home."

"So?"

"So I don't know if he'll want us to."

Ernie took a shot and hit a tree branch a few inches from a sparrow. The bird took off. So did every other bird in the tree. The boys waited for them to come back.

"Your mom and sister at the store?" Ernie asked.

"Maybe. I don't know."

"What do you mean, you don't know?"

Jimmy stared up into the tree. "I mean I don't know. They took off yesterday while I was at your place. They aren't back yet."

"Oh." Ernie handed Jimmy the BB gun, then picked up his lemonade and took a drink. "Family troubles, huh?"

"I guess."

"Don't worry about it."

"I think they just went to see my grandma in Oklahoma."

"Where in Oklahoma?"

"Tulsa."

The birds were starting to come back, so Jimmy and Ernie lowered their voices.

"That's where Oral Roberts University is," Ernie said. "That's where my mom wants me to go to college. They have a great basketball team."

"I wouldn't go to a college named after a goddamn preacher," Jimmy said.

Ernie made a face, as if the lemonade were sour. "I didn't say I was going to go. I said my mom wants me to. She's big on that prayer tower they have with the eternal flame. You can call in with prayers, and guys'll go up in the tower and pray them for you."

"For how long?"

"I dunno. Until the prayers get answered or the guys have to poop."

They both laughed, and the returning birds spooked.

"Hell," Jimmy said, "there they go again."

"Wait until night and put a light on them," Ernie said. He took another drink of lemonade. "You believe in God?"

Jimmy shrugged. "I guess. But I don't think preachers know any more about God than anyone else. Churches are a racket."

"Yeah," Ernie said. "You should see the money they rake in at the United Methodist. I wouldn't go, except my folks make me. But I think prayers work, sometimes."

"Grow up."

Ernie spit a lemonade-goober at the ground. "Not the prayer tower and church and stuff. Just telling God what you think."

"I've tried it. It don't work."

"Maybe you tried to do it the way the preachers say you should. Maybe you never tried it your own way. Just saying what you want. Or what you think about things."

Jimmy grunted. He didn't like it when Ernie got weird like this.

One of the sparrows came back to the tree and perched on a high, bare twig. Jimmy raised the BB gun and sighted.

"Oh God," he said, "please let me kill this fucking bird.

In Your name I pray, Amen." He squeezed the trigger. The BB gun popped. Jimmy didn't see the BB fly.

The sparrow twitched, then flopped over. One of its feet held on to the twig for a few seconds before it fell. It bounced once when it hit the ground.

Jimmy and Ernie ran over to it. There was blood on a weed it had brushed against on the way down. It wasn't moving.

"I'll be damned," Jimmy said. "God came through."

Ernie cupped his hands around his mouth and spoke in a booming voice.

"Thou art welcome," he said.

Ernie left at five o'clock. Jimmy rode alongside for the first mile, then said good-bye and turned back. He was within a quarter mile of home when Dad's truck pulled up beside him.

"You were told to stay home!" Dad yelled. His face was greasy with sweat.

"I did," Jimmy said. "Ernie came out and I just rode partway back with him."

"You were told to stay home!" Dad yelled again. The pickup burned rubber and went past.

Dad was waiting beside the truck when Jimmy entered the driveway. He yanked Jimmy off the bike and dragged him into the garage.

"When I give an order," Dad said, "I expect to be obeyed." He took down the piece of fiberglass fishing rod from its nails. "Drop your pants."

Jimmy forced down his fear. Not this time, he thought. He wouldn't do it this time. But then Dad would beat him up even worse.

"Mom called," Jimmy said. His voice quavered like Ernie's mother's. But at least he wasn't crying.

The switch wasn't cutting through the air the way it always did. It remained still in Dad's hand.

"What did she say?"

Jimmy didn't care what he told Dad then. He would say anything. He would say anything and keep on saying it as long as it kept the fiberglass rod still. He was thirteen. He was too old to be switched. He was too old to be treated like some goddamn baby.

"She said she was at Grandma's. She said she wouldn't be home tonight, but not to worry. She said to tell you she was sorry she got mad and she'll be back tomorrow."

"Tomorrow?" The switch lowered.

Jimmy licked his lips. "She said she hopes tomorrow, but maybe the next day. She said Grandma was really glad to see her and she couldn't just show up and then leave right away, so it might not be tomorrow but the next day. But not to worry because the car's okay and she's sorry she got mad. And she said to tell you there's pot pies in the freezer."

Dad closed his eyes for a second and rubbed his mouth with his free hand. "Anything else?"

Jimmy tried to think of something more. He couldn't. Much more would sound like the lie it was, anyway. Mom wouldn't have talked a long time on Grandma's phone bill.

"No, sir. Except she said we shouldn't call Grandma's house because Grandma's in a bad mood." Dad would believe that.

Dad snorted. "Like I would," he said. "Turn around and bend over. You still got a whipping coming. You got to start doing what you're told."

Jimmy turned around and bent over. Dad gave him five, but they weren't hard. And he hadn't had to drop his pants. He had won, so long as Dad didn't find out that he'd lied. And it hadn't been a total lie, anyway. Where else would Mom be but at Grandma's?

He and Dad had turkey pot pies for supper. The crust was black on the edges, but it still tasted okay. Jimmy burned his tongue on the filling. He always did that.

Afterward, he and Dad watched a John Wayne cowboy

movie on TV. There was a dab of ice milk left in the freezer, and they ate it.

When Jimmy went to bed, the burned patch on his tongue tingled, keeping him awake. He thought about the sparrow he had shot that afternoon. Mom had said more than once that God counted every sparrow that fell. Mom didn't approve of him shooting them. He wondered what she would think if she knew that he had prayed to kill this one.

The next day was a Friday. Mom and Jasmine didn't come home. They didn't come home Saturday either. Dad went out Saturday evening and didn't come home himself until Sunday afternoon. He smelled of beer and was angry. Jimmy knew that Dad was looking for an excuse for another whipping, so he said that Mom had called again. She had decided to stay with Grandma a few more days to help with some housecleaning and sewing. She and Jasmine would be home by Wednesday.

That had to be safe, Jimmy thought. Wednesday would be a whole week. Mom wouldn't stay away longer than that.

On Monday, Dad left in the morning. Jimmy was again to tell Mom, if she returned, that Dad would be home for supper. Dad didn't tell Jimmy to stay home, but Jimmy figured that he should anyway. Sometimes Dad meant orders given one day to be followed weeks or months later as well.

Ernie rode his bike out and brought lunch again. Jimmy was glad of that. He and Dad had eaten the last of the macaroni and cheese the night before, and there was nothing left in the house that either one of them knew how to fix. They were even out of bread for toast. Dad hadn't said anything about buying groceries, so Jimmy doubted that he would. Ernie had brought bologna sandwiches and Cheez Curls again, but also two packages of chocolate cupcakes and two bottles of Coke. He was wheezing when Jimmy met him in the driveway.

"Maybe you should see a doctor," Jimmy said. "You don't sound so good."

Ernie dropped his bike and staggered to the porch. He was wearing cutoffs, like Jimmy, and his matchstick legs were wobbly. He took off his backpack and sat down. "I just got hay fever," he said. He pulled a crumpled handkerchief from his cutoffs and blew his nose into it. He held it up. "See?"

"Jeez, why don't you show me your shit too?"

"Queer."

"Let's eat."

Jimmy was out of BBs, so after lunch they decided to go swimming. They mixed up the last package of Kool-Aid lemonade and poured it into two Mason jars. They put the jars into Ernie's backpack along with the leftover Cheez Curls and set off. The jars clanked and sloshed. Some of the chickens tried to follow the boys, so they yelled and threw clods until the birds took off squawking.

They climbed through the barbed-wire fence behind the windbreak of evergreens and tramped through prairie hay that came up to their waists. The ten-acre meadow belonged to Dad, but the man from whom he had borrowed a mower and baler last year had died. So this year the hay would stay tall. It tickled and scratched. The boys' legs became criss-crossed with red lines. They went up over the hill and down to the second fence, where they crossed into the pasture. This was seventy acres and was owned by a man named Claussen, who kept thirty head of beef on it. Jimmy pointed at the cattle when they topped a rise. The black and brown steers were two hundred yards away, clustered around salt blocks that Claussen had dumped on a grassless patch of earth. The steers switched their tails at flies.

"We'll have about two hours to swim before they come down and muck it up," Jimmy said.

"How do you know?"

"I watched them. They go down when it gets really hot,

about two-thirty or three. Then they stay there until it gets cool in the evening. Sometimes they spend the night there, I think. They graze in the early morning and hang out at the salt after that. Until it gets hot again.''

''I didn't know cows had schedules,'' Ernie said.

''Not cows. Steers. Bulls without balls.''

''No wonder you know all about them.''

Jimmy punched him in the shoulder. They went down to the pond.

The pond was surrounded by brown mud banks. The earthen dam rose at the east end. At the west end, the pond narrowed into a swampy stand of weeds.

''There're snakes in the weeds,'' Jimmy said, pointing. ''We need to stay away from that end.''

They stripped off their shirts and went in. They left their shoes on. The water stayed blood-warm until it was waist-deep. Then there was a layer of coolness down low. The bottom was mud that sucked at their sneakers, but there were also sticks and things that felt like broken glass and tin cans. The water didn't come up to their necks until they reached the center. Jimmy found one hole where the water was over his head. He dropped into it and opened his eyes, but all he could see was a brown haze. When he looked straight up, it turned reddish. The water in the hole was cold, and something slimy slithered past his legs. He surfaced and moved back to shallower water.

He and Ernie swam and splashed each other until they tired, and then they moved to where the water was shallow enough that they could sit with the waves lapping at their chins. The sun was hot on Jimmy's head, and when his hair started drying, he dunked himself to wet it again.

''Hey, look,'' Ernie said when Jimmy surfaced. He was pointing toward the dam.

Jimmy blinked the water out of his eyes. A small brown dog with a narrow head was sitting on top of the dam, watching them. It was panting.

"I think he wants a drink," Ernie said.

"So why doesn't he get one?"

"Maybe he's scared of us."

Jimmy stood. The breeze on his chest was cool for a few seconds, then turned hot. "Come on, pup," he called, bending over and patting his thighs. "Come on down. We won't hurt you. Come on."

The dog cocked its head.

"You know him?" Ernie asked.

"Never saw him before."

"How come you don't have a dog, anyway? Out here in the country you could have three or four."

Jimmy shrugged. "Dad doesn't like them. He says they just cost money for feed." Sort of like chickens, he thought. Only not as stupid. He started walking through the water toward the dam.

The dog stood, ready to run.

"It's okay, pup," Jimmy said. "Don't be afraid. We're your buddies. Don't be a chickenshit." He kept on walking until he was within a few feet of the base of the dam. "Come on down, pup. The water's fine."

The dog took a few steps toward the water, then returned to the top of the dam. It sat down again and panted.

"Here come the cows," Ernie said.

Jimmy looked. The steers were moving down the slope toward the pond like slobber-nosed tanks. Jimmy slogged back to Ernie, and they got out of the pond. Ernie opened his backpack and brought out one of the Mason jars. They each took a long drink of Kool-Aid, and then the steers were close. A chunky black one bellowed at them. The boys moved away toward the dam, and a brown streak shot past them, heading toward the cattle.

It was the dog. It charged the black steer, and the steer turned and ran, thudding into another member of the herd. Then all thirty of the steers were running back the way they had come, their hooves rumbling. The dog stayed after them, dashing first at one and then another.

Jimmy and Ernie laughed. The steers disappeared over the rise, and the boys went back into the water. After a while the dog came back and took a drink while they were out in the middle.

"Thanks, pup!" Jimmy called. The dog looked across at him and grinned, its jaw dripping. It took several more laps from the muddy water, then trotted back to the top of the dam. It stayed there and watched Jimmy and Ernie until they got tired and left.

Jimmy's mother didn't come home that day. In the evening, Dad smacked Jimmy in the head for not doing the dishes. Dad hadn't even told him that he should, but that didn't seem to matter.

On Tuesday, Dad was gone before Jimmy woke up. There wasn't a note. Jimmy took care of the chickens and boiled a couple of eggs. After eating, he cleaned up the kitchen and bathroom, then dragged out Mom's canister Hoover and vacuumed the living room. It was boring as hell, but he wanted to head off Dad's temper if he could. The only room he didn't clean was Mom and Dad's bedroom. The door was shut. He wouldn't have gone in even if it had been open.

When he had finished cleaning the house, he went outside and mowed the yard until the mower ran out of gas. The fuel cans in the garage were empty, so there was nothing more he could do. He left the mower where it had died and went into the house to splash water on his face and arms. He was dusty and covered with bits of dry grass that itched. When he felt better, he took some comic books to the porch. It was too hot in the house. He sat on the concrete step, his legs in the sun, his head in the shade.

Ernie showed up while he was reading *The Flash*. Ernie had brought lunch again. Jimmy was embarrassed that Ernie kept having to feed him, but there wasn't much he could do about it. He didn't have any money to buy groceries, and Dad would kill him if he went into town anyway.

They ate lunch and then hiked back to swim in the pond again. The little brown dog appeared after they had been there about twenty minutes. It sat on top of the dam and watched them as it had the day before. Jimmy and Ernie went to the base of the dam and called it, but it still wouldn't come down. It moved away whenever one of them took a step up the dam. They gave up and went back into the water.

"What kind of dog is that, anyway?" Jimmy asked.

"Heinz fifty-seven," Ernie said. "He's got some terrier in him, though."

"What kind of terrier, you figure?"

"Rat."

"I wonder who he belongs to."

"If he belonged to anybody, he wouldn't be here, stupe."

Jimmy splashed Ernie in the face, and they got into a terrific war. They moved into deeper water and floated on their backs, kicking brown and white plumes at each other. Then something brushed against Jimmy's shoulder, and he stood up in the chest-deep water.

The dog had swum out to them. It paddled around Jimmy in a circle, holding its triangular head up at an angle. Its mouth was closed. Jimmy heard air puffing in and out of its wet black nose. Its expression was one of serious concentration.

Ernie stopped splashing and stood. He stared at the dog. It swam around him and back to Jimmy.

Jimmy put a hand under the dog's chest and lifted, buoying it. The dog stopped paddling. It didn't try to get away. It remained still, letting Jimmy hold it. It kept its head pointed up and its mouth closed. Jimmy could feel its heart beating fast.

"You're a brave one, pup," Jimmy said, and let it go. It paddled across to the muddy bank, climbed out, and shook itself so hard that some of the spray reached the boys.

Ernie shook his head. "That's a weird dog."

"I like him," Jimmy said.

"How you know it's a him?"

"Look, moron."

The dog still wouldn't come to them when they left the water, but it trotted after them when they started back toward Jimmy's house. It stayed well back.

"What's the matter with him?" Ernie asked.

"He's smart," Jimmy said. "He wants to make friends, but he wants to make sure we want to make friends too."

"So why'd he swim out to us?"

"He's a good swimmer. He probably figured he could get away if we tried to hurt him."

"Why would he think we wanted to hurt him?"

"How should I know? Maybe people have hurt him before."

They continued toward the house. A cottontail rabbit spooked, and the dog took off after it. The boys ran after them, whooping, cheering the dog on. The wind burned past Jimmy's face. It felt great.

The rabbit led them to the salt lick. The dozing steers looked up, startled, and saw the dog. They bellowed and ran into each other trying to get away. The dog didn't even notice them. It was after the rabbit. The cattle fled, kicking up dirt.

The rabbit zigzagged and ran into a salt block. Jimmy saw it happen, and heard the *thunk*. The rabbit stopped cold. It might have been able to recover, but it didn't have time. The dog caught it by the head and shook it.

The steers' hooves rumbled. Dust boiled into the sky. The little dog stood in the center of chaos, victorious, shaking the cottontail. Jimmy stopped at the edge of the salt lick, breathing hard. He laughed and clapped. Ernie came up beside him, coughing.

The dog tore open the rabbit and lay down in the center of the bare patch of earth to eat. Jimmy and Ernie went toward it, and it growled. They stopped and watched it for a while. It was as serious about eating as it had been about swimming. Jimmy had never seen a human being with such singleness of purpose. He admired the little dog.

"Guess he doesn't go hungry," Ernie said.

"He's too smart for that," Jimmy said. They went on to the house. The dog stayed behind and ate.

Jimmy and Ernie were reading comic books on the porch when Dad came home. It was four o'clock. Jimmy hadn't expected him home until after five.

Dad lurched out of the pickup. His foot slipped on the gravel, and he almost fell. He came up cussing. He started toward the house, saw Jimmy and Ernie, and looked disgusted. Jimmy glanced at Ernie. Ernie looked scared.

Jimmy stood up. "Hi, Dad," he said.

Dad looked across the yard. "What the hell you mean leaving that mower out?" he yelled. He sounded as if his tongue were too thick. "Supposed to goddamn rain. Ain't I told you to put it back when you're finished?"

"I was going to," Jimmy said. He was miserable.

"And you stopped with the job half done," Dad said. "What kind of lazy shit did I raise, huh?"

Jimmy's misery became rage. "It ran out of gas," he said. His voice was loud. "And there wasn't any more."

"I better go home," Ernie mumbled. He put down the comic book he had been reading and started toward his bike in the driveway.

"You talking back to me?" Dad bellowed.

Ernie looked back at Jimmy. His lips formed the word "Pray." Then he hurried to his bike and pedaled away. He had forgotten his backpack. It lay on the porch beside the comic book.

"You talking back to me?" Dad bellowed again.

Jimmy's skin was hot all over. He jumped off the porch.

"I'll talk to you any way I like," he said, "you son of a bitch."

Dad lunged for him. Jimmy dodged, and Dad banged his shin against the porch. He turned toward Jimmy. His face was purple.

Jimmy ran to the backyard and past the chicken coop. The chickens scattered as he passed. Feathers flew. Jimmy could hear Dad's footsteps behind him. Dad wasn't yelling, wasn't saying anything. That scared Jimmy. Why couldn't he have kept his mouth shut? If he had kept his mouth shut, Dad would have smacked him once or twice. Big deal. Now Dad wanted to kill him. He really wanted to kill him. Jimmy could tell.

He crashed through the evergreens and clambered over the barbed-wire fence. His cutoffs caught and tore. A barb scratched his thigh. He didn't stop. Dad was coming through the trees. Jimmy dropped to the hay meadow and ran hard for the second fence.

Hay whipped his legs. His heart slammed against his chest. Hot wind scraped his throat. He ran as fast as he could, up and over the hill and down. He couldn't hear Dad behind him anymore. As he climbed over the second fence, he risked a glance back. Dad had stopped at the top of the hill and was watching him.

Jimmy dropped into the pasture and kept running north, over the rise and down toward the pond. His arms were heavy and tingling. His head hurt. But he couldn't stop. He had called his father a son of a bitch. He passed the salt blocks. Some of them had smooth channels where they had been licked over and over again. He kept running.

The cattle were at the pond. Most of them stood in the shallow part beside the flat bank. The rest were lying on the mud. They saw Jimmy coming and tensed. He ran wide around them, up onto the dam. They didn't spook, but they watched him. They didn't trust him.

He stopped halfway across the dam and looked back. Dad

was nowhere in sight. Jimmy stood there awhile, breathing hard and blinking away sweat. Then he sat down among the dry weeds. He hooked his elbows around his knees and grasped his right wrist with his left hand. He watched the steers watching him.

"Moo," he said.

The steers stared back with dull eyes.

"Moooo," Jimmy said.

Before long the steers were ignoring him. They drank the fouled water, lay on the mud, and switched their tails at flies. It was hot. Flies started buzzing around Jimmy, too. He pursed his lips and blew at them. Dad could go fuck himself with a crowbar.

His butt began to itch, but he didn't want to stand up. He leaned to one side and scratched, then leaned to the other side and scratched. It didn't help much. His underwear and cutoffs were still damp from swimming. They were sticking to his skin. He tried to pull them away, but they sucked right back. Short of stripping them off, there was nothing he could do that would help. He tried to ignore the irritation, but he couldn't. He scratched and pulled.

Ernie had said "Pray." Ernie believed in that stuff. Maybe there was something to it. Preachers were full of shit, but maybe God didn't have anything to do with that. God had, after all, seemed to answer Jimmy's prayer about the sparrow. And he hadn't even been serious. Maybe God had been telling him that he should be. Or maybe he'd just had a lucky shot.

If Mom didn't come home soon, he might as well run off or die. Mom coming back was the only thing that would keep Dad from killing him. Why was she staying away so long, anyway? What was she trying to prove? Did she think Dad would get all pitiful and go running after her, begging oh please come home I'm sorry I'm sorry I'm sorry? It would be a cold summer in hell when Dad ever did anything like that. Goddamn her anyway. Goddamn both of them. Bitch and son of a bitch.

Jimmy closed his eyes. The sun was so hot on his head that it hurt. He started to pray.

"God," he said. "Lord." He didn't know how to do this. The prayers he had learned when he was little had all been poems. God is great, God is good, Let us thank Him for our food, Amen. Pass the gravy, pass the meat, pass the taters, Lord, let's eat. Amen.

He felt the crying coming up tight in his throat. He didn't want to let it happen. He had spent years training himself not to let it happen. Men didn't cry. Men who cried were queer. Pussies and fairies and faggots.

"God," he said. He hated his voice. It wasn't a voice at all. It wasn't even his. It was a baby's. "I'll do anything You want. I'll pay any price You want me to. But make Mom come back. Please."

He didn't know what else to say. He sat there and cried. Finally he remembered to say "Amen." He pulled up the bottom of his shirt and blew his nose.

The weeds off to his right whispered. He looked and saw the brown rat terrier. It was sitting six or seven feet away. It was grinning and panting. It seemed to be glad to see him.

"Hey, pup," Jimmy said. "Was that a good rabbit?"

The dog came closer, wagging its tail. It was a funny-looking thing. Its tail was stumpy and mud-caked. Its head was like a furry wedge of wood.

"Don't you have a home?" Jimmy asked. "Don't you have people to feed you and pet you?"

The dog came closer still. It was two feet away now.

"I'd be your people if I could," Jimmy said. He reached out. "But my dad doesn't like dogs. Maybe he'd change his mind if he knew you could feed yourself."

He touched the top of the dog's head. The fur was short and stiff. The dog flinched, but didn't move away. Jimmy spread his fingers so that his palm rested on the dog's head. The head felt warm and strong.

Jimmy told the dog about the latest adventures of Green Lantern and Spider-Man. The dog sat down and grinned while Jimmy petted it. They sat there a long time.

Just before sunset, Jimmy had to take a crap. Some trees lined a dry creekbed west of the pond, so he went there and found a fallen trunk. It was propped a few feet off the ground, held up by its dead branches. Jimmy shucked down his cutoffs and underwear and sat with the backs of his thighs on the narrow trunk. He lost his balance and grabbed a branch to keep from falling. The dog was sniffing around underneath.

"Get away," Jimmy said, swinging his legs at it. It looked up, then resumed sniffing. Jimmy broke off a stick and threw it across the creekbed. The dog went to investigate, and Jimmy strained to finish before it returned. He used leaves for toilet paper.

Then he stood and pulled up his pants. He kicked dead leaves and dirt over the turds. He was disgusted. The dog had returned and was curious about what he was doing. Jimmy started back toward the pond. The dog sniffed and dug a little, then followed him.

They returned to the dam, and Jimmy watched the sun go down. It was a golden evening. The pond shimmered. The water looked pure in this light. Jimmy threw a clod into it and watched the ripples glint. A breeze came up, smelling of cattle and prairie hay. The steers began to wander off.

Jimmy supposed that he would have to sleep on top of the dam. He wished that he'd thought to grab Ernie's backpack. There had been some Cheez Curls left.

"Want to catch me a rabbit?" he asked the dog. The dog cocked its head and grinned.

Jimmy thought about round steak and mashed potatoes with brown gravy. He thought about cherry Popsicles and chocolate ice cream. He would die of hunger if he had to stay on the dam all night.

It was getting dark. Jimmy stood up. He would go on reconnaissance. He would see if the pickup was still in the driveway. Or maybe the station wagon would be back. Maybe God had answered his prayer. It had been several hours. Maybe Dad wasn't even mad anymore.

Jimmy came down from the dam, and the little brown dog came with him. They headed south, toward home. Just to check it out. Jimmy would be ready to run back if he had to. Or maybe he would grab his bike and head for town. He could stay with Ernie. Ernie's mom would feed him.

The dusk had become full dark by the time they reached the hay meadow. A yellow light from the house shone through the windbreak, but the white yard light wasn't on. This might mean that Dad wasn't home. Dad always turned on the yard light when the sun went down, to scare off thieves. Jimmy had always wondered what a thief would want to steal, but had never said so.

He and the dog continued across the meadow. The ground was uneven, and Jimmy tripped and fell. The dog snuffled his face. Jimmy pushed the dog away and stood. His ankle had twisted, but it only hurt a little. He went on. The dog came with him. The night noises had started. Crickets fell silent as Jimmy and the dog passed.

They crossed the next fence and went through the trees into the backyard. The hens made soft noises in the coop. Jimmy saw a dark lump on top of the coop and knew it was the rooster. The hens wouldn't let the thing sleep with them. The dog paused and whined as Jimmy passed the coop.

"Come on if you're coming," Jimmy whispered. The dog trotted fast to catch up.

Light shone from the kitchen and living room windows, and the TV murmured. Dad's pickup was still in the driveway. The lawnmower was still in the yard.

79

Jimmy crept up to the porch. He had left his bicycle leaning here, but it was gone now. Maybe Dad had put it in the garage. Jimmy had to walk on the driveway gravel to get there, and it made noise. He hoped that the TV was loud enough that Dad wouldn't hear.

The side door of the garage was open. Jimmy reached inside and groped for the flashlight that Dad kept hanging on the wall. He took it down and turned it on. Its light was orange. His bicycle leaned against the shop-rag barrel. He started toward it.

Frantic squawks stopped him. Out in the coop, the chickens were going crazy. Jimmy looked around the garage for the dog. It wasn't there. He ran outside, the orange oval of light wavering before him.

Chickens were scrambling from the coop. They thumped against the plywood walls in their rush for the doorway. Feathers floated down orange. Jimmy ran to the coop, colliding with a few hens on the way. He went inside and swept the light around.

The dog was in the far corner. A dead rat, its head a bloody mess, lay at the dog's feet. The rat was huge. Another rat, almost as big, struggled in the dog's mouth. The dog whipped its head back and forth, and then the rat was still. The dog dropped it beside the first.

"What the hell's going on?"

Jimmy's chest clenched. Dad was behind him. He looked back and saw the shadow.

"This dog followed me home," Jimmy said. His voice hurt his throat. "He found these rats in here and killed them. I think the rats were eating the eggs."

Dad took the flashlight from Jimmy and stepped closer to the dog. The dog picked up one of the rats and growled.

"Git," Dad said, waving the flashlight. The dog growled again, then carried the rat past Dad and Jimmy and out the door.

Dad picked up the other rat by the tail and took it outside.

Jimmy followed. Dad threw the rat toward the windbreak. Jimmy heard it hit the ground. He looked around for the dog, but didn't see it.

The light in Dad's flashlight was dying. The filament was a dull squiggle. Jimmy couldn't see Dad's face.

"Scrambled eggs in the skillet on the stove," Dad said. "Get in and eat and get to bed."

Jimmy went in. He ate. The eggs were cold, but he didn't care. He went to bed. He knew he was lucky that Dad had decided not to kill him, but his prayer still hadn't been answered. He prayed it again. He wanted Mom to come home. He even missed Jasmine. Things were too weird without them. Things weren't all that great with them around, but at least he knew what to expect.

He had no doubt that the little brown dog had saved his life. He was grateful.

The next day was Wednesday. Mom and Jasmine had been gone for a week. When Jimmy awoke he thought about calling Grandma to see if they really were there. But he couldn't do that unless Dad left. He could hear Dad snoring.

He dressed and went outside to feed the chickens and gather the eggs. He found three more dead rats near the coop. Two of them were half eaten. As Jimmy carried the eggs to the house, the dog trotted around the garage with yet another rat in its mouth. It dropped the rat and came to Jimmy to be petted. Jimmy obliged and then took the eggs inside.

Dad was in the kitchen. He wasn't wearing a shirt. His eyes were bloodshot, and his face was slack. His sparse hair stuck up at odd angles.

Jimmy put the eggs into the refrigerator. "That dog killed four more rats," he said. "He eats them. I saw him eat a rabbit too."

Dad lit the burner under the skillet that had held cold eggs the night before. "Scramble some eggs," he told Jimmy.

Jimmy did as he was told, and they ate the eggs without talking. Then Dad left the kitchen and went into his and Mom's room. He closed the door. Jimmy waited for him to put on a shirt and come out again, but an hour passed, and he didn't. Jimmy took some comic books to the porch and sat down to read. The dog appeared and hopped onto the porch to lie beside him. Jimmy scratched the dog behind the ears and noticed that it smelled like the pond, with a sharper smell mixed in. It wasn't a good smell, but Jimmy didn't mind.

He had read all of the comic books before, so he went into the front yard and threw sticks for the dog to chase. The dog had no idea what he was doing and just watched him from the porch. The lawnmower was still sitting where he had left it the day before, so he pushed it into the garage. The dog came with him.

Jimmy took some shop rags from the barrel and piled them on the dirt floor between the barrel and the wall. "You can sleep here at night," he told the dog. "This is your own personal bed." The dog sniffed at the barrel, lifted a hind leg, and pissed on it. Then it sniffed at the rags and tromped on them, turning around and around. It flopped down and grinned up at Jimmy.

Jimmy went into the house to call Ernie. The dog tried to follow him inside, but he kept it out. Dad would never allow a dog in the house. Jimmy was sure of it.

He called Ernie. "You know that dog at the pond?" he said. "It came home with me."

"No lie?" Ernie sounded hoarse again. His breath whistled in the receiver. "What did your dad say?"

"Nothing. I don't think he cares, because it kills rats." Jimmy hesitated. He was still embarrassed about the day before. "You want to come out this afternoon?"

Ernie's breath whistled a few times before he answered. "I can't. I got a doctor's appointment. I told my mom it's just hay fever, but she made the appointment anyway."

"Maybe he'll give you something for it."

"Yeah. Your mom back yet?"

Jimmy twisted the phone cord around his finger. "No."

"Well, my mom called that prayer tower for you," Ernie said. "I guess it can't hurt."

They talked a little more. New comic books were due at Nimper's IGA on Friday. They agreed to meet at Ernie's house and go down to Nimper's to make their purchases together. Then they would read the comics in Ernie's room or on the water tower catwalk.

After hanging up, Jimmy sat looking at the dusty black phone for a while. He could hear Dad snoring. Maybe it would be all right if he was quiet. He got Grandma's number from the inside cover of the phone book, where Mom had written it in ink. Tulsa's area code reminded him that this would show up as a long-distance call on the bill. But if Mom came back soon, that would be okay. She did the bills.

He dialed the number and waited. The line clicked and popped. Then there was a hiss, followed by a loud busy signal. He replaced the receiver in its cradle. He was breathing hard. He felt guilty.

He went to his room and shut the door. He didn't turn on the light. He lay down on the bed with his face in the pillow. He was a liar and a sneak. No wonder Dad was always mad at him. No wonder Mom had taken his sister and run off. No wonder God didn't answer his prayers. No wonder his best friend was a sissy like Ernie.

Far away, the chickens squawked. Jimmy put his head under the pillow. The last thing he wanted to be reminded of was the filthy fucking chickens.

He could still hear them. They wouldn't shut up. He started humming, then singing. It was a song he had heard at Ernie's house. It was about an astronaut named Major Tom. Ground control was having trouble with him.

Something exploded.

Jimmy threw off the pillow. He held his breath and listened. There was another explosion. It came from outside. It was Dad's shotgun.

Jimmy ran from his room, through the kitchen, and out the back door. A chicken rushed past, flapping madly. Dad was standing beside the chicken coop. He still wasn't wearing a shirt. He was holding his Remington twelve-gauge. He pumped it, and a spent shell went flying. It tumbled in a red arc. Dad lowered the gun. His shoulder was pink where the stock had rubbed it.

Dad's eyes and mouth were narrow. Jimmy stopped several feet away. He couldn't stand to look at Dad's face. He looked down and saw the rooster dead on the ground. Its head was gone. A hen lay a few yards away. Its head was gone too.

"Did you shoot them?" Jimmy asked. His eyes throbbed.

"Hell, no," Dad said. "I shot that goddamn dog. Son of a bitch ran off before I could finish it."

The throbbing spread into Jimmy's skull and became a roar. He couldn't feel his body. He heard a voice screaming no and no and no.

The ground was spinning. Dad grabbed him. They were in the driveway now. The shotgun lay back on the grass. Dad squeezed his left arm hard. Jimmy could feel it now.

"It was killing chickens," Dad said. "The goddamn dog was killing my chickens."

Jimmy heard the voice scream again.

"You didn't have to shoot him, you bastard!"

Dad's hand went up and came down. Jimmy fell. Dad's hand clamped onto his neck and pressed his face into the gravel.

Jimmy closed his eyes. After a while he realized that Dad's hand was gone. He got up to his knees. He was alone.

Jimmy brushed gravel from his face and stood. Gravel was embedded in his knees, and he brushed that away too. He was crying again, the same way he had cried at the pond. He hated it. He wanted to stop and couldn't. All he could do was hide. He went into the garage. He held on to the rim of the shop-rag barrel and hunched over. Something cold touched his leg.

It was the dog. It seemed to be okay. It was looking up at him the same way as before. Then it turned. The fur and skin on its left side were gone. The flesh was raw and red and open. A rib showed.

"Why'd you have to do it, pup?" Jimmy asked. He was sobbing. It was disgusting. "Why couldn't you have stuck to rats and rabbits?"

The dog whined. It limped onto the shop-rag bed Jimmy had made for it and lay down on its right side. Every breath was a short whimper. Black BBs were embedded in its side. Quail shot.

Jimmy knelt and stroked the dog's head. It licked his wrist. That was the first time it had done that.

There was nothing he could do. He couldn't drive. There was no way to get it to a vet. All a vet would do was put it to sleep anyway. All Dad would do was shoot it with bird-shot again. Fucking redneck idiot.

He stroked the dog's head a little longer. It wasn't right to let it keep hurting. He stood and wiped his face on a shop rag, then looked around the garage. Dad's toolbox was on the workbench. He went over to it. The dog stayed on the bed of rags, panting.

Jimmy opened the box. The tools were jumbled. He reached in and grabbed a hammer. Wrenches and screw-drivers came out with it. He took the hammer over to the dog. He heard gravel crunch outside.

He knelt again and put down the hammer. He pulled a few rags out from under the little dog's head, then turned the head so that the jaw lay flat against the floor. He stroked the top of the head. The eyes looked up at him. He stroked from the nose up over the eyes so that they closed.

He kept stroking with his left hand. The eyes stayed closed. He picked up the hammer in his right.

85

Jimmy had stopped crying. Now that he knew what to do, he could control himself. There was no point in prolonging pain. It would have to be one blow. It would have to be perfect. Perfection allowed no tears, no trembles.

"That's a sweet pup," Jimmy said. He raised the hammer.

A shadow fell over him. He took his left hand from the dog's head. He brought the hammer down.

It was one blow. It was perfect. Jimmy pulled the hammer free, then looked away.

His sister Jasmine was in the doorway. He stood and faced her. She turned and ran.

Mom was in the kitchen when Jimmy went inside. She hugged him and told him she'd missed him. She was going to make a special supper of smoked pork chops, and there would be ice cream for dessert.

Jimmy pulled away from the hug and looked at her. She looked the same.

Jasmine was standing with Dad beside the kitchen table. She was hanging on to Dad's leg and staring at Jimmy. Dad had his hand on her head. He still wasn't wearing a shirt.

Jimmy's prayer had worked. It had worked in just the way he had prayed it. He had told God that he would pay any price to have his mother back. Now the little brown dog was dead, and Mom was home. It made sense.

He went back to the garage and bundled the dog's body in shop rags. He carried the bundle out behind the chicken coop. There was a dead rat lying there. He set the bundle down beside it, then fetched the shovel and started to dig. The ground was packed hard. It was stiff with chickenshit. He kept at it.

A shadow passed over the hole. He looked up and saw Jasmine. She was the only one who was innocent. She was the only one he could love. He wouldn't let anyone hurt her, ever, as long as he lived.

"I saw you kill that dog," Jasmine said. "I hate your guts." She went back to the house.

Jimmy kept digging. He dug until his hands blistered, and then until the blisters opened. The hole still wasn't deep enough.

VICTIM NUMBER SEVEN

For the first seven weeks, Blackburn's job in the Automotive Department of Oklahoma Discount City went well enough. He unpacked cardboard cases of parts, stocked shelves, and helped customers find things. His boss wouldn't let him run the cash register, but that was fine with him. It was too much responsibility. He preferred work that allowed him to think about other things, and to go home and watch TV when he was finished. There wasn't much else to do in Oklahoma City, but he'd had enough partying for a while anyway. Austin had worn him out.

Blackburn's TV was a twelve-inch black-and-white that he'd bought with his first paycheck. The folks over in the

Electronics Department had given him a few dollars off because he was an employee. He thought that was a pretty fair deal. In fact, he thought Oklahoma Discount City in general was a pretty fair deal. Then his boss retired, and the store hired a man named Leo to manage the Automotive Department.

Leo didn't like Blackburn. For one thing, he thought Blackburn's hair was too long, and called him a hippie. Blackburn replied that he couldn't be a hippie, because it was 1978 and all the hippies had been declared dead in 1967. Leo grimaced and spat on the floor of the stockroom. Leo was about fifty, and he wore a black toupee. He had lines around his eyes, and liver-colored lips. He looked pissed off all the time, and he sneered at any customer who paid using a lot of pennies.

It was because of Leo that Blackburn lost his job. Leo had only been the department manager for a week and a half when he accused Blackburn of stealing a case of Quaker State 10W-30 Multi-Viscosity Motor Oil.

"I'm sorry, sir," Blackburn told him in the stockroom. It was early on Thursday morning. Leo had just accused him. They were the only ones there. "I didn't steal any Quaker State. I didn't steal anything."

Leo's face twitched. "I saw you take it out of the store last night," he said. "Then I stayed late to count the sales slips, and I came in early this morning and did it again. It's short. You're a goddamn liar and a thief."

Blackburn became irritated. He was a lot of things, but a liar was not one of them. He took a breath and closed his eyes. There was no point in getting upset. All he had to do was tell the truth. Then he could get to work and think about other things.

He opened his eyes. "May I explain, please?"

Leo's eyebrows rose. They were thin and gray. They were how Blackburn knew that Leo wore a toupee. The toupee was thick and black.

"May you?" Leo said, mocking. *"May* you? Listen, punk, you can 'explain' by paying for that case of oil and then getting your ass out of here before I call the cops."

"That hardly seems fair."

"I could care less," Leo said.

"Couldn't."

"Huh?"

"Couldn't. Saying that you could care less means that you actually do care. Saying that you couldn't care less means that you don't really give a shit."

Leo sneered. "Listen to the college boy. You sound like my wife. Thinks she's Albert fuckin' Einstein 'cause she had a year of juco. Maybe I should straighten you out like I do her." Leo raised his right hand in a fist.

"Your wife's name is Lorraine, isn't it?" Blackburn asked.

"How'd you know that?" Leo's voice was low.

"I heard you talking to her on the phone."

Leo shook his head. His toupee moved. "A liar, a thief, and an eavesdropper. Pay for the oil and get out."

"But I was carrying the oil for a customer, sir."

"Bullshit. You didn't ring it up—"

"I'm not allowed to use the register."

"—and nobody paid no money for it. You're lucky I didn't just call the cops right off the bat. This way I'm giving you a chance to get out with your ass intact."

Blackburn became more irritated. "There wasn't any money because it wasn't a cash transaction," he said. "I gave him credit."

"What?" Leo's Adam's apple bobbed. "Who? On what card?"

Blackburn stepped closer to Leo. He could smell stale cigarette smoke. "I'm getting upset, sir," he said. "You have to let me explain."

Leo bared his teeth. They were gray stumps. "So explain. Explain all you damn well please."

"A man came in last night needing oil," Blackburn said. "He had to change the oil in his truck so he could drive to Oregon to take care of his dying aunt. He needed at least five quarts for the change, and his truck burns a lot, so there's no telling how much he might need for the drive. We figured a case would do it for sure, so that's what I sold him. He gave me an IOU." Blackburn took the folded slip from his shirt pocket. Red stitching above his pocket said OK—DARREL. Darrel was the name he had given the store when he'd hired on. A man in a bar had sold him a birth certificate and Social Security card with that name.

Leo took the IOU slip and opened it. Then he crumpled it and threw it on the floor. He spit after it. "It's a goddamn worthless scrap," he said. "Can't even read the goddamn writing."

Blackburn squatted to pick it up. "He promised he'll send the money from Oregon as soon as he gets a job."

Leo put his foot on Blackburn's shoulder and pushed. Blackburn fell back on his rump. He sat on the floor and looked up at Leo.

"Christ Almighty Jesus God," Leo said. "I suppose you'd believe it if I told you I needed a free case of oil for *my* health, huh?" He started toward the swinging doors to the retail area. "Get out. I'll mail your last check, minus the price of a case of oil. Won't leave much." He glanced back. "Go on. I'm sick of looking at you."

Blackburn stood up. "I'm sorry to hear about your health, sir," he said.

"Huh?"

Blackburn lunged forward and grabbed Leo around the waist. He squeezed hard. Leo tried to yell, but it came out as a wheeze. Blackburn wasn't any bigger than Leo, but his arms were strong. He had been lifting cases of automotive equipment for eight and a half weeks. He lifted Leo and carried him across the stockroom to where the cases of oil were stacked. Leo pounded at Blackburn's head and back, but he couldn't pound hard. He couldn't breathe.

Blackburn dropped him and ripped open a case of Quaker State 10W-30. He removed a quart and punched two holes in the top of the can with his pocketknife. He had bought the pocketknife over in the Sporting Goods Department. The folks there had given him a few dollars off.

Leo was on the floor. His face was purplish. His mouth was open, gasping. He seemed almost able to move again when Blackburn squatted and poured the amber stream into his mouth. Leo choked and turned his head to spit it out. Blackburn clamped a hand over Leo's mouth and turned his face upward again.

"Swallow," Blackburn said.

Leo's face was changing colors. It went from purplish to a pale shade like dough, and then to a strange, veiled blue, like veins under skin.

"Swallow," Blackburn said again.

Leo swallowed, and Blackburn gave him more.

"Goood boy," Blackburn said. "Make-ums alll better."

Leo threw up after the first quart and lay in the puddle, his arms and legs working feebly. Blackburn stood up and poked around the stockroom for an oil can spout. He had spilled too much pouring free.

He found a spout and came back to Leo, who was crawling toward the swinging doors. Blackburn turned him onto his back again, sat on him, and plunged the spout into another quart. He put the spout to Leo's lips, but found that Leo's teeth were clamped together.

"It's for your own good," Blackburn said. "You're not at all well."

Leo shook his head.

"Come on," Blackburn said. "Open up for the good medicine."

Leo kept shaking his head.

"Open up," Blackburn said, "or I'll shove the spout through your teeth."

Leo relented. Blackburn finished that quart and started another. And then another. Leo threw up three more times. Blackburn had to jump out of the way. It took awhile before it was over.

Blackburn wrote a note on the back of the IOU to leave with Leo, then headed for the door to the loading dock. He paused there and looked back. The green-and-white cans gleamed in the slime on the floor.

"Hope you're feeling better," Blackburn said, and went out.

The police found the note in Leo's pocket. It read:

> *Dear Lorraine. I am no good, as well you may have imagined. I have been jealous because you are smart and I am stupid as a stump. I have no hemlock and don't even know what hemlock is anyway on account of I am so damn dumb, so will make do with motor oil. Goodbye. Leo.*

The Oklahoma County Coroner ruled it a suicide.

FOUR

BLACKBURN PULLS THE TRIGGER

No one was home at the house beside the Nazarene church. Jimmy knocked again to be sure, then sat on the porch step to wait. It was his seventeenth birthday. He had time. Wantoda was green and quiet, and the air smelled of new grass. The 4 SALE sign in the window of the black Ford Falcon had an exclamation point. Mr. Dunbar would be home soon, and Jimmy would get a good deal. The six-hundred-dollar wad of cash in his jeans pocket was most of the money he had earned working after school at the turnpike Stuckey's. He would spend no more than four hundred on the Falcon. It had been sitting in the Dunbars' yard for weeks.

Jimmy had the afternoon off from Stuckey's because

Ernie was sick with asthma and couldn't give him a ride. Jimmy had wanted to take the time off anyway, it being his birthday. The car would be his present to himself. It was a safe bet that it would be the only present he got. Dad had been laid off from the machine shop again, so Mom didn't have money to spend on things like birthdays. And Jasmine wouldn't even speak to him without shrieking, much less give him a present. Mom might manage to throw a cake together, but that would be it.

It was enough. He didn't want anything else. He was seventeen. He wanted to be responsible for himself, to be in control. He wanted to buy a car. He wanted to buy a car and drive all over Tuttle County before dark. He wanted to stay away from home until his family wondered where he was.

Besides, he needed the car. He had a date for the Junior-Senior Prom on Saturday. Mary Carol Hauser had said yes just this morning. Jimmy knew that she had put off her answer in hope of a better offer, but he didn't mind. He liked Mary Carol. She was smart and foul-mouthed, with green eyes and swollen lips. It was imperative that he buy the Falcon this afternoon so he would have a chance to clean it before Saturday.

Jimmy heard a car approaching. He stood, hoping it was Mr. Dunbar. Then the blue Blazer emerged from the shadows of the trees that overhung the street, and Jimmy sat back down. The Blazer was Officer Johnston's new cop car. It was a four-wheel-drive enclosed truck with a siren, red-white-and-blue roof lights, knobby tires, a public-address system, a searchlight, a shotgun, and black windows all the way around. Just why the town had bought it was a mystery. In eleven years, Johnston had never done any police work beyond setting speed traps and harassing parked teenagers. He sure didn't need a brand-new truck for that.

The Blazer slowed. The driver's-side window slid down, and Officer Johnston leaned out. He was wearing mirrored sunglasses. His veined nose seemed to throb. A burning cigarette hung from his lower lip.

"Who's that on the porch?" Johnston demanded. The Blazer came to a stop at the mouth of the Dunbars' driveway.

Jimmy stood. "Jimmy Blackburn, sir."

Johnston frowned. "Oh, yeah. Mr. Firecracker." Three years ago he had hauled Jimmy, Ernie, and two other boys to City Hall for throwing firecrackers into trash cans. "What you doin' on the Dunbars' porch?"

Jimmy nodded at the Falcon. "I'm going to buy that car, sir, but nobody's home yet."

"Uh-huh." Johnston took the cigarette from his mouth and spat. "I get any complaints from Mr. Dunbar, I'll know who to look up."

"Don't worry, sir."

"I ain't the one needs advice, Mr. Firecracker," Johnston said. "You watch yourself." The tinted window slid up, and the Blazer moved on.

"Asshole," Jimmy muttered. He was careful not to let his lips move. Johnston was known to keep an eye on people in his rearview mirror and come back if they cussed him.

When the Blazer was gone, Jimmy gazed at the Falcon and imagined himself in the front seat with Mary Carol snuggled up beside him. He doubted that she was much of a snuggler, but he could imagine it. He could imagine almost anything.

A squirrel appeared on the Falcon's roof. It seemed to have materialized from the air. Its tail fluffed, and it deposited a brown pellet on the black paint.

"Hey!" Jimmy yelled. "Not on the car!"

The squirrel chittered and deposited another turd.

Jimmy stepped off the porch and started across the yard, but stopped when a blob of gray fur shot past him. It rushed to the Falcon and leaped up, slamming against the left rear door. It fell to the ground and leaped up again, barking. It

96

was the filthiest dog Jimmy had ever seen. It leaped at the squirrel over and over again. The squirrel dashed about the roof looking for an escape.

Jimmy watched, considering. He felt a little sorry for the squirrel, but sorrier for the dog. Even though its fur was thick and shaggy, its ribs showed. It couldn't belong to the Dunbars; it had to be a stray that had stopped to rest in the cool dirt under their porch. It was so hungry that it was crazed. Jimmy went into the yard and looked for a rock to throw. Maybe he could knock the squirrel to the ground, and the dog would have time to be on it.

He found a half-buried chunk of brick. He kicked it loose and picked it up, but as he cocked his arm to throw, the squirrel jumped to the Falcon's hood and from there to the ground. It started for a cedar, but the dog cut it off. The squirrel zigzagged and fled toward the Nazarene church. The dog charged after it.

Jimmy threw the chunk of brick, hoping to at least slow the squirrel down. He missed and hit the dog. The dog flinched but didn't slow. Jimmy was angry at himself then, and impressed with the dog's determination. He swore that the dog would dine on squirrel meat before evening.

The squirrel crossed into the churchyard and ran up the church's concrete steps toward the white double doors. Then it disappeared. The dog leaped up the steps and ran headlong into the left double door. There was a loud bang and a rattle. The dog fell back, then leaped up again. It clawed at the door and barked.

Jimmy crossed into the churchyard and climbed the steps. He saw that the left door's bottom right corner was chipped and ground down, making a small hole. The squirrel had escaped into the church.

The dog moved aside as Jimmy reached the top step, but continued to bark. Jimmy knocked on the right double door. He didn't know if the Nazarenes would be home on a Wednesday afternoon, but it was worth a try. He knocked hard so he would be heard over the dog, and the door swung inward. The dog stopped barking and ran inside.

Jimmy pushed the door open wider. "Hello?" he called. "You have a squirrel loose in the church!"

No one answered, so Jimmy entered and went through the vestibule into the sanctuary. There were no windows, and the place was dark and cool. It reeked of Pine-Sol. Even with a shaft of afternoon light stabbing through the open doorway, Jimmy couldn't see anything clearly. He heard the dog's toenails clicking somewhere ahead, but that was all.

He looked back into the vestibule for light switches and saw none, so he ran his hands over the paneled sanctuary walls on either side of the vestibule. There were no light switches here either. Maybe they were up front near the pulpit. He stepped away from the vestibule and walked straight ahead, up what he guessed was the center aisle. He was beginning to see long shadows that must be pews.

The dog's toenail clicks stopped, so Jimmy stood still and listened. There was a growl and then a squeal, followed by rattles and clangs. Then the toenail clicks returned. Jimmy felt the dog's furry body brush against his jeans. He turned back toward the vestibule and saw the dog trot into the sunshine. It was carrying a limp squirrel.

Jimmy clapped and whistled. He watched the dog start down the concrete steps, its tail wagging.

Then a loud *crack* cut the air. There was a spatter of blood. The dog fell over and lay still, halfway down the first step.

Jimmy stared at the dog's rump. He couldn't see its front half. He couldn't see the squirrel. The dog's rump didn't move. Its tail didn't wag.

Officer Johnston stepped into the rectangle of light and looked down at the dog. He was dressed in brown, with a black belt and boots. He was wearing his mirrored sunglasses. He was hatless, his thinning hair slicked back with grease. He held his big blue pistol in his right hand. He cocked it with his thumb and pointed it at the dog.

"Trespasser," he said.

Johnston prodded the dog with a boot. The dog's rump slid off the landing, leaving only a little blood. Johnston looked into the church, and Jimmy felt the cop's mirrored eyes probing.

"That must be you in there, Mr. Firecracker," Johnston said. "Come on out."

From the moment of the gunshot, Jimmy had been numb. Now, in the glare of the twin mirrors, the numbness burned off like frost before a flame. He hated the cop more than Satan hated God. He would not obey that bastard. Johnston wasn't his old man. Johnston wasn't shit.

Jimmy crouched and moved to his right, groping for a pew. He would get underneath and crawl toward the vestibule. Then he would wait until Johnston came well into the sanctuary, and dash out. If he was quiet and quick, Johnston wouldn't see him. There would be no way to prove who had been inside the church with the dog.

Johnston came inside. Jimmy hurried to get under a pew and banged into metal.

There were no pews. There were metal folding chairs instead. There was no way to hide under them and crawl to the door. The Nazarenes were a cheap-ass denomination.

Johnston stopped just inside the sanctuary and stood straddle-legged. He raised his cocked pistol. "Hey! Boy! Freeze!" His breath rasped. He smoked too much.

Jimmy knew that Johnston couldn't see him. Not without lights, and wearing mirrorshades. Jimmy backed up the aisle. As long as he didn't run into any more chairs, he didn't think Johnston would be able to hear him over the cop's own breathing.

Johnston came forward, fanning his pistol before him. He was looking back and forth, searching. He kept his sunglasses on. He didn't see Jimmy.

Jimmy came up against the dais at the front of the sanctuary and stepped onto it. It stood a foot off the floor and was covered with what felt like artificial turf. Jimmy glanced to his left and saw the shadow of the pulpit. He got down on all fours and crawled to hide behind it. Once there, he discovered that it was hollow. The hollow was covered with a cloth. Jimmy pushed through the cloth and crawled inside.

His left hand came down with his full weight on something soft and furry. The thing squeaked. Jimmy pulled his hand back and drew his legs into the pulpit. He sat with his knees hugged to his chest and tried to keep his breaths shallow and quiet.

The dais creaked as Johnston stepped onto it. His footsteps went toward the back wall, then stopped. Outside the pulpit, lights came on. They shone through the cloth. The cloth was white. It didn't hang all the way to the floor. Jimmy looked down and saw that the furry thing was a squirrel in a nest of shredded paper. It wasn't moving. He had crushed it. There was a bloody mess behind and beside it, and tiny pink babies. They looked dead too.

Johnston's footsteps resumed. They were loud thumps on the thin plywood. The platform groaned. The light dimmed, and the scuffed leather toes of Johnston's boots appeared below the edge of the white cloth.

"Come on out, boy," Johnston's voice said from above. "You're under arrest for trespassing."

Jimmy didn't want to leave the pulpit. He looked away from Johnston's toes and stared at the dead mama squirrel and her babies instead. He smelled blood.

"You know, Mr. Firecracker," Johnston said above, "I don't know for a fact that it's you in there. Could be a professional church thief. Could be a convict. Nobody'd blame me if I acted in self-defense. I could put a bullet through the pulpit and nobody'd question it. Not a soul."

Jimmy stared at the dead mama squirrel. Something was happening inside his head and chest. It knotted in his gut. Today was his birthday, and he had wanted to buy a car. Then he had tried to help a hungry dog, and the town cop had killed the dog for no reason. Now the cop wanted to kill him too. Because he was hiding in a pulpit.

"I could shoot you," Johnston said above, "just like I shot that damn dog."

There it was. The dog was dead. Jimmy had tried to help it, and Dad had made him drop his pants and had switched him with the fishing rod. The dog had killed rats, and Dad had shot it. The blind man had said that Jesus would help, but Mom had left, and the dog was dead. The dog had killed a squirrel, and Johnston had shot it. The blind man had not heard the voice of Jesus, had made it all up, had lied to him. Jimmy had swum in the pond with the dog, and now it was dead. Dad had hit Mom in the mouth. Jasmine had screamed at monsters in the night. Jimmy had hit the dog with a hammer so it wouldn't hurt. But Jasmine had seen. He had come into the church with the dog, and now it was dead. Jesus had not listened to him even though he was saved on Easter. Glass had broken in the living room. He had awakened in the morning with his sheets glued to his legs in lines of blood. Boss Stud had taunted his sister and stomped his kite. Johnston had kicked the dog down the steps. Jimmy had wrapped the dog in shop rags to bury it, and it was all his fault because he had made a deal with God. Jasmine came to him to say that she hated him. Dad pushed his face into the gravel, and Mom came back and served smoked pork chops. The dog swam out to where he and Ernie splashed and then the sound of the shotgun and the red splash on the concrete in front of the Nazarene church.

There it was.

The dog was dead.

Jimmy waited a moment longer, to feel the tightness of the change inside, to know it was right. It meant never seeing Mom again. Or Jasmine. Never goofing off with Ernie. Never trying to snuggle with Mary Carol Hauser. Never graduating from high school.

And then there was Dad.

A moving shadow told him that Johnston was reaching for the white cloth.

That was all, then. He could let Johnston pull away the cloth, or he could do it himself. Nothing he had ever done had made anyone behave any better, so the only choice left was how he would behave himself. But if Johnston pulled away the white cloth before he did, even that choice was taken away.

Mom. Jasmine. Ernie. Mary Carol.

Dad.

None of them was worth as much as this.

None of them was worth as much as the life of a dog.

He took the dead mama squirrel in both hands. It was warm and limp. One of the babies slid onto his wrist. He was surprised that he wasn't scared. He was trembling, but not from fear.

That was important.

Johnston's fingertips brushed the white cloth.

Jimmy's life was over.

Blackburn lunged through the cloth, thrusting the dead mama squirrel into the cop's face. The light was brilliant. The squirrel's eyes gleamed from each lens of the mirror-shades. Johnston gave a gargled scream. Blackburn shoved the squirrel into Johnston's mouth.

Johnston stumbled back. Blackburn went with him, trying to shove the squirrel down his throat. Johnston's pistol came up. The muzzle grazed Blackburn's cheek. It was hot. The engraving on the blue barrel was an inch from Blackburn's eyes. He saw the word COLT. He saw the word PYTHON. He saw the numerals 3, 5, and 7. It was a revelation. It was a God speaking to him on the green-turfed dais of the Nazarene church. He let go of the dead mama squirrel and reached for the pistol's blue perfection.

Johnston coughed out the squirrel and pointed the pistol at Blackburn's mouth. Blackburn grabbed it. He and Johnston fell together. The oil in Johnston's hair had the sharp smell of Vick's Vapo-Rub. A clump of black strands tickled Blackburn's upper lip. He spat the clump away and saw droplets appear on Johnston's sunglasses.

"Little prick," Johnston said. His breath was the essence of wet cigarettes. His teeth were yellow scabs.

Blackburn tried to pull the pistol away, but Johnston wouldn't let go. He was stronger than Blackburn. Johnston rose to his knees, pulling Blackburn with him. They knelt with their hands locked on the pistol between them. Blackburn tried to stare past his own reflections. He imagined the cop's eyes as milky white.

"You're under arrest, you piece of shit," Johnston said. He was breathing hard. He could hardly talk.

Blackburn smiled at him. "Nobody likes you," he said.

Johnston stopped breathing. His mouth opened. Blackburn leaned forward and kissed him. Johnston's grip weakened. Blackburn wrenched hard and fell.

He lay on his back, looking up at the white lights in the ceiling above the pulpit. He raised his hands over his face. They were wrapped around the body of the Python.

Johnston appeared above him, blocking the lights. He was standing. He was huge, but nothing more than a shadow. Nothing more than a ghost.

"Give me the gun, son," the cop said. A huge shadow hand reached down.

Blackburn turned the Python and held it two-fisted the way the cops on TV did. His right index finger curled around the trigger. It was hot. It felt right. His finger was happy. The hammer was already cocked. He pointed the muzzle at the shadow's head.

"No," he said.

The shadow moved away. Blackburn sat up, keeping the pistol steady. The Python was heavy, but the weight gave him strength.

The shadow brightened as Blackburn sat up, resolving

into Officer Johnston. Johnston held his hands out before him. He backed away.

"Stay where you are," Blackburn said.

Johnston stopped. "Now, son," he said, "you're making things awful bad for yourself." His voice quavered.

Blackburn was disgusted. Big tough man. Big tough man with a gun. Big tough man killing a hungry dog.

Blackburn got to his feet. "Take off your shades," he said. "Take off your shades and drop them."

Johnston took off his shades and dropped them. They clattered on the green turf beside the dead mama squirrel. Johnston blinked. His eyes were dirt brown. They watered. The left eye had a spidery red blotch in the white.

"Get down on your hands and knees," Blackburn said.

Johnston shook his head. "Son, you're diggin' yourself in deeper and deeper."

"Hands and knees," Blackburn said.

Johnston got down on his hands and knees. Blackburn kept the gun trained on him.

"Bark like a dog," Blackburn said.

Johnston barked like a dog.

"Now pick up the squirrel."

Johnston lifted his right hand and reached for the squirrel.

"With your mouth."

Johnston lowered his hand. His lips pulled back from his teeth. Then he put his head down and picked up the dead mama squirrel with his mouth.

"Trespasser," Blackburn said, and pulled the trigger. The explosion rang from wall to wall in the empty church. The Python jumped. It almost hit Blackburn in the face.

Johnston fell over with the squirrel in his mouth. He landed on his right side. His legs twitched. After a few seconds they stopped.

Blackburn stood still for a while. His wrists tingled, then ached. His ears hummed. There was a stink of gunpowder, and then of gunpowder and shit. Blackburn lowered the Python and stepped forward to stand over Johnston. Johnston's eyes were open. His teeth were clamped on the dead mama squirrel, compressing its body in the middle. His legs had drawn up, and his hands were in front of his chest, the wrists bent. Dark blood was spreading through his shirt. Some of it was seeping from a hole under the left pocket. Blackburn thought he saw the cop's chest move a little, but only once.

Officer Johnston was dead.

Blackburn took a deep breath through his nose and let it out through his mouth. He started to feel a little scared, but squelched it. There was no point in being scared now. He hadn't even known that he was going to pull the trigger until it was already done, but once done, he couldn't take it back. He didn't think he would want to anyway.

He squatted and picked up Johnston's mirrorshades. They were in good shape. He might as well keep them.

Blackburn turned away from the body and stepped down from the dais. The humming noise in his ears faded as he walked up the aisle. When he reached the vestibule, he realized that he would have to hide the Python. He put on the mirrorshades and then pulled out his shirttail with his free hand. He loosened his belt and tucked the pistol into the back waistband of his jeans. The shirttail covered it. It was uncomfortable, but it would have to do for now.

He left the church and closed the door behind him. He went down the steps past the dog. The dog still had its squirrel in its mouth too. It was grinning and looked happy. Blackburn felt better.

Johnston's Blazer was parked down the block. Its tinted windows were up. Anyone who noticed it would assume that Johnston was inside. As Blackburn stepped onto the sidewalk, a new Plymouth sedan appeared on the street and turned into the Dunbars' driveway. Blackburn crossed into the Dunbars' yard.

A stooped man in coveralls emerged from the Plymouth and eyed Blackburn. He didn't look happy. Blackburn supposed that the mirrored sunglasses and untucked shirt made him look delinquent.

"Mr. Dunbar?" Blackburn said, coming close. "You still selling that car?" He nodded toward the black Falcon.

Mr. Dunbar looked wary. "Uh-huh."

"How much?"

"Five hundred."

"Give you four."

Mr. Dunbar shook his head.

Blackburn reached into his pocket and pulled out the wad of bills. "Four hundred cash money."

Mr. Dunbar started to shake his head again. Blackburn shifted the cash to his left hand and reached behind him. His fingers touched the butt of the Python.

"Well," Mr. Dunbar said. His headshake became a nod. "Fair enough."

Blackburn was relieved, and pleased. He was proud of himself for holding firm. He gave Mr. Dunbar eight fifties.

Mr. Dunbar removed two keys from a ring and handed them to Blackburn. "Hang on a sec and I'll fetch the title," he said. He stepped onto the porch.

"Could we do the title tomorrow, sir?" Blackburn asked. "I sort of have a date, and I thought maybe I could use the car. I'm kind of late as it is."

Mr. Dunbar shrugged. "I'll be home tomorrow about four-thirty again." He peered down at Blackburn. "What's your name?"

Mr. Dunbar had seen Blackburn plenty of times, but the sunglasses probably made him hard to recognize. Mr. Dunbar might not have known his name anyway. And that was fine with Blackburn.

"Sam," Blackburn said. "Sam Colt."

"Glad to do business with you, Sam," Mr. Dunbar said. He went into his house.

The Falcon's door creaked when Blackburn opened it, and the seat sank almost to the floor when he sat down. But the engine fired after only fifteen seconds of whining. Blackburn put the car into gear and drove through the shallow ditch onto the street.

The muffler had a hole. It was loud. And there was only a quarter tank of gas. But the steering was smooth, the acceleration fine. It was a decent car. Too bad he would have to get rid of it soon. It wouldn't be long before the Falcon was a wanted vehicle. He wondered if it would be hard to steal another car. He had never stolen anything bigger than a candy bar and wasn't sure how to go about it. He would have to devise a plan during the next few hours, while he drove.

Before hitting the highway, Blackburn cruised the side streets of Wantoda, past Ernie's house, past Todd Boyle's house, past the grade school. He wished that he could risk the time to drive out past his own home too. It would be nice to honk good-bye. But the faster and farther he could get away, the better. Mom and Jasmine wouldn't have known it was him anyway. And Dad probably wasn't home yet. He tended to keep working hours even when he was laid off. The taverns were open.

Blackburn stopped for a moment at the west edge of town, where the Potwin road ran north toward Clay Hill and the water tower stood guard over the town and its people. He looked up and saw himself on the catwalk, eyes stinging in the wind, spitting at the road below. He saw the silver tank burst at its rusted seams, the water exploding, sweeping him from the catwalk, ripping away the catwalk itself. He saw the water rush down as a wall, crushing the homes of Wantoda, drowning the inhabitants in froth. He saw his body at the crest of the leading wave as it smashed schools and cars and ripped up trees like brittle weeds.

Then he looked away and drove south, past the Methodist and Baptist churches. He turned east on K-132 and blasted past Nimper's IGA and the Volunteer Fire Station at sixty miles per hour, heading for the Ozarks. The wind tore through his open window and whipped his hair back. He didn't figure that there would be a speed trap today.

Once he was clear of Wantoda, he realized that the Python was digging into his spine. He steered with his left hand and leaned forward so he could reach back and pull the gun from his waistband with his right. As he did so, he glimpsed himself in the rearview mirror. The vision was startling and ugly.

It was the mirrored sunglasses. They made him look like a cop.

Blackburn put the Python under the seat, then took off the sunglasses and examined his face in the mirror. That was better. The eyes were clear. They were eyes that wouldn't hide anything, that wouldn't lie. They were eyes that only fools would doubt.

He threw the sunglasses out the window, and they disintegrated on the grille of a Peterbilt heading the other way. He smiled. He had heard the lenses break. The sound inspired him, and he sang ''Happy Birthday'' and ''I Saw Her Standing There.'' He hoped that Mary Carol wouldn't be hurt at being stood up.

Blackburn leaned to the right to look at his face again. Yes. His eyes were meant to be seen.

He just wasn't a mirrorshades kind of guy.

VICTIM NUMBER EIGHT

Blackburn came to a suburb of the City of Brotherly Love and found it full of garbage. The sanitation workers were on strike, and trash heaps lined the streets. The sidewalk in front of the house where Blackburn stayed was unwalkable. It was buried under cans, bottles, newspapers, disposable diapers, and rotting food waste. The stench and the noise of flies were constant. Blackburn resisted the urge to bring out his Colt Python and shoot the occasional rat that showed itself.

He was reading a sci-fi paperback and eating corn chips on a Tuesday evening when the doorbell rang. He had never heard it before. He stopped reading and listened. It rang again, playing the opening notes of "Greensleeves." Blackburn put down the book and stood. His bare skin peeled from the fabric of the easy chair. The weather was sticky, and the house had no air-conditioning.

Blackburn went to the door. There was no security peephole, so he hesitated, thinking of cops. But he opened the door. A man in a cream-colored suit stood on the stoop, holding a black case in his right hand. His skin was sallow, his teeth brownish. His hair was a little darker than his teeth.

"Good evening, Mr. Talbot," the man said. "I'm Randall Wayne. I've brought the information you requested regarding the *Encyclopedia Europus*. I'm sorry it's taken me so long to reach your neighborhood. The garbage situation has made traffic difficult."

"I understand," Blackburn said.

Randall Wayne stood there, smiling. He seemed to be waiting for something. Blackburn leaned against the doorjamb and waited with him.

"May I come in?" Wayne asked at last.

Blackburn considered. "No," he said, and shut the door.

The doorbell rang again before Blackburn could return to his chair. He reopened the door. Wayne was still there.

"I'm sorry to bother you again, Mr. Talbot," Wayne said, "but you asked for an in-home presentation. The free two-volume reference set is included, of course. I'll only take a few minutes of your time." He held up a printed postcard. Blackburn saw that Mr. or Mrs. Talbot had filled out the blanks on the card, which did indeed state that an in-home presentation was involved.

He supposed that he should fulfill the Talbots' obligation, although he doubted that they would have fulfilled it themselves. He had painted the house as they had ordered, complete with trim, and then they had refused to pay him. They wouldn't even reimburse him for paint and materials. They just didn't like the way it looked, they had said. They were the sort of people who would send in a postcard for a free two-volume reference set and then refuse the in-home presentation.

Blackburn was cut from more honest cloth. "Come on in, then, Mr. Wayne," he said.

The salesman came inside, and Blackburn closed the door and returned to his chair. Wayne stood in the center of the room, looking around and smiling.

"Nice home you have here," he said. "Nice new coat of paint outside."

"Thank you," Blackburn said.

Wayne licked his lips. "I wonder if I might trouble you for a glass of water."

Blackburn frowned. An obligatory presentation was one thing; a glass of water pushed the boundaries. He stood up. The chair fabric stuck to his skin again. "Be right back," he said, and went into the kitchen. While he was running water into a glass, the floor thumped under his feet. He shut off the water, and the floor thumped three more times. He stamped his foot, and the thumping stopped. He returned to the living room with the water.

Wayne took the glass. "What was that noise?" he asked.

"Rats," Blackburn said.

Wayne nodded. "It's the garbage." He drank the water, then eyed the glass. "Good cool water," he said. "Ice would have been redundant."

"You're welcome." Blackburn sat down in his reading chair.

Wayne gestured at the divan across the room. "May I have a seat?"

"Sure."

Wayne sat and opened his black case. He pulled out a shrink-wrapped pair of paperbacks. "This is your free reference set, the best dictionary and thesaurus in the English language." He placed the package on the cushion beside him. "But, as good as it is, it only deals with words. It's no help with detailed information concerning people, places, and world events. Suppose you needed a nutshell description of Einstein's Theory of Relativity. Could you find it in a dictionary or thesaurus, Mr. Talbot?"

Blackburn didn't want to rise to the bait, but the presentation might last longer if he didn't. He would have to play along. "My guess would be no," he said.

The salesman shook his head. "Of course not. And where would your son look for information if he had to write a school theme on mollusks, or the moon landings, or Sacco and Vanzetti, or Pocahontas, or the Treaty of Versailles?"

"I don't have any children," Blackburn said.

Wayne took the postcard from his jacket pocket. "Your card says you have a son."

"Oh, him. He's away at college. Pitt."

Wayne peered at Blackburn. "You look young to have a son in college, Mr. Talbot."

Blackburn decided that the salesman had been there long enough. "The boy's my stepson," he said. "And, really, my wife is the one you want to talk to, since the encyclopedia would be for her kid. She's away right now, but she'll be back in a few weeks. You could talk to her then."

Wayne remained seated. "I'll be happy to do that, Mr. Talbot," he said. "But as long as I'm here now, I'd like to show you the many features the *Encyclopedia Europus* has to offer. Then, when your wife returns, you can fill her in." He reached into the black bag and pulled out a thick, oversized volume bound in brown leather.

"I don't think—" Blackburn began.

Wayne interrupted. "This is Volume Fourteen, *Lalo to Montpar.* This volume alone contains seven hundred and eighty-seven entries on nine hundred and twelve pages and weighs two kilograms, or four point four pounds. It includes six hundred and three photographs and illustrations, two hundred and sixty-two in full color. Like each of the other twenty-eight volumes, it includes its own index—and that's in addition to the comprehensive index, which is a separate volume. This binding is full leather, but we also offer simulated leather, buckram, simulated buckram, and Carthaginian cork.''

"How much?'' Blackburn asked. He had become curious.

Wayne stood and carried *Lalo to Montpar* across the room to Blackburn. "Just feel that leather, sir. And the paper's acid-free. It'll last for centuries.''

"I don't think my stepson will need it that long,'' Blackburn said.

"No, but his children and their children will, Mr. Talbot.''

"Won't it be out of date by then?''

The salesman shook his head. "*Europus* publishes its yearbook every February, so your encyclopedia can stay perpetually current.''

Blackburn was beginning to think that maybe this encyclopedia was something the Talbots could use. On the other hand, if they wouldn't even pay a man for painting their house, they wouldn't spend much money on a set of books. It would have to be a bargain.

"How much?'' Blackburn asked again.

Wayne placed *Lalo to Montpar* in Blackburn's lap. It fell open to an illustration of the lymphatic system. "Far less than you would think, Mr. Talbot. *Europus* has an easy monthly payment plan.''

Blackburn stared up at Wayne's eyes. "How. Much. For. The. Least. Expensive. Set.''

"Your monthly payments would only be—''

Blackburn shut the volume and stood. "Total price,'' he said. He was becoming irritated.

"Two thousand eight hundred and twelve dollars. But when you consider—''

"My wife will never agree to that,'' Blackburn said. "I'm sorry.'' He held out the volume with both hands. He expected Wayne to take it and leave.

113

Wayne did neither. Instead, he tilted his head and gave Blackburn a sly look. "How old are you, Mr. Talbot?"

Blackburn was taken aback, but he saw no reason not to answer. "I'm twenty-one."

Wayne chuckled. "Smart. Very smart."

Blackburn didn't know what the salesman was talking about. "Excuse me?"

"Not that I blame you," Wayne said. "If I could find a nice older woman with a few bucks—"

"Please take your book," Blackburn said.

Wayne held up his hands. "Hey, I'm not putting you down. You're the smartest guy I've run into all day."

"Thanks."

"You're welcome," Wayne said. "So. Two thousand eight hundred is going to be too much for your wife. I trust your judgment on that. Hey, if you don't know what she'll spend, who does? Just tell me what you think she *will* spend."

Blackburn considered. How much would the encyclopedia be worth to the Talbots? "Maybe a thousand," he said.

The salesman laughed. "Is Talbot a Jewish name?"

Blackburn considered. "No. It's a werewolf name."

"Just kidding," Wayne said. "But look, you're going to have to make an offer I can take to the company without them pissing on my shoes." He leaned in close. "Then maybe you can sell me something too, you know?"

"Beg pardon?"

"Come on." Wayne's voice lowered. "A young guy like you? With an older lady? With nothing else to do all day? What do you deal—smoke or snort?"

Blackburn smiled. He was beginning to understand. He wasn't wearing a shirt, and his hair was a little long. That made him a gigolo and a drug dealer. He thought twenty-eight hundred dollars was too much money for an encyclopedia, so that made him a Jew.

"Let's you and me do some business," Wayne said. "If

114

you can get your old lady to spring for the leatherbound, four thousand five hundred, I can bounce five hundred back to you. Free money, no taxes. She gets an encyclopedia for her college boy, you get some untraceable working capital, I get my commission. Everybody's happy. How about it?"

Blackburn hefted *Lalo to Montpar*. It was good and heavy. Solid.

"Not good enough?" Wayne said. "Okay, so how about this: I go into a lot of people's houses. These houses contain expensive items. Sometimes I leave a house and happen to find something small but valuable in my pocket. Other times I notice how bigger things might be taken away. Perhaps you could use such information."

Blackburn was appalled. "You steal from the people you sell to?" Blackburn himself sometimes stole when he had no other choice, but he never did so under false pretenses.

Wayne shrugged. "I'd call it putting knowledge to work. Hey, that's the whole concept behind the *Encyclopedia Europus* in the first place."

Blackburn nodded. "I understand," he said. He raised *Lalo to Montpar* and clubbed the salesman over the head.

Wayne staggered backward. "Hey!" he yelled. "What the fuck do you think you're doing?"

"Putting knowledge to work," Blackburn said, and went after him.

Blackburn tried to drive Wayne out the front door, but Wayne went into the kitchen instead. Blackburn got in five more blows, and then Wayne found a filleting knife in a magnetic rack. The salesman stood with his back against the refrigerator and held the knife as if to stab Blackburn in the chest. Blackburn raised his encyclopedia volume and pressed the attack.

The knife struck the book, glanced downward, and speared into Wayne's upper left thigh. It went in deep.

"Shit," Wayne said. He slid down the refrigerator to the floor. He tried to pull out the knife and failed. Soon there was a great deal of blood. It surged out around the blade. The floor thumped.

"Oh, shut up down there," Blackburn said.

"Help me," Wayne said.

Blackburn squatted beside him. "I think you hit the femoral artery."

"Please."

Blackburn sighed. "All right. Close your eyes."

Wayne closed his eyes. Blackburn went into the living room to retrieve the Python from under the chair cushion, then changed his mind. Why waste a cartridge? They were hard to come by. He looked at the encyclopedia volume in his hands. The filleting knife had sliced the leather on the back cover, but the board underneath was intact. It really was a well-made book.

Blackburn returned to the kitchen. Wayne was still alive, but the puddle of blood on the linoleum was growing. Blackburn stepped around it and knelt beside Wayne's head. He placed the spine of the book on the salesman's throat and pushed down. Wayne's eyes opened wide. His tongue stuck out. Then *Lalo to Montpar* crushed his trachea, and he was dead. Blackburn took the car keys from the body, cleaned up the mess as well as he could, and waited for night.

Just after eleven, Blackburn went out to the sidewalk trash pile and found a moldy twin-size mattress. He dragged it into the house, placed the salesman's body on it, and covered the body with newspapers, coffee grounds, and banana peels. Then he returned the mattress to the trash pile. It was hard work. When he came back inside, he had a glass of iced tea and a pastrami sandwich.

After eating, he tucked the filleting knife under his belt and stuffed his possessions into a gray duffel bag he found in the utility room. He carried the duffel and the Python outside and put them into the salesman's Vega. He locked the car, then took a hacksaw and a flashlight from the Talbots' garage and went around behind the house. He had to put down the saw and flashlight to pull the concrete blocks away from the gap in the foundation. Then he got down on his belly, grabbed the tools, and crawled in.

The place smelled like a public toilet. Mr. and Mrs. Talbot had messed their pants. They were still slouched against the stanchion to which they were chained. There was a shallow hole in the dirt beside Mr. Talbot, and he now held a chunk of two-by-four in his bound hands. That explained why the kitchen floor had been thumping.

Blackburn used the filleting knife to cut the Talbots' gags and to free their wrists from the nylon clothesline he had used to bind them. Mrs. Talbot began screaming. Mr. Talbot tried to club Blackburn with the two-by-four, so Blackburn scooted away and then tossed them the hacksaw.

"I couldn't find a key for the padlock," he said. "I'll leave you the flashlight, though."

"Lousy bastard," Mr. Talbot said.

"Hey," Blackburn said, "you got your house painted for nothing, and there's a free two-volume reference set in the living room. Don't bitch."

By the time he reached the Vega, he could no longer hear Mrs. Talbot's screams or Mr. Talbot's curses. The car started easily, and Blackburn pulled away from the trash. When he reached I-95, he took the encyclopedia volume from his duffel and caressed the leather. It felt wise. Maybe he had never graduated from high school, but within a month he would be an expert on everything from *Lalo* to *Montpar.*

Seven weeks later he read a dateline-Philadelphia story buried deep inside the Washington *Post.* The garbage on Mr. and Mrs. Talbot's street had finally been picked up.

FIVE

BLACKBURN THE
BREADWINNER

Blackburn met Dolores in a San Francisco record shop four days after his twenty-second birthday. They reached for the same copy of *The Kids Are Alright* at the same moment. It was the last one in the bin.

"Toss you for it," Blackburn said.

"Bet you can't," Dolores said.

Blackburn bought the album, and Dolores came to his apartment to listen to it. Blackburn hardly heard the music even though it made the windows rattle. His senses were full of Dolores. She was wearing running shorts and a halter top. She had golden hair, green eyes, a brown stomach, and long legs. She was California incarnate, and Blackburn was not pleased with himself for wanting her. But there it was. He was horny as a mule deer.

"My name is Eddie Reese," he said. That was the name on his new driver's license and Social Security card.

"Got anything to eat?" Dolores asked. Her voice was like honey poured over an apple.

Blackburn fed her pepperoni slices and Cheetos. Then they kissed, and Dolores said she would stay the night if Blackburn promised to use protection. Blackburn promised.

That night Blackburn told Dolores that he loved her. He had never said that to anyone, and it surprised the hell out of him that he said it to Dolores. Then he said it again, and again. He couldn't stop himself. It was as if a live wire were plugged into his lower spine, and the signal jolted its way through his vertebrae to his mouth. Dolores could do whatever she wanted with him. She could cut him open and bite holes in his heart with her fine pearl teeth. He would twine his fingers in her hair and hold her there.

The next day Blackburn went to his job at a Taco Tommy franchise and made burrito after burrito without having any orders for burritos. The manager came into the food preparation area and chewed him out for his wastefulness. Blackburn stood there and took it without wanting to kill the manager or even hurt him. After all, he was right. Overnight, Blackburn had become an idiot. His hands had been on automatic. The stack of burritos reached halfway to the ceiling.

As the manager yelled at Blackburn, the girl running the counter gave a yelp. Blackburn and the manager turned to look. A busload of Jews for Jesus had pulled up outside, and its occupants poured out like water. They came into the Taco Tommy and ordered one hundred and forty-four burritos to go. The manager stared at them, and then at Blackburn. Blackburn began stuffing the burritos into paper bags.

It was a miracle. Blackburn didn't believe in God, but he had to believe in a miracle when he saw one. At the end of his shift, he went home, telephoned Dolores, and asked her to marry him. Dolores laughed and suggested a second date instead.

They ate hamburgers and saw *Melvin and Howard*. Then they went to Dolores's apartment and made love five times between 11:00 P.M. and 6:00 A.M. Dolores fell asleep then, but Blackburn lay awake, studying Dolores in the glow of her Tom & Jerry night-light.

Her tan lines made her look as if she were wearing an ivory bikini. Blackburn hadn't noticed the phenomenon the night before, because they had made love in the dark. But now that he could see her entire body, he became fascinated with it in more than just a sexual sense. Her tan was absolute; there was no gradual fade to pale, but sharp demarcations between dark and light. She looked both naked and clothed. If it weren't for her nipples and pubic hair, she could go out in public.

Dolores turned in her sleep, snuggling her rump against Blackburn's abdomen. His erection returned. He would eat nails for this woman.

After the Jews for Jesus incident, the Taco Tommy's manager decided that Blackburn had the psychic ability to predict when unusual quantities of food items would be required. Blackburn almost believed it himself when he made eighty tostadas while lost in another reverie, and then sold them all within forty-five minutes. The manager gave him a nickel-an-hour raise and told him to keep up the good work.

Blackburn did his best. For the first time, he believed he was making progress toward the kind of moral, independent life he wanted to lead. He had even been able to save a little money. Saving money, he had decided, was important. He was determined to repeat his marriage proposal just as soon as he could do so from a position of financial strength. He had discovered that Dolores respected financial strength.

He saw her every evening, and they never fought. This amazed him. He hadn't thought it would be possible to spend so much time with another person without finding just cause to paste that person's brains on the wall. However, despite what his childhood had trained him to expect, his relationship with Dolores was euphoriant.

Blackburn was happy. That in itself was a new and strange experience. It made him stupid.

He reveled in it.

The Taco Tommy's evening supervisor quit in late June, and the manager offered the job to Blackburn. It meant a dollar-an-hour raise, but it also meant working 3:00 P.M. to 12:00 A.M. every day except Sundays. Blackburn hesitated to take the job at first, because it would spoil his evenings with Dolores. Then it occurred to him that the extra money might make marriage possible right away. He accepted the promotion, then went to Dolores's apartment and waited for her to return from her own job. When she arrived, he explained that his earnings would now be great enough that she could stop working if she liked. All she had to do was marry him.

Dolores said she wanted to think about it. They went out to eat, and over fried shrimp, she said yes. Then they rushed to Blackburn's apartment and screwed like mad.

"Oh, Ed," Dolores said. "You're the best."

Blackburn felt like Jimi Hendrix: He could kiss the sky.

Dolores quit her job and moved in with Blackburn the following week, right after they opened their joint checking account. Blackburn put his clothes in the dresser, and Dolores took the closet. They spent the Fourth of July in bed. The week after that, on Thursday, July 10, they were married at noon by a judge. They had celebratory sex at home, and then Blackburn went to work. There, he had an inspiration and made a pile of over a hundred sanchos.

But the Jews for Jesus didn't return. The sanchos cooled. It was the slowest night since Blackburn had started. He figured he was allowed one mistake.

The newlyweds planned a honeymoon trip to Marin County for the first Sunday after the wedding, but then a Taco Tommy employee fell ill, and Blackburn had to work. He pointed out to Dolores that he would be paid time-and-a-half for the extra hours, so they could take an even better trip later. Dolores said that was fine, as long as the trip wasn't the next weekend. That was when her parents were coming up from Los Angeles to meet her new husband. Blackburn was not looking forward to the meeting, and he wished that Dolores had given him the same wedding gift he had given her: He had told her that his parents were dead.

When the visitation weekend arrived, Dolores and her mother spent all day Saturday shopping while Dolores's father watched baseball games on Blackburn's TV. He only spoke once, to compliment Blackburn on the Old Milwaukee beer in the refrigerator. When Blackburn left for work, Dolores's father was still in front of the TV.

There was another employee shortage at the Taco Tommy the next day, so Blackburn only saw his in-laws for a few minutes in the morning when they came over from the motel. Then he had to go to work again. Dolores's father complimented him on his initiative, and her mother said that he certainly was a catch. They were gone when he returned that night, and Dolores locked herself in the bedroom and cried. Blackburn drank Old Milwaukee and watched TV until she emerged and ravished him on the couch.

Blackburn was glad to be Eddie Reese. He was glad to have a horny wife and a steady job. He was glad that he no longer had to survive on the run. He hadn't killed anyone since Philadelphia, almost a year ago, so there was no reason to leave San Francisco. Most people here were polite, and the dirtballs, if they existed, weren't running into him. Or maybe he just didn't mind them so much now that he had Dolores. Thank goodness for Dolores. Thank goodness his old life was over.

Things didn't start to go wrong until he had been married almost a month.

The rent came due on Friday, August 1, and Blackburn wrote a check for it. A week later his landlord telephoned him at work to tell him that the bank had returned the check for insufficient funds. Blackburn didn't understand it. He promised his landlord that he would clear up the problem.

When Blackburn came home that night, Dolores was asleep. He didn't wake her to make love, as was his habit, but instead sat at the kitchen table and went through his checkbook register. He triple-checked the math and then looked at the pad of checks themselves. There were three missing that weren't accounted for in the register. He remembered the shopping trip that Dolores and her mother had taken. He hadn't been home when they had returned, so he hadn't seen what, if anything, Dolores had bought.

He went into the bedroom and turned on the light. Dolores mumbled and stuck her head under her pillow. Blackburn opened the closet and found three empty shopping bags on the floor. The attached receipts were dated July 19 and added up to over four hundred dollars. The checking account was overdrawn even without counting the rent.

Blackburn went to the bed and knelt on the floor beside Dolores. "Sweet love," he said, taking the pillow from her head, "our checkbook is overdrawn. The rent is past due. You spent too much shopping and didn't record the checks."

Dolores's eyes opened. "Sorry," she said.

"Can you take any of the merchandise back?" he asked.

Dolores stretched, twisting onto her back. The sheet slid

down from her breasts. Blackburn started to have an erection.

"Don't think so," Dolores said.

Blackburn couldn't help staring at her rib cage, her breasts, her throat. He wanted to hold her and force his molecules in between hers. "That's all right," he said. "We have enough in savings to cover the deficit, but that's all. So we'll have to be careful for a few months. There won't be any money to spare. We'll have to skip movies and eat lots of Rice-a-Roni." His cock ached for her. It was like a grenade with the pin pulled. "But only until we can save a little again."

"Do I have to go back to work?" Dolores asked. She seemed to be waking up.

"Not if you don't want to."

Blackburn didn't know how it was possible, but their lovemaking that night was better than ever. He really did believe that his molecules mingled with hers and engaged in a million microscopic copulations with simultaneous orgasms.

Money was meaningless.

Blackburn depleted their savings account, paid the August rent, and then worked his ass off, logging as many overtime hours as his boss would allow. He wanted to be sure that he and Dolores would have enough money to get by in September. Most days he worked double shifts, leaving home by eight-thirty in the morning and returning more than sixteen hours later. He worried that Dolores would feel neglected, but she assured him that was not the case. She was proud of him. However, she did get bored sitting at home, so would it be all right if she went out with her girlfriends now and then?

He felt guilty that she should even ask such a question. He had been too harsh about the checkbook error. So he held her shoulders, looked into her eyes, and told her that marriage was not slavery. She could do whatever she liked. He only asked that she take care of herself.

They made love, and Blackburn went to work. When he came home at 1:00 A.M., Dolores was gone. He sat up in bed and waited for her. She came in a little before four, wearing a belted leather jacket that Blackburn had not seen before. Dolores noticed him looking at it and remarked that she had it on loan from one of her girlfriends. She took it off, then stripped naked and leaped on him.

Blackburn went to work four hours later and had trouble keeping his eyes open and making his fingers coordinate. His burritos and tacos fell apart. In the afternoon, he fell asleep in the walk-in refrigerator and woke up shivering. His head ached for the rest of the shift. Dolores was waiting for him when he went home, but for the first time, he didn't want to do anything but sleep. Dolores called him ''poor baby'' and cuddled his head between her breasts. He dreamed of cotton candy.

He felt better the next morning, but called the Taco Tommy manager and said he wouldn't be in until the afternoon shift. After hanging up the phone, he began licking Dolores all over.

''Why aren't you going in?'' Dolores asked.

Blackburn looked up from her belly button. ''I'd rather do this.''

''Glad to hear it.'' Dolores leaned back and didn't talk for a while. Then she said, ''But I have a lunch date with my friend Lisa.''

''Okay,'' Blackburn said. He didn't know Lisa. He didn't know any of Dolores's girlfriends.

''I'm supposed to meet her downtown at ten-thirty,'' Dolores said. ''It's really more of a brunch date, I guess. Then she wants me to help her shop for shoes.''

Blackburn looked at the clock radio on the dresser. It was nine-twenty. ''We still have a little time,'' he said.

''I know. I just wanted to warn you.''

They did it fast and furious. Then Dolores showered, dressed, and left. She wore the leather jacket. Blackburn wondered if it was Lisa's, and if Dolores had to return it already. He resolved to buy her one just like it as soon as he could afford to.

With Dolores gone, Blackburn had nothing to do until three o'clock. He dozed, then turned on the TV and found only game shows and soap operas. He ate some Post Toasties dry. No wonder Dolores liked to get out during the day. The apartment was no fun when you were alone.

He was brushing his teeth when the phone rang. He ran to the living room to answer it and said a garbled "Hello."

"Dolores?" The voice on the other end of the line belonged to a man. Maybe Dolores's father.

Blackburn spat out his toothbrush and swallowed the foam. As he was swallowing, the voice spoke again.

"Dolores, you there? You said twelve-thirty. It's after one. Where are you?" It was not Dolores's father.

Blackburn said nothing.

"Dolores? Dolores?"

The phone clicked, and Blackburn replaced the receiver in its cradle. He picked up his toothbrush and went into the bedroom. He sat on the bed and studied the drying paste in the toothbrush bristles. He sat there for an hour, then went to work.

By the time Blackburn came home that night, he had concocted and rejected a dozen explanations for the voice. A few of them had been innocent. Lisa's boyfriend, perhaps, had confused ten-thirty with twelve-thirty. But Dolores hadn't said anything about Lisa's boyfriend joining them. Blackburn thought she would have said something about that. So most of the explanations he had concocted had been vile. He had always thought of himself as cool-headed, and it irritated him to realize that he had fallen prey to something as intemperate as jealousy.

Dolores was sitting in bed with the sheet pulled up, reading a paperback romance. The borrowed leather jacket covered her shoulders. When she saw Blackburn in the bedroom doorway, she dropped the book and jumped up. The sheet and the jacket fell away. She was wearing a white teddy. Blackburn sucked in his breath.

"Comeherecomeherecomehere," Dolores said, grabbing his wrists and pulling him to the bed. "Sit down. Sit down and close your eyes. Oh, come on, Eddie, do it!"

Blackburn sat on the edge of the mattress and closed his eyes. He saw orange blood vessels. Dolores put something in his lap.

"Okay, open your eyes."

He kept them closed. He was tracing the pattern of the blood vessels.

Dolores's hands touched his face, and he shuddered. Her fingertips were hot. She put her thumbs on his eyelids and pushed them open.

A cardboard box lay in his lap. Dolores removed the lid. Inside, nestled in tissue, were black cowboy boots. They were tooled with designs representing prairie grasses.

"Happy month-and-a-half anniversary," Dolores said. "I would have done it at the actual month anniversary, but I didn't see these until today."

Blackburn was astonished. This was the first gift he had received since he was sixteen. He picked up one of the boots. It was solid. It was his size.

"Cowboy boots?" he said.

Dolores bounced on the balls of her feet. "Well, you said you were born in Wyoming, and I figured, you know, *cowboys,* right?"

The Wyoming lie had brought him a present. But there had been cowboys in Kansas too; it didn't matter. He picked up the other boot. The box slid off his lap. "How?" he asked. He'd had a sudden thought of money.

Dolores turned her eyes toward the ceiling. "Oh, I've been

saving my pennies," she said. "And Mama sent a check. I didn't use our account, if that's what you're worried about."

Blackburn stood and put his arms around her. The boots clunked together behind her back. She loved him. She had proven it every day. She had just done so again. He was a bastard to have concocted vile thoughts about her.

"I'm not worried about anything," he said, and kissed her. "I'll wear them always."

Dolores grinned. "Not to bed, you won't." She made him drop them, then pushed him down.

The next day was Sunday, but Blackburn worked anyway. Seven-day-a-week double shifts were becoming a steady thing. He wore his new boots to work and was proud of them.

The day after that was September 1, and Blackburn paid the rent and the bills. There was enough money left over for him to give Dolores twenty dollars and to set aside another twenty toward a two-month anniversary celebration. He was determined that it would be a special occasion.

In retrospect, he supposed that it was.

On Wednesday, September 10, Blackburn left the apartment in the morning as if he were going to his first shift at the Taco Tommy. Dolores was still in bed, curled like a kitten. She had switched to a new shampoo and smelled of apples and cinnamon. Blackburn licked her neck before he left. She squirmed.

Blackburn got into his Rambler and headed for a mall in Oakland. He had seventy-six dollars that he had saved by skipping lunches and shaving the household budget. He hoped to spend forty or fifty on a gift, and the rest on a surprise lunch at a nice restaurant. He would have liked to make it dinner, but he had to work that evening. Money was still scarce—too scarce, really, to spend any on a two-month anniversary. But it would be worth it. He wanted to prove his love with more than words and sex. He hadn't given

Dolores anything since her wedding ring, and that hadn't been much. Someday he would buy her a better one.

He didn't have the money for that today, or for a leather jacket either, but he could still get her something nice. Maybe a sweater. Dolores had only moved from L.A. to San Francisco in April, and she didn't have much cold-weather clothing. The breeze off the Bay was already chilly. Something to keep her warm would be a fine symbol of his love.

He arrived at the mall right after it opened, and he found the sweater fifteen minutes later at the J.C. Penney store. The sweater was thick and gray, with a knitted belt and wooden buttons. The color would bring out Dolores's eyes and set off her hair. It cost thirty dollars. He bought it and had it gift-wrapped, then found a flower shop and spent another fifteen dollars on a dozen red sweetheart roses in a glass vase. The vase had vines and butterflies cut into it. The engraving looked a little like the tooling on his boots. Dolores would appreciate that. And he still had money left for the restaurant. He was pleased with his success.

He carried the package and flowers to the Rambler, listening to his footsteps on the asphalt. The boots were almost broken in. In another few days, they would feel fine indeed. They already looked and sounded good. Their pointed toes caught the sunlight, and their thick heels made solid *chunk* noises.

As he walked, Blackburn experienced a rush of exhilaration that started in his belly and swelled into his chest and head. The air became crisp, and the outlines of cars and lampposts sharpened. Colors brightened. The sensation was so strong that it made him dizzy. When he reached the Rambler, he set his things on the hood and leaned against the fender. He hadn't felt anything like this since he was ten years old and almost fell from the Wantoda water tower. He had tried to recapture the feeling then, and had failed.

In the years since, he had learned that joy never came when he looked for it. When it came at all, in whatever strength, it took him by surprise. While he was falling, or listening to his boots. Or looking for a copy of *The Kids Are Alright*. Or eating fried shrimp. It would never be in the same place twice.

After a few minutes, the sensation ebbed enough for him to feel safe driving. But some of the joy remained, and he would take it home to Dolores. That would be the best present of all.

He drove back across the Bay Bridge, to ruin.

In some ways, it was a classic scenario: Husband comes home unexpectedly. He brings a gift. He finds wife in bed with another man.

In other ways, it wasn't. Blackburn was unfamiliar with classic scenarios.

He entered the apartment with the package and flowers hugged to his chest, taking care that the front door didn't squeak. It was only ten-thirty, and Dolores might still be asleep. He didn't want to wake her with noise, but with kisses. Once inside, he heard Led Zeppelin playing on the clock radio back in the bedroom. "Gotta wholotta love." Bwaaaah. "Gotta wholotta love." Bwaaaah. "Ah-a-aaah, Ah!"

Blackburn closed the front door and walked through the living room and kitchen to the bedroom door. It was closed. He had left it open, so Dolores must be up. Led Zeppelin was getting louder. Blackburn hesitated, wondering if Dolores might be dancing to the music. He could picture her spinning naked atop the bed. He was afraid that he might embarrass her if he just walked in.

Led Zeppelin faded into Bachman-Turner Overdrive's "You Ain't Seen Nothin' Yet," and Blackburn heard a final "Ah-a-aaah, Ah!" It was louder than the radio. It was the voice of a man.

Blackburn's heart twisted. The only word in his head was *rape*.

Then he was in the bedroom. The glass vase lay in shards on the hardwood floor at the foot of the bed. The roses and water were spread out in the shape of a fan. The J.C. Penney package was crushed in the crook of his left arm. Its blue wrapping paper was ripped. The white bow dangled.

On the bed, a naked man with a hairy back was on top of Dolores. His face was in her crotch. Hers was in his.

Dolores looked up from between the man's buttocks. "Uh-oh," she said.

The word *rape* left Blackburn's head. Then he wanted it back. Then he felt evil for wanting it back. Then that went away too. Everything that he had become in the past four months went away with it. He heard the hiss.

He dropped the package and went to the clock radio to turn it off. Bachman-Turner Overdrive stopped in midstutter. Blackburn was standing at the head of the bed now, looking down at Dolores. Her hair was tangled and damp. Her lips were puffy. The naked man had rolled away and was crouching on the floor on the other side of the bed. Blackburn gave him a glance, then looked back at Dolores.

"Hello," he said. He blinked. His eyes were stinging. That wouldn't do. He made them stop. "I brought flowers."

"Thank you," Dolores whispered.

He looked at the rest of her body. The bikini patches glared. She looked ridiculous in her naked non-nudity.

Blackburn returned to the foot of the bed and squatted to pick up the roses. The naked man's feet appeared among them, and then Blackburn saw that the naked man's clothes were there too. The naked man stooped to collect them, his body bending so that his cock vanished under his belly. Blackburn looked up at the naked man's eyes and tried to see into his brain.

"Look," the naked man said. He was wringing out his briefs. "I never took nothing I never paid for."

Blackburn finished gathering the flowers and stood up.

Dolores was sitting against the headboard now. She had pulled the sheet up to her throat.

"Money's so tight, Ed," she said. "It doesn't mean anything. I was just trying to make things easier."

"So tight," Blackburn said. He turned back to the naked man. "See my boots, naked man?"

The naked man had dropped his wet briefs and was starting to pull on his pants. "What about them?" he asked.

"I think you bought them for me," Blackburn said.

The naked man had one hand on the waistband of his pants. He straightened a little, and the pants came up partway. He smiled.

"Hope you like them," he said.

Blackburn nodded. Then he took a step and kicked. The pointed toe of his right cowboy boot caught the naked man under the balls and drove upward. The naked man's back arched, and his mouth opened. Blackburn stepped away. The naked man crumpled. He hit the floor and lay curled in the water and broken glass. He made a gurgling noise.

Blackburn returned to the head of the bed. He held the roses in a clump in his left hand. "I brought you some flowers," he said again.

Dolores said nothing. Part of the sheet was crammed into her mouth.

"They're sweetheart roses," Blackburn said. "There aren't many thorns. Here." He selected a rose and held it out to her. The tight petals brushed her cheek.

Dolores's right hand came up from the sheet. She took the stem between her thumb and fingers.

"Would you like to smell it?" Blackburn asked.

Dolores nodded.

"Put it up your nose," Blackburn said.

By the time he gave Dolores the last rose, the bedroom smelled like the flower shop. The naked man was throwing up. Dolores was convulsed in a fit of sneezing.

Blackburn went to the closet and took down all of

Dolores's clothes. He threw them on top of the naked man, who was trying to crawl out of the room. The clothes slowed him down. Blackburn shut the door to stop him. Then he turned toward Dolores again.

Dolores was on her knees on the bed. Her eyes were wet. "Eddie, I love you," she said. "I really—" A sneeze cut off her last word.

Blackburn wanted to kill her. The Python would be the best way. It was in the Rambler, wrapped in rags under the back seat. It would be an effort to go out and remove the seat, retrieve the pistol, and bring it back. But he could be fast. His life before Dolores had taught him to be fast. He wouldn't even have to tie her up first. He could put one behind her ear before she could get away.

Her sweet, perfect-for-tonguing ear.

He wanted to kill her.

He wanted to make love to her.

He wanted to kill her.

Dolores had betrayed him. She had treated him as one human being should never treat another. She had violated his rules in the most severe way possible. It was as simple as simple could be.

One behind her ear.

Blackburn started for the door. The pile of clothes with the naked man under it was in his way. He stopped. Then he turned back and crawled onto the bed. He crawled up until his nose was a millimeter from Dolores's nose. Her eyes converged. She turned away. He gave her one kiss behind her ear.

Then he dragged her to the closet and bound her ankles to the clothes rod with the belt from the leather jacket, which he didn't think was borrowed after all. Her head just touched the floor. She began yelling for help, so he opened the box from J.C. Penney and took out the sweater. He used its belt to gag her, then wrapped the sweater around her head. He put his hands against the sweater and felt her breath. She would be all right. He straightened, stepped back, and closed the closet door. He would not be using the Python today.

No matter what she had done, no matter what his rules, Dolores was his wife. And a good husband did not put a bullet into his wife's brain. He had already done too much as it was. He was already too much like his father.

Blackburn stuffed a few things into his duffel bag, then kicked the pile of clothes off the naked man and helped him to his feet. The naked man was bleeding where the glass had cut him. He had trouble standing upright. His hands clutched his cock and balls. His eyes were wide and white.

"Come on," Blackburn said. He slung his duffel over his shoulder and pulled the naked man toward the door.

"I gotta," the naked man gasped, "get my clothes."

"You won't need them."

"People will see me." The naked man was hairy and had a gut. His legs were skinny below the knees. He didn't look good in the nude.

"No, they won't," Blackburn said. "You're riding in the trunk."

When Blackburn opened the trunk on the Golden Gate Bridge, the naked man was screaming "You're going to kill me! You're going to kill me!"

"Am not," Blackburn said. He pulled the naked man from the trunk. The Rambler was parked next to the guard rail.

The naked man hopped from one foot to the other, his stomach jiggling. The bridge had gathered solar energy and was hot.

"So you're not going to kill me?" the naked man asked.

"No," Blackburn said. "You'll have to blame that on the fall."

The naked man stopped hopping. "Huh?"

"Maybe drowning. But it's a long way down."

134

The naked man tried to run into traffic. The cars honked. Blackburn caught him and dragged him back to the guard rail. When the naked man came up against the rail, he fought. But he was naked, his crotch was bruised, his cuts were bleeding, and the bridge was hot. Cars kept honking. Some of the drivers pointed. Blackburn waved to them.

He didn't watch the naked man all the way down to the Bay. Instead he pulled off the black cowboy boots and tossed them over the rail too. The naked man had paid for them; they were his.

He put on his sneakers in the Rambler and then had a narrow escape from the police cars that wailed onto the bridge from San Francisco. He sped into Marin County and blasted north on Highway 101. He had a hard drive ahead of him. He would have to switch cars as soon as he had a few moments out of sight. The Python was on the seat beside him, just in case.

"Good-bye, Dolores!" Blackburn called out the window as he headed toward Oregon.

He decided to give up on love.

VICTIM NUMBER TEN

I-70 through eastern Colorado was as bleak as a bald tire.
Blackburn was still over a hundred miles from the state line
when billboards for the first Kansas tourist attraction began
appearing. SEE THE WORLD'S LARGEST PRAIRIE DOG! they said. PET
THE BABY PIGS!

"Welcome home," Blackburn told himself. But in fact he
wouldn't go anywhere near Wantoda. It was far off in the
southeastern part of the state, and he would be sticking to
I-70 all the way to Kansas City.

He wiped his forehead with a handkerchief that was already wet. He was driving an old Valiant that he had stolen
in Longmont, and it didn't have an air conditioner. The

wind blasting through the open windows scorched rather than cooled. Blackburn was out of soda pop and food, and the little cash remaining in his jeans pocket would have to go for gas. He couldn't even afford to see the world's largest prairie dog or to pet the baby pigs. But that was okay. As a child, he had heard from his friend Ernie that the prairie dog was a ripoff. It was a statue made of concrete. The baby pigs were probably real, but he doubted that petting them was much of a thrill.

His mouth was dry, and his stomach was a knot against his backbone. Money or no money, he would have to refuel his body as well as the car. Seventeen miles into Kansas, he came to the town of Goodland and decided that its name was an omen. It would give him nourishment. He left the interstate, filled the Valiant's tank, and then cruised up and down the dusty streets. He was looking for a community barbecue or church picnic to crash. It was a summer Saturday, so he figured the odds were good.

He didn't find a barbecue or picnic, but as he drove past a Lions Club hall, he saw that its parking lot was packed with cars and pickup trucks. The people going inside were dressed as if for Sunday services, and they carried packages wrapped in silver and white. These were the signs of a wedding reception, so Blackburn went around the block and pulled into the lot. He wouldn't find an actual meal here, but he could at least score a piece of cake and something to drink. He was sure of success when he saw that the license plates in the lot were divided between Kansas and Illinois. It was unlikely that all of the Illinois folks knew all of the Goodland contingent, and vice versa. The groom's family would think Blackburn was related to the bride, and the bride's family would think he was related to the groom. He buttoned the top button of his short-sleeved cotton work shirt, put on a wrinkled black necktie from his duffel bag, and went inside. He looked like trash, but that would give the families something to talk about later. It would be his present.

The reception line was still in progress when Blackburn came into the main room, so he hung back to wait for the cake to be served. The air-conditioning system was cranking full blast, and the cold air felt wonderful. Blackburn's sweat began to dry. He was already glad he had stopped.

When the reception line dwindled, the bridesmaids hustled the bride and groom over to the cake table, and the newlyweds did the traditional things with cake and punch that Blackburn had never been able to figure out. What was the point of linking your arms in order to spill punch down each other's front? What was the point of mashing cake up each other's nose? Maybe, he thought, those acts were supposed to be symbolic of what the couple had to look forward to in their married life.

He got in line for cake, nodding to the middle-aged woman in front of him when she gave him a raised-eyebrow look. She turned away quickly. Blackburn hadn't shaved in three days, and the long drive in the sun hadn't done his body odor much good. But he was wearing a tie, so no one would have the guts to kick him out. He accepted a glass plate with a sliver of cake, then stopped at the nut and mint bowls and loaded up. He picked up a cup of orange punch at the end of the table, then finished his refreshments in two minutes and got in line again. He noticed that the middle-aged woman was whispering to another woman and pointing at him. His gift was in effect already.

His second piece of cake was bigger than the first, so by the time he finished it and another cup of punch, the edges had worn off his hunger and thirst enough for him to realize that he had to go to the bathroom. He spotted a hallway leading off one corner of the room, so he left his plate and cup on a chair and headed in that direction. On the way, a burly man with a red face clapped him on the back and asked how he was doing. Blackburn answered that he was doing just fine and that it had been a heck of a wedding. The burly man agreed. His breath was pungent with beer, and he looked happy even though his shirt collar was too tight for his neck.

"Don't go nowhere," the burly man said. "Larry's settin' up the music box for dancin'. Too many purty girls to leave now."

"Just going to the necessary room," Blackburn said.

The burly man laughed. "Necessary room!" he bellowed. He was still laughing as Blackburn left him and slipped into the hallway.

The hallway was dim, so Blackburn let his fingertips trail along the paneled wall while his eyes adjusted. A door marked LADIES opened as he touched it, and a bridesmaid stepped out. His fingers brushed her bare shoulder and across the crisp fabric over her breasts. She gasped.

He drew back. "Pardon me," he said. It really had been an accident, and he hoped she realized it. He could imagine the ruckus if she accused him of copping a feel.

"S'all right," the girl mumbled, and hurried past. Blackburn didn't think she would tell anyone. She probably assumed that he was a friend of the groom, and she wouldn't want to embarrass her friend the bride.

Blackburn raised his hand to his lips and blew on his fingertips. The bridesmaid's skin had been smooth. Not as smooth as Dolores's had been, but smooth enough. He wondered if she was over the age of consent, then decided that it didn't matter. He didn't have time to seduce a bridesmaid in western Kansas. He had to take a whiz, eat another piece of cake, and get on down the road.

The hallway ended in a door marked GENTLEMEN. Blackburn tried the knob, but it didn't turn. He leaned against the wall to wait, and before long the pressure in his bladder became painful. He tried the knob again, knocked, and then put his ear to the door. He thought he heard muffled sounds from within, but he couldn't be sure because of the noise from the reception.

"Hello?" he called. "Everything all right in there?" There was no answer, so he assumed that the door had been locked by accident. He gripped the knob, put his shoulder to the door, and shoved. It didn't budge, so he took a few steps back and rammed it. The door popped open with a *spang*. The latch plate flew inside, ricocheted off the closed toilet stall, and landed in the urinal. Blackburn stepped into the rest room and shut the door behind him. It didn't latch, but it stayed closed.

He went to the urinal, unzipped, and urinated. As he finished, he heard a giggle, followed by a "Shh!" There were people inside the toilet stall. He zipped up and washed his hands, then squatted to look under the stall door. Someone wearing dark-blue pants and black shoes was sitting on the toilet. Someone with bare legs and feet was sitting on that person's lap. A pair of yellow high heels and a crumpled wad of panty hose lay on the floor.

Blackburn stood. This was none of his business.

There was a squeal, and then the stall door flew open. A man and a woman tumbled onto the floor at Blackburn's feet.

The man looked up. "Lost our balance," he said.

Blackburn recognized him. He was the groom. His tuxedo pants were down around his knees. His ruffled white shirt was twisted.

The woman underneath the groom was not the bride. She was wearing a yellow dress that was bunched around her waist. The woman looked up at Blackburn in terror and struggled to pull up the top part of her dress.

Blackburn wanted to leave, but he couldn't. The woman's head was in front of the rest-room door, so he couldn't open it without braining her. He leaned back against the sink to wait.

The groom untangled himself and stood. Blackburn

140

averted his eyes while the groom pulled up his underwear and pants. The woman was still adjusting her dress while lying on the floor. When she finished, the groom lifted her to her feet and handed her the high heels and panty hose. She opened the door a crack to peek into the hallway, then hurried out. The door swung shut after her. Blackburn stepped forward and put his hand on the knob.

"Hang on a second," the groom said.

Blackburn paused. "Why?"

"I want to explain." The groom took his tuxedo jacket from a hook inside the stall and put it on. One lapel had an orange stain and a smear of white frosting. The groom produced a flat pint bottle of Wild Turkey from an inner pocket, took a drink, and offered the bottle to Blackburn. Blackburn shook his head and started to open the door. The groom pushed it shut.

Blackburn took his hand from the knob. "Last guy who did that," he said, "can't tie his shoes now."

The groom stepped between Blackburn and the door. "Look, I can understand you being pissed off as a first reaction," he said. "You're Eleanor's cousin, right?"

Blackburn said nothing. He put his hands in his pockets as a precaution. He didn't want to hurt the groom. There were a lot of people between the rest room and the parking lot, and he wasn't armed.

"Okay, you don't have to say anything," the groom said. "And I'd appreciate it if you wouldn't say anything to Eleanor either. It wouldn't make sense. Once you stop being pissed, you'll see what I mean."

"I don't follow," Blackburn said.

The groom tapped his wedding ring against the whiskey bottle. "You married?"

"I was," Blackburn said. He assumed that Dolores had arranged a divorce by now. If she hadn't, it was all the same to him. They were divorced as far as he was concerned.

"Was," the groom repeated. "Man, then you've got to

know what I'm talking about." He took another drink. "What's your name?"

"Carl."

The groom extended his right hand. "I'm Steve. But I guess you knew that."

Blackburn kept his hands in his pockets.

The groom lowered his hand. "Well, shit, Carl. Remember getting married? You stand up there with this girl, in front of a church full of relatives, and the preacher makes you swear to 'forsake all others.' And that ain't natural, but there's all those relatives, so what are you gonna do? You're trapped. And then an hour later—"

"You're banging somebody in the bathroom," Blackburn said.

The groom grinned. "Not on purpose. But there in church, I was thinking, Man, is that it? I mean, look, I'm not ashamed to say that I love Eleanor. I don't want to be married to anyone else. You know?"

"If you say so."

"It's the truth. But women, you know, their brains are screwed. They think that being in love and getting laid are the same goddamn thing. And it ain't so. Am I right?"

Blackburn considered. "I don't know that women think they're the same."

The groom took another swig of Wild Turkey and shook his head. "Well, when you marry one of them, that's what she thinks. At least, that's what Eleanor thinks."

"How do you know?" Blackburn asked. "You only just now married her."

The groom shrugged. "We talked about it when we got engaged. I mean, *she* talked about it. She's got this little girl's idea about one man, one woman, happily ever after, all that fairy-tale bullshit. It's a weird attitude for her to take too, because before we got together, she wasn't exactly—" He hesitated. "Well, shit, the truth's the truth. She wasn't exactly, you know, a virgin when we started dating."

"So?"

"Exactly my point," the groom said. *"Everybody* screws around. It's like eating or breathing. It doesn't mean anything. Getting laid is just getting laid, and that doesn't change because you have some piece of paper. It doesn't mean you don't love your wife. It's not like you're going to leave her or anything. Right?"

"Guess not," Blackburn said. He glanced at the stall. "But it does seem like you're getting a head start."

The groom snickered. "Oh, yeah, well. That was Cindy. We went steady when I was fourteen, and we never did much back then, so we were sort of wondering how it would've been. You know. Last chance to find out. Doesn't mean anything."

"If you say so."

The groom drained his pint and shoved the bottle into the wastecan. "The thing is, see, I told Eleanor I'd be faithful. And I will be, in the true sense of the word. I'll take good care of her, and I'll never hurt her. So I'm asking you not to tell her about this. It'd just upset her. It shouldn't, but it would. That's the way she is."

"She won't hear it from me," Blackburn said.

The groom reached out and squeezed Blackburn's shoulder. "Thanks, man," he said. Then he opened the door and went out.

Blackburn shut the door, then went into the stall and shut that door too. He wiped the toilet seat with a strip of tissue and sat down to think. The groom's philosophy almost fit what had happened between him and Dolores, except the genders were reversed. Maybe that meant that men and women were, in fact, alike. Maybe the normal condition for both sexes was a constant desire to copulate with as many different partners as often as possible, which would mean that people like him and Eleanor were mutants. Maybe it was perverse to fixate on one person and to want that person to return the perversion. Maybe he had been unreasonable to expect Dolores to refrain from fucking hairy strangers in the middle of the day, and Eleanor was being unreasonable to expect Steve to refrain from fucking Cindy at their wedding reception.

Maybe. He couldn't decide. The issue was complex, and he had too little information. He needed additional input before he could make up his mind.

He left the restroom and went to the end of the hall as "The Tennessee Waltz" began playing in the main room. He watched the bride and groom take their spotlight dance. The bride's dress swirled, and the groom's hair was mussed just enough to make him look charming. They gazed into each other's eyes and grinned. As the song ended, they kissed, and their friends and relatives applauded.

The next song was also a waltz, and other couples joined in the dancing. Blackburn entered the room and walked around the dancers to the cake table. He ate a third piece of cake while he watched the dancers turn and twirl. The frosting was already starting to get crusty, but Blackburn didn't mind. He ate yet another piece after that, and drank two more cups of punch. By the time he finished, a dollar dance was in progress. For a dollar, anyone could dance with the bride. The collected money would go toward honeymoon expenses.

Blackburn took his remaining cash from his pocket and counted it. Four dollars and sixty cents. Spending a dollar here would make reaching Kansas City a real stretch. On the other hand, he wanted to talk to the bride, and this was his best chance. He put three dollars and sixty cents back into his pocket and got into the dollar-dance line.

The dollar dances were short, lasting a minute or less apiece, so Blackburn's turn came soon. As he approached the bride, he knew that all eyes in the room were on him, and that most of their owners were wondering who the hell he was. As he took the bride's warm hand in his, he saw the groom give him a nod. The groom had confidence in Blackburn's discretion.

"Hello, Eleanor," Blackburn said. "Congratulations."

"Thank you," she said. Her face was frozen in a smile, but Blackburn could see that behind it, she was pretty. She was shorter than she had appeared from a distance, and small-boned. She seemed so light that Blackburn had the impression that a strong hug would crush her. Her dark-blond hair was permed into ringlets. Blackburn leaned in close to speak to her, and the ringlets brushed his cheek.

"So now you're Steve's wife," Blackburn said.

She rolled her eyes. "It hardly seems real yet."

"Till death do you part," he said. "I suppose you've thought a lot about that."

"Pardon?"

"The till-death-do-you-part business."

"Well," the bride said, "that's what marriage is all about."

"I was married too," Blackburn said. "But it didn't last till death. Not hers or mine, anyway. She became involved with someone else. Of course, that sort of thing couldn't happen to you and Steve."

The bride stiffened and looked away. Blackburn could see that she wanted him to leave now, but he couldn't. Not yet.

"It does happen, though," he said. "Sometimes it's the woman, sometimes the man. I guess they have their reasons."

The bride looked back at him. Her smile had vanished. "I can't imagine what. There's a Commandment against it."

"I know," Blackburn said. "But what if something happens anyway? What if someone has a good, loving spouse, and he or she goes astray just the same?"

The bride's cheeks flushed. She was angry. Blackburn was ruining her dollar dance.

"Then he or she should be shot," she said. She pulled her hand from Blackburn's. "Thank you for the dance."

Blackburn went outside and began to sweat again, so he rubbed his hands on his jeans to keep them dry. He went to the Valiant and took the Colt Python from under the front seat. The grip and trigger were hot. He returned to the building. It was too late to do anything for himself, but he could still do something for Eleanor.

Once inside again, he took a breath of air-conditioned air and cocked the Python. Then he yelled "Steve!" loud enough to be heard over the music.

Heads turned. People saw the pistol. There were shouts. Some of the men started toward him. The music stopped.

The groom was standing on the far side of the room. It was a longer shot than Blackburn had ever tried. But the middle of the room had been emptied for the dollar dance, and the man dancing with the bride pushed her to the floor and lay down on top of her. The people near the groom moved away from him. Blackburn had a clear line of fire.

He used a two-handed grip and aimed for the head, squeezing the trigger as the groom started to run. The groom dropped and screamed. The men heading for Blackburn stopped and turned to look. The groom lay on his back, doubled up, rocking. Blackburn sprinted across to him, jumping over the bride and her dollar-dance partner.

The groom held his crotch with both hands. Blood was soaking his tuxedo pants.

"Damn," Blackburn said, and cocked the Python again.

"Where's my dick?" the groom asked.

"I'm sorry," Blackburn said. "Bad shot." Then he fired into the groom's right eye.

He turned and saw that the exit was clogged with people squealing and squirming like baby pigs. Other people were standing and staring like concrete prairie dogs.

"Welcome home," Blackburn told himself.

At that moment the burly man who had clapped Blackburn on the back charged toward him. Blackburn pointed the Python at him. "Stop," he said, and the man stopped.

146

"Lie down," he said, and the man lay down. So did everyone else, except for a few who still struggled to get outside. Blackburn let them go.

The bride crawled out from under her dance partner and stood. She looked at the groom, then ran at Blackburn. He lowered the gun and waited for her. When she reached him, she scratched his face. Then she hit him in the chest with her fists.

"Why?" she asked. She asked it over and over again.

Blackburn looked around until he saw the woman in the yellow dress. She was lying under the cake table. He went to her, and the bride came along, hitting him and asking her question.

"Cindy," Blackburn said, nudging the woman under the table with his foot. "Come out and tell Eleanor why I shot Steve."

The woman didn't move, so Blackburn cocked the Python. Then she came out and stood. The bride stopped hitting Blackburn and faced the woman.

"Why?" the bride asked.

The woman in the yellow dress began crying.

Blackburn thought that was a copout, but he supposed that she would have to confess sooner or later. He left her there with the bride and headed for the door, which was clear now. Halfway there, a boy on the floor clutched his ankle and held up a cloth bag.

"Is this what you want?" the boy asked.

"No," Blackburn said.

"Is this what you want?" the boy asked again. He asked it three more times, so Blackburn took the bag to shut him up. The boy released his ankle, and Blackburn went outside.

In the parking lot, a man behind a pickup truck took a shot at Blackburn with a rifle. The bullet went through the cloth bag and sprayed bits of masonry from the wall of the Lions Club building. Blackburn ran for the Valiant, firing two shots into the pickup truck.

He threw the bag and the pistol into the Valiant, jumped in, and started the engine as the rifleman came out from behind the pickup. Blackburn grabbed the Python with his left hand and fired out the window. The rifleman ducked back behind the truck. Blackburn backed the Valiant from its parking space, put it in Drive, and stomped the accelerator. He saw the rifleman again in the rearview mirror, so he reached outside and fired the Python's last shot backward. The recoil hurt his wrist, but the bullet shattered the pickup's side window, and the rifleman dove behind another car.

Blackburn sped north out of Goodland, away from I-70, watching for sheriff's deputies and the Kansas Highway Patrol. He steered with his knees while he reloaded the Python. He was operating on an intense sugar buzz. He turned east when he reached U.S. Highway 36 and switched cars in the town of Atwood. It was only then that he looked into the cloth bag that the boy had given him.

It contained the money from the dollar dance. Some of the men had paid tens and twenties to dance with the bride. There was even one fifty.

Blackburn couldn't go to Kansas City or anywhere else along I-70 for a while, so instead he headed into Nebraska via a tortuous route of county and country roads. As he drove, he considered finding out Eleanor's last name so he could mail the money to her. After all, he wasn't a thief. He did steal the occasional automobile, but that was a necessity. He hadn't meant to steal from Eleanor. He had only meant to see her receive justice. He wouldn't want her to think otherwise.

After consideration, however, Blackburn decided to keep the money himself. Eleanor, he had realized, wouldn't want it. There wasn't going to be a honeymoon anyway.

SIX

BLACKBURN CHOOSES STERILITY

On the day after he killed his eleventh man, Blackburn decided to have a vasectomy. That was because the Monday *Kansas City Times* reported that the victim had been a father of four. Blackburn didn't enjoy reading it. He wished that he had stayed behind the grill instead of taking his morning break.

It wasn't that he regretted what he had done. Late Sunday, Number Eleven had run over a dog and had made a hash mark in the air with his finger, so Blackburn had driven after him and killed him at the next red light. It had been quick— one .357 bullet through the side window, and the light had changed. Blackburn had rolled up his own window and driven on. No one had seen. Kansas City was dead on Sunday nights.

Number Eleven had deserved what he had gotten, but Blackburn thought it sad that the man had fathered four children who would now be warped by his cruelty in life and his ugly death. With that thought, Blackburn realized that he himself would not make an exemplary father and that he might die an ugly death of his own.

After his experience with Dolores, he doubted that he would ever take another wife. But he had a sex drive as strong as that of any other twenty-four-year-old man, and women found his sandy hair and blue eyes attractive, so there would be girlfriends and one-nighters. He could not allow himself to impregnate them.

Paying for the operation might be a problem. Upon arriving in Kansas City in September, he had spent most of his cash on documents identifying him as Arthur B. Cameron, and the rest on a scabrous 1970 Dart. He had then landed his job at Bucky's Burgers, but in two months of work, he had saved only fifty dollars. He would have to find a clinic that performed cheap sterilizations.

During his afternoon break, he went into Bucky's office and looked through the Yellow Pages. He found what he needed under the heading of "Birth Control":

Responsible Reproduction of Kansas City
Pregnancy Testing
Birth Control/Family Planning
Abortion Counseling and Services
Vasectomies
Fees Scaled to Income
Open Noon to 10:00 P.M. Weekdays

The ad was followed by a telephone number and a midtown address. Blackburn's one-room basement apartment had no phone, and he didn't want to call from Bucky's, so he decided to visit Responsible Reproduction after work. He spent the rest of the afternoon in a state of anticipation, knowing that he was about to give a great gift to the world.

Stinking of deep-fryer grease, Blackburn pushed open a glass door embedded with wire mesh and found himself in a room illuminated by fluorescent tubes. Plastic chairs lined the walls. Most were occupied by women, a few of whom clutched the hands of nervous men. Three toddlers sat on the linoleum floor playing with G.I. Joe dolls. An odor of medicine mixed with Blackburn's own smell.

He approached a middle-aged woman who sat at a desk beside a doorway. A sign on the desk read ELLEN DUNCAN. "Ms. Duncan," Blackburn said, "my name is Arthur Cameron. I want a vasectomy."

Ms. Duncan opened a drawer and brought out a pamphlet that she pushed across to him. It was entitled "Facts to Consider About Vasectomy (Male Sterilization)."

Blackburn took the pamphlet and gave it a glance. "Thank you," he said, "but I've considered the facts, and I've decided to have the operation. Could you tell me how much it will cost?"

Ms. Duncan frowned. "Our urologists charge Responsible Reproduction a hundred and ninety-five dollars. The amount that we pass on to the patient varies according to what he can afford." She paused. "Pardon me for asking, but have you discussed this with your spouse?"

"I'm not married."

"Are you in a long-term relationship?"

"No."

"Have you any children?"

"No." Blackburn wondered what these questions had to do with anything.

"Mr. Cameron," Ms. Duncan said, "our mission is to make family planning services available to those who couldn't afford them otherwise. We provide vasectomies to men who have consulted with their partners, whose families are complete, and whose incomes must support those families. We prefer that single men who have fathered no children see private physicians . . ."

A woman in a white smock appeared in the doorway. "Melissa," she called. "We're ready."

Across the room, a girl of sixteen or seventeen stood up. As she stepped around the children, she trembled.

". . . but, in any case, you should read the pamphlet," Ms. Duncan was saying. She opened the drawer again and brought out a sheet of paper. "Then I hope you'll contact one of the physicians on this list." She put the list on the desk and looked at Blackburn as if she expected him to take it and leave.

He watched the girl named Melissa disappear down a hall.

"Why is she going back there?" he asked.

Ms. Duncan stared. "That's none of your business."

Blackburn stared back. "Does she have a family? Must her income support it? Did she consult with her partner?"

Ms. Duncan's face flushed. "Please leave."

"Why?"

"Because I don't think you're here for information. I think you're one of those who stand outside and shout horrible things at the people who come to us for help. You're here to harass us."

Blackburn shook his head. "No. I'm here because I don't want kids. I have no partner to consult, but since I work as a short-order cook, I also have no savings account or health insurance."

Ms. Duncan studied him. "All right," she said, picking up a pen and poising it over a calendar. "You'll have to meet with our staff counselor."

"I don't need—"

"It's required. The discussion will deal with your reasons for this decision and with the nature of the procedure. Your cost will be calculated then." She looked at the calendar. "Could you come back tomorrow at five forty-five?"

"I'll be here."

"I'm glad I was able to help you," Ms. Duncan said.

Blackburn was glad too. When Ms. Duncan had begun asking her irritating questions, he had decided to kill her if she turned him away. He had never killed a woman before, and he had not been happy at the prospect.

The sun had gone down, and the air was cold. As Blackburn left the building, he put his hands into the side pockets of his jeans jacket and gazed at the concrete walk. He didn't see the people who blocked his way until he was almost upon them. They hadn't been there when he'd arrived.

There were eight of them, clustered beside the drive that led to the clinic parking lot. Each held a burning candle in one hand and a handmade sign in the other. The letters shone in the glare of the streetlights.

Blackburn stopped and read the signs. GOD COUNTS THE CHILDREN, said one. SAVE THE UNBORN, said another. ABORTION IS MURDER, said a third.

A man stepped out of the cluster and asked, "Have you come from in there?" He pointed with his candle, and the flame faltered. "There where they butcher babies?"

"I've just been inside," Blackburn said, "but I don't know anything about any butchering."

A slender woman joined the man. She was dressed in a gray coat with matching gloves, muffler, and cap. Her eyes and lips gleamed with reflections of her candle flame. Wisps of brown hair quivered beneath the edge of her cap.

"If you've been in there, you know about it," she said. Her voice had a rich timbre but was hoarse. "They do abortions."

"They didn't do one to me," Blackburn said. "Now, please, let me pass. My car is across the street."

"So why are you here?" the woman demanded. "Did you

153

drop off your girlfriend so she could let them kill your baby? Or—'' The flames in her eyes brightened. ''Or have you killed babies yourself? Are you going to a home paid for with the flesh of infants?''

Blackburn had heard enough. These people were lucky that after his close call with Ms. Duncan, he didn't feel much like killing anyone tonight. He strode forward.

The man who had confronted him jumped aside, and the cluster of six did likewise. The woman in gray stayed where she was.

Blackburn stopped again to decide whether to shoulder his way past her or to try to go around.

The woman dropped her candle and reached into a pocket, bringing out a vial filled with dark liquid. She pulled out the stopper with her teeth (perfect teeth, Blackburn saw; white, smooth), then spat it out and screamed ''Murderer!'' She snapped the vial toward Blackburn as if it were the handle of a whip.

The liquid hit him in the face and got into his left eye and his mouth. He took his hands from his jacket pockets, and as he rubbed his eye, he tasted what was on his tongue: blood. Cow's blood, pig's blood, maybe even blood that the woman had drawn from her own veins.

She remained before him, holding the vial like a weapon. It was not empty.

Blackburn took a step. The woman stood her ground. He reached out and plucked the vial from her glove, raised it to his lips, and drank. When the blood stopped flowing, he put his tongue inside and cleaned the glass.

Then he dropped the vial to the sidewalk and crushed it under his foot. The edge of his shoe caught the discarded candle as well, flattening it.

The woman gaped at him.

Blackburn walked around her and crossed the street to his car. Once inside, he turned on the interior light and examined the smears on his fingers. He almost reached for his

Colt Python, which was nestled under the seat, but did not. He was calling it even with the woman in gray.

When he returned the next evening, the protesters were pacing, their breath wafting in faint clouds. He parked the Dart where he had the day before and walked across, but they ignored him as he passed.

Inside, Ms. Duncan gave him a personal information and medical history form to fill out, and when he had completed it (having lied where necessary), she led him to a cubicle where the staff counselor, a black man in his mid-thirties, was waiting. Ms. Duncan introduced the counselor as Lawrence Tatum.

"Call me Larry," Tatum said as Ms. Duncan left. He was sitting at a desk covered with a jumble of books, pamphlets, and folders. "I'll take that data sheet off your hands."

Blackburn handed him the form and sat down. The desk was against the wall, so the two men faced each other with nothing between them.

Tatum examined the form, then looked up and asked, "What happens if you decide to get married, your wife-to-be wants kids, and you've had your balls disconnected?"

Blackburn tried to imagine the situation, but the only wife-to-be he could picture was Dolores, she of the perpetual white bikini patches. "I won't be a father," he said, remembering how his own father had shot his dog and then pushed his face into the gravel for crying. "Any woman who knew me and still wanted to have children by me would make a poor wife."

"A vasectomy is permanent, Arthur. What if you turn thirty and all of a sudden, *blam,* you want to be a daddy?"

Blackburn doubted that he would live to be thirty, but he considered the question anyway. "That'll be tough shit for me, I guess," he said.

Tatum wrote on the form. "Okay. Let's talk about what'll

happen during the operation, and then Duncan can schedule you for surgery."

Blackburn was surprised. "That's it?"

"For you it is. Couples take longer." Tatum began to rummage through the mess on his desk. "Besides, I figure that any guy who would be sterilized without understanding the consequences is a guy who shouldn't be spreading his dumbass genes around anyway."

It was the most honest statement Blackburn had ever heard. He liked Tatum.

Tatum found a card with a diagram of male genitalia and held it up. "You'll be given two shots of local anesthetic in the scrotum, one on either side of the base of the penis." He pointed with his pen. "After they take effect, the doctor will make a vertical incision midway between the vas deferens tubes. He'll pull one vas over to the incision, put a permanent clamp on it, and cut away a section. Then he'll repeat the procedure for the other side and close the incision with a few self-dissolving stitches. The whole thing takes about twenty minutes. Any questions?"

Blackburn stood. "How much will it cost?"

Tatum glanced at the form. "You'll need to bring a money order or cashier's check for ninety bucks." He picked up a telephone receiver and punched a button. "Ellen? When Mr. Cameron comes out, could you arrange the pre-vasectomy sample and schedule him for surgery? Thanks."

"What's a pre-vasectomy sample?" Blackburn asked.

"Semen specimen," Tatum said, hanging up the phone. "You'll need to take it to a medical lab within a half hour of ejaculation. We do the post-op sperm counts here, because then it doesn't matter whether we find the sperm alive or dead, only that we don't find any. For this one, though, we need a live count. You never know—maybe you won't have any."

"What are the odds of that?"

Tatum chuckled. "About the same as the odds of the

Royals winning the Series next year. If you don't hear from us before your surgery date, assume that your count's in the normal range."

Blackburn thanked him and went out to Ms. Duncan, who gave him the address of the lab and told him to deliver his sample on Thursday morning. She also told him that his surgery would take place in one week, at 5:20 P.M.

"Soon," he said. "That's good."

"Every Tuesday," Ms. Duncan said. "There are two underway upstairs right now."

"Could I observe?"

Ms. Duncan said that she didn't think so. Then she gave him two instruction sheets and a baggie containing a single-bladed, blue plastic safety razor. The first instruction sheet told him what it was for.

Before going to the Dart, Blackburn stopped among the protesters and spoke to the woman in gray. "You have the wrong night. There's no baby-butchering today."

"I suppose you call it 'choice,' " she said.

Blackburn smiled. "No. Tonight it's 'crotch-cutting.' Or maybe 'scrotum-slicing.' "

"I can have you arrested for obscenity," the woman said.

Blackburn laughed and crossed the street. As he unlocked his car, he heard footsteps on the asphalt. Turning, he saw that the woman in gray had followed him. She had left her sign and candle on the sidewalk.

"Are you going to throw more blood?" Blackburn asked as she drew close.

The planes of her face seemed frozen. "You already have so much on you that it'll never wash off."

"Yet blood washes away sin."

"What would you know about that?"

He knew plenty, but instead of telling her so, he said, "I'm not an abortionist."

"It doesn't matter. If you work there, if you're *in* there,

157

you're one of them. Condoning it is the same as doing it. It's evil."

"So why come over here? Shouldn't you be afraid of evil?"

She tilted her head. "I need to understand you if I'm going to fight you. How can you believe in what you do, and *do* what you do?"

For a moment, the sureness of her tone made Blackburn fear that she knew who he was, and knew the things he really had done. Then he remembered that she didn't even know him as Arthur Cameron, let alone as James Blackburn.

"You're wrong about me," he said. "In fact, I'm making sure that I'll never be the cause of what you're fighting." He took the baggie containing the plastic razor from his jacket. "This is to shave the hair off my scrotum. I'm having a vasectomy next week."

The planes of the woman's face crumpled, and she spun and stumbled into the street. A car was coming fast and would have hit her, but Blackburn pulled her back.

He was startled at what he had done. He didn't save people from themselves. He left people alone . . . unless they angered him, in which case he either punished them if the offense was slight, or killed them if it was great.

In the past seven years, the only exception to this rule had been that he had not killed Dolores.

The woman in gray clawed at his hands until he released her, and she rushed into the street again.

"Could I have that back?" Blackburn called.

She stopped. Her right hand was clutching the baggied razor. She dropped it and ran to her fellow protesters.

Blackburn retrieved the razor, got into the Dart, and drove to his apartment. All that night, the woman in gray filled his thoughts. He was afraid that he might be in love with her.

* * *

On Wednesday, Blackburn worked twelve hours at Bucky's. He needed the money.

On Thursday morning, he ejaculated into an empty breath-mint box and took it to the medical lab. He was embarrassed, not because he was delivering his own fresh semen, but because he had conjured up the ghost of the woman in gray to produce it. She had thrown blood on him, and then they had rolled together, each staining the other.

After a ten-hour shift behind the grill, he drove to Responsible Reproduction. The woman and her friends were there, but none of them seemed to recognize his car. He parked a short distance down the block, and for the next hour he watched them shout at everyone who went in and out of the building. The voice of the woman in gray rose above the rest.

On Friday night, after cashing his paycheck, he approached the clinic from the opposite direction and parked across the street from where he had the night before. He watched longer this time. At nine-thirty the protesters blew out their candles and stacked their signs in a station wagon. Blackburn slouched low as they went to their cars.

The woman in gray crossed the street alone to a maroon Nova. When it left the curb, Blackburn followed.

He lost the Nova in traffic on the city's east side, but spotted it as he drove past a side street. It was parked under a streetlight, and the woman was standing on the porch of a small house. Blackburn pulled over and adjusted his rearview mirror so that he could see her.

A light came on in the house, glowing yellow through the shades, and the door opened. A thin, backlit figure handed the woman something, and the door closed.

The woman returned to her car carrying bunches of red roses, their stems wrapped in green florist's paper. She cradled them as if she were carrying a child, but when she reached the Nova, she put them into the trunk.

Blackburn followed her again as she drove away. She went far west, into Kansas, but he didn't lose her.

The Nova stopped in the parking lot of an apartment complex in Mission, and Blackburn watched as the woman left her car and entered the complex through a security gate. A bank of mailboxes filled a wall beside the gate, so if he had known her name, he could have discovered her apartment number. But he didn't know her name.

He went to his own apartment and stayed up listening to the radio. The figure who had given the roses to the woman had looked male, but he was not her lover, Blackburn decided. She hadn't gone into his house, and she had left the flowers in the trunk of her car. At most, he was a friend. A friend with roses.

Blackburn worked another ten-hour shift on Saturday, then drove past Responsible Reproduction. The lights were on, but there were only five protesters outside. The woman in gray was not among them. In bed that night, Blackburn lay awake wondering if she had abandoned her post because she had a date.

The next evening there were no protesters at all. The street was empty, the clinic dark. Sunday in Kansas City.

He went to the apartment complex in Mission, thinking of breaking into the woman's car to find its registration slip and discover her name, but the Nova wasn't in the lot. He wished that he'd had the idea two nights ago.

Shivering and dozing, he waited for her to return. Once he dreamed of shooting a backlit figure and awoke at the Python's report.

The Nova didn't appear, so Blackburn left at dawn and drove to the house of the roses. The woman's car wasn't there either, but he parked the Dart and watched the house until a skinny man who wore glasses came out and drove away in a Pinto.

Blackburn walked up to the porch and saw that the name

on the mailbox was "R. Petersen." He pressed the button beside the door and heard the bell ring. Inside, a dog barked. Blackburn pressed the button again, and the dog kept barking. No one came to the door.

Blackburn went to work. While on his midmorning break, he read in the *Times* that a pipe bomb had exploded at Responsible Reproduction during the night. It had been set off outside the front door.

The police suspected that the bomber's intent had been to cause minor building damage, but the explosion had done more than that. A counselor named Lawrence Tatum had been doing paperwork in an inner office, and the police speculated that he had heard a noise and investigated.

They had found him in the waiting room with pieces of glass in his flesh. They thought that he had been starting to open the door when the bomb had gone off.

At press time, Tatum was in critical condition at St. Luke's. He had not regained consciousness. The police had no suspects. Ellen Duncan of Responsible Reproduction had announced that the clinic would continue its usual services.

After work, Blackburn bought a six-pack and a *Star,* which said that Tatum was still alive. The police had questioned some people, but they still had no suspects.

Blackburn went to his apartment. Five beers later, he was able to sleep.

On Tuesday, Blackburn left Bucky's at midafternoon. He stopped at a branch post office and bought a ninety-dollar money order.

At his apartment, he took off his work clothes and showered. Then he sat on the edge of the bathtub, soaped his scrotum, and shaved with the blue razor. It was a slow process because his testicles kept drawing up, but he persevered. His only alternative was to use his electric.

By the time he had dressed, it was five o'clock. He took

the money order and the razor and drove to Responsible Reproduction.

More than thirty protesters were pacing the sidewalk when he arrived, and there were so many cars along the curbs that he had to park almost two blocks away. As he started to walk to the clinic, he saw the woman in gray emerge from a van with six others. He waved to her.

He had almost reached the building when he realized that he had left his money order in the Dart. He ran back to get it, and the woman and some of her companions stepped off the sidewalk to avoid him.

"Tonight I do it!" he shouted as he ran past. The woman averted her eyes.

When he reached his car, he glimpsed a bit of color on the pavement and squatted to pick it up. It was a rose petal. The edges were black and curled, but the center was bright. He crushed and dropped it, then grabbed the money order and hurried back to Responsible Reproduction. Several protesters yelled at him, but the woman in gray was quiet.

The glass-and-wire-mesh door was gone, and in its place was a slab of plywood with a handle. Blackburn opened it and went inside.

He lay on a padded table that was covered with blue paper. His naked buttocks rested on a pad of the stuff.

His knees were supported by saddle-shaped pieces of plastic atop metal posts, and his feet hung in the air, chilling. He wished that he had left his socks on.

The crewcut medical assistant took a spray bottle from a counter and bathed Blackburn's crotch in a cold mist. Blackburn gasped.

"Antiseptic," the assistant said. He returned to the counter, opened a packet, and pulled out another pad of blue paper. When he unfolded it, a hole appeared in its center. He laid it over Blackburn's crotch and pressed down so that the scrotum pushed up through the hole. The upper half of the paper became a curtain between Blackburn's thighs.

"Doctor'll be in soon," the assistant said, and left.

Blackburn lowered his head and stared up. Above him, attached to the ceiling with thumbtacks, was a poster of a kitten clutching a knot in midair. Underneath the kitten were the words:

> *When you've reached the end of your rope,*
> *HANG ON!*

Blackburn wanted to tear it down. He wasn't in the mood for cute bullshit.

Then, as the antiseptic evaporated and made his testicles feel as if they were packed in ice, it occurred to him that this room was used for vasectomies only on Tuesday evenings. On other evenings, it was used for other things.

He was lying on a table where women had lain for abortions.

He thought of the girl named Melissa. Would the kitten have meant something to her, or would she have thought it as stupid as he did?

The assistant returned with the doctor, who was wearing a green smock over chinos. The doctor had thinning hair and looked about forty. "Let's get to it," he said.

Blackburn raised his head and watched as the assistant brought a cart and a stool to the foot of the table. When the cloth over the cart was removed, he saw a syringe and an array of stainless-steel instruments.

"You'll be more comfortable if you keep your head relaxed," the doctor said.

Blackburn lowered his head again, but he was no more comfortable. With peripheral vision, he saw the assistant pick up the spray bottle again. A second cold mist hit his scrotum and hissed against the blue paper. The assistant placed the bottle on the cart, then opened a package of latex gloves and helped the doctor put them on.

The doctor nudged the stool with his foot and sat down between Blackburn's legs. Blackburn could see his face, but his hands were hidden behind the blue paper.

"I'll check on the other guy," the assistant said. "The jerk showed up half shaved." He left the room.

The doctor grasped Blackburn's testicles, pulled them away from the body, and began rolling the skin above the right testicle between his thumb and forefinger. Blackburn's calf muscles contracted, and his feet cramped. He had to grab the edges of the table to hold himself down.

"I have to find the vas," the doctor said.

Blackburn clenched his teeth and glared at the kitten.

"Got it," the doctor said. "Now I'll give you the first shot of anesthetic. It's procaine hydrochloride, like the Novocain you get at the dentist's."

Blackburn had been to a dentist twice, and both times he had suffered. Novocain did not work well on him.

"Here it comes, in the top right side," the doctor said. "It'll feel like a bee sting."

It was worse than that. Blackburn's back arched, and his thumbs tore through the paper covering the table. He strained to keep from pulling his legs off the posts and kicking the doctor in the face.

The needle withdrew, and the doctor began manipulating the left side as he had the right. "One more," he said, and the needle went in. Sweat trickled into Blackburn's ears.

"Try to hold still," the doctor said.

The needle withdrew again. Blackburn lay still for a moment, then raised his head to see what was happening.

The doctor was looking up at his face. "How old are you?" he asked.

"Twenty-four."

"Ah. How many children do you have?"

Blackburn wanted to hurt him. "None. So what?"

"Ah," the doctor said again. He shifted on the stool, and his right hand appeared above the blue curtain. It held a blood-smeared scalpel.

"What does 'ah' mean?" Blackburn asked.

The doctor laid the scalpel on the cart and picked up another instrument, moving it behind the paper before Blackburn could see what it looked like.

"Never mind," the doctor said, looking down at his work again. "I'm going to pull the right vas over to the incision now. You might feel a slight tug."

It was as if a vein in Blackburn's abdomen were being yanked out through the scrotum. Blackburn rose on his elbows.

"Please hold still," the doctor said.

Blackburn wished that he could feel justified in killing the doctor, but he knew that he couldn't. He had asked for this.

Much later, the doctor said, "You seemed to experience some discomfort, so I'll give you another shot before I do the left vas. It won't be as bad this time, because you're already somewhat deadened."

The kitten was a yellow blur. Blackburn tried to brace himself, but it didn't help. The woman in gray, he thought, had better appreciate this.

When the stitched wound was covered with gauze, Blackburn got down from the table and put on his clothes and jacket. He couldn't feel the pressure of the athletic supporter, or of his jeans. It was as if he had no genitals.

The doctor gave him a prescription for tetracycline and left the room. Blackburn started to leave as well, but paused at the foot of the table. He was surprised at how much the blue paper on which he had lain was blackened.

The assistant came in with a trash bag and began taking up the paper. He glanced at Blackburn and said, "You're finished, aren't you?"

Blackburn went out. Downstairs, Ms. Duncan smiled at

him. "We'll see you in a few weeks for your first sperm check, Mr. Cameron."

"Right." He moved toward the plywood door.

"Oh, you might like to know that I just called the hospital about Larry Tatum," Ms. Duncan said. "He'll lose two fingers and maybe his right eye, but he's out of danger and joking about the whole thing."

"That's good," Blackburn said, and left.

Outside, among the protesters, he stopped before the woman in gray. "I'm sterile," he said.

"Get away from me." She was surrounded by candles, and her face wavered between dark and light.

Blackburn looked back at the clinic. "A bomb went off here two nights ago. A person was hurt."

"That's what they'd like us to think," the woman said, "but it's a lie to make it look as if *we're* in the wrong. If we stopped marching, we'd be giving in to that lie."

Blackburn's wound began to throb. "I admire your strength," he said, and walked on to the Dart. Each step hurt more.

The van wouldn't bring the woman home for at least two more hours, and no one approached Blackburn as he opened the trunk of the maroon Nova. When he was finished, there would be no evidence that he had done it. Trunks were easy.

A bulb came on as the lid lifted, and a heavy scent reminded Blackburn of compost and funerals. In addition to a tire and a jack, the trunk contained three bunches of wilted roses.

The paper around one bunch was loose, and a few flowers had fallen free. Blackburn picked up this bunch and pressed his face into the dead petals, then put it down and reached for another. This one was heavier, so he left it on the floor of the trunk and unwrapped it.

Among the rose stems was a twelve-by-two-inch iron pipe that was capped at both ends. A cord almost as long as the pipe hung from a hole in the center of one of the caps. Blackburn picked up the pipe and shook it, listening to the rattle. He had used something similar once, so he knew that the pipe contained a stick of dynamite and a blasting cap. This was the simplest sort of pipe bomb, a bangalore torpedo. When he opened the third bunch of flowers, he found another.

His pulse was trying to break through his stitches, so he began to hurry. He unbuttoned a jacket pocket and took out the razor, dropped it, and stamped on it. He used the freed blade to slice off half of each fuse.

After rewrapping the pipes into their flower bundles, he closed the trunk and gathered up the razor's plastic shards. On the way to the Dart, he dropped them into the gutter.

He had his prescription filled at an all-night pharmacy. Then he went to his apartment, took four aspirin, and lay in bed with an ice pack on his crotch. He couldn't sleep, so he read the "Instructions to Follow After a Vasectomy" sheet over and over.

Instruction #8 said that it would take from fifteen to thirty-five ejaculations to clear the sperm from his tubes. After fifteen ejaculations, he was to bring a specimen to Responsible Reproduction for examination.

Blackburn doubted that he would remain in Kansas City long enough to do that.

The name of the woman in gray, the next Monday's *Times* said, had been Leslie Bonner. She had shared her apartment with her mother.

She had placed her second bomb outside the door of an obstetrician/gynecologist's office in Overland Park. It had gone off when she was twelve feet away, and her head had hit the sidewalk when she fell.

Her car had been found nearby, with another bomb in the trunk. The police were investigating to discover the source of the dynamite.

Blackburn looked at the picture of Leslie Bonner for his entire morning break.

Either she hadn't noticed that the fuse on her second bomb was shorter than the one on her first, or she had thought that it didn't matter. She had trusted the maker. She had failed to understand the consequences.

No one had saved her from herself.

Blackburn dropped the newspaper into the garbage. He worked until the end of his usual shift and left Bucky's without cleaning the grill.

At his apartment, he gathered his possessions and put them into his duffel bag. Then he lay on the bed and waited for night.

She hadn't looked like a Leslie. If anything, Blackburn would have guessed her to be a Lisa, or a Lydia. Thinking about her, he started to have an erection, but the stitches pulled at his skin and stopped it.

At eleven o'clock, he went into the bathroom and examined his incision. The swelling was gone and the stitches were dissolving, but his scrotum was still bruised. He put a new gauze pad over the wound, pulled up his jeans, and took his duffel bag out to the Dart. The weight made him ache. He wasn't supposed to carry anything heavy yet.

He drove to the east side of the city and parked a few blocks from the house of the roses. He tucked the Python into the back waistband of his jeans so that it was hidden by his jacket, then walked the rest of the way. The street was quiet, the homes dark.

The house's shades were drawn, but there was a light on inside. As Blackburn stepped onto the porch, he heard the sound of televised laughter. R. Petersen was watching David Letterman.

Blackburn took the pieces of fuse from his pocket and tied them together. He lit one end with a match, then held the knot in his left hand while he took the Python into his right.

He pressed the revolver's muzzle against the doorbell button.

When the door opened, he tossed the fuse inside. R. Petersen turned toward it, and Blackburn hit him behind the ear with the Python. Petersen fell.

Blackburn went inside and closed the door as Petersen crawled across the hardwood floor toward the fuse. Blackburn stepped around him and turned up the volume on the television set.

Petersen reached the fuse and slapped at it.

Blackburn took a pillow from a chair, pressed it over Petersen's head, and fired one round through it. The fuse sputtered out by itself.

He found a roll of tens and twenties in a dresser drawer in the bedroom, and a half-grown, black-and-white mongrel pup in the kitchen. He found a box containing dynamite, blasting caps, crimpers, and fuse hidden among junk in the basement.

When he was ready to go, he carried the box outside and dumped it on the street. Then he returned to the house and lit the fuse he had looped around the living room. That done, he took the pup and left. The pup was heavier than she looked, and she squirmed. By the time Blackburn reached the Dart, he was sore and had to take aspirin.

He didn't think that the single stick of dynamite in Number Twelve's mouth would endanger the neighboring homes, but he stopped at a pay phone and called 911 anyway. He didn't know the house's exact address, but he told the dispatcher which street and block.

Then he drove north on I-35. He would dump the Dart in Des Moines, acquire another car, and go on to Chicago. He had never been there.

"Chicago sound good?" he asked the pup.

The pup gnawed on the butt of the Python and growled.

Blackburn was having trouble thinking of a good name for her. Maybe he wouldn't give her one.

VICTIMS NUMBER FOURTEEN AND FIFTEEN

The '68 Fury that Blackburn had bought in Joliet was running rough, and the dipstick was the color of road tar. What was needed, he decided, was a tune-up and an oil change. He would have to pay someone else to do it, though. He had no tools. Tools were too heavy to take along on sudden departures.

So he looked in the Greater Chicago Yellow Pages and called garages. When he had called a dozen, he picked the cheapest one and drove the Fury there on a Monday morning. He had three hundred and ten dollars in his jacket pocket. Monday was his day off from the Chi-Town Chicken Hut, so he planned to do his laundry when the car was done.

With luck, he would be home before Dog peed on the carpet.

He enjoyed the drive to the garage. Chicago was cold, and the gray sky hung low. Blackburn liked it. Blue skies and sunshine made him feel as if there were no place to hide. But when everything was the color of cold flesh, he could dissolve into a wall if he had to.

Ed & Earl's Auto Service was a concrete-block building with two garage-bay doors. Blackburn parked the Fury in the lot out front at 8:30 A.M. and went inside through a glass door marked CUSTOMER ENTRANCE. This brought him into a waiting room that smelled of the new tires stacked along its walls. The only sound was the hum of the pop machine. No one was behind the service counter. Blackburn waited a few minutes and then went to a second glass door that led to the garage itself. Through this door he could see a car on a hydraulic lift and another car on the floor beyond it. But no people were in sight.

Blackburn pushed open the door and stepped into the garage. It stank of grease and cigarette smoke, and was warmer than the waiting room.

"Hey!" a voice called. "No customers in here!"

Blackburn looked to his left. Four men in green coveralls sat on folding chairs in the back corner. They were drinking coffee and smoking cigarettes. Two of them looked like teenagers, with long hair and sparse mustaches. The other two were older. One was a big man with dark hair and dense beard stubble. An oval patch on his chest spelled "Ed" in red thread. The other man was shorter but heavier, with a crewcut, thick forearms, and an enormous gut. His patch said "Earl."

"I've brought my car in," Blackburn said. "I spoke to someone here on Saturday. On the phone."

Ed stood, dropping his cigarette and grinding it out on the cement floor. He was about six foot four, and solid except for a beer belly. He looked angry, but Blackburn thought that might be because of his black eyebrows.

171

"No customers allowed in the work area," Ed said. His voice was like gravel.

"Sorry," Blackburn said. "But no one's in the other room."

"Be there in a minute." Ed turned away and flipped a switch on an air compressor. The compressor rattled to life, filling the garage with its racket.

Blackburn returned to the waiting room and watched the Dr. Pepper clock over the pop machine. The sweep hand went around eight times before Ed came in and stepped behind the counter. Ed took a clipboard from a nail on the wall, inserted a printed yellow form under the clip, and spoke to Blackburn without looking at him.

"What's the problem?" he asked.

"I need a tune-up and an oil change," Blackburn said. "It's the Fury out front."

"What's wrong with it?"

"It just needs a tune-up and an oil change."

Ed looked up from the clipboard, scowling. "What's it doing?" he asked.

Blackburn guessed that he had committed an error similar to a patient's telling his physician what treatment he wanted, rather than what his symptoms were. "It's running rough," he said. "And the oil's dirty."

Ed wrote on the yellow form. "What's the model year?"

" '68."

"How long since the belts and hoses were changed?"

"I don't know. I just bought it last month. They seem fine, though."

Ed looked up scowling again. "We'll take a look," he said. "If you'll fill out your name and phone number—" He turned the clipboard around and dropped his pen on the counter. "—we'll get to it in an hour or two and give you a call."

Blackburn wrote down the information, using his current

172

alias, Donald Wayne. "You still running the twenty-nine ninety-five tune-up special?" he asked.

"Yeah."

"That's what I want, then. And an oil change."

Ed tapped the bottom of the yellow form. "Need a signature. And your car key."

Blackburn signed the form, then put his key on the counter. "See you in a while," he said.

"Uh-huh." Ed replaced the clipboard on its nail, put the key in his pocket, and returned to the garage.

Blackburn went outside. He had a few hours to kill, and his apartment was too far away for him to walk there and back. But he had passed a multiplex cinema ten blocks away. He patted the Fury's fender and headed down the street.

He saw an early show, ate lunch, and was back at Ed & Earl's at one o'clock. The Fury was sitting where he'd left it. He went into the waiting room and found Earl drinking coffee in a swivel chair behind the counter.

"Excuse me," Blackburn said. "Have you had a chance to work on my Fury yet?"

Earl grimaced and stood. "What's the name?"

"Donald Wayne."

Earl took the clipboard from the wall, put it on the counter, and clicked his tongue. "You got problems, Mr. Wayne," he said. "Your radiator cap's not sealing, your belts and hoses are worn, your distributor cap's cracked, your air cleaner's dirty, your shock absorbers are weak, your fuel pump's shot, and you need a new ignition rotor, spark plugs, and points. New plug cables would be a good idea too, because your insulation's brittle. And you need an oil change and filter, a cooling system drain and flush, and fresh transmission fluid and seals. We also recommend a brake job and new tires. When Ed drove it, he said the brakes felt mushy, and your tires are just about running on cord due to underinflation. If you want to put off fixing the brakes, they might last another thousand miles. But it's best not to gamble when it comes to brakes." Earl looked at Blackburn.

Blackburn was confused. The Fury was parked where he had left it. But he supposed that Ed could have reparked it there. "Did you do the tune-up and oil change?" he asked.

"No, sir," Earl said. "We don't do anything until we get your say-so. We tried to call you, but you weren't home."

"I already authorized the tune-up and oil change," Blackburn said. "They were supposed to be done by now."

Earl shrugged. "I don't know anything about that. Ed said you wanted the car checked over, and then we were supposed to call you. See, we never do work without the customer's approval."

"No, of course not," Blackburn said. He was replaying his conversation with Ed in his mind. It was possible that Ed had misunderstood his wishes. "How much will it cost to fix everything on that list?"

Earl punched numbers into a calculator. The numbers added up to $1,117.67.

"No," Blackburn said.

Earl squinted at him. "Well, sir," he said, "that's why we wait for your say-so. We think that these things need to be done to make this a safe car, but we'll only do what you want. What should we leave out?"

Blackburn considered. The Fury seemed to ride and stop just fine to him, and he had a spare tire in the trunk. "No shock absorbers or brakes," he said. "And no tires."

Earl shook his head as he crossed the items off the yellow form. "You're the boss," he said. He punched the calculator buttons again. "That leaves us at three hundred ninety-four dollars and thirty-one cents."

It was still too much. "Look," Blackburn said, "all I want is a tune-up and an oil change. No radiator cap, no coolant change, no transmission fluid, no spark plug wires, no belts, no hoses."

"Gotta have a new distributor cap for the tune-up," Earl said. "And the rotor, plugs, and points."

"Okay. How much will that come to?"

Earl punched the buttons. "One hundred seventy-six dollars and twenty-three cents. Tax included."

"The tune-up's supposed to be twenty-nine ninety-five," Blackburn said. "You don't charge a hundred and fifty for an oil change, do you?"

Earl gave him a stern look. "Twenty-nine ninety-five is the cost of our labor. We have to pass the cost of the parts on to the customer, or we'd go broke. And you're getting the premium oil change, which includes a crankcase flush and a Fram filter."

Blackburn gave up. "Do it," he said.

Earl wrote the final total on the form. "You need to initial this," he said, pushing the clipboard across the counter.

Blackburn initialed the form. "When will it be ready?"

Earl replaced the clipboard on its nail. "An hour or two."

Blackburn looked through the glass door into the garage. The same cars were still there. The two younger mechanics were leaning over the engine of the car on the floor. Ed was nowhere in sight.

"I'll wait here," Blackburn said. He sat down on a folding chair. "I want to watch you work."

Earl went into the garage and pressed a button on the wall. The nearer bay door opened. Ed appeared beside Earl then, and the two men talked for a while. Ed scowled through the door at Blackburn. Blackburn waved.

Ed pressed another button, this one on a metal box hanging on a cable from the ceiling, and the hydraulic lift brought its car down to floor level. Earl got into the car and backed it out. Then he drove Blackburn's Fury inside and gestured to one of the younger mechanics. That mechanic came into the waiting room, took the clipboard from the wall, and returned to the garage. Ed and Earl spoke to him and then headed toward the back of the garage, out of Blackburn's view. The young mechanic opened the hood of the Fury and got to work.

Blackburn bought a Dr. Pepper from the pop machine, picked up an old copy of *Motor Trend* from the table beside his chair, and alternated between reading and watching the activity in the garage. Metal clanked and pneumatic wrenches whirred. The air compressor chunked on and off. There was an occasional shouted cuss word.

As Blackburn finished his soda, he heard a car pull into Ed and Earl's lot. A minute later a small, elderly woman came in through the Customer Entrance. She paused inside the door, looked at Blackburn, and smiled. Blackburn smiled back. The woman went to the counter and waited. She stood there for eleven minutes, and then Blackburn went to the door to the garage and pushed it open.

"Hey!" he yelled. "You got another customer!" He returned to his chair and smiled at the woman again.

Ed came into the room and stepped behind the counter, his dark brow looking darker than ever. "What can I do for you, ma'am?" he asked, ignoring Blackburn. He brought out another clipboard and yellow form from under the counter.

"It's my Chevy," the woman said. Her voice was thin and fragile. "It shoots black smoke out the tailpipe. My son fixed it last time, but he's in Florida now."

"What's the model year?" Ed asked.

"1962."

"How long since the belts and hoses were changed?"

"I think my son did that at Christmas. Not this past Christmas, but the one before."

Ed wrote on the form and turned the clipboard around. "Fill this out. We'll get to it in an hour or two and give you a call."

The woman filled out and signed the form. "I'll be at home. I only live a few blocks from here."

"Don't forget to listen for the phone," Ed said. He hung up the clipboard and returned to the garage.

The woman stood there looking bewildered for a moment, then started for the door. She paused beside Blackburn. "Thank you for announcing me," she said. "I thought I'd take root." She held out her hand. "I'm Mrs. Stopes."

Blackburn took her hand. It felt like ash. "Pleased to meet you," he said. "I'm Don Wayne."

"Pleased to meet you too, Mr. Wayne." She looked outside. "That's my Chevy. My husband bought it brand new. It was the first new thing we ever owned."

Blackburn looked. The Chevy was robin's-egg blue, and immaculate. "That's a good car," he said.

"Well, I'd sell it if I had any other way to get around," Mrs. Stopes said. "If the buses were safe. But you're right, it is a good car. It just needs to be fixed up now and then." She smiled again. "Just like people."

Blackburn watched Mrs. Stopes walk past her Chevy and down the street. She walked as if her hips hurt. When she was out of sight, he returned to his magazine. He didn't think that Ed had been nice enough to Mrs. Stopes, but that was none of his business. As long as Ed and Earl did what they were supposed to do with his Fury, they could deal with others however they liked.

Thirty minutes later, he looked up and saw green water pouring from under the Fury's front end. He went into the garage and tapped the mechanic on the shoulder. "What are you doing?" he asked.

The mechanic gave him a dull stare. "What's it look like?"

"It looks like you're draining the radiator."

"Good guess, man."

"You weren't supposed to drain the radiator."

The mechanic picked up the clipboard from the Fury's fender. "Says here: Drain, flush, and refill cooling system."

177

He showed Blackburn. Earl had not crossed it out, but underlined it.

Earl appeared beside them. "What's the problem?"

Blackburn took the clipboard from the mechanic and showed Earl the problem. Earl turned to the mechanic.

"Can't you goddamn see?" Earl asked. "I crossed that out. You keep on screwing up and you can go look for a job on the South Side. Now get over there and help Sonny with that starter. I'll finish this myself."

The young mechanic went to the other car, muttering. Earl got down on the floor to replace the Fury's radiator drain plug.

"It wasn't his fault, Earl," Blackburn said. "Your cross-out looks like an underline."

"Customers aren't allowed out here," Earl said.

Blackburn returned to the waiting room and picked up a seven-month-old issue of *Newsweek*. At three-thirty, Ed came into the room, went behind the counter, and made a phone call. "Mrs. Stopes?" he said. "Yeah, this is Ed down at Ed & Earl's Auto Service. You brought your Chevy in around lunchtime? Well, I'm afraid you have some problems."

Ed seemed to be implying that he or one of the other mechanics had examined the Chevy. But Blackburn was sure that no one had gone near it. He hadn't kept a close eye on it, but he would have heard if anyone had opened its hood or started its engine.

"Well, ma'am, your belts and hoses are old," Ed said, "and your radiator cap's not sealing right. Your coolant's worn out and should be replaced, and your air cleaner's dirty. Your distributor cap's cracked, and you need new plugs, points, and a rotor. I'd also suggest new spark plug wires, because your insulation's brittle. You should also have a new fuel pump, and your transmission fluid and seals need to be changed. And for your safety, we strongly recommend that you replace your shock absorbers and have a complete brake job. When Earl drove it, he noticed some bounce and said that the brakes were mushy. As far as basic maintenance goes, you need an oil change and a new oil filter, and a tune-up. And frankly, ma'am, you should be getting all four tires replaced; they're just about running on cord. Probably due to underinflation."

Blackburn went to the pop machine and bought another Dr. Pepper. He spilled some of the soda and then stared at the can until it was steady.

"I'll have to add it up for an exact figure," Ed was saying, "but it's going to be around a thousand dollars. Yes, ma'am, but how much is your safety worth? Well, with that much work, we need a deposit of two hundred dollars. If you could have that to us before six, we might be able to get started today. No, ma'am, we can't give you a ride. We only have four mechanics, and they're all hip deep in work. Well, yes, you could bring the deposit in the morning, but we couldn't start work until then."

Blackburn went to the counter. "I'll pay the deposit," he said.

Ed waved a hand at Blackburn. "Just a minute, buddy, I'm on the phone."

"I said I'll pay the two hundred dollars for Mrs. Stopes," Blackburn said. "Let me talk to her."

Ed, scowling, looked from the phone to Blackburn and back at the phone. Then he handed the receiver to Blackburn.

"Mrs. Stopes," Blackburn said. "This is Donald Wayne. We met here this afternoon. I'm going to pay your deposit money so you don't have to make an extra trip. You can pay me back tomorrow, when your car's done."

Mrs. Stopes protested, but Blackburn insisted. Then he put the receiver on the counter and turned away. He took a long drink of Dr. Pepper and felt the coldness of it behind his eyes. He heard Ed say a few more words to Mrs. Stopes, but he didn't pay attention to them. Out in the garage, Earl was installing the Fury's new distributor cap. Blackburn sat down and picked up a ripped copy of *Sports Illustrated*.

Ed came around the counter. "Well," he said. His voice was murderous.

Blackburn unbuttoned his jacket pocket and took out his cash. He handed it to Ed.

Ed counted it. "There's three hundred here."

"The extra hundred's a gift," Blackburn said. "If both my car and the old lady's are done by six, you can keep it."

Ed locked the money into a drawer under the counter and went back into the garage. Blackburn watched him open the far bay door and speak to the two young mechanics. A moment later the two were pushing the car they'd been working on out of the garage. One of them drove Mrs. Stopes's car inside. They closed the bay door, opened the Chevy's hood, and got to work.

At twenty minutes after six, the mechanics closed the Chevy's hood, and one of them opened the bay door while the other one backed the car out. Then they both got into the car that had been on the hydraulic lift that morning and drove off. Earl slammed the hood on the Fury a few minutes later and closed the bay door that the young mechanics had left open. He wiped his hands on his coveralls and came into the waiting room with his clipboard.

"Gotcha all set," Earl said.

Blackburn dropped his magazine beside the two crushed Dr. Pepper cans. "Glad to hear it," he said, standing.

Earl went behind the counter and punched buttons on the calculator. He scribbled on the work order. "And the damage comes to two hundred twenty-seven dollars and eighteen cents," he said.

Blackburn went to the counter. "What happened to the hundred and seventy-six you quoted this afternoon?"

"Well, things got more complicated than we expected," Earl said. "And we did flush your radiator."

"I told you not to do that."

"Yes sir, but our boy misread the work order, and the work did get done. It wouldn't be fair if we didn't charge for work that got done."

"So why'd you have me initial the one seventy-six?"

"That figure was an estimate. Your initials just authorized us to start working."

"Then what was my signature for?"

"That was to authorize us to look at the car in the first place. We have to be careful."

Blackburn laughed. These guys were hilarious. They should be dressed up in polka dots and milk-white makeup, tumbling out of a car in a center ring somewhere. Their belief in gullibility was so absolute, so crystalline, that it would be childlike if it had to do with, say, the existence of the Easter Bunny rather than with ripping off old ladies.

"What's so funny?" Earl asked. He sounded pissed.

Even the question was hilarious. Blackburn laughed so hard that his stomach hurt. He pounded his fists on the counter. His eyes blurred. Earl was a ruddy blob. Blackburn howled.

He heard the door to the garage open, and another blob, bigger and darker, joined Earl behind the counter.

"What's so funny?" Ed asked. He sounded pissed too.

Blackburn dropped to his knees and leaned his head against the counter. His body shook. He had never laughed like this before. It was as miraculous as an orgasm.

"I said, what's so funny?"

Blackburn looked up and saw two smears that he knew were Ed and Earl's heads. They were looking over the counter at him. He allowed himself one last burst of laughter, then wiped his face on his jacket sleeve. "I'm not going to pay you," he said.

Ed and Earl glanced at each other. Then they glared down at Blackburn.

"You sure as hell *are*," Ed said.

"Bet me," Blackburn said, and then reached up and whacked their heads together.

Ed and Earl bellowed, and Blackburn jumped up and ran into the garage. He grabbed the metal box hanging from the ceiling and punched the green button marked UP. The Fury began to rise beside him. Ed came into the garage then, shoving the glass door so hard that it shattered against the wall. Earl came in behind Ed, cursing.

Blackburn released the UP button, and the hydraulic lift stopped. He ran around the Fury, which had risen about three feet, and put his thumbs in his ears. He waggled his fingers and stuck out his tongue at Ed and Earl.

Ed took a crescent wrench from a tool cabinet. He came stomping around the Fury holding the wrench like a club. "You don't know who you're fucking with," he said.

"Sure I do," Blackburn said. "It says 'Ed' right on your chest." He backed away, keeping ten feet between him and Ed, until he bumped against the parts rack along the far wall. The rack wobbled, and packaged spark plugs rained down on Blackburn's head. Blackburn looked to his left and right and saw that the rack's shelves sagged with mufflers, starters, alternators, brake shoes, bearings, and assorted other parts. The rack was bolted to the wall, but some of the brackets meant to hold it there had torn.

Blackburn spread his arms wide and grasped two of the rack's vertical supports. Earl had stayed on the far side of the Fury, blocking the way back into the waiting room, but Ed was now almost close enough to strike. The wrench was rising.

"You don't know who you're fucking with, either," Blackburn said. "Ever hear of Samson?" He strained forward, and the parts rack shrieked. A starter, a muffler, a box of clamps, and several hoses hit the floor. Then more spark plugs rained down, mixed with distributor caps, plug wires, and rolls of electrical tape.

"Son of a bitch!" Ed yelled, and lunged for Blackburn.

Blackburn let go of the rack, ducked Ed's wrench, and sprinted for the Fury. He dove under the car, coming to a stop in the trough below the hydraulic lift's right brace. He saw his warped reflection in the lift's silver post.

He heard crashes and curses, and turned his head to see what had happened. The parts rack had not fallen, but it had tilted forward enough that most of the parts had slid off their shelves. Ed was down on one knee. Something had conked him, and his scalp was bleeding. When the parts stopped falling, he stood up and looked around until he saw Blackburn. Then he started for the Fury. He looked sluggish and dizzy, but he still held the wrench.

Blackburn scrambled past the silver post as Ed crawled underneath the car after him, and Ed's wrench only glanced off the sole of his shoe. But as Blackburn came out from under the left side of the Fury, Earl yelled and lumbered toward him. So Blackburn rolled onto his back and kicked Earl in the crotch. As Earl doubled over, Blackburn got to his feet and jabbed his thumb into Earl's throat. Earl dropped to his knees, and Blackburn grabbed the dangling control box again. He pressed the red button marked DOWN.

Ed had crawled halfway out from under the Fury when the hydraulic lift's left brace came down across his back. He gurgled, looking angrier than ever, and then spat a red glob at Blackburn. It missed. The hydraulic lift whined and settled.

Blackburn released the button. Earl was on his hands and knees against the broken waiting-room door, coughing. There was a puddle of drool on the floor under his mouth.

"You sound underinflated," Blackburn said. "Keep that up and you'll be running on cord." He grasped the collar of Earl's coveralls and began dragging him to the rear of the garage. As they passed Ed, Earl grunted and grabbed Blackburn around the knees, bringing him to a halt. Blackburn became irritated. These guys had wasted his day, and now Earl was trying to draw things out even longer. Blackburn kicked free, knocked Earl's head against the floor, and resumed dragging him.

Blackburn propped Earl in a sitting position against the back wall, then pulled the valve from the end of the air-compressor hose. The hose hissed, and the compressor kicked on. Blackburn put the hose into Earl's mouth and shoved it down as far as it would go. Then he sealed Earl's mouth and nose with electrical tape, wrapping the tape around and around Earl's head.

When he ran out of tape, Blackburn went to the front of the garage, opened the left bay door, and got into the Fury. The key was in the ignition, and the car started on the first try. He backed it out, then turned it off and came back inside to close the bay door. He took a ring of keys from Ed's pocket, went into the waiting room, and unlocked the cash drawer. In addition to Blackburn's three hundred, the drawer contained two hundred and forty-two dollars in cash and over fifteen hundred in checks. Blackburn took the cash. Then he pocketed the yellow forms for the Fury and for Mrs. Stopes's Chevy.

Something out in the garage went *pow*. Blackburn didn't bother to go see what it was.

He drove Mrs. Stopes's Chevy to the small house at the address on her yellow form. He parked it in the driveway and left the two hundred and forty-two dollars in an envelope on the dash. He enclosed a note that read, "You are our thousandth customer. Here is your prize. Your car is fixed. You do not need to come back. Best, E. & E."

Then Blackburn walked back to Ed & Earl's Auto Service. It was dark now, and a cold mist was falling. He pursed his lips to suck in the moisture. It had been a beautiful day. He wished that he hadn't had to spend most of it cooped up in Ed and Earl's waiting room.

When he reached the garage, he could hear the air compressor running inside. But he had turned off the lights before leaving, so the place looked empty. The windows in the bay doors showed him his own face under a streetlight halo. He got into the Fury and drove to his apartment.

Dog was waiting for him, dancing in a black-and-white whirl. She had peed on the carpet again. This time Blackburn didn't mind.

"We're going for a ride," he told her, and packed his duffel bag. There wasn't much to pack. His dirty laundry was in the Fury's trunk.

The Fury overheated on the way to Minneapolis, and Blackburn discovered that Earl had failed to refill the radiator. Blackburn did so and drove on.

The next day the car blew steam from its tailpipe and died on Marshall Avenue in St. Paul. Blackburn had it towed to a discount store with an auto service center, where he was told that the engine block had cracked because of the overheating incident. The Fury was a total loss.

Blackburn had to spend all of his money on a 1974 AMC Hornet. For the first time, he wished it were possible to kill someone twice.

SEVEN

BLACKBURN KISSES THE OLD MAN

The water tower lay in pieces. Blackburn pulled the Hornet onto the far shoulder of the Potwin road and stared at the wreckage.

He had passed the new one out on K-132. It was a mushroom-shaped thing with letters that spelled TUTTLE CO. RURAL WATER DISTRICT #8 instead of WANTODA. It had neither a catwalk nor graffiti. It was ugly.

He let Dog out of the car to take a piss, and she jumped into the ditch and rolled in the burrs. Blackburn got out and yelled at her. She ignored him.

Blackburn crossed the ditch and climbed into the field, shading his eyes. The tower looked like a dead robot. As he approached, he saw that its legs were only partially dismembered. If he had come two days sooner, he might have seen it still standing. Two days later, and he might not have seen it at all. But today was Sunday, and the carrion eaters were at rest.

He stopped beside the rust-smeared silver tank. Here were the letters WAN, peeled and almost gone. And here were graffiti, although he remembered none of the phrases. ZZTOP, they said. AC/DC. '84 RULES. PINK FLOYD THE WALL. KATHY BITES. JESUS IS LOVE. LOVE THIS. Beside this last was an arrow pointing to a red spray-paint drawing of a giant cock and balls. Blackburn pressed his lips and tongue to the tank's skin. The taste of paint and metal, at least, hadn't changed.

A truck rumbled past on the road, and Dog charged after it. Blackburn ran back to the Hornet, shouting. Damn stupid Dog had no sense. She would get herself killed. He blamed her first master. A mistreated pup never recovered.

After a while she came to him, looking happy. He shoved her into the car and then sat and talked to her. She put her head in his lap and slobbered on his jeans. He pointed at the crumpled tower.

"I used to climb that," he said. "I was king of the world."

He wished that the tower would reassemble and leap up, like a film run backward. He wished that the mushroom out on 132 would shrivel into the dirt. He wished that the town of Wantoda were as it had been when he had left it. He had wanted to think of this trip as a visit to the past, as a time-travel story about a man confronting his idiot ancestors. He had wanted May '84 to be a rerun of May '75.

But then tomorrow would be his seventeenth birthday instead of his twenty-sixth. It was better to be older. It was better not to be afraid.

Blackburn looked away from the remains of the water tower and started the Hornet. He steered back onto the pavement and drove down the Potwin road to kill his father.

* * *

187

Even for rural Tuttle County, the house was cruddy. The siding was blotched with orange, and the wooden shingles looked like scabs. The porch sagged. Dad had let the place go to hell.

A blue Celica sat in the dirt driveway behind a battered white GMC pickup. Dad had a visitor. That was too bad. Blackburn parked the Hornet against the Celica's rear bumper, then reached under the seat for his Colt Python. It had slid back, and he had to bend low and stretch before his fingers closed on the grip.

Dog barked in his ear, making him bang his head on the steering wheel. He yelled, and Dog barked again. Blackburn slapped at her with his free hand. Then he sat up, holding the pistol, and saw his mother on the porch. She was wearing a cream-colored summer dress like the ones she had always looked at in the Penney's catalog. Her hair touched her shoulders. Blackburn was amazed. He had thought she was in Oregon, or possibly dead. He ducked to hide the gun under the seat again.

When he rose, she was walking across the yard toward him. The south wind pressed the dress against her legs, and her hair blew back from her face. Her face was smooth.

Then she was at his window, and in her scowl he saw that she was not his mother after all. She was his sister. Dog barked at her.

Blackburn rolled down the window. "Jasmine," he said.

"Jimmy." She stepped back. She looked surprised.

Blackburn opened his door and got out. Dog cowered against the passenger door.

Jasmine was several inches shorter than her brother. He looked down at her. "You have breasts," he said.

Her eyes narrowed. "You don't."

Blackburn realized that he had said a stupid thing. But he had left when she was twelve, and now the twelve-year-old's eyes and mouth were pasted on a different body. Maybe he should have said "You're taller" or "You're bigger." Or "You look like Mom." But that would have been worse. She wasn't supposed to be here, anyway.

He pointed behind him with his thumb. "That's my dog."

Jasmine looked around him. "Black and white. Is she a border collie?"

"Beats me."

"What's her name?"

"Dog."

Jasmine looked back at him. "You're the same," she said.

Blackburn thought he knew what she meant. "You still hate me."

She shrugged. "I don't know you."

"But you said I was the same."

"You are." She glanced at the house. "Want to see Dad?"

Blackburn stared past her. "He isn't dead yet?"

"No." Her scowl darkened. "How'd you know he was sick?"

"Saw his name in the hospital lists in the Wichita paper. But when I went to the hospital, they said he'd left. They wouldn't tell me what he was there for."

"I'm surprised that you cared."

"Oh yeah," Blackburn said. "I care." He took a few steps toward the house, then stopped. "Is Mom here?"

"God, no."

"Any idea where she is?"

Jasmine gave him a sharp look. "We've been in Seattle for years, Jimmy. I'm a senior at the University of Washington."

"Outstanding." He started toward the house again.

Jasmine came along. "I would have graduated this spring, but I took incompletes so I could come down here."

"Why'd you want to do that?"

"Because he doesn't have anyone else."

Blackburn stepped onto the porch. "Of course he does."

He nodded to his reflection in the storm door. Dad wouldn't like his haircut. "He has me."

Jasmine touched his elbow. "Jimmy. Are the police after you?"

"I don't know," he said. It was the truth.

Jasmine closed her eyes. When she opened them again, she looked different. Softer. "I haven't seen you in so long," she said. "I guess I should at least give you a hug." She put her arms around him and pressed close.

Blackburn didn't like it. He pushed her away, and she looked at him, blinking.

"Dog!" Blackburn called. Dog jumped from the Hornet and came running. Blackburn opened the storm door, and Dog sped into the house. Jasmine gasped.

Blackburn went inside.

The house smelled of ham and potatoes. Blackburn found the old man at the kitchen table, swiping at Dog with a butter knife. He was wearing blue work pants and a red plaid shirt. His face was still florid and stubbled, with the same broad nose and small, pale eyes. But he was skinnier, and he breathed with a phlegmy wheeze. His sparse hair had turned gray. Patches of scalp were visible, like dead leaves seen through mist.

"Hi, Dad," Blackburn said.

The old man glanced up, furious, and then looked back at Dog. "Get it out of here," he said. His voice shook. It wasn't as deep as Blackburn remembered. "Get the son of a bitch out of my house."

"Just 'bitch,' " Blackburn said.

Jasmine came past him and grabbed Dog's collar. Dog bolted. Jasmine lost her grip, and Dog collided with the old man's chair. Dad bellowed and tried to stab Dog in the neck, but his hand hit the edge of the table. The knife spun away and clattered on the linoleum. Dog whirled and ran from the kitchen.

Dad sat hunched over, gripping his hand. Jasmine reached toward him, but drew back when he started banging his fist on the table. Plates and glasses jumped. Then Dad swiped his arm across the tabletop, flinging a Pyrex bowl of salad. It would have hit Jasmine in the face, but Blackburn knocked it away. It slammed into the sink and shattered.

"Who let a dog in my house?" Dad yelled.

Blackburn squatted before his father. "She followed me home, Daddy," he said. "Can I keep her?"

Dad's eyes focused on him. Blackburn waited, letting the old man stare. *Old man.* Only forty-eight. But he looked ancient enough to be God.

The old man raised a hand and smacked his son in the mouth.

It was a harder blow than Blackburn had expected. His head jerked. He probed with his tongue and found that his teeth had cut into his lip.

Then he hit back. He had been saving it. Dad and his chair went over onto the floor.

Jasmine rushed to help him up. "What's the matter with you?" she shouted at Blackburn. "Can't you see he's sick?" She eased the old man into his chair again.

Blackburn stood. "What are you sick with, Dad?"

Dad glowered. His cheek was red. "Not a damn thing. I can still whip your ass any day of the week."

"So you aren't sick?"

"I just said I ain't. Ate some bad meat is all. They pumped my stomach and let me go."

"That's not true, Daddy," Jasmine said.

Dad looked at the table and muttered.

Blackburn sucked on his lip for a moment and then left the kitchen. Dog was waiting at the front door. Together, they went outside. Blackburn took a pair of wirecutters from the Hornet and walked to the telephone junction box on the west side of the house. After severing the cord, he returned

191

to the driveway and let the air out of the tires of the GMC and the Celica.

Jasmine came outside as he was finishing with the Celica. "Jimmy! Just what do you think you're doing?"

Blackburn stood. "Giving the family time to get reacquainted."

He looked toward the house. Dad was staring out through the storm door. Blackburn supposed that he should count the old man as Number Sixteen, but he couldn't help thinking of him as Number One. And it only made sense that Number One would be the hardest.

As Blackburn started across the yard, the old man withdrew from the doorway, fading like a ghost.

Blackburn opened the storm door and gestured for Dog to go inside again. Dog did so, avoiding Jasmine.

"You know he doesn't like dogs," Jasmine said.

Blackburn said nothing. He went into the house and held the door open behind him so Jasmine could catch it. He was trying to be considerate.

Dog scurried back and forth across the living room, sniffing the tattered couch and recliner. Then she stopped in the center of the green carpet and squatted.

Dad emerged from the hallway to the room that had been his and Mom's. He was carrying his Remington pump twelve-gauge. He pumped it once, snapping a shell into the firing chamber.

Blackburn remembered lying in his tiny pantry room, reading a comic book, and hearing that sound outside. He remembered the explosion, and the shriek. He remembered running outside and going into the garage. He remembered finding the terrier hiding behind a pile of Dad's shop rags.

He hadn't understood what was wrong until the little dog had stood up. Then he had seen that its left side had no skin. The dog had come to him, trembling.

Now Dad was aiming at Dog. Again. And now Blackburn

was fully ready to kill him. But he had left the Python in the car. Jasmine had distracted him, had made him stupid.

He grabbed the shotgun barrel with both hands, jerking it upward. As he wrenched the weapon from the old man's grasp, it roared with a flash of blue fire. Ceiling plaster exploded. Dog tried to scramble outside and ran into the base of the storm door. Jasmine backed against a wall and covered her ears. Dad collapsed onto the couch.

Blackburn went to the door and let Dog out. Then he pumped the shotgun, ejecting the spent shell, and fired upward again. He continued pumping and firing until the magazine was empty. The air filled with white dust and stank like the Fourth of July. Blackburn's skull rang.

He threw the shotgun at his father. The old man ducked, and the gun hit the wall and fell behind the couch.

"You don't kill a man or a dog with quail shot!" Blackburn yelled. He could hardly hear himself, so he yelled even louder. "You do it with a bullet! One bullet to the head!"

Dad sat up straight. "Damn dog was pissing on my floor!"

Blackburn came close and leaned over him. "Piss doesn't matter. Chickens don't matter. *Dogs* matter."

Dad looked confused. "You're crazy," he said. "I raised a goddamn crazy man."

Jasmine, her face pale with dust, stepped across the broken plaster. "He's talking about that terrier," she said.

The noise in Blackburn's skull was starting to subside. "Yeah," he said. "That terrier."

Dad lurched up from the couch. "Gonna call the sheriff."

Blackburn caught his arm. "I cut the wire. We never had much quality time when I was little, so I thought we should have some now."

The old man's eyes were as steady as a snake's. "If you'd turned out to be worth a crap, I'd've done it then."

Blackburn tightened his grip. "You never did know much about 'worth.' You thought the chickens were 'worth' something, but all they did was shit and eat. That little dog, on the other hand, killed rats. One bite through the head, and then he went for the next one. And then the next. But one day he happened to kill a couple of chickens. Two stupid chickens. So you took your shotgun and blew a hole in his side. Blew a big hole. Very psychosexual, Daddy. Very Freudian."

"Your mother overprotected you," Dad said. "You always were a sissy."

"I made him lie down on the garage floor," Blackburn said. "And then all I could find to help him was a hammer. Afterward I wrapped him in shop rags and buried him behind the chicken coop. I hoped he would haunt you."

The old man made a snorting noise. "Am I supposed to feel guilty? Is that why you came back?"

Blackburn smiled. "Not exactly. See, I've figured it out: It wasn't just that dog. It was everything. Every time I got to liking something, you'd blow a big hole in it. Kill it. But what you really wanted to kill was me."

Jasmine tried to step between them. "That's not so, Jimmy. You're his son."

She had grown breasts and gone to college, but Jasmine was still as dumb as a dirt clod. "Sure I'm his son," Blackburn said. "That's why he did it." He fixed his eyes on the old man's. "And that's why I've come back."

He released Dad's arm, and the old man ran into the kitchen.

Blackburn started after him. He glanced back at Jasmine. "Very psychosexual," he said. "Very Freudian." He followed Dad into the kitchen and out the back door.

Dad scuttled under the sheets on the clothesline, then ran across the backyard and through the windbreak of evergreens on the north. Blackburn stopped at the windbreak and watched through the trees as Dad crawled under the barbed-wire fence into the hay meadow. The old man's shirt tore.

Blackburn waited until Dad disappeared behind the crest of the hill. Then he turned and walked to the Hornet. Jasmine emerged from the house as he brought out the Python.

She froze at the edge of the porch, and Blackburn saw that she thought he was going to shoot her. This saddened him. He had never been a perfect brother, but she should have realized long ago that he never did anything to anyone who didn't deserve it.

"Don't be afraid," he said. "It isn't even cocked."

She didn't relax. "What are you going to do with it?"

Blackburn started toward the meadow. "Retroactive gene-pool maintenance."

Jasmine jumped from the porch and ran to him. She grabbed his wrist and tried to make him stop. He kept walking. Jasmine wasn't very strong.

"Jimmy, there's no point," she said. "He's got cancer, and he won't accept treatment. He told the doctors to go to hell. They said he only has three to five months."

"Then this is my last chance," Blackburn said.

"But he's paying *himself* back for the things he did. All you have to do is let him!"

Blackburn shook his head. "People can't punish themselves for their sins. Only the people they've sinned against can do that."

"The Bible says only *God* can do that."

"The Bible's full of chickenshit." He pulled free and sprinted for the windbreak. He heard Jasmine running after him. "Don't make me lock you up!" he shouted.

The sound of her footsteps stopped. When Blackburn reached the evergreens, he looked back and saw her getting into the Hornet. He wasn't worried. He had the keys. Even if she knew how to hot-wire, he would be finished before she could have anyone else here.

He climbed over the fence and ran up the hill. When he

reached the top, he spotted Dad and Dog a few hundred yards away to the north. Dog was dancing around the old man, nipping, and Dad was kicking at her. As Blackburn watched, the old man kicked himself off balance and fell into the prairie hay. Dog darted in and slobbered on his face, then darted away again.

Blackburn slowed his pace to a walk. He cocked the Python.

"Hey, Daddy!" he called. "Wanna play catch?"

There was no fear in the old man's face, and Blackburn was glad. Fear might have made things difficult. It occurred to Blackburn that this was the first time Dad had ever made anything easier for him.

He stood over his father and aimed the Python at the old man's forehead. Then Dog came up and slobbered on Dad's face again. Blackburn yelled and chased her away. When he turned back, he saw that Dad had gotten up and was trying to run toward the house. Blackburn almost put a slug into the ground at Dad's feet, and then was ashamed of himself. He hadn't played around with any of the others. When he killed, he killed clean. Mostly. To do otherwise would be to behave as the old man would.

Dad was a pitiful runner. Blackburn caught him and grabbed his shirt where it had been torn by the barbed wire. Dad twisted around, flailing, and hit Blackburn's gun hand. The Python went off, the shot echoing. Blackburn stumbled, and he and his father fell together. Dad tried to scramble away backward, and his shirt ripped open wide, exposing his torso. Blackburn let go, and the old man collapsed onto his back. Blackburn, on his knees, straddled him.

Dad's narrow chest, rising and falling as the old man wheezed, looked hollow. The ribs stuck out. The hair and skin were as white as milk.

Except for the tumor.

It was a pink egg above the left nipple. Red capillaries,

thin as spiderwebs, laced through the skin over and around it, vanishing beneath the whiteness a few inches away.

Then the whiteness melted as if the sunlight were X rays, and Blackburn saw the capillaries spreading throughout his father like a living net. He saw the heart stumbling. He saw the lymph glands strangling. He saw the kidneys shuddering, failing.

Blackburn looked up at his father's face. He couldn't see beneath the skin here, but he didn't have to.

"You have breast cancer," he said.

Dad's eyes flashed. "I ain't!" His breath stung. "I ain't got no woman's disease!"

Blackburn pointed at the tumor. "There it is."

The old man swung a fist. Blackburn blocked it with his arm.

"I ain't!" Dad yelled. "It ain't possible!"

"Why not?"

"Because I'm a man!"

The words struck Blackburn as hilarious, and he laughed and laughed. The tumor shook. It seemed to be growing as he watched, as if a cosmic clown were filling it with divine breath. As if it were a sacred balloon.

When Blackburn could laugh no more, he saw that Dad was crying. It was a miracle. Blackburn was stunned. He got off the old man and laid his pistol in the grass. He knelt there, hands clasped, and knew that judgment had been rendered. Punishment had been meted. The universe had proven that it was sometimes perfect, and he would not alter perfection. This one time, seeing it was enough.

As the old man wept, Blackburn bowed down and kissed his breast. The pink egg was hot. Blackburn wanted to always remember how it felt.

"You don't have to get me a birthday present," he murmured.

Then he stood and looked around for Dog. He spotted her

lying fifty feet down the hill. He called to her, but she didn't move. He remembered then that the Python had fired.

When he went to her, he found that the bullet had gone through her skull behind the eyes. She hadn't even yelped. There hadn't been time for pain.

Blackburn couldn't cry for her. When there was no time for pain, there was nothing to cry about. Truly, in this place, in this moment, the universe was perfect.

He slowed the Hornet when he saw Jasmine. She was running toward town, coming up on the old water tower. She stopped and turned when she heard the car. Blackburn pulled the Hornet onto the shoulder, got out, and walked to her.

Jasmine was breathing hard. She had run two miles. Her dress was damp and dirty. She had fallen.

"That dress is too long for running," Blackburn said.

She didn't seem to hear him. "Well?" she asked.

"Well what?"

She wiped hair from her forehead. "Did you do it?"

He gazed at the remains of the water tower. It had been his hideout, his Rosetta stone, his starship. He had stood on its catwalk and watched his sister, the size of a doll, playing in the field below.

"Remember the snowball war we had here?" he asked. "You and I built a fort, and some of the town kids built another one. Ours was up against the tower fence. We pretended the water tank was our doomsday bomb."

Jasmine still wasn't listening. "Did you hurt him?"

"And in the spring and summer we flew kites. I made them myself. You were always kind of in the way."

"Did you do something to Daddy?"

Blackburn looked at her again. Had he done anything to Daddy? He supposed that he had.

Just after finding Dog's body, he had heard the Python's hammer click. He had turned to see that Dad had pointed the gun at his own chest. Blackburn had gone over and taken it away. Then he had gathered up Dog and left. At the windbreak he had looked back. The old man had still been kneeling in the same spot.

"All I did," Blackburn told Jasmine, "was kiss him good-bye."

Jasmine stared. "I don't believe you."

Blackburn went back to the Hornet. He retrieved the Python from under the driver's seat and tucked it into his jeans. Then he took his duffel from the back seat and tossed it into the ditch. He threw the shovel that he had taken from the garage down beside it. Finally, he lifted Dog's body from the passenger seat. It was wrapped in a sheet he'd pulled from the clothesline. Only a little blood had leaked through.

Carrying Dog, he returned to Jasmine. "You can take the car back to the house," he said. "See for yourself."

Jasmine was eyeing the bundle in Blackburn's arms. "Don't you need it?"

"No." He would steal another car in town. It was time for a switch anyway.

Jasmine went to the Hornet, then faced her brother again. "Tomorrow's your birthday, isn't it?"

"Yes."

Jasmine tried to smile. It didn't suit her. "Well," she said. "Happy birthday, then."

"Thanks." He turned toward the ditch. "Say hi to Mom for me." He heard the Hornet start as he climbed into the field. By the time he reached the fallen tower, Jasmine was gone.

He laid Dog beside the rusted tank, then retrieved his duffel and the shovel. As he dug the grave, he told Dog about the lessons he had learned from the things he had read and done here. A car on the Potwin road slowed, and its occupants stared at him as it went by.

When Blackburn lowered Dog into the grave, he saw an earthworm writhing in a corner. This reminded him of another story, and he told Dog about the one time that he and Dad had gone fishing together. He wondered if Dad ever went fishing anymore. He doubted it.

He patted Dog through the sheet and filled in the grave. He threw the shovel among the pieces of the water tower's legs, then slung his duffel over his shoulder and walked toward the heart of town.

His family had vanished into the past. For the first time in his life, Blackburn was alone. The perfection of the universe, embodied in the quiet Sunday evening of Wantoda, lay before him. He felt weightless, as if he were falling. Or flying.

Cars were pulling into the parking lot at the Methodist church, and ghosts were emerging from them. Blackburn's lips pulsed with warmth. He took out the Python and cocked it.

It was good to be home.

VICTIM NUMBER SEVENTEEN

The bookstore was crowded. So many people were in line ahead of Blackburn that he couldn't see the author. He was surprised. He had thought he would be one of only a few people in St. Louis who would appreciate Artimus Arthur's *The Guy Who Killed People.*

He gazed at the book in his hands. He had bought it here the week before, and now had brought it back to be autographed. The dust jacket was black, with the title embossed in letters of bleeding crimson. At the bottom, in small white type, were the words A NOVEL BY ARTIMUS ARTHUR. Blackburn liked that. It indicated that Arthur, as famous as he was, still considered the book more important than his name.

There wasn't even a photograph of him on the back of the jacket, although there was a small one on the flap. The back of the jacket was an unbroken expanse of black. It was a statement in itself, worthy to shroud the words inside.

Blackburn had never before read anything so full of truth. *The Guy Who Killed People* told the story of a man who was sick of the world, and who set out to make it right. In the process, he had to do away with liars, fiends, bad drivers, politicians, vice cops, dope dealers, and civil servants. Blackburn was fascinated and impressed, although he found some of the death scenes unrealistic. For one thing, The Guy Who Killed People was able to obtain barrels of caustic chemicals with more ease than Blackburn was able to obtain .357 Magnum cartridges. But that didn't really matter; the book was fiction, and its death scenes were metaphors. The Guy Who Killed People was Everyman, and the child-abusers, state legislators, and morons that he wasted weren't meant to represent real child-abusers, state legislators, and morons, but their dark spirits.

The photograph on the back flap was of a bearded man whose facial lines seemed to cut to the bone. His eyes were deep-set, as if they had seen so much of life that they wanted to retreat. Blackburn was anxious to meet the man. If his real-world face was like the face in the photograph, and if his real-time thoughts were as piercing as those in his novel, Artimus Arthur might well be the wisest man on the planet. And wisdom was not his only power. While reading *The Guy Who Killed People,* Blackburn had felt that Artimus Arthur was there with him, probing his mind and exposing his soul on the pages of the book. It was as if Arthur had written the novel about Blackburn himself.

He was convinced that no one—not his family, not Dolores, not even Ernie—had ever understood him as Artimus Arthur did. No one he had ever met had even grasped concepts as simple as freedom and justice. So how could they have understood him? Artimus Arthur, on the other

202

hand, had mastered those concepts and more. Otherwise he could never have written *The Guy Who Killed People*.

As he waited to have his book signed, Blackburn imagined Arthur looking up from the autograph table and recognizing in an instant that Blackburn was a man like the protagonist of his novel, a man of independence and conviction. The two of them would go off to a coffee shop and discuss the book, emphasizing the questions of morality and responsibility that it raised. Finally, when the coffee shop was about to close, Arthur would look at Blackburn and say, "There are laws deeper and more rigid than those shaped by the inconstant fools who place themselves above us, and a man who knows and keeps those laws is beyond the judgment of such fools. That man must never seek absolution, for where no absolution is needed, none can be given." Then Artimus Arthur would leave the coffee shop and Blackburn would watch him walk into the night, a woolen scarf wrapped around his neck, snowflakes falling behind him. The snowflakes would sparkle in the white cones cast by the streetlamps.

The line was moving now, and Blackburn stepped forward. His book's dust jacket gleamed under the fluorescent lights. Blackburn looked up, blinking, and saw Artimus Arthur.

The writer's skin was paler than the photograph had suggested, the beard less dense. His eyes were not deep-set, but encircled by dark flesh. He was wearing a gray suit that was too big, and his shirt had an orange stain on the collar. He slumped in his chair. Even so, no one could fail to recognize him. Reality was never as pristine as a photograph. Blackburn didn't like things pristine anyway.

Arthur was signing a book for a shaggy man who was speaking in a loud voice. "—and I'm planning to discuss what I call the 'poetics of postmodern psychopathy' as imagized in both this novel and your *Purple Silence, Pink Death* in the Contemporary Literature course I'm teaching this semester, and I was wondering—"

The shaggy man yammered on even after Arthur had finished signing his copy of *The Guy Who Killed People*. He wanted Arthur to come to his class and describe his "thematic impulses" for his students. Arthur gave him a blank look, saying nothing. Then a bookstore employee hustled the man away, and the next person in line stepped up. This person was an attractive young woman.

Artimus Arthur sat up straighter and smiled. He took the woman's copy of his novel and then kissed her knuckles. The woman laughed. Arthur wrote a long inscription in the book and then asked, "Would you care to come around?" He patted the folding chair on his left. "It gets dull sitting here by oneself." His voice was higher-pitched than Blackburn had imagined, and he slurred some of his words.

The woman accepted the invitation. Artimus Arthur scooted his chair closer to hers and leaned over to whisper in her ear. She flinched, but laughed again. Arthur signed three more books in quick succession, and then it was the turn of another attractive woman. He chatted with her and wrote another long inscription.

"Would you care to come around too?" he asked. "I'm sure we could find a third chair." Another employee brought a chair and set it up on Arthur's right. The new woman went around the table and sat down. Arthur's hands disappeared.

Blackburn dropped his book. When he squatted to pick it up, he could see under the autograph table. Arthur was squeezing the women's knees. Blackburn stood and saw that the women were flustered, but didn't want to make a scene. Arthur brought his hands up and signed the next book.

Blackburn's nylon coat had become too warm, so he unzipped it partway. Then he opened the back cover of *The Guy Who Killed People* and read the "About the Author" note under Arthur's photograph. The note said that he lived in Long Island, New York, with his wife of thirty-four years, Irma. Blackburn looked up at the real Arthur again and tried to guess what Irma must be like.

Arthur leaned to his right and whispered into the ear of Attractive Woman Number Two. She stood, thanked him for signing her book, and left. He smiled, leaned to his left, and whispered into the ear of Attractive Woman Number One. She scooted her chair a few inches away but didn't leave. Arthur signed another book, and another. Now only four people remained between Blackburn and the autograph table, but Blackburn had decided that he didn't want his copy of *The Guy Who Killed People* signed just yet. He got out of line and went into the science fiction aisle, where he could observe Arthur's behavior.

The novelist wasn't himself. No one whose written words contained such wisdom could be the sort of fool that he appeared to be now. His slurred speech suggested that he had been drinking, and that in turn suggested that it was his intoxication that was making him come on to women who weren't his wife of thirty-four years, women who were in fact young enough to be his children. It was repulsive and pitiful, but it wasn't the real Arthur doing it.

Another young woman approached the table, and Arthur told her that he would only sign her book if she gave him a kiss. She looked around as if searching for an escape route, but then leaned down and gave Arthur his kiss. He invited her to join him behind the table, but she declined and fled. Attractive Woman Number One, still seated to Arthur's left, had a trapped look in her eyes. Arthur whispered in her ear again. From Blackburn's vantage point, he could see Arthur's hand come down to rest on her thigh.

Blackburn was sickened. He went up the aisle to the wall and followed the wall to the front door. He went out to the February chill and stuck his book into his coat on the right-hand side. The left side was already bulky; his Colt Python was tucked there in a pouch he had sewn in. He zipped up the coat and jammed his hands into its pockets. The sun had set, and the downtown streets held no warmth. He started for the bus stop two blocks down.

On the way to the bus stop he came across a coffee shop, so he went inside and ordered a grilled cheese sandwich and french fries. As he ate, he reread the first two chapters of *The Guy Who Killed People* and began to feel better. Artimus Arthur deserved a second chance to be himself, and Blackburn deserved a chance to meet him. The fact that Arthur understood human folly didn't mean he was immune to it. He was bound to backslide now and then.

Blackburn returned to the bookstore and waited outside, stamping his feet to keep warm. He had decided that he would not meet Artimus Arthur under the artificial conditions of the autograph session. Not only was Arthur less able to be himself under such conditions, but Blackburn would not be able to reveal his own true self either. There were too many other people around, too many leather yuppies and nouveau beatniks who, Blackburn had realized, were only buying Arthur's book because it was the hip thing to do, because they were intellectual blanks who craved not wisdom but a brush with celebrity. Most of them wouldn't even read the novel and wouldn't appreciate its truth if they did. Blackburn did not want Arthur to see him as one of them. So he would approach him when the autograph session was over, when the winter air had cleared the writer's head and neither he nor Blackburn would have to behave as anything other than what they were.

But more than a dozen of Arthur's admirers remained when the store closed at seven o'clock, and they all came outside with him, clustering around him like viruses attacking a healthy cell. The cluster moved down the street, and Blackburn followed. He was frustrated and cold.

The entourage swept Arthur into the coffee shop where Blackburn had eaten dinner. Blackburn watched through the window while they shoved tables together. Arthur stood apart, gripping the arm of Attractive Woman Number One. He swayed, looking as if he might fall if he released her. The woman was giving him a fixed smile and nodding at whatever he was saying.

As Arthur and his admirers sat down, Blackburn entered the shop and walked past them, taking a booth in the back. He unzipped his coat, and his copy of *The Guy Who Killed People* fell onto the table. He stared at the book to keep from staring at its author. Now was still not the time for them to meet, and he didn't want to draw Arthur's attention.

"Weren't you in a while ago?" a voice asked.

Blackburn looked up. A hairnetted waitress was standing beside the booth.

"Yeah," he said. "Decided I wanted some dessert. Banana cream pie."

The waitress scribbled on her pad. "That a good book?" she asked, nodding at *The Guy Who Killed People*.

"It's okay."

The waitress waved a thumb at Artimus Arthur's group. "One of those people writes books. At least, that's what they told me. If you're interested."

"Thanks."

The waitress left. Blackburn opened the novel and reread Chapters Three and Four, and half of Five. Then he glanced up and saw that his pie was on the table and that Arthur and his entourage were leaving. He closed the book and wolfed down three bites of pie, then dropped money on the table and went out.

Outside, the entourage was disintegrating. Some of the people were walking toward the bus stop, and others were getting into cars parked along the street. Artimus Arthur was still hanging on to the arm of the attractive woman and was speaking to two young men.

"I appreciate the offer, gentlemen," he said, "but Stephanie has offered to see me safely to my hotel, and I have full confidence in her abilities. Thank you for coming. I enjoyed our conversation." He didn't sound drunk anymore.

The two young men turned and left Arthur with the woman. They passed by Blackburn.

"Think she'll fuck him?" one of them whispered.

Blackburn didn't hear the reply. He followed Artimus Arthur and Stephanie. There weren't many people on the sidewalks tonight, but there were enough that Blackburn didn't think he'd be noticed.

Arthur and the woman walked five blocks east to 4th Street and then down three blocks to the Clarion Hotel. Blackburn had dropped back until he was almost fifty yards behind them, and he ran to catch up when he saw them enter the hotel. If they were going to get on an elevator, he wanted to be sure he was on it with them.

They were still in the lobby, standing between a row of pay phones and the elevators, when Blackburn came inside. Arthur was leaning toward Stephanie and murmuring something, and Stephanie was leaning away, smiling and shaking her head. Blackburn went to the pay phone closest to them and pretended to make a call.

Stephanie kissed Arthur on the cheek, then walked past Blackburn and out of the hotel. "If you change your mind," Arthur shouted, "I'm in Room Twenty-one Fourteen!" But Stephanie was already outside. Blackburn was glad to see her go.

Arthur stepped into an elevator with three other people, so Blackburn didn't try to get there before the doors closed. He wanted to meet Arthur alone, and now that he knew the writer's room number, he could be sure that he did. He went to the elevators after Arthur's car had gone and pushed the UP button.

The door to Room 2114 opened on the fourth knock, and Artimus Arthur stood there grinning. Then he saw Blackburn, and the grin disappeared. He leaned out and looked up and down the empty hallway. "Oh," he said. "I was expecting someone else."

Blackburn smelled liquor. He didn't like it. "Hello, Mr. Arthur," he said. "I can't tell you my name, but I've read your novel, *The Guy Who Killed People*, and I wondered if you would sign the title page for me." He unzipped his coat and pulled out the book. "I'd also like to talk a while, if you have time."

Arthur stepped back. "You have the wrong room," he said, and started to close the door.

Blackburn put a hand on the door to hold it open. "I really think you'll want to talk to me," he said.

Arthur glared at him. "I'm doing a signing tomorrow at a Waldenbooks in St. Charles. Talk to me then." He tried to shove the door shut, but it didn't move.

Blackburn shook his head. "I was at your signing today," he said. "It was awful. None of those people knew your work, or what it means. And you . . . were drunk. Probably so you wouldn't have to think about those people."

"If you don't leave right now," Arthur said, "I'll yell for help. There are a lot of people on this floor, and they'll call hotel security. Or the police."

Blackburn held out *The Guy Who Killed People*. "This book is about me," he said.

Arthur's eyebrows rose. "Excuse me?"

"The man in the book," Blackburn said. "The guy who kills people, but only when they deserve it. I'm him."

Arthur's hands slid from the door, and he took another step back. "You don't say."

"If you'll give me a few minutes, you'll believe me," Blackburn said. He entered the room and closed the door. "You're the first person I've told about this. You can imagine why."

Arthur's grin was creeping back. "Oh, yes," he said. He went to the nightstand and picked up an open fifth of Jack Daniel's. He grasped the bottle by the neck and took a drink.

Then he looked at Blackburn. "So you've sprung to life from the pages of my book, is that it? Must have been an easy birth. No water breaking, no straining. No blood."

"That's not what I mean, sir," Blackburn said. "I'm not a lunatic."

"I wasn't suggesting you were." Arthur went around the bed to the window, taking the bottle with him. He opened the drapes. The Gateway Arch was visible on the far side of I-70. "To believe you've been given life by words isn't lunacy. But to try to parachute down to land on top of that thing—" He pointed at the Arch. "Now, *that's* lunacy."

Blackburn didn't know what Arthur was talking about. "What I meant to say, sir," he continued, "was that I share the values and behavior of your nameless protagonist. I am a real-world analog of The Guy Who Killed People."

"Oh," Arthur said. "Well, in that case, you *are* a lunatic. Go parachute onto the Arch." He took a swig from the bottle.

"Please listen," Blackburn said. "Once I saw a man beating his wife, so I shot him. Another time I saw a man run over a dog on purpose. So I shot him. Another time I caught two mechanics cheating an old lady, so—"

"Let me guess," Arthur said. "You shot them."

"No. I would have, but I didn't have my gun with me. I crushed one of them under a hydraulic lift and blew up the other one with an air compressor."

"That was very resourceful." Arthur took a long drink. The bottle was almost empty. "Now get out of here before I call hotel security."

"You still don't believe me."

Arthur laughed, and it became a cough. He bent over and hacked, then spat and straightened up. His face had turned red. "You want to know the truth?" he asked.

Blackburn stepped toward the writer, holding *The Guy Who Killed People* before him like a holy icon. "Yes," he said. "I found truth in this book, so I know you're a man who understands what truth is.''

''You bet,'' Arthur said. He drained the bottle and coughed again.

Droplets hit Blackburn's face. He breathed bourbon, and his lungs burned. He was glad the bottle was empty. Maybe things would go better now.

Arthur pushed Blackburn aside and returned to the night-stand. He set down the bottle and put his hand on the telephone. ''The truth is that I don't care whether you ever killed anybody, or whether you're using my book as an excuse to hallucinate. Either way, you're nothing to me but a pain in the ass. I've met you a thousand times, and I only put up with you for the first hundred. So you can walk out of this room, or I can call someone to drag you out.''

Blackburn was beginning to despair, but he had to keep trying. ''I'm not like those others,'' he said, coming around the bed. ''They want your fame to rub off on them. I don't. I only want to let you know that your vision isn't in vain.''

Arthur looked puzzled. ''What vision is that?''

''The vision in this book,'' Blackburn said, holding out *The Guy Who Killed People* again. ''The vision of a man who understands the meaning of independence and justice, and who isn't afraid to act on that understanding.''

Arthur picked up the empty bottle and tried to take another drink. Then he brought it up to his right eye and peered through the glass at Blackburn. ''You are not only a lunatic,'' he said, ''but a lunatic who can't read his way out of a wet paper bag.''

''I don't know what you mean,'' Blackburn said.

''Of course not.'' Arthur lowered the bottle and shook it at Blackburn. ''That's because you're a lunatic. Just like the man in my book. He's worse than a serial killer, worse than evil. He's *stupid,* which is the worst lunacy of all. The reader isn't supposed to sympathize with him. The reader's supposed to *loathe* him. *I* sure as hell did.''

It was as if Blackburn had been slugged. "But the people he killed all deserved it," he said. The words hurt his throat. "They were horrible."

"We're all horrible!" Arthur yelled, waving the bottle. "I'm horrible, you're horrible, the President of the United States is horrible! Mother stinking Teresa is horrible! A newborn baby will be horrible as soon as it gets a chance! Trying to fight that isn't noble. It's *futile*. Why do you think I killed him off at the end, anyway?"

"To . . . make him a martyr?"

Arthur came close to Blackburn and bellowed in his ear. "BECAUSE HE WAS A PAIN IN THE ASS, THAT'S WHY!"

Blackburn flinched away. He was angry now. "I see," he said. "Thank you for your time, Mr. Arthur."

"Drop dead," Arthur said. "But get out first."

Blackburn went to the door, but then turned back toward the writer. "You know what I think?" he asked.

Arthur stood beside the bed, his shoulders slumped. The Jack Daniel's bottle dangled from his hand. "Not only do I not know," he said, "but I don't give a shit either."

"I think," Blackburn said, "that you've lied to me. I think you know you've written the truth, and you're afraid of it. I think you're so afraid of it that you have to get drunk to be brave. And then you lie to fight off your own truth."

Arthur's eyes opened wide. He raised the whiskey bottle over his head. "I said get—" He lunged forward. "—the FUCK OUT!"

Blackburn dodged, and the bottle clipped his shoulder. He came up against the wall and dropped *The Guy Who Killed People*. Arthur swung again, and the bottle bounced off Blackburn's skull. Blackburn saw a white burst like a flash-bulb. He dropped to his hands and knees and scrambled. He didn't know which way he was going until he ran into the bed. He turned around and saw Arthur coming at him.

"You're not like the man in my book," Arthur said. His voice was thick with contempt. "But *I* am."

212

Blackburn got onto the bed. "I thought you said that you loathed him."

Arthur grinned. "Sure. Any man who doesn't despise himself hasn't looked close enough." He charged toward the bed and swung the bottle.

Blackburn lurched away, and the bottle missed him. He fell off the bed on the far side, landing on his rump.

Arthur bounced on the bed on his knees and glared down at Blackburn. "I've always wanted to kill people," he said. He hefted the bottle. "I've just never had the guts. So I write about it instead. But maybe I can at least hurt you."

Blackburn stood and reached into his coat. He opened the Velcro flap over the Python's pouch, then pulled out the pistol. He didn't point it, but he cocked it.

"I can't let you hit me again," he said. "No matter who you are or what you mean to me. Nobody hurts me."

Arthur lowered the bottle. His face sagged. "All right, then," he said. "Take your blue-metal dick and leave me alone."

Blackburn looked at the Python. "This isn't a dick," he said. "It's justice. That's in your book. It's what The Guy says about the rifle he uses to kill the school board."

"I know what's in my book," Arthur said. He came off the bed and stood facing Blackburn. "You don't have to tell me what's in my own goddamn book."

Blackburn stared into the black depths of Arthur's eyes. "I think I do. I think you've fogged your brain so much that you can't remember your own wisdom."

Arthur sneered. "Screw you," he said. He gripped the neck of the Jack Daniel's bottle with both hands and swung it at Blackburn's face.

Blackburn raised his arm to block it, and the Python fired. The bottle exploded.

Blackburn stumbled backward and slammed against the window so hard that it cracked. He turned toward the glass and saw two reflections of his face, one on either side of a snaking silver line. Then he noticed that each face had a fragment of whiskey bottle stuck in its cheek. He reached up to brush the fragment away. It stuck to his fingers for a moment before falling.

"My hands," Arthur said.

Blackburn turned toward him. Arthur was lying on his back on the bed, holding his hands above his face. The fingers were curled into claws. Blood welled out everywhere. It was soaking Arthur's sleeves.

"My hands," Arthur said again.

Blackburn replaced the Python in its pouch and went around the foot of the bed toward the door. The meeting hadn't gone at all the way he had hoped.

"You'll be all right, sir," he said, picking up his copy of *The Guy Who Killed People* from the floor. "If you died, I'd have to count you as one of my victims, and I don't want to." He stared down at the black dust jacket. "You didn't even sign my book."

"Open it."

Blackburn looked up. "What?"

"Open it and bring it here."

Blackburn opened the book to the title page and took it to the bed.

"Under my hands," Arthur said.

Blackburn held the book under Arthur's hands, and a few drops of blood spattered on the paper. Blackburn closed the book and stepped back.

"You are a great man," he said.

Arthur made a noise in his throat. "I've pissed my pants," he said.

Blackburn left the room. Despite the gunshot, the hall was still empty. He went down to the lobby and called for an ambulance from one of the pay phones, then got out of there. He wondered if Arthur had any children, and if so, whether they felt as much kinship for the man as he did.

He was bruised and sore the next morning, and the cut on

214

his face throbbed. But he forgot all of that when he turned on the radio. According to the newscaster, novelist Artimus Arthur had died the night before when he leaped through the glass of his hotel room window and fell to the street. A paramedic had told him that his wounded hands might be crippled for life.

Blackburn wept.

EIGHT

BLACKBURN SINS

The deadbolt wasn't set, so Blackburn broke into the apartment with a six-inch metal ruler. A lamp was on inside. He scanned the living room, but wasn't interested in the TV or stereo. This was a second-story apartment with outside stairs, so he couldn't take anything big. The VCR was small enough, but he decided against it anyway. He wasn't proud that he had turned to thievery, so he preferred to steal only those things that were of no use or pleasure to their owners. But that rule tended to limit him to class rings and junk, so he didn't always stick to it.

He didn't bother with the kitchen. Apartment dwellers didn't own silver. He pulled his folded duffel bag from his coat and stepped into the hallway that led to the bedroom. Bedrooms were good for jewelry. Houston pawn shops paid cash for gold chains and silver earrings.

The bedroom door opened, and a man stepped out. Blackburn froze.

The man closed the door behind him. He was tall. His face and most of his body were shadowed. His right hand was empty, but Blackburn couldn't see his left. It might be holding a weapon.

"What are you doing here?" the man asked. His voice was of moderate pitch. He didn't sound upset.

Blackburn was confused. He had watched this building for three days, noting the occupants of each apartment and their schedules. This unit's occupant was a woman who had left for her night shift at Whataburger twenty minutes ago. He was sure that she lived alone. The man at the end of the hall should not exist.

"Don't be afraid," the man said. "I just want to know why you're here."

Blackburn took two steps backward. His Colt Python was in its pouch in his coat, but he couldn't reach for it without dropping the duffel bag from his right hand. Then it would take two or three seconds to reach into the left side of his coat, open the Velcro flap, and pull out the pistol. If the shadowed man had a gun or knife, Blackburn might be dead before getting off a shot. So his best option was to leave, but he had to do it without turning his back.

"Tell me why you're here," the shadowed man said, "and I won't hurt you. But if you don't stand still, I will."

Blackburn stopped. "I was going to steal things," he said, "but I'm not going to now."

"What things were you going to steal?"

"Jewelry. Rings, necklaces. Maybe a musical instrument, like an old trumpet or an out-of-tune guitar."

"Why out of tune?" the shadowed man asked.

"A guitar that's in tune is in use," Blackburn said. "I don't like to steal things people use."

The shadowed man gave a short chuckle, almost a grunt. "A burglar with a moral code," he said. "But people use jewelry too, you know."

"It just hangs there," Blackburn said. "It's stupid."

"In your opinion."

Blackburn started to relax his grip on the duffel bag. He had decided to try for the Python. "Yes," he said. "In my opinion."

"And that's the only opinion that counts."

"Yes." The duffel began to slip from Blackburn's fingers.

"Don't reach for your pistol, Musician," the shadowed man said.

"I don't have a pistol."

"You have a lump in your coat. It's big, but the wrong shape for an automatic. I'm guessing a three fifty-seven. A forty-four would be awfully heavy."

Blackburn tightened his grip on the duffel bag again. "All right. I won't reach for it."

"Good. If you did, I'd have to kill you. And that would be a shame, because I agree with you. Your opinion is the only one that matters. *My* opinion is the only one that matters too."

"That's a contradiction," Blackburn said.

"Why? You create your world, I create mine. Contradictions only exist for people who aren't bright enough to do that. When they come up against someone who is, it's matter and antimatter. Know what I mean?"

"Yes."

"I knew you would," the shadowed man said. "I'm going to come toward you now so we can see each other. I'll move slowly, and you won't move at all. All right?"

"All right."

A smell of deodorant soap preceded the man as he stepped from the shadows. He had long dark hair, shot through with gray. It was pulled back from his face. His skin was sallow, his eyes a greenish brown. He was wearing a hooded black pullover sweatshirt, black sweatpants, and gray running shoes. His left hand held a small paper bag. There was no visible weapon.

Blackburn dropped his duffel and brought out the Python. He cocked it and pointed it at the man's face.

The man stopped. "You agreed not to move," he said.

"I lied."

"That doesn't seem consistent with a moral code."

"I've created my own world," Blackburn said. "In here, it's moral." He stepped backward.

"You don't have to leave empty-handed," the man said. He shook the paper bag, and its contents clinked. "See, I'm a burglar too. I don't know that I'm as moral as you, but I'm willing to split the take."

Blackburn paused. He eyed the paper bag. "I was watching this place. How'd you get in?"

"Through a window in the bathroom. On the back side of the building."

"Someone might see your ladder."

The man shook his head. "I climbed the wall. Plenty of space between the bricks." He turned the paper bag upside down. Rings, necklaces, and earrings fell to the carpet. "This has to be fifty-fifty, so don't cheat."

"Why let me have any of it?" Blackburn asked.

The man knelt on the floor and bent over the tangle of jewelry. His ponytail hung down over his shoulder. "So you won't turn me in." He looked up and smiled. "And so if we're caught, I can plea-bargain the punishment over your way."

Blackburn replaced the Python in its pouch. "I'll take that class ring."

The man flicked it toward him. "You can call me Roy-Boy."

"I don't need to call you anything," Blackburn said,

squatting to pick up the ring. "I won't be seeing you again."

"The best laid plans, Musician."

"I'm not a musician."

"In your world, maybe not. In mine, you play electric guitar. You want to sound like Hendrix, but you're too white and you don't do enough drugs."

Blackburn said nothing. He took the ring and three gold chains, then picked up his duffel bag and left. He crossed the street and hid behind a dumpster to watch the apartment building. He wanted to see if Roy-Boy left too.

A few minutes later Roy-Boy appeared under a streetlight and looked across at the dumpster. He pointed his right finger and waggled his thumb to mimic a pistol. Then he walked away.

Blackburn waited until Roy-Boy was out of sight before walking the four blocks to his Plymouth Duster. The back of his neck tingled. He looked in all directions, but saw no one. He thought he smelled deodorant soap, but decided it was his clothes. Maybe he had used too much detergent.

Two nights later, on Friday, Blackburn stuffed his pockets with cash and drove to The Hoot, a bar near the Rice University campus. His coat felt light without the Python, which he had hidden in his closet. He wouldn't need a gun tonight. His goal was to seduce one of the college girls he had met at The Hoot the week before, preferably the thin brunette who was a flute player in the marching band. The last time he'd had sex had been behind a barbecue pit at a Labor Day picnic, and here it was almost Christmas. He was afraid the top of his head might blow off.

The Hoot was crowded. It smelled of moist flesh and beer, and throbbed with canned rock 'n' roll. The flute player was there. Blackburn went to her and made the comment that the Rice football team could have had more success the previous weekend had it used the band's woodwind section in place of its defensive line. The flute player laughed. She remembered him and called him Alan, the name he was using now. Her name was Heather. It seemed to Blackburn that at least half of the twenty-year-old women in the world were named Heather, but he didn't tell her that. He liked her. She had a fine sense of humor. It had been her idea, she said, for the Marching Owl Band to cover their uniforms with black plastic trash bags and lie down on the football field at halftime to simulate an oil slick.

Heather was a steady drinker, and Blackburn felt obliged to match her. After half an hour he had to excuse himself for a few minutes. When he came out of the men's room, he saw that someone had taken his place at the bar and was leaning close to Heather. Blackburn couldn't see this person's head, but he could tell from the way the jeans fit across the hips that it was a male.

Heather saw Blackburn and waved. "Hey!" she called. "Everything come out okay?"

The man beside her raised his head, and Blackburn saw that it was Roy-Boy.

Roy-Boy smiled as Blackburn approached. "Musician," he said. His ponytail was wet. It glistened in the neon glow.

Heather looked from Blackburn to Roy-Boy. "You guys know each other?"

"We're in the same business," Roy-Boy said. He turned on his bar stool so that his knee touched Heather's thigh.

Blackburn's teeth clenched. The sharp scent of Roy-Boy's deodorant soap was cutting through the other smells.

"Really?" Heather said. "What do you do?"

"We sell discount merchandise," Roy-Boy said. "We're competitors, actually."

Heather looked concerned. "Does that mean you don't like each other?"

"No," Roy-Boy said. "In fact, we can help each other."

"I'm thinking of getting into another line of work," Blackburn said. But if he stopped stealing, he would have to take a job at yet another fast-food restaurant. It was the only legal work he was qualified to do. He had fried burgers or chicken, or stuffed burritos, in every city he had ever stayed in more than a few days. He was sick of it.

"I'd be sorry if you did that, Alan," Roy-Boy said.

Blackburn looked at Heather. "Did you tell him my name?" He realized after he said it that it sounded like an accusation. The beer had made him stupid.

"No," Heather said, frowning. "Why would I? You know each other, right?"

"We've never exchanged names," Roy-Boy told her, "but I got curious and asked around about him. Has he told you he's a guitar player? He plays a left-handed Telecaster."

Heather's frown vanished. "You in a band?" she asked Blackburn.

"No," he said. "I mean, not right now."

"He was in three bands at once when he lived in Austin," Roy-Boy said. "He even played with Stevie Ray a couple of times."

Heather was gazing at Blackburn. "Why'd you quit?"

"No money in it," he said.

Roy-Boy got off the bar stool. "That reminds me," he said. "I have some work to catch up on." He dropped a five-dollar bill on the bar. "Next round's on me."

"Oh, that's sweet," Heather said.

"Yeah," Blackburn said.

Roy-Boy clapped Blackburn on the shoulder. "Happy to do it," he said. "Us old guys got to stick together." He headed for the door.

Blackburn imagined making Roy-Boy eat his own eyes.

"Bye, Steve!" Heather called. Then she grinned at Blackburn. "How old are you, anyway?"

Blackburn sat down on the empty stool. It was warm from Roy-Boy, so he stood up again.

"Twenty-seven," he said. "How about you?"

Heather raised her beer mug. "Twenty-one, of course. You don't think I'd come into a bar if I wasn't, do you?"

222

"Guess not."

"I'd love to hear you play sometime."

Blackburn's tongue tasted like soap. "I don't have a guitar now," he said.

Heather shrugged. "Okay, I'll play for you instead. You like flute music?"

"You bet," Blackburn said. The back of his neck tingled, and he turned.

Roy-Boy was standing outside, looking in through the cluster of neon signs in the front window. He pointed his finger at Blackburn and waggled his thumb.

"So, you want to have another beer?" Heather asked. "Or would you like to hear some flute?"

Blackburn turned back to her. "Flute," he said.

They stood to leave. Roy-Boy was gone from the window. Blackburn left the five-dollar bill on the bar.

In the morning Blackburn awoke with Heather's rump against his belly. Since the end of his marriage, it was rare that he spent an entire night with a woman, and even rarer that he let it happen at his place. But as he and Heather had left The Hoot, she had said that her apartment was off-limits for sex because her roommate was a born-again Christian. So they had decided to put off the flute recital, and Blackburn had taken Heather to his studio crackerbox in the Heights. After a few hours they had fallen asleep together.

He slid out of bed and went into the bathroom. He didn't flush, because he didn't want to wake Heather. When he came out, he saw that she had rolled onto her back. Her mouth was open, and strands of her hair were stuck to her face. She wasn't a beauty, as Dolores had been, but she was fun. Blackburn didn't remember ever having laughed in bed before.

He dressed and went out. His plan was to bring Heather a surprise for breakfast. In the night, she had told him a story about a Rice fraternity that had been getting noise

223

complaints from the sorority next door. One morning the sorority women had received a box of donuts from the fraternity, along with a note saying that the donuts were the men's response to the complaints. The women had eaten the donuts for breakfast and then had received another delivery from the fraternity. It was a photograph of all seventy-two men in their dining room, each one naked except for the donut on his penis. Heather thought the story was hilarious, so Blackburn wanted to have a box of donuts waiting for her when she awoke.

The sun had risen, but the air had the sting of a winter night. Blackburn hadn't thought Houston ever got so cold. He breathed deep, and the chill cut into his throat. When he exhaled, his breath was white. He hurried across the parking lot to the Duster, hoping it would start. Its windows were opaque with frost. Blackburn didn't have an ice scraper, but maybe the defroster would do. He unlocked the driver's door and got inside, letting the door slam shut after him. The interior smelled of deodorant soap.

Roy-Boy was sitting in the passenger seat. He was wearing the black sweatsuit again. The sweatshirt's hood was up over his head, and his hands were inside the pouch.

"Morning, Musician," he said, peering out from the hood. "Happy Pearl Harbor Day."

Blackburn was annoyed. "Get out," he said, "and don't come near me again. If you do, you won't do anything else."

"Now, come on," Roy-Boy said. "You're a moral guy, and I haven't done anything to you. You wouldn't whack me for looking at you wrong, would you?"

"You broke into my car," Blackburn said. "In Texas, it's legal to shoot people who break into your car."

"But I didn't break in. This door was unlocked."

"Doesn't matter. You didn't have my permission to enter. So I can shoot you."

"But you don't have your gun."

224

"I can get it."

Roy-Boy took his hands from his sweatshirt pouch. His right hand held a .22-caliber revolver. "You can try," he said.

Blackburn saw that the .22 was a cheap piece of crap. But at this range, it could kill him just as dead as a .357.

"What do you want?" he asked.

"Right now, to get warm," Roy-Boy said. "Then I want to talk a little. Let's drive, and crank the heater."

Blackburn put the key into the ignition. The Duster whined for a while, then started. The engine sputtered, and the car shook.

"Sounds like ice in the fuel line," Roy-Boy said. "Put a can of Heet in the tank. If you can find it in this city." He opened his door. "Hang on and I'll scrape your windows." He got out, leaving the door open.

Blackburn considered trying to run him over, but decided against it. A bullet might make it through the windshield. So he waited while Roy-Boy scraped. Roy-Boy's scraper was a long, pointed shard of glass with white cloth tape wrapped around one end. Roy-Boy had pulled it from his sweatshirt pouch. He was scraping with his left hand. His right hand, with the pistol, was in the pouch. Blackburn could see the muzzle straining against the fabric. It was pointing at him.

When the windows were clear, Roy-Boy got back inside and closed the door. He licked ice crystals from the glass shard, then replaced it in his pouch and looked at Blackburn. "What're you waiting for?" he asked. He pulled out the .22.

Blackburn drove onto the street and headed for I-10. He would wait for his chance. It would come. It always did.

"So, how was she?" Roy-Boy asked as the Duster entered the freeway.

"Fine."

"I'm glad. I was afraid I'd ruined things for you at The

Hoot, so I tried to fix them before I left. Guess I did. What're you gonna do with her now?''

Blackburn glanced at him. ''What do you mean?''

''Are you gonna fuck her again, kill her, or what?''

''Why would I kill her?''

''Because you're a killer, boy. That's what you do, right?''

Blackburn's neck tingled. ''What makes you think so?''

Roy-Boy leaned close. When he spoke, his breath was hot on Blackburn's face.

''Takes one to know one,'' he said.

Blackburn flinched away, bumping his head on the window.

Roy-Boy returned to his previous position. ''Don't worry,'' he said. ''I promise not to stick my tongue in your ear or bite through your cheek.'' He pointed outside. ''You just passed a Day-Lite Donut store. If you take the next exit you can cut back to it.''

Blackburn stared at him.

''Watch the road,'' Roy-Boy said.

Blackburn took the next exit. He parked at the donut shop, then put his keys into his coat pocket and clenched his fist. Two keys jutted out between his knuckles. He watched Roy-Boy.

Roy-Boy smiled. ''You want to kill me now. You're hoping I won't notice your hand in your pocket.''

''You seem to know me pretty well,'' Blackburn said.

''Oh, yeah. I know you, Musician.'' Roy-Boy put his pistol into his sweatshirt pouch, then held up his empty hands. ''So I also know that if you think about it, you'll decide not to kill me after all. I pulled a gun on you, but only because you pulled a gun on *me* Wednesday night. I figure we're even.''

That made some sense to Blackburn, but it only went so far. ''How did you know I was going for donuts?''

''Well, I was shooting the shit with Heather last night,'' Roy-Boy said. ''You know, at The Hoot, while you were in the can. She was telling me about this donut gag some frat pulled. Then you came out this morning with a shit-eating grin on your face, so I thought: donuts. A dozen glazed be okay?" He got out of the car and went into the shop.

Blackburn waited. There was no point in leaving. Roy-Boy knew where he lived.

Roy-Boy returned with a white cardboard box. "I got a few extras," he said, exhaling steam as he entered the car. "Some jelly and some creme. Want one?"

"No."

Roy-Boy opened the box and took out a filled donut. Chocolate creme oozed when he bit into it. He gestured at the Duster's ignition switch. "Don't let me hold you back," he said around a mouthful of pastry. "We can talk while you drive."

"I'd like to sit here awhile," Blackburn said. "If that's all right."

"Sure," Roy-Boy said. He reached up and pushed his sweatshirt hood from his head. "I'm warm now. I just thought you might want to get home to your three fifty-seven. Why'd you take it out of your coat, anyway? Were you afraid Heather might feel it when she hugged you? Or did you shoot her and then leave it in her hand to make it look like suicide?"

"I wouldn't kill a woman."

Roy-Boy's eyebrows rose. "How come? Haven't you run across any who deserved it?"

Blackburn thought of Dolores. "It's just a rule I have."

Roy-Boy shook his head. "Sexist," he said.

"Maybe. But a man's got to have his rules."

Roy-Boy stuffed the rest of the chocolate-creme donut into his mouth. "Yeah," he said, his voice muffled. "If you say so."

"Have *you* ever killed a woman?" Blackburn asked. His fist tightened around his keys. The windows had fogged. No one could see in.

"No," Roy-Boy said, chewing. His eyes were steady, fixed on Blackburn's. "In fact, I've never killed anyone. But I'm still a killer, because I'd do it if I had to. If it was me or him. Or her."

"Why'd you think I killed Heather?"

"I didn't. I just thought it was a possibility. See, she's got a rep for screwing guys over. Narking on them, taking their money, leaving teeth marks, shit like that. I figured if she did it to you, you'd fix her." Roy-Boy swallowed. "But I was unaware of your rule."

Blackburn didn't know whether to believe what Roy-Boy said about Heather. He sounded like he was telling the truth, but some people were good at that. And Heather didn't seem like the kind of woman who would screw over a lover. On the other hand, Dolores hadn't seemed like that kind either.

"Any other probing questions before you decide whether to poke holes in me with your car keys?" Roy-Boy asked.

"One," Blackburn said. "Why are you bugging me?"

Roy-Boy grinned. There were chocolate smears on his teeth. "Am I bugging you? That's not my intention. I just think we can help each other, like we did Wednesday. I take half, you take half. See, if we hit places together we'll have less chance of trouble, because we'll both be watching for it. And we could carry the big stuff. You see the advantages?"

"Yes."

Roy-Boy held out his hand. "Then it's a partnership."

"No. I can see the advantages, but I don't want them."

Roy-Boy lowered his hand. "Why not? Because you don't want to take 'things people use'? Man, people use everything. They just don't *need* all of it. If it'll make your moral code happy, then I promise we won't steal any insulin kits or dialysis machines. But a TV set ought to be fair game."

"My moral code doesn't have anything to do with it," Blackburn said. "The problem is that I'm leaving town." It wasn't really a lie. He hadn't been planning to leave, but he hadn't been planning to stay either.

Roy-Boy looked surprised. "How come?"

"I never stay anywhere more than a few months." That was most often because he had no choice, but Roy-Boy didn't need to know that. "And I've been here since August, so another week and I'm gone. By Christmas for sure."

"Where to?"

"Don't know yet."

Roy-Boy looked away and sighed. "Ain't that the way it goes. I find a partner with morals, and he's no sooner found than lost." He opened the door and got out, leaving the box of donuts on the seat. "No hard feelings, though, hey?"

Blackburn said nothing.

"You don't still want to kill me, do you?" Roy-Boy asked. His hand went into his sweatshirt pouch.

"No," Blackburn said.

Roy-Boy stooped and peered in at him. "You should grow your hair into a ponytail," he said. "All of the great states-man-philosophers had ponytails. Thomas Jefferson, for example, who philosophized about independence and freedom, and owned slaves. What a great world *he* created." Roy-Boy straightened. "Have a good trip, Musician, and enjoy the donuts. I'm gonna get some more for myself. See, I only have one testicle, so I have to eat twice as much as most men in order to manufacture enough jism for my needs." He turned and walked toward the donut shop.

Blackburn leaned over to pull the door shut, then wiped the fog from the windshield and watched Roy-Boy enter the shop. He still had the feeling that he should kill Roy-Boy, but he couldn't think of a good reason why. All Roy-Boy had done was pester him. That might have been enough to warrant death, had it cost Blackburn anything, but it had cost him nothing but a little time. And now he had a free box of donuts, which pushed Roy-Boy's behavior even further into a gray area.

He started the Duster. No matter what he felt, he would not kill someone for behavior that fell into a gray area. He required a clear reason. If he started killing people without such reasons, he would be in violation of his own ethics. It was bad enough that he had become a burglar. A man had to have his rules.

On the way home, he stopped at a convenience store and bought a can of Heet, which he poured into the Duster's tank. Then he drove to his apartment and carried the box of donuts inside. Heather was in the bathroom with the door shut.

When she emerged, Blackburn was lying on the bed wearing nothing but a donut. Heather stayed two more hours, then said that she had to get home to study for finals. Blackburn was going to drive her, but the Duster refused to start. So Heather took a cab. After she had gone, Blackburn realized that he didn't have her phone number or address. He might be able to find her at The Hoot again, but he wasn't sure that he should. He liked her a lot, and he knew what that could lead to.

Blackburn was still in Houston the next Friday evening, watching a three-story apartment building in Bellaire. He had decided to leave the city by Christmas, but he needed traveling money. He had also decided that he had to stop breaking into houses and apartments, even if it meant working in fast food again. If he found some worthwhile items tonight, this would be his last day as a burglar.

He had not returned to The Hoot to look for Heather, and she had not come by his apartment to look for him. That was all right. They'd had twelve good hours together, which was twelve more than he'd had with most people, and he had the sense to leave well enough alone. It didn't feel good, but good feelings had nothing to do with good sense.

The sun had set, and lights in some of the apartments had come on. Blackburn, sitting across the street in the Duster, noted the number of cars in the building's lot and the number of apartments that were lit. He compared these numbers to those he had counted at other times since midafternoon, when he had started watching. He had been careful—sometimes driving by, sometimes parking a few blocks away and walking, and now parked under a broken streetlight—but he hadn't observed this building for two or three entire days, as was his habit. He had figured that some of the residents would have already left for Christmas vacations, and their apartments would be easy to spot. He had been right. Two apartments on the top floor were staying dark, as were three on the second floor, and one on the first. Two other apartments had lights that had been on since he'd started watching, and he didn't think anyone was home. He would wait a few more hours to be sure. He could turn on the radio now and then to keep from getting bored.

He was listening to a ZZ Top song when the back of his neck tingled. He looked around and saw a man standing under a streetlight in front of the apartment building. The man was wearing a black sweatsuit, and his hair was pulled back in a ponytail. He was pointing at Blackburn and waggling his thumb. It was Roy-Boy.

Blackburn turned off the radio. He gave Roy-Boy a violent sidearm wave, trying to tell him to go away. But Roy-Boy stayed put, still pointing. Someone would drive by and notice him before long. Blackburn changed his wave to a "come here" gesture, then unzipped his coat and reached inside. He opened the Velcro flap over the Python's pouch.

Roy-Boy jogged across the street, his ponytail bouncing. He had put his hands into his sweatshirt pouch, so Blackburn had to take his own hand out of his coat to let him into the car. The smell of deodorant soap was even stronger than before. Blackburn wondered what Roy-Boy was trying to cover up.

"Evening, Musician," Roy-Boy said. "Happy Friday the thirteenth."

"I was here first," Blackburn said.

Roy-Boy shook his head. "I've been watching that building since last Saturday. It's mine." He grinned. His teeth looked as if they were still stained with chocolate creme from the week before. "Unless you want to share. Two of the apartments on the top floor are rented by college students who've taken off for winter break. I've heard their stereos, and they sound expensive. They probably have VCRs and Sony Trinitrons too. We could clean 'em both in fifteen minutes, hit my fence in the morning, and be done."

"I don't use fences," Blackburn said. "They're crooks. And I already told you I'm not interested in teamwork. If you've been planning on this place for a week, you can have it. I'll leave."

Roy-Boy gave his gruntlike chuckle. "But don't you see, Musician? That won't work now. If you take off with nothing, I'll be afraid that you'll call the cops on me. So in self-defense, I'll make a call of my own after I've done the job. I'll describe you and your car, and when the cops ask the neighbors, some of them'll remember seeing you hanging around. And we've got the same situation in reverse if you stay and I go. One or both of us gets screwed. You know where that leaves us?"

Blackburn was keeping his eyes on Roy-Boy's, but his right hand was creeping back into his coat. He didn't want to shoot Roy-Boy while they were inside the Duster, but he would if he had to.

"Where?" he asked.

"MAD," Roy-Boy said. "As in mutual assured destruction." His right hand came out of the sweatshirt pouch with the .22. He pointed it at Blackburn's face.

Blackburn froze with his hand on the Python's butt.

"This is how I see it," Roy-Boy said. "I have the advantage, but I'd have to waste you instantly, with one shot, or suffer retaliation. In other words, although you might be mortally wounded, you could still do me with your superior

232

weapon. So our only choices are to work together or be destroyed. You feel like being destroyed?''

"No," Blackburn said. He saw Roy-Boy's point. "I'll work with you this one time, but I can't promise anything else. I still want to leave town."

Roy-Boy nodded. "Fair enough. We've achieved diplomatic relations. Now comes the disarmament phase. Take out your pistol, slow. You can point it at me if you want, but I'll be watching your hand. If the fingers start to flex, I'll shoot. MAD, get it?''

Blackburn pulled out the Python and held it so that it pointed down at his own crotch.

"Careful or you'll wind up like me," Roy-Boy said. "A one-ball wonder. Of course, mine's the size of an orange."

"Mine aren't. I'd just as soon keep them both."

"Then put your gun on the seat between us. I'll do the same. Our hands should touch, so we'll each know if the other doesn't let go of his weapon. This is known as the verification phase." Roy-Boy turned his pistol so that it pointed downward. "Begin now."

They moved as slow as sloths. The pistols clicked together on the vinyl seat. The men's hands touched. Blackburn waited until he felt Roy-Boy's hand begin to rise, and then he lifted his own hand as well.

"So far so good," Roy-Boy said. "Where's your tote bag?''

"Under the seat."

Roy-Boy clucked his tongue. "I can't have you reaching under there. We'll have to find a grocery sack or something in the apartment. That acceptable to you?''

"I suppose so."

"In that case," Roy-Boy said, "we can get out of the car. Doors open at the same time."

"We can't leave the guns on the seat," Blackburn said. "Someone'll see them."

"No, they won't. Once we're outside, take off your coat

233

and throw it back inside to cover them. That'll also assure me that you aren't packing another piece.''

''What's to assure me that *you* aren't?''

''Good point. Okay, as you take off your coat, I'll take off my sweatshirt. The pants too, if you want. I'm just wearing shorts and a T-shirt underneath.''

Blackburn took his keys from the ignition. ''All right,'' he said. ''Lock your door on the way out.'' He and Roy-Boy opened the doors and got out. Blackburn took off his coat while watching Roy-Boy pull off his sweatshirt on the other side of the car. It was like a weird dance. Cars going by on the street illuminated the performance with their head-lights. Roy-Boy's face went from light to dark to light again, and then disappeared as the sweatshirt came up over his head. But even while Roy-Boy's head was inside the sweat-shirt, the eyes were visible through the neck opening. They didn't blink.

Blackburn tossed his coat into the car, covering the pis-tols. Roy-Boy tossed his sweatshirt in on top of the coat. Then they closed the doors. The Duster shuddered.

''What's in your shirt pocket?'' Roy-Boy asked.

''Penlight.''

''Okay. It's a tool of the trade, so keep it. Now put your keys away, and we can meet at the rear bumper. It'll be our Geneva.''

Blackburn put his keys into a jeans pocket, and he and Roy-Boy walked behind the car. Blackburn was wearing a long-sleeved shirt, but he was cold. He crossed his arms for warmth. Roy-Boy's gray T-shirt was cut off at the midriff, but he seemed comfortable. His bare arms swung at his sides. When the two men met at the bumper, Roy-Boy held out his right hand. Blackburn kept his arms crossed.

''Pants,'' he said.

Roy-Boy shucked off his sweatpants and turned around to show Blackburn that he was unarmed. His legs were pale and hairless. They looked shaved.

234

"That's enough," Blackburn said, suppressing revulsion. Roy-Boy pulled his sweatpants back on, then held out his hand again. "Ratify our treaty," he said, "and I won't ask you to take off your pants too. I'll believe that your moral code won't allow you to hide a second weapon from me. That ruler in your back pocket I'll let go, since it's a tool of the trade too."

They shook hands. Roy-Boy's was dry and cold. He held on too long. Blackburn pulled free.

Roy-Boy looked across the street at the apartment building. "Top floor, second unit," he said. It was one of the apartments that had stayed dark. "Two bedrooms. Its collegiate occupants have gone home to Daddy for Jesus' birthday and left all their shit behind."

"Jewelry first," Blackburn said. "Then I'll help you carry one big thing, and that's all. Once I'm out, I'm not going back in. And my car's not for hire to haul freight. You have a vehicle?"

"Yeah. That black Toyota in the lot. Yesterday its former owner rode away in a car with snow skis on top. So it's mine now."

Blackburn couldn't object. He had stolen cars himself, and didn't think he was in any position to cast a stone.

Blackburn and Roy-Boy crossed the street and climbed the stairs that zigzagged up the face of the building. It was almost midnight, but TVs and stereos were turned up loud in some of the lighted apartments. Blackburn was glad. Two burglars would make more noise than one, but the ambient sound might cover it. And every apartment's drapes were closed, so none of the residents would see them.

They reached the top balcony and apartment 302. "You're the front-door specialist," Roy-Boy whispered.

Blackburn tried the knob. The door had a half inch of play. As at his last burglary, the deadbolt hadn't been set. People who didn't set their deadbolts were asking to be robbed. He reached into his back pocket and pulled out the metal ruler. In a few seconds the door popped open, and Blackburn and Roy-Boy went inside.

Blackburn took the penlight from his shirt pocket and turned it on. The pale circle of light revealed that the apartment was well furnished. A thick carpet muffled the men's footsteps.

"Ooh, lookee here," Roy-Boy said. "A Sony Trinitron. Tell you what—I have great night vision, so I don't need the light. I'll unhook the TV cable and look around in here, and you see what you can find in the other rooms."

Blackburn couldn't think of a reason against the plan, so he went into the blue-tiled kitchen and took a black plastic trash bag from a roll under the sink. Then he stepped into the hall. Here the penlight revealed four doors, two on each side. The first door on the right was open, and he saw more blue tile. The bathroom. He opened the door across from it and found a linen closet stacked with towels. It smelled like a department store, so he leaned inside and breathed deep. It wasn't a smell he was crazy about, but it cleared his head of Roy-Boy's deodorant-soap stink.

He continued down the hall and opened the next door on the right. This was a small bedroom, as clean as a church. There was a brass cross on the wall and stuffed animals on the dresser. The window was open, and Blackburn's neck tingled from the cold. White curtains puffed out over the narrow bed. The bed had a white coverlet with a design of pink and blue flowers.

A jewelry box on the dresser contained only a small silver cross on a chain. It was worth maybe thirty dollars at a pawn shop, but Blackburn left it. He himself had given up on Jesus while still a child, having seen more evidence of sin than of salvation, but he didn't want to mess with someone else's devotion. He found nothing else of value in the room, so he started back into the hall. Then he paused in the doorway.

The window was open. Even the screen was open. But no one was home.

He looked at the closed door across the hall and turned off his penlight. Then he stepped across, dropping the trash bag, and turned the doorknob. He moved to one side as the door swung inward, and caught a whiff of rust and vanilla. He stood against the wall and listened for a few seconds, but heard only Roy-Boy rummaging in the living room and the dull thumping of a stereo in another apartment.

Then he looked around the doorjamb. Except for the gray square of a curtained window, the room was black. He turned the penlight back on and saw the soles of two bare feet suspended between wooden bars. The toes pointed down. He shifted the penlight and saw that the wooden bars were at the foot of a bed.

A nude woman lay on the bed face-down, spread-eagled, her wrists and ankles tied to the bedposts with electrical cords. She was bleeding from cuts on her back, buttocks, and thighs. Strands of her brunette hair were stuck to her neck and shoulders. Her legs moved a little, pulling at their cords with no strength.

Blackburn sucked in a breath, then entered the room and closed the door. He dropped his penlight, found the wall switch, and turned on the ceiling light. He began to tremble. What he had smelled was blood and semen, and sugared pastry. There was a white cardboard box on the floor, and half-eaten donuts on the floor and the bed.

He stepped closer and saw a long shard of glass on the bed between the woman's knees. One end of the shard was wrapped in white cloth tape. The glass and the tape were smeared with blood.

On the woman's back, in thin red lines, were the words HI MUSICIAN.

Blackburn went to the head of the bed on the left side and knelt on the floor. The woman's wrists were tied so that her arms angled upward. Her face was in her pillow. Even this close, he couldn't hear her breathing. But he saw her back moving. There were teeth marks on her shoulders.

He lifted her head and turned her face toward him. The face was Heather's. Her eyes opened, and they widened as she recognized him. Her mouth was covered with duct tape. He pulled the tape away and then saw that a donut had been stuffed into her mouth. She tried to cough it out, but couldn't.

Blackburn lowered her head to the pillow and dug out the donut with his fingers. The smell was thick and sweet. His trembling became violent. He tried to untie the cord around Heather's left wrist, but his fingers were clumsy and numb. He was worthless, useless, a sissy, a pussy. Little Jimmy, dropping his pants and grabbing the rim of the wheel well. He could hear the fiberglass rod cutting the air. Its hiss became a scream, and it bit into his flesh. His skin caught fire.

Then his hands spasmed, and his fingers sank in. It wasn't the rim of a wheel well. It was the edge of a mattress.

He wasn't little Jimmy anymore. He had learned better. He had no father, no mother, no sister, no friends. His only trust was in himself. He could see not only what was, but what should be. He was Blackburn.

And Blackburn always knew what to do, and how to do it.

He tried the cord again. Heather's left wrist came free, and her arm fell to the bed. Her fingernails scratched his face on the way down. The pain was sharp and pure. His trembling stopped.

"Nasty," a voice said. "But maybe she didn't mean it."

Blackburn looked up. The bedroom door was open, and Roy-Boy was standing in the doorway. He was holding a small silver pistol. He gave his chuckle, his piglike grunt.

"Look what somebody left behind the TV," he said. "A twenty-five-caliber semiautomatic. Who woulda thought?"

Blackburn stood. "This is what comes of committing a sin of omission," he said.

Roy-Boy's expression became quizzical. "Omission of what?"

"Your death," Blackburn said. "I could see its place in the pattern of my world, but I left it out because I didn't understand why it needed to be there. Now I see that the reason was obvious. Maybe even to you. Do you know why I should have killed you?"

"Beats me," Roy-Boy said. "But now you can make up for it with a surrogate. I was grooming her for myself, but when I saw you watching the place, I decided to save her for you. See, you need to become aware of the superiority of *my* world, and to do that you've got to live in it a while. In your world you've got your stud attitude, and she's got her bouncy little ass . . . but when you try to pull that shit on me, it's a different story. I'm Thomas Jefferson, and you're slaves."

Blackburn took a step toward him. "So command me."

"Stop," Roy-Boy said. He pointed the pistol at Blackburn's face. "And pick up my ice scraper."

Blackburn stopped. He was at the foot of the bed, four feet from Roy-Boy. He reached down between Heather's knees and picked up the glass shard.

"Now cut her," Roy-Boy said. "Anywhere you like. But cut deep, or I'll shoot you."

"You'll shoot me anyway."

"No, I won't. I promise. I'm a moral guy too."

Blackburn gripped the taped end of the shard with both hands. The sharp end was pointed up.

"Why should I have killed you?" Blackburn asked again.

"Maybe because I threaten your masculinity," Roy-Boy said. "So stick the glass between her butt cheeks. That should make you feel like a stud again."

Blackburn placed the point of the shard under his own chin and began to push upward. It hurt, but like Heather's fingernails on his face, the pain was pure, cleansing. He thought again of Dad's fiberglass rod. No matter how much he had hated it, it had contributed to his creation. This new pain reminded him of that truth.

Roy-Boy grimaced. "Not *you*, Musician," he said. He took a step toward Blackburn and pointed the silver pistol at Heather. "*Her*. Just turn around and—"

Blackburn thrust his fists out and down, cutting his chin, and slashed Roy-Boy's right wrist.

Roy-Boy shrieked. He swung his pistol toward Blackburn again.

But Blackburn was already lunging. He sank his teeth into Roy-Boy's slashed wrist. With his left hand he grabbed the silver pistol and tried to yank it away. With his right hand he used the shard to rip and stab. Roy-Boy stumbled backward. He was screaming things that might have been words, but Blackburn didn't listen to them. The only voice he listened to now was his own, the voice that told him what needed to be done.

They fell to the floor in the hall. Blackburn kept his teeth clamped and his left hand on the pistol, but concentrated on driving the shard into Roy-Boy's eyes, throat, belly, and groin. The odor of soap was overwhelmed by stronger smells. Before long the pistol came free.

Blackburn rolled off Roy-Boy and squatted beside him. He threw the shard into the living room. Then he looked down at what remained of Roy-Boy's face.

"You'd like to believe you're evil," Blackburn said. "But you're only stupid. Anyone who's done it seriously knows there's only one good way to kill: a bullet to the head. Of course, with the smaller calibers, it might take more than one." He placed the muzzle of the silver pistol against Roy-Boy's forehead. "Do you know the answer to my question yet?"

One of Roy-Boy's hands flopped aimlessly.

"It's simple," Blackburn said.

He cocked the pistol.

"Because I felt like it."

He squeezed the trigger until the gun was empty.

Blackburn dropped the pistol on Roy-Boy's chest and stood. He was dizzy for a moment and steadied himself against the wall, leaving a handprint. He was a mess. There had been a lot of blood some of the other times, but never this much. He wanted to brush his teeth and take a shower. He wanted to scrub and burn incense until Roy-Boy's stink was gone.

On the floor, the carcass twitched. Its ponytail had come loose, and the hair was spread out like a fan on the trash bag Blackburn had dropped. The plastic was keeping most of the hair off the wet carpet. Blackburn thought of taking the scalp, then rejected the idea. He didn't want a trophy. He wasn't proud of the way things had gone with Roy-Boy.

He heard a noise in the bedroom and turned to look. Heather was up on her knees. She had managed to free her right wrist and was now trying to loosen the cords around her ankles. She wasn't having any success. She was unsteady, swaying.

Blackburn went to her. "I can do that," he said.

She looked up at him and tried to say something, or to scream. All that came out was a moan.

Blackburn wiped his hands on his shirt. It didn't help. His shirt was wet. "This is mostly his," he said.

Heather looked away as Blackburn untied the cords around her ankles. When she was free, he tried to help her up, but she pulled away and got off the bed on the other side. She stumbled into the hall.

Blackburn pulled the top sheet from the bed. The apartment was cold, and he thought Heather should cover herself. He went into the hall and saw her step over Roy-Boy's body. She didn't seem to notice it. He followed her into the kitchen and turned on the light. Then he draped the sheet over her shoulders, and she didn't even glance at him.

He saw that she was no longer the Heather who had slept with him, and he knew that he was responsible. For the first time in his life, he was horrified at himself. Not for what he had done, but for what he had failed to do. In that failure, he had become an accessory to torture and rape. Killing was not always murder, and stealing was not always a crime . . . but torture and rape were absolutes.

Heather lifted the receiver from a wall telephone and pushed 911. Blackburn heard the dispatcher answer the call, but Heather didn't put the receiver to her ear. She stared at it as if trying to figure out why it was making noise.

"Let me," Blackburn said. He reached for the receiver.

Heather jerked it away, then hit him in the face with it.

His eyes filled with tears. The receiver had struck his nose hard. "Let me talk to them," he said. "You're hurt. You need to go to the hospital."

Heather dropped the receiver and yanked the telephone from its wall jack. The sheet fell away, and Blackburn saw the red lines that her wounds had left on it.

She swung the telephone and hit his head. Then she hit him again, and again. The telephone clanged, and the receiver bounced on its cord, thunking against the floor.

Blackburn backed up against the refrigerator and then stood there, letting Heather hit him. He should never have begun stealing for a living. That moral slip had led to the next one, and that in turn had led to this. So he would take his punishment. It was the only punishment he had ever received that made sense.

"I'm sorry," he told Heather. She had become a blur. "I'm sorry, I'm sorry."

The telephone clanged. Heather began to grunt with each clang, and then to shout. There were no words. Only the voice of her rage.

Blackburn heard it and knew it was just. He slid to the floor. The tiles were like cool water against his cheek.

* * *

And so the State of Texas took him, and healed his face, and charged him with rape and murder. He let the rape charge stand. Murder, however, he could not accept. He had killed, but he had never committed murder. This went double in the case of Roy-Boy.

His court-appointed attorney said that this was not a suitable defense.

Homicide investigators from across the nation came to Houston to question Blackburn, but he was only able to help two of them. Most of the others were trying to track down serial killers of women, and Blackburn had nothing to tell them about that sort of thing—except to say that there were a lot of bastards out there, and he should know, having killed a number of them.

Then the State of Texas charged him with murder again.

He was told that on the night that he and Roy-Boy had met, there had been a woman in the bedroom from which Roy-Boy had emerged. Blackburn had not known of her existence because she had been sick in bed for a week. She had been the sister of the apartment's other occupant, the woman who worked the night shift at Whataburger.

The sick woman had been tortured, raped, and killed.

And since Blackburn admitted that he had been in her apartment on the night of her death, he was accused of the crime.

Blackburn was astonished. "I've never killed a woman," he told his interrogators.

"Yet you've confessed to raping a woman," one of them said.

Blackburn shook his head. "No. What I confessed to was *responsibility* for that rape. And I won't let you use that as grounds to blame me for something else." He turned to his attorney. "You have to make them see my point."

"What point is that?" an interrogator asked.

Blackburn looked at him.

"One sin," he said, "is more than enough."

VICTIM NUMBER NINETEEN

The rape charge and one of the murder charges were dropped in April when Heather announced that she would not testify against Blackburn. It had taken her three and a half months of therapy and hypnosis, she said, but now she had grasped the reality of what had happened on the night she was attacked: Blackburn had not been her rapist, but her savior. While he had arrived too late to stop the rape, he had prevented the rapist from killing her. In order to do that, he'd had no choice but to kill the rapist. It had been justifiable homicide.

Blackburn read Heather's statement in the *Houston Chronicle* over and over again. His first thought was that she was overlooking some basic facts—such as that he should have killed Roy-Boy a week earlier, and that he had broken into her apartment in Roy-Boy's company. But then some of her words began to resonate in his brain.

"While I might wish that Mr. Blackburn had acted sooner," she said, "I cannot condemn him for not having done so. He is only human. He did the best that he could."

That was the key. Blackburn had fallen short of perfection . . . but no one was perfect. To be human was to fail, and Blackburn could not escape his own humanity. So if Heather was willing to absolve his sin, he had to be willing to forgive himself for committing it.

The State of Texas, however, was peeved. To make up for the charges it had lost, it added a new rape charge to the remaining murder charge.

This pissed Blackburn off.

"I didn't kill that woman," he told his attorney, "and I didn't rape her either. I didn't even go into the bedroom. I didn't even know she was there."

"I believe you," his attorney said.

Blackburn found no comfort in that. "It doesn't make sense. They've known all along that she was raped before she was killed, so if they were going to charge me with it, why didn't they do it when they charged me with her murder?"

"Because the physical evidence didn't support it," his attorney said. "The tests showed that the rapist had a different blood type."

"Roy-Boy's."

"Yes. But now the prosecution will argue that you and he committed the crime together—that you also raped her, but didn't ejaculate. You see, even though there's no physical evidence, the jury's likely to believe you did it just because the state accuses you of it. And that'll help the prosecution push for a conviction and a capital penalty on the murder charge."

"But there's no evidence for the murder charge either," Blackburn said.

The attorney looked down at his notes. "Well, there's no physical evidence," he said. "But you've already confessed to killing a man in Goodland, Kansas, in 1981, and another in Kansas City in 1982. You haven't been charged with those crimes, but the prosecution will make a big deal of them anyway. Furthermore, you've admitted to being in the murdered woman's apartment on the night she was killed, and the police found a homeless man who'll testify to seeing you enter the premises within fifteen minutes of the time of death. That's close enough for a jury."

"But I didn't enter with Roy-Boy," Blackburn said. "He went in through a window in the back, where the woman was. Didn't anyone see him?"

"Apparently not. But even the state admits he was there, so that's the route we'll take during the trial. We'll try to make the jury believe that he did it, and that you entered the apartment several minutes later."

"Well, that's what happened," Blackburn said.

"I believe you," his attorney said.

This time Blackburn not only found no comfort in the statement, but heard that it was a lie. His instincts told him that if he was going to get out of this mess, he would have to do it himself. This time, he would listen to them.

The hearing on the new rape charge took place on Wednesday, May 14, 1986, Blackburn's twenty-eighth birthday. His lawyer arranged for him to be allowed to wear a suit and tie instead of jail fatigues, but he was transported to the courthouse in handcuffs and leg shackles. His lawyer was not allowed to accompany him in the van.

He sat on a wooden bench in the van's rear compartment. Three Texas Department of Public Safety troopers serving as guards sat on a bench across from him. They wore cowboy hats and mirrored sunglasses. They reminded him of Officer Johnston.

246

"You know that needle they stick in your arm," one of the troopers said. "Supposed to be painless, but it ain't." Another trooper nodded. "It's as big around as a garden hose." "Sometimes they have to dig for twenty or thirty minutes to find the vein," the third trooper said.

Blackburn watched them. They were pretending to be talking to each other, but their message was for him.

"Personally," the first trooper said, "I wisht they hadn't gone to the needle at all. It hurts some, but not enough. Not as much as this boy hurt that woman he killed."

"I've never killed a woman," Blackburn said.

The troopers turned toward him. Their mirrorshades reflected his face six times. The van went over a bump, and the reflections jiggled.

"Shut up, boy," the second trooper said. "Don't speak unless you're spoken to."

"You were speaking to me," Blackburn said.

The third trooper reached across with his rubber baton and jabbed Blackburn in the stomach. Blackburn saw it coming and tensed his muscles for it, then doubled over to make the trooper happy.

"Don't puke on them shiny shoes," the first trooper said. "The judge won't like it."

"Judges frown on puke," the second trooper said.

Blackburn sat up and smiled.

"Wipe that grin off," the third trooper said, "or I'll give you another politeness lesson. You hear?"

"Yes," Blackburn said. "Thank you."

The troopers glanced at each other—or seemed to; it was hard to tell with the mirrorshades—and then laughed.

"'Thank you,'" the first trooper repeated. "Ain't that polite?"

"Polite as Sunday school," the second trooper said.

"Why you thanking us, boy?" the third trooper asked.

"For giving me a reason," Blackburn said.

247

"A reason for what?" the first trooper asked.

Blackburn said nothing.

The van stopped in a tunnel under the courthouse, and the troopers hustled Blackburn to a courtroom where the third trooper took a set of keys from his shirt pocket and removed Blackburn's handcuffs and leg shackles. That was another concession that Blackburn's attorney had won for him. It was to be the last one.

The hearing was quick. Blackburn's attorney protested the rape charge, but the judge let it stand. Since Blackburn was to be tried for murder anyway, the judge said, the state might as well kill two birds with one stone and try him for rape at the same time. If the charge had no merit, the jury could say so. Bail was denied. Blackburn's attorney sighed and said nothing more.

Five minutes later Blackburn was in handcuffs and shackles again. Five minutes after that he was back in the van with the three DPS troopers, waiting on the driver and shotgun rider. The driver and shotgun rider had not expected to be needed again so soon, and had gone to the courthouse cafeteria. One of Blackburn's troopers called them on a walkie-talkie, but they replied that it would be a few minutes before they could return to the tunnel.

The troopers didn't seem to mind.

"Tough break in court today," the first one said in mock sympathy.

"Guess you won't be raping anyone else," the second said.

"I've never raped anyone," Blackburn said.

The third trooper jabbed him with the baton again. This time Blackburn didn't double over.

"I've never raped anyone," Blackburn repeated, "and I've never killed a woman. Men, yes. But never a woman."

"How many men?" the first trooper asked.

"Just so we know how scared we should be," the second said.

"Eighteen," Blackburn said. "So far."

The troopers laughed.

" 'So far,' " the third one said. "Whoo, this boy's a mean one."

"You remember them all, do you?" the first trooper asked. "Every man you killed, every way you did it?"

"Yes," Blackburn said.

"Well, hell, enlighten us," the second trooper said. "We got time. Who was your first one? A cripple in a wheelchair?"

The troopers were chuckling. They thought Blackburn was a psychopathic freak who needed to hurt women to feel strong. They didn't believe he had killed any men.

Blackburn stared at his six reflections. "The first one," he said, "was a cop."

The troopers stopped chuckling.

"It was my seventeenth birthday," Blackburn said, "eleven years ago today. It was even a Wednesday. He was the city cop of my hometown in Kansas. He shot a dog on the steps of the Nazarene church, so I took his gun and killed him. The gun was a Colt Python with a four-inch barrel." He nodded at the third trooper. "Like the one in your holster. Most people with three fifty-sevens have Smith and Wessons, but I was always glad to have a Colt."

"There's nothing wrong with Smith and Wessons," the first trooper said.

"Hell, no," the second said.

"I never said there was," Blackburn said.

The third trooper stood, crouching because of the low ceiling, and shoved his baton into the loop on his belt. His hand went to the butt of his pistol. "Boys," he said, "if you would like to go for a cup of coffee, I would be happy to stay with the prisoner."

The first trooper looked up at him. "You know we can't do that."

"He's shackled," the third trooper said. "And you don't have to be gone long."

The second trooper shook his head. "Anything you want to do, you can do with us here. We won't say a word."

"Two minutes," the third trooper said. "That's all I want. You can stay close to the van if you're worried."

The first trooper shrugged. "What the hell. I ain't worried."

The second trooper shrugged too. "Okay. What the hell."

The first and second troopers left the van and shut the door. The third trooper unsnapped his holster's safety strap and removed his pistol. It was identical to Blackburn's old Python.

"You want to take this from me?" the trooper asked, holding up the gun.

Blackburn saw no point in lying. "Yes," he said.

"You want it bad enough to kill me for it?" the trooper asked.

Blackburn considered. "No," he said. "I do want to kill you, but taking the gun would be incidental."

The trooper cocked the Python and pointed it at Blackburn's face. "Why do you want to kill me, then?"

Again, Blackburn saw no point in lying. "Because you're a sadistic prick."

The trooper came close and placed the gun muzzle against Blackburn's left cheek. "You got an answer for everything," he said. "So answer me this: Why do I want to kill *you*?"

The muzzle pressed upward. It hurt, but Blackburn ignored it.

"Because you're a sadistic prick," he said.

The trooper took the muzzle away from Blackburn's cheek and then hit him on the other side of the face with the Python's butt. Blackburn fell and lay on the bench. He heard the roar of blood in his skull.

"I just got done healing," he said, trying not to wince.

"Don't you think people will notice a new bruise on my face?"

"You're wearing shackles," the trooper said. "You tripped, you fell. Happens all the time. Besides, nobody cares if you get hurt. Folks *want* a shit like you to get hurt. You've for damn sure caused enough hurt yourself."

Blackburn pushed himself back up to a sitting position. "I've never killed anyone the world wasn't better off without," he said. "Maybe a few wives and kids have suffered some grief from what I've done, but not as much as they would have suffered if I'd let the sons of bitches stay alive."

"My uncle wasn't no son of a bitch," the trooper said.

Blackburn was taken aback. "Excuse me?"

"He was a cop in Liberal, Kansas," the trooper said, "and some punk shot him. We never knew who." He pointed the pistol at Blackburn's face again. "Now I know."

Blackburn frowned. "I've never been to Liberal. The cop I killed was in Wantoda."

"Never heard of it."

"That proves it, then," Blackburn said. "You've got the wrong punk."

"Maybe." The trooper lowered the Python and uncocked it. Then he replaced it in his holster and pulled out his baton. "But you'll do for now. And don't worry, I'll stay off your face."

Blackburn compressed himself into a ball. The trooper beat him on the back and legs for a while, then kicked him off the bench. Blackburn lay on the metal floor, staring at the trooper's boots. The trooper beat him some more, then stopped, breathing hard.

"Get up," the trooper said.

Blackburn managed to rise to his knees. The trooper hit him in the face with a forearm, and he fell again.

"I told you to get up," the trooper said.

Blackburn didn't move. "You said you'd stay off my face."

The trooper spat on him. "Pussy," he said.

Blackburn struggled up to his knees again. As he did so, the door made a noise, and the trooper turned toward it. Blackburn found himself at eye level with the butt of the trooper's Python. The trooper had not refastened his holster's safety strap.

The door opened. The first and second troopers began to climb into the van. The third trooper began to say something to them.

Blackburn brought up his manacled hands and pulled the Python from the holster. His right thumb cocked it, and his index finger curled around the trigger.

The third trooper turned back, thrusting his baton at Blackburn's face.

The Python fired as the baton glanced from Blackburn's forehead. The bullet caught the trooper in the breastbone, and he spun into his companions. All three troopers fell to the pavement outside the van.

Blackburn got to his feet and shuffled to the open door, pointing the pistol down at the troopers. Their sunglasses and hats had been knocked away. The third trooper lay prone across the other two, who lay on their backs. Blackburn jumped down and landed on his knees on the third trooper. The two troopers underneath groaned. The third trooper was quiet.

Five men stood nearby at the courthouse entrance. Two of them were uniformed police officers. The officers turned toward the van and reached for their weapons. As they did so, Blackburn cocked the Python again and placed its muzzle against the nose of the first trooper.

"Gunfire would make me twitch," Blackburn shouted. His voice rang from the tunnel's concrete walls.

The officers froze with their weapons still in their holsters.

"Your friend was hurting me," Blackburn told the two

252

troopers on the pavement. "I had to defend myself. You understand that, don't you?"

The troopers stared up at him.

"Doesn't matter, then," Blackburn said. He pressed down on the Python, flattening the first trooper's nose. "Get his keys and unlock my handcuffs. If you're slow, or if either of you tries to take out his Smith and Wesson, I'll assume that you mean to hurt me. You have ten seconds. One thousand one. One thousand two."

The first trooper unbuttoned the third trooper's shirt pocket and pulled out the keys. They were wet with blood. One of the second trooper's arms, pinned under the third trooper, moved a little.

"If you jostle me," Blackburn said, interrupting his count, "my Colt might go off." It wasn't a threat, but a statement of fact. This Python had a more sensitive trigger than his old one.

The second trooper lay still.

"One thousand eight," Blackburn continued.

The first trooper unlocked the handcuffs. Blackburn pulled his left hand free and took the keys. Then, keeping the Python against the trooper's nose with his right hand, he reached back with his left and unlocked the leg shackles without looking at them. He had been paying close attention when they had been removed earlier.

"This won't solve anything, James," a voice said.

Blackburn looked up and saw his attorney approaching. The attorney's hands were spread, and his forehead gleamed. He stopped a few feet away.

"Put down the gun before things get any worse," the attorney said.

Blackburn was amused. He had just shot and killed a Texas DPS trooper. From a legal standpoint, things were as bad as they could get.

"You have a car in the parking lot?" Blackburn asked.

"No," his attorney said. It was a lie. Blackburn had gotten

good at telling when his attorney was lying. It was most of the time.

"Take me fishing for my birthday?" Blackburn asked.

His attorney looked confused. "I don't think so."

"Oh, come on," Blackburn said. "I haven't been fishing since I was a kid." He stood, but kept the Python pointed at the first trooper's face. "Let's go."

His attorney looked from side to side, as if for help. No one else in the tunnel moved. "Taking a hostage won't improve your position," the attorney said.

"What hostage?" Blackburn said. He stepped off the troopers and gripped his attorney's arm. "If I wanted a hostage, I wouldn't use a lawyer. The whole point of hostage-taking is to pick someone the police don't want to shoot." He shifted the Python's aim so that its muzzle touched the attorney's left ear. "Anyone who follows us outside," he shouted, "will be sued by this man's estate."

Blackburn and his attorney walked backward out of the tunnel into hazy sunlight. The air was thick with Houston steam and smelled of automobile exhaust and mold. Blackburn wondered what had ever possessed him to move down here in the first place. Except for one sweet night with Heather, Houston had been a bad idea.

The attorney's car, a Chrysler New Yorker, was parked close to the courthouse in a space reserved for the handicapped.

"You're not handicapped," Blackburn said, pushing his attorney around to the passenger side of the car.

"I'm not going to take lessons on morality from a man who just blew open another man's chest," the attorney said.

"I was trying to aim for his head," Blackburn said, "but this thing has a hair trigger. Now get in and slide over. You're driving."

They entered the car, and the attorney drove out of the parking lot into downtown traffic. "I can't believe they haven't tried to pick you off yet," he muttered.

254

"Whose side are you on, anyway?" Blackburn asked. He wiped his hands on the velour seat, then reached into his attorney's jacket and took out a wallet. He removed the cash and stuffed it into his own jacket.

They were only four blocks from the courthouse when sirens began wailing. The attorney wasn't driving fast enough. At the next red light, Blackburn tucked his new Python into the back waistband of his slacks and left the car, tugging his jacket down to make sure it hid the pistol. As he ran between cars to the sidewalk, the Chrysler's horn blared.

Blackburn ran up one street and down another, then ducked into a hotel. He stepped into an elevator and rode up to the eleventh floor with a fat businessman who had a parking-garage ticket sticking up from his breast pocket. He followed the man to his room, pushed his way inside when the man opened the door, and then tied the man's wrists to the shower curtain rod with his belt and gagged him with a hand towel. He stole the man's car keys and parking-garage ticket, then left the room and took the stairs down to the garage. There was a car-alarm remote control on the key ring, so he pressed the button and followed the chirps to a Mercedes sedan. The parking attendant didn't even glance at him while handing him his change.

He left the Mercedes in a Wal-Mart parking lot on the city's northern edge and stole a rusting Ford pickup whose owner had left the keys in the ignition. It was only after he was on a crumbling two-lane, heading northeast through the Texas countryside, that he realized his face and body ached from the third trooper's beating. Also, the Python was digging into his spine.

He pulled the gun from his waistband. It fit his hand as if it were part of it.

Today was his birthday, and he had just killed a cop who wore mirrored sunglasses. Maybe he would head for the Ozarks again. But first he would find a telephone and call Information for the numbers of Houston-area handicapped-persons' organizations. He would tell them about his attorney's parking habits.

Blackburn put the Python under the seat and then gazed down the road. He had never been here before, but the road looked just like a thousand other crumbling two-lanes he had driven. After eleven years, nothing had changed.

And if that meant that the world was still the same, at least it meant that he was too.

NINE

BLACKBURN AND THE LAMB OF GOD

When he was clear of Houston, Blackburn tried to head for northern Louisiana. But he couldn't keep his direction constant because he was sticking to back roads. After nightfall he used some of the money he had taken from his attorney to buy gas, a candy bar, and a cheap digital watch at a small-town convenience store. The Ford's odometer said that he had driven three hundred and sixteen miles, but because of his route he doubted that he was any farther than two hundred miles from Houston.

Clouds moved in to cover the stars as he resumed driving, and by 2:00 A.M. on Thursday, May 15, he was lost on a dirt road in an East Texas forest. Then rain began to fall, and he discovered that the pickup's windshield wipers didn't work. He pulled over to the edge of the road and tried to nap, but lightning and thunder kept him awake. Each flash lit up the pines and dogwoods and cast their shadows across the road. As thunder rattled the truck, Blackburn imagined the trees catching fire in white bursts.

The rain fell until daybreak, and when the clouds cleared, the rising sun showed Blackburn that the dirt road ran north and south. It had become a narrow sea of mud. Blackburn started the Ford and tried to continue driving, but the truck slid into the ditch and sank until mud covered its rear axle. So Blackburn took his Colt Python, climbed to the road, and struck out northward on foot.

The road sucked at his shoes, so he jumped across the ditch and walked in the weeds next to the trees. The ground was uneven and thickets of brush were frequent, so it was slow going. The humidity was high, and the temperature was rising fast. Blackburn took off his suit jacket and necktie, but that didn't help much. The shirt his attorney had given him to wear to court was polyester, and the slacks were wool. The Python was too heavy in his waistband and kept trying to slide down, so he removed it and rolled it up in the jacket, carrying the bundle under his arm. He sweated and itched and was sure that he was breaking out in boils. When he became thirsty he licked rainwater from leaves. He also had to use leaves as toilet paper. By midmorning he was plagued by swarms of gnats and flies. Added to all this was his growing hunger; except for the candy bar, he had not eaten since breakfast the day before.

Blackburn began to think he was being forced to pay penance for his one sin. He wondered if he should start believing in God.

The woods on both sides of the road were unbroken by buildings or clearings. There weren't even any fences. After hours of walking, Blackburn crossed another mud road, and then another, and in the early afternoon came to a two-lane strip of pavement. He stepped onto it and stamped his feet to knock the mud from his shoes.

As he stamped, he heard the hum of an automobile approaching from the east. He looked toward the sound and saw that there was a hill between him and the vehicle. If he wanted to, he could run into the trees and hide. But his clothes were sticking to his skin, and his feet were blistering. There was a chance that the vehicle contained a Texas Department of Public Safety trooper—but he would take that chance rather than slog back into the mud. He crossed to the north side of the asphalt and slipped his right hand into his rolled-up jacket, curling his fingers around the butt of the Python. His muscles tensed, and he waited.

The vehicle turned out to be a slow-moving white van. Blackburn relaxed a little as he watched it come over the hill, and then he took his hand from his jacket and waved. The van pulled to the edge of the pavement and came to a stop beside him. Black lettering on its side panel said RUSK STATE HOSPITAL RUSK TX 75785.

Blackburn looked at the two men inside the van and tensed up again. The plump, balding man in the passenger seat was wearing a short-sleeved yellow shirt, but the driver was a younger, thinner man wearing a blue uniform that made him look like a cop. Blackburn didn't see a gun, though, so he didn't put his hand back into his jacket.

The plump man rolled down his window, and Blackburn felt a puff of air-conditioning. He stepped closer.

"Having trouble?" the plump man asked.

Blackburn forced a smile. He had to look friendly, like someone who deserved to be helped. "Yes. I was exploring some of these back roads looking for dogwood blossoms to photograph." He pointed at the mud road. "But I didn't realize that one was in such bad shape until I was on it. My car bogged down, and I had to leave my camera equipment so I could walk out."

"You're about a month late for dogwood blossoms," the

plump man said. "The end of March and the first week of April are best."

The driver was muttering. "Dirt road after a rainstorm," he said. "Not too bright."

Blackburn ignored him. "Well, I'm a transplanted Northerner," he said to the plump man. "I just now moved down here, and I forgot to allow for the earlier spring." He squinted up at the sun. "Feels like summer already."

"It's getting warm, all right," the plump man said. "Could we give you a lift into Palestine? It's over ten miles, and you look like you've walked a piece already."

"I'd appreciate it," Blackburn said. "I drove my car out from Palestine this morning, but I was starting to think I'd be going back in a box."

The plump man started to open his door. "You're lucky we came along. This road doesn't get much use."

The driver made a noise in his throat. "Uh, Doctor, what if we find Morton?"

The plump man paused with his door open a few inches. He looked down at the asphalt and frowned. "Good point," he said. He looked back up at Blackburn. "We're searching for a patient who wandered off Monday evening. The sheriff and DPS are checking the main highways, but we thought we'd improve our chances and look along some of the back roads ourselves. If we were to run across him before dropping you off, you might be . . ."

"In the way?" Blackburn asked.

"Frankly, yes," the plump man said. "And there might be a question of liability if anything should happen."

"Morton's a handful," the driver said. His voice was flat.

"So perhaps what we should do instead of giving you a lift," the plump man said, "is to call a tow truck for you when we reach Palestine. Would that be all right?"

Blackburn tried to look politely dissatisfied. "I'm afraid my car's so far down that road, and stuck so badly, that a tow truck won't be any use until things dry out. So, well . . ." He hesitated, hoping to imply that he really hated to impose. "If you'll let me ride with you, I promise I'll get out if you find this Morton. That would still get me closer to town than I am now."

The plump man glanced at the driver. The driver shrugged, looking disgusted, and the plump man pushed his door open. "That sounds reasonable," he said. "And the odds are that we won't come across Morton anyway. But we have to try."

Blackburn squeezed past the plump man and sat on the bench seat behind him. The cool air inside the van was wonderful. "I'll be happy to pay for your gas," Blackburn said. "I'm on vacation this week, so I'm getting paid for nothing. And right now I'd rather buy a ride to town than anything else."

"No need," the plump man said, shutting his door and rolling up his window as the van started moving again. "We're going as far as Palestine anyway, and then we'll drive back to Rusk on another path less taken."

"Waste of time," the driver muttered.

The plump man looked back at Blackburn. "I hope you don't mind if we aren't too talkative. We need to keep our eyes peeled."

"I don't mind at all," Blackburn said. It was the truth. Not having to talk would mean that he wouldn't need to elaborate on his story about being a Northerner transplanted to Palestine.

"And if you should happen to see someone wearing a white hospital gown," the plump man said, "be sure to holler."

"Where should I be looking?" Blackburn asked.

The plump man gestured at the forest alongside the road. "In there. Morton likes to play in the woods." He stuck his right hand back at Blackburn. "By the way, I'm Dr. Joe Norris."

Blackburn shook his hand. "Bruce Rayburn," he said. "Just down from Iowa City."

The driver looked at him in the rearview mirror and grimaced.

"How'd you get the shiner, Bruce?" Dr. Norris asked.

Blackburn touched his right cheekbone, where the DPS trooper had hit him with the Python. It was tender. His nose was sore from the trooper's forearm, too.

"I was carrying a chair into my new house and ran into a doorjamb," he said.

Dr. Norris nodded. "That's why I always hire movers." He turned away and peered out at the trees.

The driver whispered "Dumbass Yankee" just loud enough for Blackburn to hear.

The van proceeded west at forty miles per hour. Blackburn wiped his shoes on the floor mat and watched the woods for a glimpse of a man in a white gown. If he saw him, he would keep his mouth shut.

As the van approached a state highway loop on the outskirts of Palestine, Blackburn spotted a shopping center with an H.E.B. supermarket. He asked Dr. Norris to let him off there. He would call his wife at work, he said, and she would pick him up. Norris's driver muttered something about not having been hired as a chauffeur, but he pulled the van into the H.E.B. parking lot.

Blackburn got out, and as the van drove off, he looked up and down the highway loop and saw a sign for a Best Western motel about a mile to the north. That motel would be his next stop, but first things first. He tucked his rolled-up jacket under his arm and went into the supermarket.

He bought bread and cheese, a couple of apples, a Texas highway map, a disposable razor, and a meat-tenderizing mallet. Then he went outside and bought a copy of the *Dallas Morning News* from a machine. He sat down on a bench beside the machine, made a cheese sandwich, and found

Palestine on the map. His zigzagging during the night had taken him back farther to the west than he had realized; Palestine was a hundred and fifty miles straight north of the western edge of Houston. He was no closer to Louisiana than he had been before his escape.

On the other hand, the DPS would be keeping an eye on the Louisiana border, and they wouldn't be looking for him here. Plus, Palestine had a population of sixteen thousand, which was big enough for him not to be noticed as a stranger. It was also big enough for him to find a car. As long as he wasn't spotted by a city cop, sheriff's deputy, or DPS trooper, he could rest here until after dark, then acquire a vehicle and head for Oklahoma. He didn't think the DPS would be expecting him to try for Oklahoma.

He folded the map and then looked at the newspaper while eating his sandwich. His escape had made the front page, but the article was at the bottom right corner, and there was no photograph of him. The article did mention the brown wool suit he was wearing, but nothing else that would identify him. Its lead paragraph claimed that he had escaped during a "gun battle" with police and DPS troopers. Blackburn thought it was stretching the truth to call one shot a "battle."

He finished his sandwich and was about to leave the newspaper on the bench when another article on the front page caught his eye. It said that a Texas prison inmate named Jay Pinkerton was to be executed by lethal injection at Huntsville that night. He would be the third man to be executed in Texas so far in 1986. He had been seventeen years old when he had committed rape and murder, and had now been on Death Row for four years. He had been taken to the execution chamber once before and had received a stay only minutes before the intravenous solution was to have been administered. Now his time had run out again. The article suggested that there would not be another stay.

Blackburn's sandwich lay in his stomach like concrete.

263

He too had killed at seventeen. He too was accused of rape and murder. If they had convicted him and sent him to Huntsville, would they have made him wait four years before giving him the needle?

The thought was sickening. If you had to kill someone, it was better to do it quickly. If you had a choice. And surely the State of Texas had a choice.

Blackburn felt sorry for Jay Pinkerton. Not that Pinkerton didn't deserve to die; the article made it clear that he did. He had raped and killed a woman, which put him in the same class as Roy-Boy. But Blackburn would not have made even Roy-Boy wait on his death for four years. That would have been sadism on the order of Roy-Boy's own.

He pulled the front page from the newspaper, crumpled it, and tossed it into a garbage can beside the bench. He folded the rest of the paper and laid it on the bench for someone else to read, then took his rolled-up jacket and his plastic grocery bag and walked down the shopping center's sidewalk to a sporting goods store. There he bought black shorts, a white T-shirt with ADIDAS stenciled on the chest in red, an athletic supporter, white socks, and the cheapest pair of running shoes he could find. That still left him with almost a hundred dollars of his attorney's money. His jacket, with the Python, fit inside the sporting-goods-store bag with his new clothes.

He walked to the Best Western and rented a room from the dazed old woman in the office. She didn't even glance at the phony name and auto-license number he wrote on the check-in form. Nor did she seem to notice that he was sweating and carrying two plastic bags instead of luggage. Blackburn was pleased.

His room was on the second floor on the north side of the building. Once inside, he turned the air conditioner on HIGH, stripped, and lay on the bed in the cold breeze. When his skin was dry, he sat up and ate another cheese sandwich and both apples. Then he lay back down for a nap.

264

He was exhausted, but he had trouble falling asleep. He should have passed over the *Dallas Morning News* and picked up a comic book instead.

Blackburn awoke to red and blue flashing lights and sat up gasping. He had been dreaming of drowning, and had seen the lights filtered through the water. Now he saw them filtered through the curtains over his motel room window. Except for them, the room was dark.

He slid out of bed and crept on all fours toward the window. The carpet was stiff and grungy. Beneath the window, the air conditioner was still blasting. He gulped a lungful of iced air and shivered.

At the window he peeked between the curtains and saw that it was night. Down in the parking lot, a police car sat with its lights whirling as two cops shoved a shirtless man into the back seat. Several yards from the car, a young woman in a short nightgown was standing barefoot, hugging herself and crying. Other people stood nearby, watching. Something violent had happened at the motel in the past hour, but Blackburn had heard none of it. The air conditioner had drowned it out. There must have been a siren too, but Blackburn had not heard that either. He switched off the air conditioner, and it stopped with a loud, shuddering *chunk*. The people in the parking lot looked up.

Blackburn ducked and held his breath. After several seconds he risked another look. Everyone was watching the police car again. The cops shut the shirtless man into the back seat and got into the front seat. The red and blue lights stopped flashing, and the car moved off toward the highway loop. Blackburn let out his breath and stood. The police car hadn't come for him, but sooner or later one would. He took his disposable razor from the grocery bag and went into the bathroom, where he turned on a light and looked at his watch. It was after eleven; time to get on to Oklahoma and beyond. Maybe he would give Canada a try. It was cold, but there was national health insurance.

He took a shower, then went to the sink and worked the remaining sliver of motel soap into a lather. He spread the foam on his cheeks and throat and got too much around his mouth, so he made a mad-dog face in the mirror. Then he shaved. The State of Texas would be thinking of him as a desperate, dirty animal on the run. Maybe he was, but he could try not to look like one.

After shaving, he toweled off and returned to the bedroom. The room was steamy from his shower, but he didn't turn the air conditioner back on. He put on the clothes and shoes he had bought that afternoon, then stuffed his other clothes and shoes into the sporting-goods bag. He had to hang on to them until he could dump them where they wouldn't be found. The jacket, still wrapped around the Python, went on top. Obtaining more ammunition would be a priority as soon as he was out of the state. His five remaining cartridges would be adequate for now, but they wouldn't last forever.

He picked up his plastic bags and was about to leave, but heard a knock at the door of the room next to his. He heard the door open and then voices on the balcony. He set down his bags, went to the window, and peeked between the curtains again, looking sideways. He saw the two cops who had been in the parking lot, and the old woman from the motel office. The cops were talking to a man in the next room, asking whether he had seen or heard anything unusual that evening. They were looking for witnesses against the man they had arrested.

One of the cops said, "If you think of anything, give us a call." The door closed, and the cops and the old woman started toward Blackburn's room. Blackburn backed away from the window, then stood still as they knocked on his door. He breathed in short, shallow puffs.

"Excuse me," one of the cops said in a loud voice.

"We're police officers, and we need to ask a few questions."

Blackburn squatted and reached into the sporting-goods bag. He put his hand into his rolled-up jacket, but his palm came up against the Python's muzzle. He pulled his hand out again.

"I know this room's occupied," the old woman said. "Maybe he's gone out." Blackburn heard the rattle of keys. "We'll just take a look."

Blackburn picked up his bags and went into the bathroom. "Just a minute!" he yelled. "I'm on the pot!" He put the bags into the bathtub and pulled the shower curtain across to hide them. Then he took some deep breaths. There was nothing to worry about. These cops weren't here for him. They wouldn't be thinking about him. He wasn't wearing the same clothes as yesterday. He could leave the bathroom light on, and that would draw their eyes away from his face. Even if they did look at his face, his hair was wet and looked darker than it really was. He flushed the toilet and went to answer the door.

As the door opened, Blackburn saw that the cops were young, in their early twenties. They looked grim. "Sorry to bother you at such a late hour, sir," the closest one said. He didn't sound sorry. "But we had a disturbance downstairs, and we were wondering if you might have seen or heard anything that could help us with our investigation."

"I'm afraid not," Blackburn said. "I had the air conditioner on, and I didn't even wake up until you were putting the guy into your car. I did see that."

"You slept through the disturbance, sir?" the cop asked.

"I guess so."

The other cop pointed at Blackburn's feet. "Do you sleep in your shoes, sir?"

Blackburn looked down at his new running shoes. "No," he said. "But I couldn't get back to sleep, so I thought I'd go for a jog to tire myself out."

"Jogging at night isn't advisable, sir," the first cop said. "You might be hit by a motorist."

"Oh," Blackburn said. "I won't do it, then."

"Maybe you could watch TV instead," the cop suggested.

"I'll do that."

"And if you happen to remember anything that might help us, please call the Palestine Police Department. Or tell the front desk here at the motel."

The old woman rattled her keys. "I'm sorry about the ruckus," she said. "I hope you can get back to sleep."

"Not your fault," Blackburn said.

The cops and the old woman moved on toward the next room. As Blackburn closed the door, he saw the second cop look back at him and scowl. But there was no recognition in the look, only the normal aggressive distrust of a young male.

Blackburn turned on the television so the cops would hear that he had taken their advice. He couldn't leave until he was sure they were gone anyway. As he sat down on the bed, the television screen brightened into an artist's rendering of Jay Pinkerton lying strapped to a gurney. According to the voiceover, the execution was taking place at that moment.

Blackburn got up and turned off the television. He went into the bathroom, took his plastic bags from the tub, and returned to the bed. He pulled the Python from his jacket and cocked it. Then he sat with his back against the headboard and waited.

Several minutes later he heard the cops' voices in the parking lot, and then a car starting and driving away. He waited ten more minutes before uncocking the Python and replacing it in his jacket in the sporting-goods bag. Then he picked up both bags and left the room. The sky was covered with clouds again.

Blackburn walked behind the motel and out to a tree-canopied side street. There was no traffic. He headed east, away from the highway loop, until he came to a small apartment house with a ripe parking lot. There he wrapped his polyester courtroom shirt around his meat-tenderizing mallet and broke the driver's-side wing window from an old Dodge Coronet sedan. He reached in and unlocked the door, then opened it and tossed his bags inside. He glanced at the apartment house to be sure no lights were coming on, then squirmed under the car's dashboard.

When the engine started, Blackburn came out from under the dashboard and looked at the apartment house again. There were still no lights. He settled into the driver's seat, pulled out of the lot, and drove back toward the highway loop. The Coronet's engine stumbled, but he thought it would get him to Oklahoma.

As he turned north onto the highway loop beside the Best Western, he saw that the police car was back again, parked in front of the motel. The two cops were coming out of the office. One of them seemed to stare at Blackburn as he drove past.

Blackburn watched his rearview mirror and saw the police car pull onto the loop and also head north. But it was half a mile behind him, and its flashing lights weren't coming on. Blackburn turned west at a stoplight, and although the police car turned west there too, it dropped back even farther. By the time Blackburn was out of the city, accelerating northwest on U.S. 287, there were no headlights in his mirror. It had been thirty-six hours since he had escaped from the courthouse in Houston, and he was still alive and free.

That put him two up on a lot of people. Including, by now, Jay Pinkerton.

The Coronet died soon after he turned off U.S. 287 onto Texas 19, before he could find one of the back roads that he preferred. There was a grinding noise, and then the engine quit. Blackburn let the car coast into the ditch and stopped it under an overhanging tree. God was still trying to get him to believe in Him, and had decided that he should wander on foot for a while longer.

Blackburn didn't think that would have to be for long. After turning onto Texas 19, he had passed a gravel road with a sign beside it that said PALESTINE COMMUNITY FOREST, and he had seen red taillights wink off among the trees. At least one car was parked in there.

He took his two plastic bags and trudged back toward the gravel road. The ground was moist rather than muddy, so he knew the rain had not been as heavy here. A car passed by on the highway, and he lay down in the grass at the bottom of the ditch so its occupants wouldn't see him. When he stood, his clothes were damp, and he felt bugs, probably ticks, crawling on his skin. He stopped and set down his bags to brush himself off, but it was too dark for him to see whether he was successful. The sensation of things crawling on him didn't go away, so he had to walk on and try to ignore it. He couldn't wait to get out of Texas.

When he could see the flat shadow that was the mouth of the gravel road, he climbed the slope of the ditch and entered the forest, weaving his way between the trees. The woods were alive with chirps, clicks, and scrabblings, some of which ceased as Blackburn passed by. He didn't want to think about all the ticks he was rousing, so he thought about snakes instead. Snakes could be shot.

A few hundred yards into the forest, an automobile appeared among the trees. It was a Nissan Z car that, in the darkness, appeared to be a dull gray color. It was parked in a clearing at the end of a dirt track that Blackburn assumed led back to the gravel road. The Nissan's windows were down, and as Blackburn approached, he heard slurping sounds from within. Kids making out.

Blackburn's plan was simple. He would force the Nissan's occupants out of the car and take it. But he would have to be careful. In Texas, even people in sports cars were often armed. Blackburn set down his bags among the roots of an elm, removed the Python from his rolled-up suit jacket, and stepped into the clearing.

At that moment, another man emerged from the trees on the opposite side of the clearing. This man's shirt, like Blackburn's, was white, and his legs, like Blackburn's, were bare. He stood out so sharply against the dark trees that he seemed to glow. Blackburn stopped and stared, thinking at first that he was seeing a reflection of himself, a terrestrial gegenschein. Then, as the other man continued to approach, Blackburn saw that he was small and walked in a stoop, and that his shirt was in fact a gown that stopped at mid-thigh. His gray hair was long and matted, and his beard touched his chest. He was not a reflection of Blackburn.

The man raised his hands above his head and shouted in a high-pitched, cracking voice: "Fornicators! Repent!"

Two heads popped up in the Nissan. Blackburn hissed "Shit" and stepped back into the trees. He didn't know if the people in the car had seen him or not.

The long-haired man continued to shout. "The wages of sin is death!" he cried. He was standing beside the car now, pounding its roof with his fists. "At least use a rubber!"

The Nissan's engine started, and its headlights came on. The beams stabbed into the woods and pinned Blackburn against a tree trunk. He dropped to the ground, hoping the kids were too intent on getting away to notice him. The Nissan spun its rear wheels, backed up in a half circle, and scraped against a cedar. Metal squealed as it lurched forward onto the dirt track, and then it was gone. Blackburn heard it turn onto the gravel road and roar off toward the highway.

"Oh, generation of vipers!" the long-haired man shouted, shaking a finger toward the sound of the departing car. "Who hath warned you to flee from the wrath to come? Me, that's who!"

Blackburn was perturbed. He stood, sure that he was covered with ticks again, and stepped back into the clearing.

"Hey, you!" he said. "You're Morton, right?"

The long-haired man froze, his finger still raised. Then his head swiveled, and he stared at Blackburn.

"My child," he said. His voice was hoarse.

Blackburn raised the Python and shook it as the long-haired man had shaken his finger. "You may have just ruined my chances for getting out of here alive. I'd kill you, but killing crazy people is bad luck."

The long-haired man turned so that his finger pointed at Blackburn. "I am the good shepherd," he said, "and know my sheep, and am known of mine. Thou knowest I am the Morton. Thou art mine." He lowered his hand and scratched his crotch. "As for killing me, go ahead. That's what I'm here for. But if ye seek to be set free—" He turned and shuffled toward the trees from which he had emerged. "Follow me."

Blackburn considered. Insane or not, Morton had managed to escape from a state hospital, and so far he had avoided capture for three days. Blackburn followed him into the forest.

Morton was fast, and Blackburn had trouble keeping up. Sometimes Morton vanished, then reappeared farther away, a will o' the wisp in a hospital gown. Blackburn scraped his elbows on tree trunks, and tripped and fell twice. The forest seemed endless, and Morton flitted through it as if he were composed not of flesh, but of white gases that could pass through tree trunks as easily as through air.

At last, when Blackburn was sweating and his lungs had been aching for what seemed like hours, Morton stopped in a clearing. Blackburn collapsed a few yards away from him, breathing hard, not caring about ticks. After a minute or two he was able to sit up and saw that Morton had made a small pile of sticks on a strip of bare earth. Morton was sitting cross-legged before the sticks and setting them on fire with a butane lighter. When the fire was burning well, Morton tossed the lighter over his shoulder. It landed behind him with a clink.

"Isn't it warm enough already?" Blackburn asked, rising to a crouch and moving closer. He saw now that Morton was wearing dirty high-topped sneakers with cracked soles and no shoelaces.

"Be willing for a season to rejoice in a burning and shining light," Morton said. He leaned over the blaze and grinned. "Fire *good*," he said.

Blackburn sat down across the fire from Morton and laid the Python beside him. "You said you'd set me free," he said, "and for me that means getting out of Texas. You don't happen to have a car, do you?"

Morton shrugged. "I am the way, the truth, and the life, but I got no wheels."

"So how do I get out of here?" Blackburn asked. "I'm lost."

"Yea, the son of Stan is come to save that which was lost," Morton said. "No man cometh unto the fat herd, but by me."

"What's that mean?"

"Hang out with me until the old farts come from town for their picnics tomorrow," Morton said. "Then you can snag a Buick and take a journey into a far country. But waste not your substance with riotous living unless your old man is a soft touch. Fatted calves don't grow on trees."

Blackburn decided that, at its core, Morton's plan made sense. His only alternative was to take off through the woods on foot again, and that would get him nowhere. He had no idea where the nearest road might be or what he would do even if he found it. He might as well consider himself settled in for the night.

"Speaking of fatted calves," he said, "I'm hungry. I had

some bread and cheese, but I left it beside a tree. Do you have anything?"

"I have food for the spirit, my son," Morton said.

"Anything else?"

Morton reached behind his back and produced a small foil-covered box. "A few Cracker Jacks," he said. He held the box out to Blackburn. "Take, eat; this is my body."

Blackburn accepted the box and shook some of the contents into his mouth. He had to chew for a long time before swallowing. "You're a little stale," he said.

"Watch your mouth. Know that I am indeed the Morton, the Savior of the world."

Blackburn took another mouthful of Cracker Jacks. "No fooling?"

"I shit you not," Morton said. "For lo, Stan went up from Indiana, out of the city of Goshen, into Pennsylvania, unto the city of Bethlehem. And there Bernice his espoused wife, being great with child, brought forth her firstborn son and did call him Morton, saying, This city doth reek with the fumes of many mills of steel, and it is not meet that a child of decent people should be brought up in a stinking cesspool. So Stan took the young child and his mother, and turned aside into the parts of Kentucky; and he came and dwelt in a city called Nazareth, population seven hundred. But lo, there was no labor for Stan in the parts of Kentucky thereabouts, and he didst drink of the fruit of the vine and clobber his wife and child when they didst cry out for meat. And behold, an angel of the Lord appeareth to Stan in a dream, saying, Arise, and dump yonder bitch and brat. For what dost thou need this crap? And verily, Stan did arise, and gat himself the hell out of Dodge."

"You were better off without him," Blackburn said.

"Tell me about it," Morton said. He reached behind his back again and produced a quart bottle of orange Gatorade. He held it out to Blackburn. "Drink ye all of it, for this is the blood of Morton of Nazareth, which is shed for many for the remission of sins." His eyes narrowed. "You *do* have sins, don't you? I don't want to waste this stuff. We're talking blood here."

Blackburn was thirsty, so he took the bottle. "I only have one sin," he said, "but it's a big one. A woman was raped because I didn't do anything to stop it." He shook the bottle, took off the cap, and drank. The Gatorade was warm and salty. He drank half the bottle in seven gulps, then lowered it and caught his breath.

"I said all of it," Morton said. "Whosoever drinketh of the water that I shall give him shall never thirst; but the water that I shall give him shall be in him a well of water springing up into everlasting life. So chugalug." He clapped his hands and chanted. "Chuga*lug*, chuga*lug*, chuga*lug*."

Blackburn chugalugged, draining the bottle. Then he belched.

"Attaboy," Morton said. "Now, if thou wilt confess thy sins unto me and accept me as thy Savior, thou wilt be born again of water and of the Spirit and dwell in Paradise, a small town in Utah."

Blackburn dropped the bottle, and it clanked against the Python. He saw then that the Python's muzzle was clogged with mulch from his falls in the woods, so he picked up the pistol and removed its cartridge cylinder. "I told you, I only have one sin," he said, pulling a weed and running it into the Python's barrel. "And the woman I committed it against has already absolved me, so I don't need to be born again."

Morton sat up straighter and glared. "Unless she has written permission, she can't absolve squat. And even if she does, you still need a Savior."

Blackburn continued cleaning the Python. "I don't think so. I was willing to accept a Savior when I was a kid, but everyone who tried to sell me one turned out to be peddling snake oil."

"That which is born of the flesh is flesh," Morton said,

275

"and that which is born of the Spirit is spirit. They were false prophets; I'm the real McCoy."

"The Christians say that Jesus is."

Morton snorted. "Yea, but if Jesus had to die for Christians to be saved, and Jews killed Him, then shouldn't Christians be kissing Jews on the backside at high noon instead of burying them in shallow graves at midnight? Hear then my condemnation: That light is come into the world, and men love darkness rather than light. Verily, a new, improved Savior with superior night vision is required."

Blackburn finished wiping the Python clean with his T-shirt. "You?"

"As foretold in the prophecies," Morton said. "Witness my birthplace, my home town, my ministry, my scourging, and my crown of thorns. Witness that I yearn to submit to the sacrifice, and that I shall exalt whosoever offs me as the instrument of man's salvation. I'd do it myself, but that would be an act of selfishness and would queer the deal. So pack up your doubts and troubles in your old kit bag and behold the Lamb of God, which taketh away the sin of the world!"

"I don't see a crown of thorns," Blackburn said.

Morton put his hands on his hips. "I took it off for the evening, okay? The damn thing *hurts.*"

Blackburn snapped the Python's cartridge cylinder back in place and laid the gun on the ground again. "Sorry," he said. "No offense."

Morton took his hands from his hips and pointed a finger at Blackburn. "Art thou going to confess thy sins and be saved, or aren't thou?"

"I repeat, I only have one sin."

"I'll be the judge of that." Morton cleared his throat. "To begin: Hast thou had any other Gods before me?"

Blackburn peered across the fire at Morton, studying his

dirty, lined face in the flickering light. "No," he said, "but I can't say that I've had you either."

"Close enough," Morton said. "Now for door number two: Hast thou ever taken my name in vain?"

" 'Morton'?"

"Okay, dumb question." Morton scratched his beard. "How about adultery? Ever done that?"

"No. It was done to me, though."

Morton gasped. "What'd you do to your wife when you found out?"

"I tied her upside-down in a closet. It didn't hurt her, but I guess I feel bad about it."

"You let her off easy," Morton said. "So forget it and tell me: Hast thou honored thy father and thy mother?"

Blackburn looked at the fire. "I tried to do what they said, when I was a kid. But I don't think I loved them. My mother was weak, and my father was—"

Morton interrupted. "A frustrated failure who became a mean-tempered, shit-heeled son of a bitch you wished you had the guts to kill?"

"Something like that," Blackburn said.

"Piss on 'em, then," Morton said. "*My* old man used to scourge me with baling wire, and when he left, my mom took up the slack. That's why in *my* church, commandments are conditional. Which brings me to: Hast thou killed? People and furry creatures, I mean. Serpents, bugs, and armadillos that jumped up into your transmission don't count."

"Yes," Blackburn admitted. "I've killed nineteen men."

Morton didn't seem surprised. "Did they deserve it?" he asked.

"Every one of them."

"Piss on 'em, then." Morton stood. His joints made popping sounds. "Come kneel thou before me."

Blackburn stood and went around the fire, then knelt beside a shallow hole that was just behind the spot where

277

Morton had been sitting. The hole contained the butane lighter, another bottle of Gatorade, a bag of Fritos, and a dead mole. Blackburn clasped his hands before him in a prayerful attitude.

Morton placed his hands on Blackburn's head. "Dost thou repent of all thy manifold sins?" he cried.

"Well, the one, anyway," Blackburn said.

"Dost thou promise to walk in the way of righteousness?"

"Yea, verily," Blackburn said.

"Art thou now or hast thou ever been a member of the Communist Party?"

"Not to the best of my recollection."

Morton pressed down hard. "Be thou clean!" he shouted. "By the powers vested in Me by Me, I now pronounce you SAVED!" He leaned over and gave Blackburn a wet kiss on the mouth. Then he straightened and smiled. "Son, thy sins be forgiven thee. Let's us go find the nearest body of water." He wrinkled his nose. "You smell a little gamy."

Blackburn laughed. Morton might be crazy, but his craziness was more tolerable than what most of the world called sanity. He stood and shook Morton's hand.

"Thank you," Blackburn said.

"Thou art welcome," Morton said. "Maybe someday you can do something for me."

As Morton spoke, there was a crashing noise in the forest. Blackburn released Morton's hand and jumped across the fire. He scooped up the Python and cocked it, then stood with his back to the flames and looked into the woods. He saw bobbing disks of white and yellow light.

With the lights came voices. "There!" one cried. "I see him!"

Blackburn jumped back across the fire and grasped Morton's arm. "Come on," he said. "We'll head the other way."

But as he began to pull Morton that way, lights appeared

among the trees there as well. So Blackburn turned another way, and then another. The lights were almost everywhere. Only one direction was free, but Blackburn and Morton had taken only a few steps when the sound of engines approached from there. Then headlights appeared, bearing down on them.

Blackburn stopped, and now he saw that he and Morton were standing in the same clearing where the Nissan had been parked. He had followed Morton for miles, only to be led back to their starting point.

They were surrounded. A circle of more than a dozen armed men emerged from the trees, and two vehicles with not only headlights but spotlights entered the clearing. Blackburn and Morton were caught in their beams.

Morton pulled free of Blackburn's grasp and stepped toward the spotlights. "Whom seek ye?" he shouted.

One of the spotlights was blocked as a man stepped in front of it. "Morton," he said.

"Morton who?" Morton demanded.

The man came toward Morton, and Blackburn saw that it was Dr. Norris from the Rusk State Hospital.

"Morton of Nazareth," Dr. Norris said.

Morton's shoulders sagged. "I am he."

Then a voice behind Blackburn spoke. "You in the shorts," it said. "Drop that weapon and lie face-down."

Morton whirled around. "I have told you that I am he!" he shrieked. "If therefore ye seek me, let this schlemiel go his way!"

A figure dashed from behind the spotlights and charged toward Morton as if to tackle him from behind. Blackburn saw that it was Dr. Norris's blue-uniformed driver.

Blackburn raised the Python. "Stay away from him!" he yelled.

The driver came on, so Blackburn aimed and fired. The driver screamed and dropped to his knees, pressing a hand over his right ear. Some of the men in the circle shouted and raised their weapons, but Blackburn knew none of them could fire at him without the risk of hitting the men across from them.

Morton jumped at Blackburn and threw his arms around him. "Put up thy three fifty-seven into the sheath," he said. "The cup which my Father hath given me, shall I not chugalug it?"

The circle of men tightened, and Blackburn saw among them the two cops who had questioned him at the motel. The one who had scowled at him was carrying the plastic bags containing Blackburn's clothes and food.

"My ear!" Norris's driver was shrieking. "He shot my fucking ear!"

"Don't bitch," Blackburn said. "I was aiming for your fucking skull."

Dr. Norris came closer. "Morton," he said in a syrupy voice. "Come along, now. You know we can make you better."

Morton twisted his head back. "How can Satan cast out Satan?" he yelled. "Dipshit!"

Blackburn looked for an escape route and did not see one. He cocked the Python again, but Morton was holding him so that he couldn't aim, and there were too many armed men anyway. All of them were pointing their guns at him. If he fired again, they might not worry about hitting each other.

"We're screwed," he told Morton.

Morton looked up at him. The Savior's hair fell back from his forehead, and Blackburn saw the cuts and scratches that the thorns had left.

"Do not forsake me unto them," Morton whispered. "Their soldiers smite me with coat hangers, and their concubines mock me. I cannot preach. I cannot wander in the wilderness of Palestine." He clutched Blackburn's right wrist and pulled it up so that the Python's muzzle touched his chest. "Ought not Morton to have suffered, and to enter into his glory?"

Blackburn tried to pull the gun away. "No," he said. "You don't deserve to die."

Morton was stronger than he looked. He held Blackburn's hand and pistol tight against his chest. "The beggar died and was carried by the angels into Abraham's bosom," he said. "The rich man also died, and fried like a sliced 'tater. Pull the trigger, asshole."

"Drop the weapon *now*!" a man in the circle bellowed. "If it moves any way but down, I'll blow your brains out!"

"It'll be all right, Morton," Dr. Norris cooed.

Blackburn decided that the question of whether Morton deserved to die wasn't the question he should be asking.

"Are you sure?" he whispered.

Morton nodded. "Verily, I say unto thee: Let's do it."

Blackburn pulled the trigger. The noise was a loud thump.

The men in the circle fell silent, unsure of what they had heard.

Morton closed his eyes and smiled. Blackburn lowered him to the ground.

"Let us go over unto the other side of the lake, Jimmy," Morton murmured. "We gonna catch us a whopper."

Then something hit Blackburn in the head, and he fell. A man with a rifle stood over him, tall as a tree. Others appeared beside him.

"I said drop the gun," the man with the rifle said.

Blackburn considered killing him and decided not to. The man's voice held no cruelty, only a resigned determination to do his job. That wasn't worth a bullet.

He let his fingers relax. The Python was taken away, and then the men jerked him to his feet.

"I know you now," the cop who had scowled said. "You're Jimmy Blackburn."

Blackburn looked down at Morton, and at the red spot on the white gown. Morton wasn't breathing. Even though

Blackburn had not been able to make it a head shot, Morton had died fast.

"Yes," Blackburn said. "But I never told him my name, and he called me by it anyway. He said we'd go fishing."

He looked up at the angry faces, lit by white and yellow flashlight beams and orange flickers from the dying fire. He had to let them know what had really happened this night in the wilderness of Palestine.

"Truly," he said, "this was the Son of God." He looked down at Morton again. The smile was still there. "I shit you not."

VICTIM NUMBER TWENTY-ONE

Jasmine came to see him in February. Blackburn was surprised. She hadn't written to tell him she was coming. He almost said that he wouldn't see her, but then decided it would be worth it to get out of his cell for the walk to the visitation area. Ever since he had been reclassified from "death row work capable" to "death row segregation," his legs had been stiff.

"Jimmy. Hi." Jasmine was wearing a dark blouse, and her hair was cut just above her shoulders. She sat with her shoulders hunched, as if afraid of being hit. She looked more like Mom than ever.

Blackburn sat down. He hadn't been here before. A Plexiglas panel and a metal grating were set into the wall, and there were wide counters on both sides. Brother and sister were six feet apart. Blackburn didn't mind. He wouldn't have wanted to be closer.

"Hi," he said. "Welcome to Ellis Unit."

Jasmine frowned. "Is it bad?"

Blackburn tried not to laugh. He didn't want to insult her. But he couldn't help smiling.

"I'm sorry," Jasmine said.

"You don't have anything to be sorry for," Blackburn said. "Did you come all the way from Seattle?"

"I'm in Spokane now. I'm a C.P.A."

"Doing okay?"

"Not bad. I make enough."

"I'm glad. You didn't have to spend it to come here, though. But as long as you did, you ought to hit the Huntsville tourist attractions."

Jasmine's eyebrows rose. "I didn't know there were any."

"You bet," Blackburn said. "I haven't seen them myself, but I've read about them in the library. I recommend the Texas Prison Museum, featuring balls and chains, Bonnie and Clyde's rifles, and best of all, 'Old Sparky.' "

"What's that?" Jasmine asked.

"The Texas State Electric Chair, now retired in favor of a more energy-efficient method. But beloved nonetheless."

Jasmine looked down at the counter. "I don't want to talk about this."

"I'm not talking about it," Blackburn said.

Jasmine looked up. She was angry. "Yes, you are."

She was right. Blackburn didn't have any business bothering her with it. But on the other hand, he hadn't asked her to come.

"You had to know it'd be on my mind," he said.

Jasmine was quiet for a long moment. "Yes," she said

then. "But there's nothing I can do. So I was hoping we could talk about other things."

"Like what?"

"Well, I thought you might want to hear about Mom. And Dad."

Blackburn supposed that made sense on her side of the wall. "Okay. How's Mom?"

"She got married at Thanksgiving. Her husband's name is Gary. He worked at a cannery for thirty years, but he's retired now."

"That's nice," Blackburn said. "How about you? Married?"

"No."

"Shacking up?"

Jasmine reddened.

"Take precautions," Blackburn said.

Jasmine laughed. Her eyes looked moist.

"I'm not kidding," Blackburn said.

Jasmine put a black purse on the counter and took a tissue from it. She wiped her eyes. "I know you're not," she said. "That's not why I'm laughing. I'm laughing so I don't cry."

"I don't get it."

"I wouldn't expect you to."

Blackburn decided he was glad she had come. He and Jasmine understood each other.

"All right," he said. "So what about the old man?"

Jasmine crumpled the tissue. "He passed away in September."

"He lasted that long?"

Jasmine nodded. "He got better for almost two years. Then he went downhill fast. I had him at my place in Spokane when it happened. He was watching the cable news, and they were talking about you pleading guilty, but I don't think that's what did it. He just sort of dozed off. He was on a lot of painkillers by then, so I don't think he hurt much."

Blackburn sighed. It figured. Those who caused the most pain almost never suffered any themselves. But maybe that meant Blackburn could hope for an easy death of his own. "What are you going to do with the homestead?"

"Sell it," Jasmine said. "I certainly don't want it, and you—" She cut herself off. She looked scared.

"It's okay," Blackburn said. "I don't mind. All I mind is that it's taking so long."

Jasmine shook her head. "I don't understand why you don't fight it," she said. Her voice quavered. "You're the last person I'd expect to give up."

"I'm not giving up," Blackburn said. "I'm accepting reality. It's going to happen, so it might as well be soon." He gestured at the walls. "This place is no fun. For example, I was converting all the work-capable Jesus freaks to Mortonism, so the chaplain had me reclassified. Now I only get three hours a day out of my cell, five days a week. And the cell's six by nine, most of which is bed and toilet." He stood. "I'm upsetting you. I should go."

"Don't," Jasmine said. "We have time left."

"You should spend yours in Spokane." Blackburn turned and nodded to the guard.

"I love you, Jimmy," Jasmine said.

Blackburn couldn't imagine how that could be true. But he had never known Jasmine to lie. He looked back at her and said, "Thanks." Then he returned to his cell.

A week later, an attorney he didn't know came to see him. The attorney sat in the same chair in which Jasmine had sat. He looked miserable.

Blackburn took that as a good sign. "What's the word?" he asked.

The attorney, a man only a few years older than Blackburn, adjusted his crooked wire-framed glasses, making them more crooked. "I have a ruling from the Texas Court of Criminal Appeals," he said. "They upheld your sentence. I'm afraid where the murder of a Texas peace officer is concerned, the court has little compassion for the accused."

"Well, after all," Blackburn said, "I did it."

"That doesn't matter. Your case was rushed to trial, and your counsel presented no defense. So regardless of what the Texas court says, we have constitutional grounds for a U.S. Supreme Court review, and then for *habeas corpus* appeals if that fails."

Blackburn didn't like what he was hearing. "Look," he said, "my lawyer accomplished the only thing I wanted him to accomplish. The state was saying that I raped and killed a woman, and he got them to admit it was a lie. Then they said that I shot and killed a DPS trooper, which was the truth. The guy had it coming, but apparently that isn't a legal consideration. So I pled guilty, and they sentenced me. Then my lawyer said he'd argue an appeal of the sentence, and I told him to get lost. I knew it'd be pointless."

"You didn't have a choice," the attorney said. "Texas law requires an automatic review by the Criminal Appeals court whenever capital punishment is imposed. So when your counsel resigned, I was appointed to your case. I sent you a letter informing you of that. Didn't you receive it?"

Blackburn shrugged. "Maybe. I get a lot of mail. Some of it's from people who want to preserve my life, and some of it's from people who want to see me fry, even though Texas doesn't do that anymore. But most of it's from lawyers who want to use me to get movie deals."

The attorney adjusted his glasses again, and they fell off his face and clattered on the counter. He picked them up and shoved them back on, then glared at Blackburn. "I took your case because a judge ordered me to," he said, "but that doesn't mean I'm not going to do my job. And my job is to keep you alive."

"Why?" Blackburn asked. "So I can spend my life here?"

"There's parole," the attorney said. "Sometimes even for cop killers."

"You think you can get me parole?"

"It wouldn't be for a long time, but it could happen."

"How long a time? Minimum."

The attorney grimaced. "Given the nature of your crime," he said, "and given that you have another murder trial pending in this state and have confessed to killings in other states, I would say that the soonest you would be eligible for parole would be in twenty years. Now, I know that sounds like forever. But it beats dying."

Blackburn stared at the attorney. The man looked sincere, but sincerity was irrelevant. Blackburn stood.

"I've seen enough death to know more about it than you do," he said. "And I've been in one cage or another for most of the past year, so I know more about incarceration than you do. I've also done extensive reading about the execution procedures in this state, and about the psychological effects of long prison terms. Therefore, given my superior knowledge of these matters, my decision is this: The only way I will stay in Huntsville for twenty years will be as a stuffed mummy in the Texas Prison Museum, perched on Old Sparky. So unless you're going to help make this thing quick and easy, you can take your *habeas corpus* and stick it."

The attorney stood as well. "Mr. Blackburn, I can understand that you're upset. But you have to realize that you have legal options that could save your life. If you refuse to take advantage of them, you'll be killing yourself." He fumbled with his glasses. "I'll try to come back tomorrow, so you'll have tonight to cool down and think. I might even be able to arrange a consultation without a wall between us, so we can talk more comfortably."

Blackburn fixed the attorney with a steady gaze. "Please do that," he said. "Then I can tear you open where you're soft, hang you up, and watch you drain."

Blackburn didn't really do that sort of thing, but the attorney didn't seem to know that. He went away and did not return.

The execution warrant was issued on Wednesday, April 1, 1987. The execution was scheduled for Thursday, May 14, Blackburn's twenty-ninth birthday. When Blackburn saw a copy of the warrant, he thought someone was playing an April Fools' joke. But the warden sent him a letter the next day, confirming the warrant, and Blackburn knew it was serious. Two days after that, he received a letter from the attorney who had visited him, offering to apply for a stay of execution. He wrote back to the attorney, offering to have people blow up the attorney's home. He received more letters from that attorney and from other lawyers in the weeks that followed, but did not open them.

Then on Monday, May 11, Blackburn received a letter from Heather.

Dear Mr. Blackburn:

I have not written you before because my parents and friends say I should not. They say you are a killer and as such do not deserve communication from me. But my heart tells me that since you are a condemned man, you should know that you have a son.

This past September, I gave birth to a boy I named Alan. I named him after the man I thought you were when I knew you in December 1985.

I hope I have done the right thing in telling you. I hope it will be a comfort.

Your son will be eight months old this Thursday.

Blackburn was horrified. He'd had a vasectomy in 1982.

The child was Roy-Boy's.

He grabbed pen and paper and wrote furiously.

For the love of Morton drown it drown it now it is the son of a psychopath and will grow up to torture people but especially people who love it believe me it is not mine I am sterile but his the one who cut you and

289

Blackburn stopped, breathing hard, his chest thundering. When he could, he read what he had written. Then he tore the paper to shreds.

"You okay, Blackburn?"

Blackburn looked up. A guard was looking in through the bars of the cell door.

"Yeah," Blackburn said. "I'm fine."

"Whatcha doing with that pen?"

Blackburn looked at the pen in his hand. "Writing," he said.

"Let's have it," the guard said.

"Why? I've had pens all along."

"Let's have it."

Blackburn surrendered the pen. A few minutes later he was taken from the cell, and two guards went through it while he watched. They brought out two more pens and three pencils.

"We don't want you hurting yourself," one of them told Blackburn as they put him back into the cell.

Blackburn was confused for a moment, and then he realized what they were talking about. He was to be executed in three days, and they didn't want him beating them to it.

"Don't worry," he said. "For verily, Morton saith: I'd do it myself, but that would queer the deal."

The prison chaplain tried to visit Blackburn that evening. Blackburn mooned him, and he went away.

At 5:00 P.M. on Wednesday, May 13, four guards removed Blackburn from his cell and took him to another building. There they put him into a holding cell. Two of the guards remained outside that cell, watching him. He lay down on the bunk and traced the cracks in the ceiling with his eyes. An hour later, one of the guards who had left returned with fried chicken, mashed potatoes, and gravy. It smelled delicious. Blackburn sat up. The meal was on a metal tray on the shelf in the cell door. Steam rose between the bars.

"Is this my last meal already?" Blackburn asked.

"That's not until tomorrow evening," the guard who had brought the food said, "but they need to know what you'll want. I'll write it down now, if you're ready."

Blackburn grinned. He knew about sphincter relaxation in freshly killed bodies, and had decided that he wasn't going to die without making sure he was remembered. He asked for a pot of chili, bran cereal with milk, celery stalks, asparagus spears, bran muffins, a half gallon of prune juice, a quart of beer, and a carrot cake with "Happy Birthday" written in pink script on white icing. The guards looked puzzled.

"Fiber," Blackburn said. "It's good for you."

He ate the fried chicken and mashed potatoes, and then slept. He awoke late in the morning with no memories of dreams. Breakfast was bacon, eggs, hash browns, and coffee. Afterward, he asked for the current issues of *Superman, The Flash, Batman, Hawkman, Spider-Man, X-Men,* and *Green Lantern.* One of the guards made a call from a wall phone, and two hours later, Blackburn had his comic books. He read them slowly. He was in the middle of *Hawkman* when lunch arrived. Lunch was a cheeseburger, french fries, and a pint of chocolate ice cream. The ice cream was good, so he asked for more. But the pint had been brought in from outside, a guard said, and there wasn't any more.

Blackburn saved *Green Lantern* until his last meal was served at 7:00 P.M. He read it while he ate, and was disappointed. It had lost something over the years. When he had eaten all of his meal that he could, he lay down on the bunk and reread *X-Men.* He was stuffed and sleepy, and wondered if he had time for a nap.

He dozed, but the guards awoke him at eight-fifteen and took him to a shower stall next to the holding cell. They had him strip and throw his clothes into a laundry bag. When he finished showering, they handed him a towel, and then clean clothes and a pair of slippers. He dressed, commenting on the fact that the shirt was short-sleeved. The guards did not respond to that, but returned him to the holding cell and told him he could relax for a few hours.

Blackburn couldn't relax. He wasn't frightened, or even nervous; he was simply wide awake. Showers did that to him. One of the guards asked if he would like a television brought in, but Blackburn asked for a *Houston Chronicle* instead. When that was provided, he skipped the news sections in favor of the advice columns and funnies. He didn't see much point in knowing what was going on out in the world; it was probably just more Iran-Contra bullshit anyway.

The warden and chaplain came at eleven-thirty, along with three men in suits whom Blackburn didn't recognize and a guard wheeling a gurney. Blackburn was glad to see that the gurney had a mattress. He was taken from the holding cell and escorted to a closed door, where he was told to unbutton his shirt and to lie down on the gurney. He did so, lying down with his feet toward the door, and the guards secured him to the gurney with six leather straps. His right arm was strapped to a board that angled out from the side of the gurney. Then the warden opened the door to what Blackburn knew was called "the Death House," and the gurney was wheeled inside.

The room had brick walls. The wall on Blackburn's left had a door that led to the executioner's room. Beside that door were two small, square holes, one above the other. Beside the upper hole was a rectangular mirror. Blackburn knew that the executioner and a doctor on the other side of the mirror would be able to see him, but he wouldn't be able to see them.

The gurney stopped under the mirror. Blackburn looked up at it and winked.

The door beside the square holes opened, and a man in a blue smock stepped into the Death House. This man was not a doctor, but a "medically trained individual." He came around the gurney to Blackburn's right side, reached across Blackburn, and took a long needle attached to a clear plastic tube from the lower of the two square holes. He pulled the tube out so that it lay across Blackburn's bare chest, then smoothed the skin on Blackburn's inner elbow and pushed in the needle.

Blackburn watched the needle go in, but had no pain. "You're good," he told the man in the smock. "I didn't feel a thing."

"Thanks," the man in the smock said. "You have good veins." Then he looked startled, and glanced at the other men in the room. They pretended not to have heard anything.

The man in the smock taped the needle to Blackburn's arm, then pulled a second tube from the lower hole. This tube was gray, ending in a metal disk that the man in the smock taped to Blackburn's chest. It was a stethoscope for the doctor.

The man in the smock returned to the executioner's room and closed the door.

"Hey," Blackburn said. "What's the top hole for?"

The warden's face appeared over Blackburn. The warden had a weak chin and a receding hairline. He wore glasses.

"We don't use the top hole," he said.

"Then why'd you put it in the wall?" Blackburn asked.

The warden didn't answer. Instead, he said, "Jimmy, you can make a statement now, if you like."

Blackburn had known this moment was coming for almost a year, and had rehearsed various statements. But he hadn't been able to pick one and one alone, and he still couldn't decide.

I have never killed a woman; Leslie doesn't count, because she lit the fuse herself.

Auto mechanics are, without exception, crooks.

No man knows love who has never had a dog.

I regret making Leo drink motor oil; I should have just come back later and shot him.

Artimus Arthur will be remembered as the greatest man of letters of the twentieth century.

Go fly a kite.

The unit of currency in Laos is the kip; in Mongolia, the tugrik.

Morton giveth, and Morton taketh away.

Tell Jasmine not to take less than sixty thousand for the homestead.

Tell Dolores I forgive her.

Tell the people of Wantoda, Kansas, that I've made them famous.

Tell Ernie's parents that if they never did anything else in their lives, they can still be proud because they made Ernie.

Tell Heather not to let Alan play with anything sharp.

All of these were worth saying, and none of them were enough.

"Jimmy?" the warden said.

Blackburn tried to shrug, but the leather straps were tight.

"*Green Lantern* isn't what it used to be," he said.

The warden frowned, then stepped away. The chaplain appeared over Blackburn then, and Blackburn made a noise in his throat as if he were bringing up phlegm. The chaplain stepped away too.

Blackburn felt something cold in his arm, and he raised his head to look at the clear tube lying across his chest. It was full of a colorless liquid. He knew that the liquid was a saline solution, with no poison in it. They would keep this going for a while, so he wouldn't know when the drugs started. The drugs would be sodium thiopental, pancuronium bromide, and potassium chloride. He didn't know what those words meant, exactly, but he had taken pride in learning them. He wasn't sure why. Maybe it was something like learning the words "Colt Python," which also didn't mean anything, by themselves. They only meant something when applied to steel and lead. Just as drugs only meant something when they slid into your body.

He became aware of a dull pressure in his bladder and bowels, and smiled. They would wish they could kill him twice.

He turned his head to the right and saw a glass panel in the far wall. The glare from the ceiling light kept him from seeing the faces of the witnesses behind that panel, but he saw their shapes. They were like ghosts. He stared at them for several minutes to make sure they were uncomfortable. Then he looked up at the ceiling light. This was taking too long.

The ceiling light was a single bright bulb. Blackburn guessed that it was at least two hundred watts. He stared at it, playing a game to see how long he could look without blinking. Then one of the men in the room appeared over him again, blocking his view.

"You're in my light," Blackburn said.

The man stepped away, and the sun was bright in Jimmy's eyes. His black fiberglass rod and Zebco 404 reel gleamed.

"Well, come on if you're coming," Dad said.

Jimmy hurried down the bank, almost falling. Dad took the lid off the Folger's coffee can, reached in, and pulled out a wriggling red worm.

"You do it like this," Dad said, holding the hook of his own rod and reel in his right hand. "You thread it on, head to ass or ass to head. You don't jab it through sideways, 'cause then the fish just bites off what he wants."

Jimmy stood close and watched. The worm bunched up on the hook as Dad pushed it on. The free end flailed.

"Does it hurt it?" Jimmy asked.

"Worms ain't got nerves." Dad took his hands away from the hook. It dangled before Jimmy's face, no longer metal, but hook-shaped flesh. "Now do yours," Dad said.

Jimmy laid his rod on the flat mud beside the water and

sat down. He dug into the dirt in the coffee can and pulled up a worm, slimy and strong. It almost slipped away. He clutched the worm in his right hand and picked up the brass hook at the end of his line with his left.

He couldn't get the hook into the worm the way Dad had done. The worm's ass or head or whatever wouldn't stay still long enough for him to push the point of the barb into the hole. He jabbed in desperation and stuck himself in the thumb.

"Ow!" he yelled, dropping both worm and hook.

Dad picked them up and squatted beside him. "I'll show you one more time," he said, "and if you don't get it right after that, we're leaving. Give me your hands."

Jimmy held out his hands, and Dad placed the worm in his left and the hook in his right. Then Dad guided Jimmy's fingers.

"Like this," Dad said. "It ain't hard."

The worm slid onto the hook as slick and easy as macaroni onto a toothpick.

In that instant, Jimmy became dizzy with a joy he had never before experienced. He didn't know what had caused it, but he didn't want it to stop, so he tried to memorize everything: the warmth of the sun on his crew-cut scalp; the coolness of the mud beneath him; Dad's rough fingers wrapped around his; and the smell of earth and blood from the worm on the hook.